# WARRIORS

## A SHADOW IN RIVERCLAN

# WARRIORS

## A SHADOW IN RIVERCLAN

**CREATED BY**
**ERIN HUNTER**

**WRITTEN BY**
**DAN JOLLEY**

**ART BY**
**JAMES L. BARRY**

*An Imprint of HarperCollinsPublishers*

WARRIORS

## GRAPHIC NOVELS

*Graystripe's Adventure*
*Ravenpaw's Path*
*SkyClan and the Stranger*
*A Shadow in RiverClan*

*Tigerstar and Sasha #1: Into the Woods*
*Tigerstar and Sasha #2: Escape from the Forest*
*Tigerstar and Sasha #3: Return to the Clans*
*The Rise of Scourge*

**Warriors: A Shadow in RiverClan**
Created by Erin Hunter
Written by Dan Jolley
Art by James L. Barry

HarperAlley is an imprint of HarperCollins Publishers.

978-0-06-294665-2 (hardcover) — ISBN 978-0-06-294664-5 (pbk)

20 21 22 23 24    SCP    10 9 8 7 6 5 4 3 2 1

First Edition

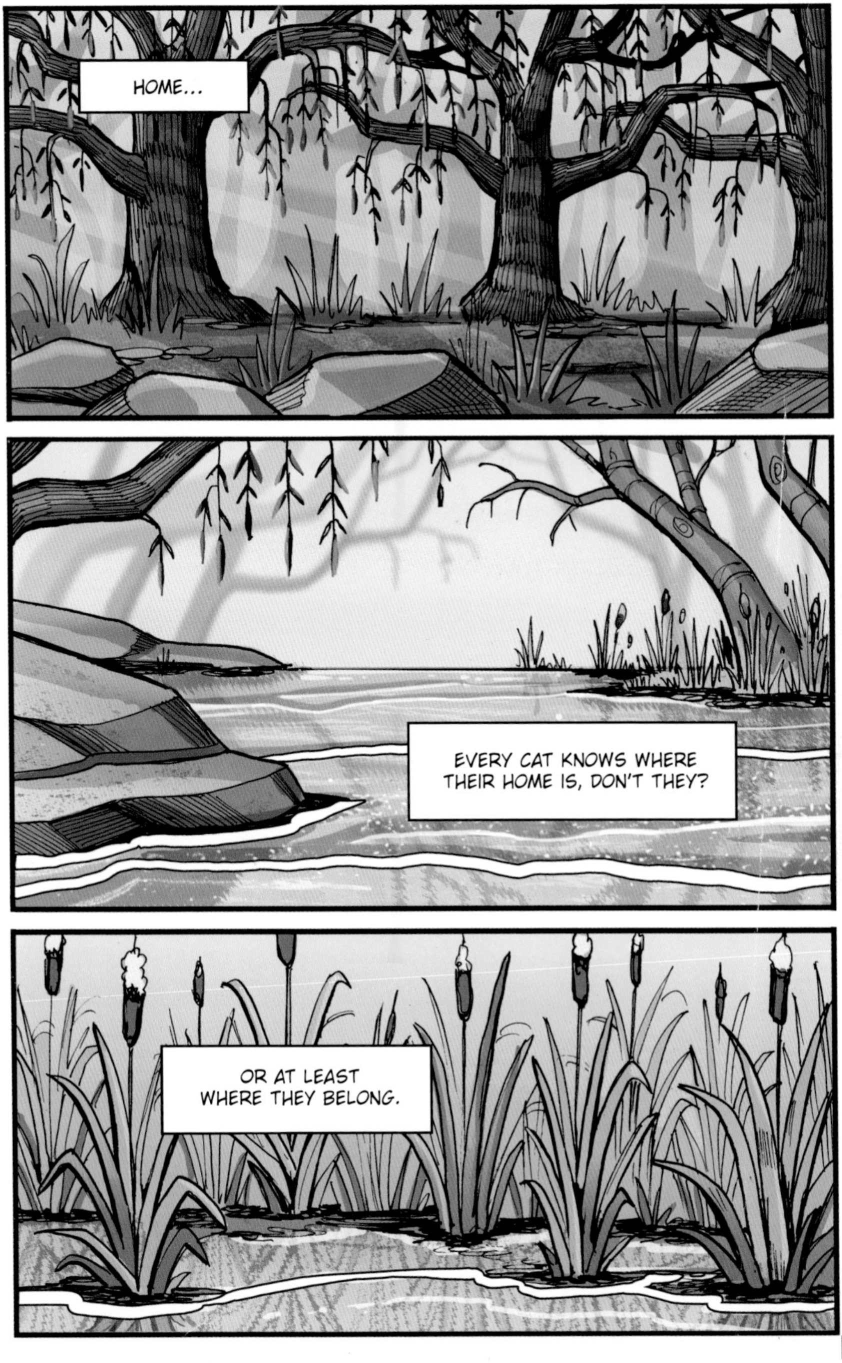
HOME...
EVERY CAT KNOWS WHERE THEIR HOME IS, DON'T THEY?
OR AT LEAST WHERE THEY BELONG.

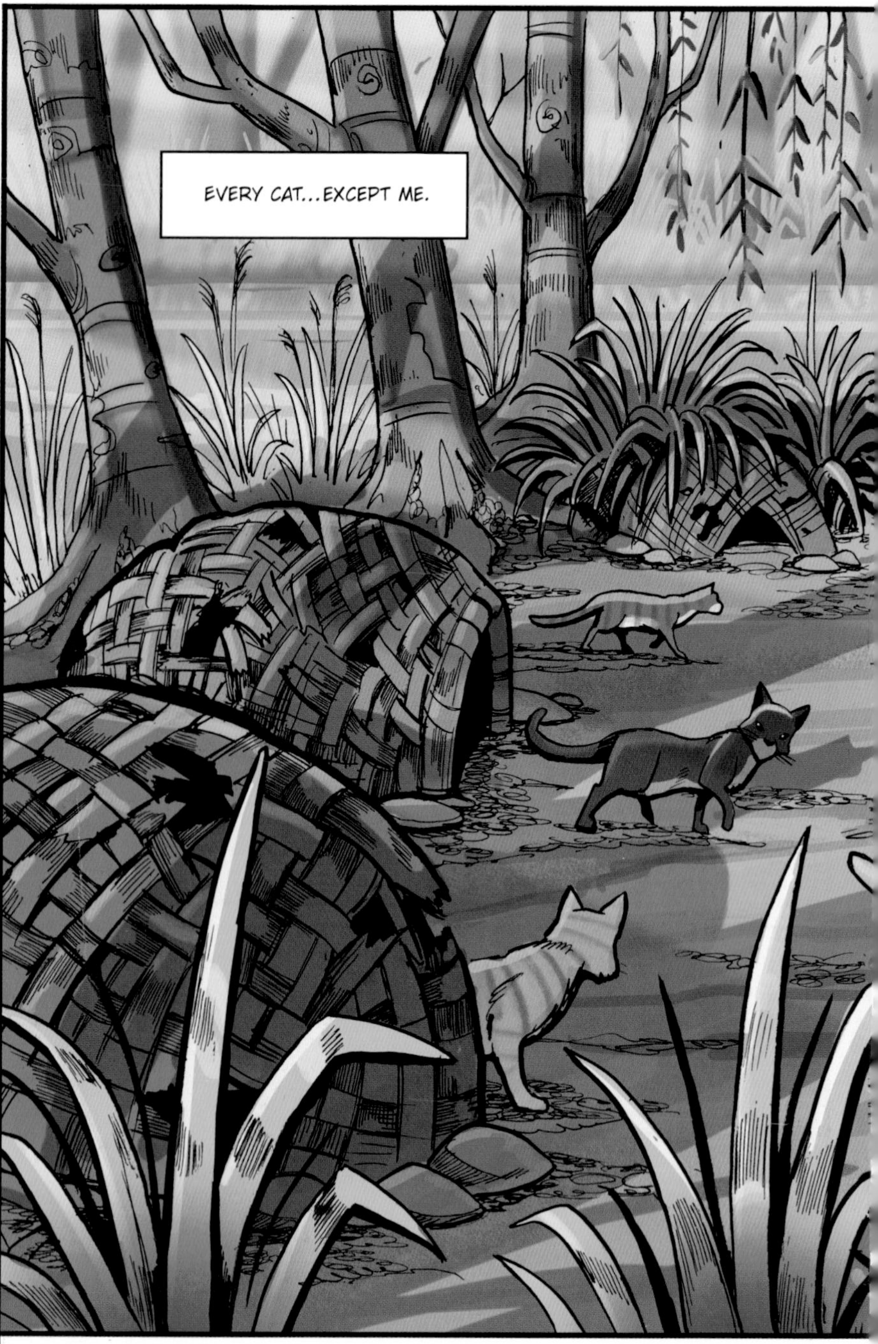
EVERY CAT...EXCEPT ME.

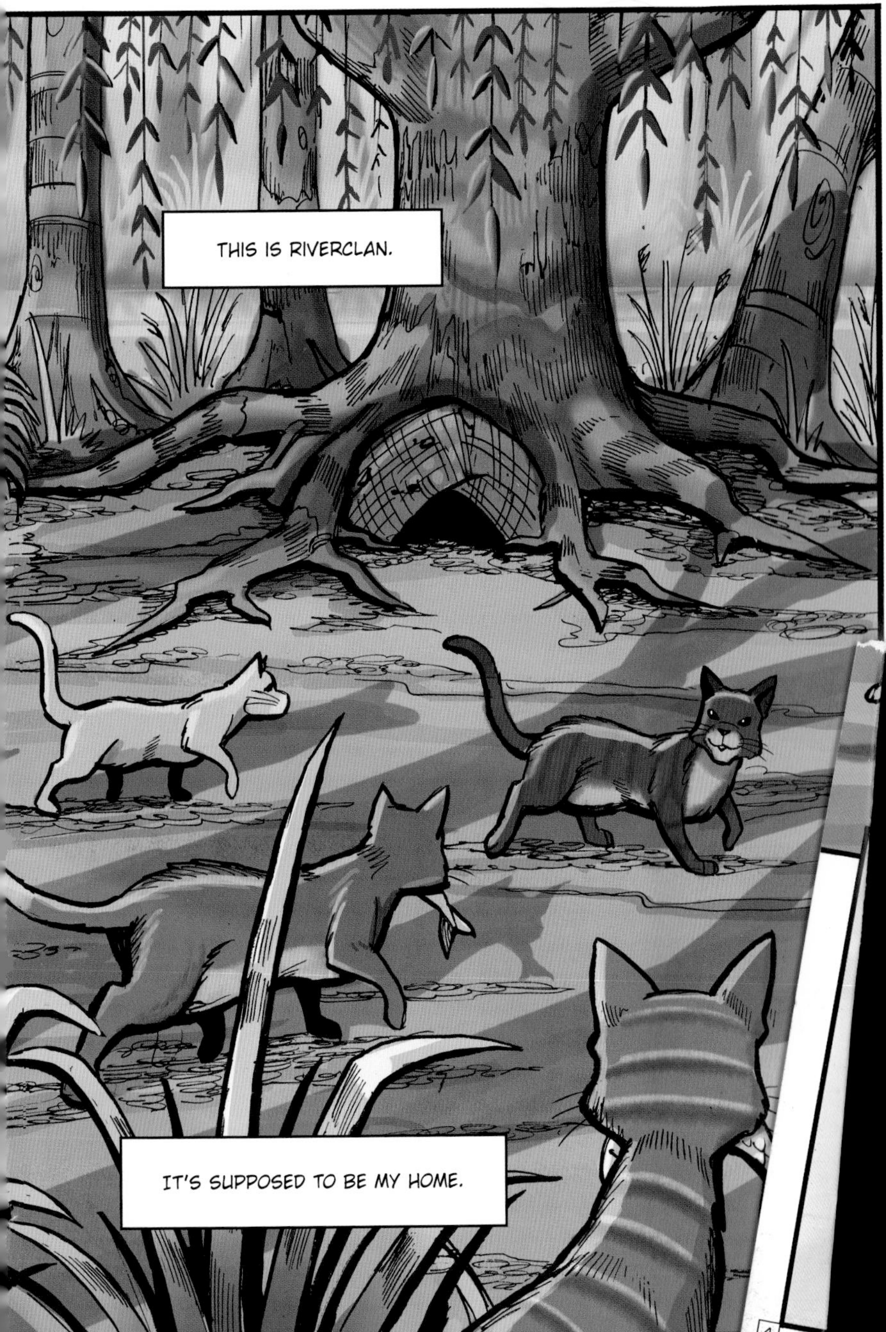
THIS IS RIVERCLAN.
IT'S SUPPOSED TO BE MY HOME.

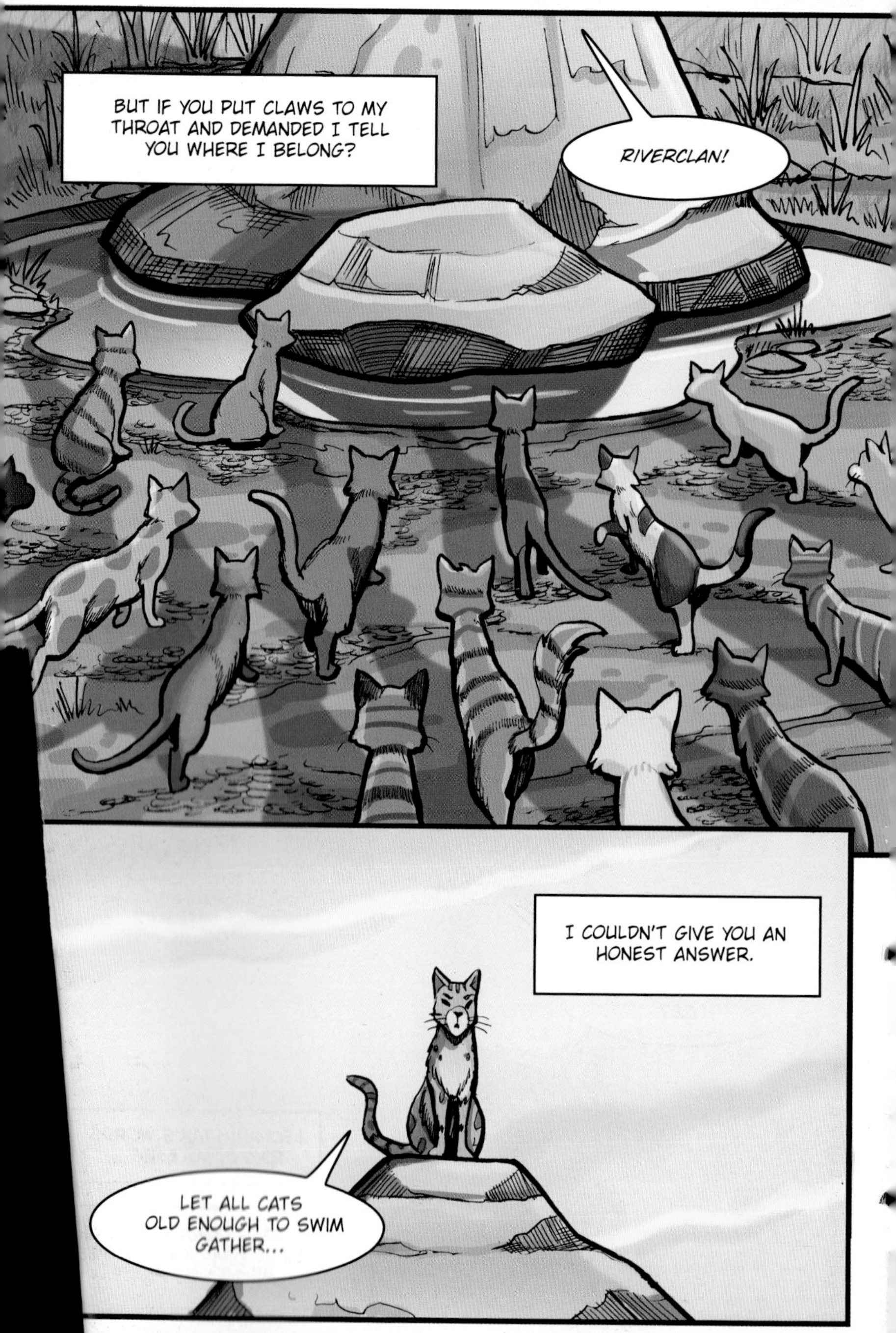
BUT IF YOU PUT CLAWS TO MY THROAT AND DEMANDED I TELL YOU WHERE I BELONG?
RIVERCLAN!
I COULDN'T GIVE YOU AN HONEST ANSWER.
LET ALL CATS OLD ENOUGH TO SWIM GATHER...

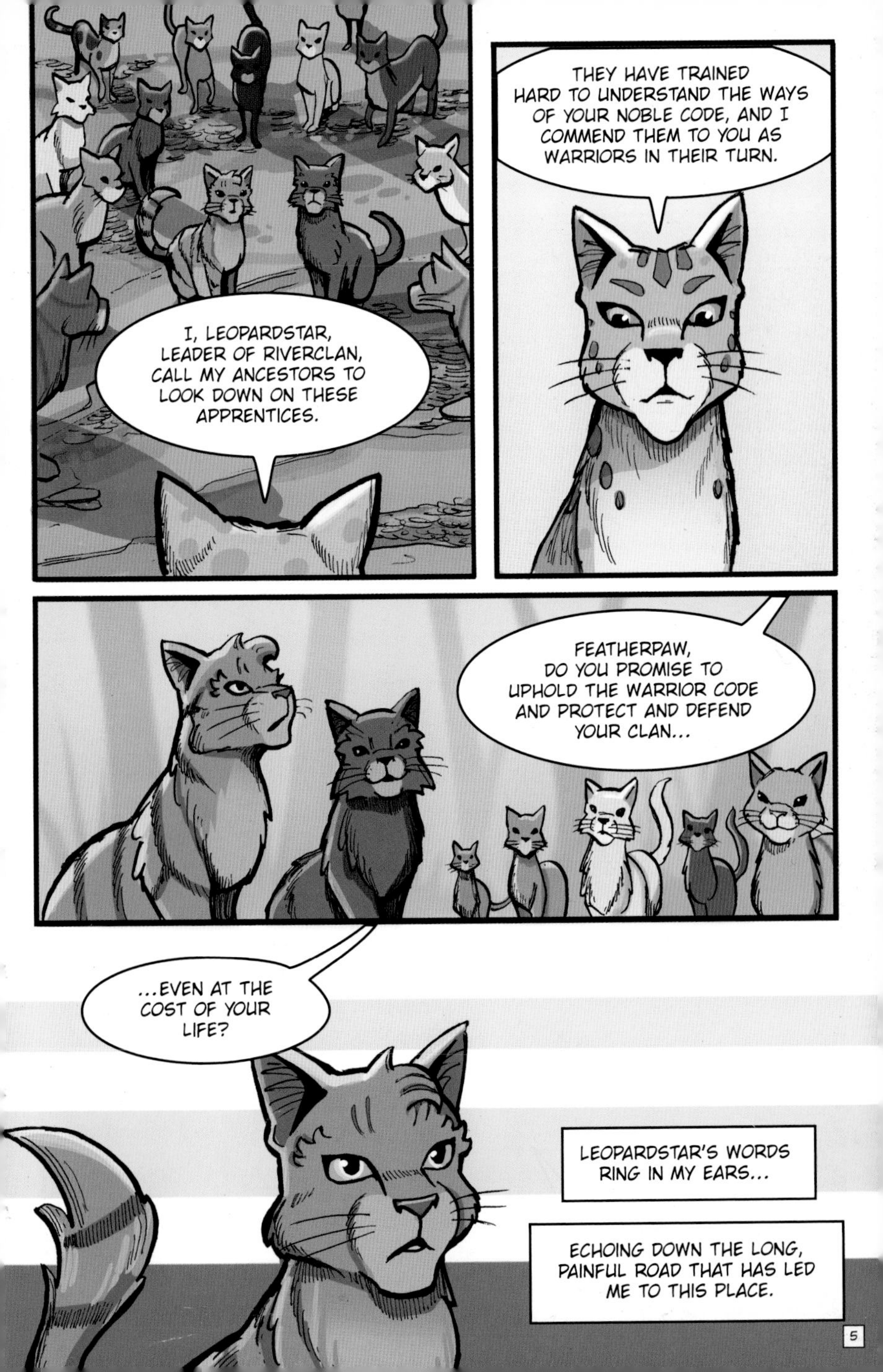
I, LEOPARDSTAR, LEADER OF RIVERCLAN, CALL MY ANCESTORS TO LOOK DOWN ON THESE APPRENTICES.
THEY HAVE TRAINED HARD TO UNDERSTAND THE WAYS OF YOUR NOBLE CODE, AND I COMMEND THEM TO YOU AS WARRIORS IN THEIR TURN.
FEATHERPAW, DO YOU PROMISE TO UPHOLD THE WARRIOR CODE AND PROTECT AND DEFEND YOUR CLAN...
...EVEN AT THE COST OF YOUR LIFE?
LEOPARDSTAR'S WORDS RING IN MY EARS...
ECHOING DOWN THE LONG, PAINFUL ROAD THAT HAS LED ME TO THIS PLACE.

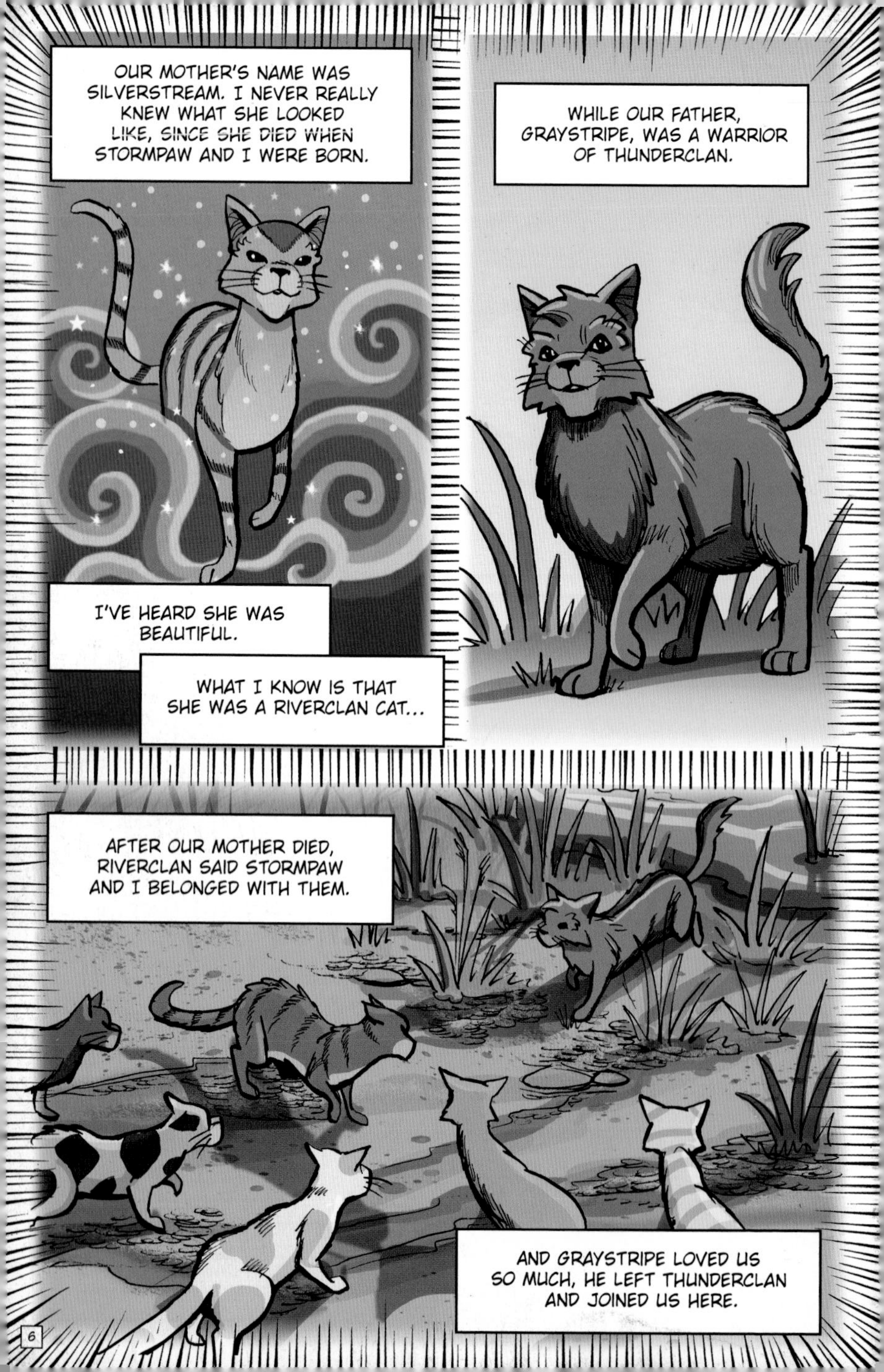
OUR MOTHER'S NAME WAS SILVERSTREAM. I NEVER REALLY KNEW WHAT SHE LOOKED LIKE, SINCE SHE DIED WHEN STORMPAW AND I WERE BORN.
I'VE HEARD SHE WAS BEAUTIFUL.
WHAT I KNOW IS THAT SHE WAS A RIVERCLAN CAT...
WHILE OUR FATHER, GRAYSTRIPE, WAS A WARRIOR OF THUNDERCLAN.
AFTER OUR MOTHER DIED, RIVERCLAN SAID STORMPAW AND I BELONGED WITH THEM.
AND GRAYSTRIPE LOVED US SO MUCH, HE LEFT THUNDERCLAN AND JOINED US HERE.

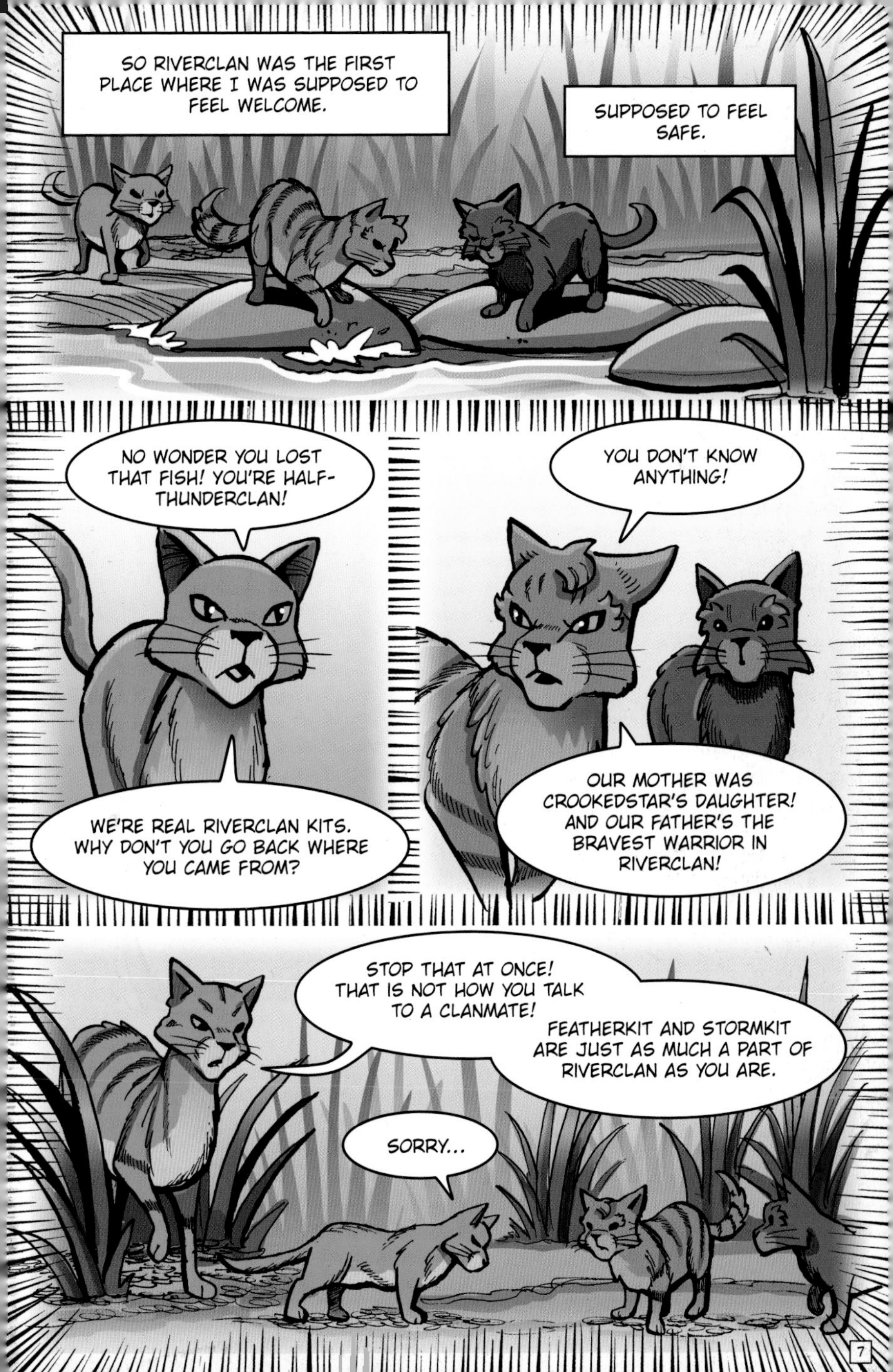
SO RIVERCLAN WAS THE FIRST PLACE WHERE I WAS SUPPOSED TO FEEL WELCOME.
SUPPOSED TO FEEL SAFE.
NO WONDER YOU LOST THAT FISH! YOU'RE HALF-THUNDERCLAN!
WE'RE REAL RIVERCLAN KITS. WHY DON'T YOU GO BACK WHERE YOU CAME FROM?
YOU DON'T KNOW ANYTHING!
OUR MOTHER WAS CROOKEDSTAR'S DAUGHTER! AND OUR FATHER'S THE BRAVEST WARRIOR IN RIVERCLAN!
STOP THAT AT ONCE! THAT IS NOT HOW YOU TALK TO A CLANMATE!
FEATHERKIT AND STORMKIT ARE JUST AS MUCH A PART OF RIVERCLAN AS YOU ARE.
SORRY...

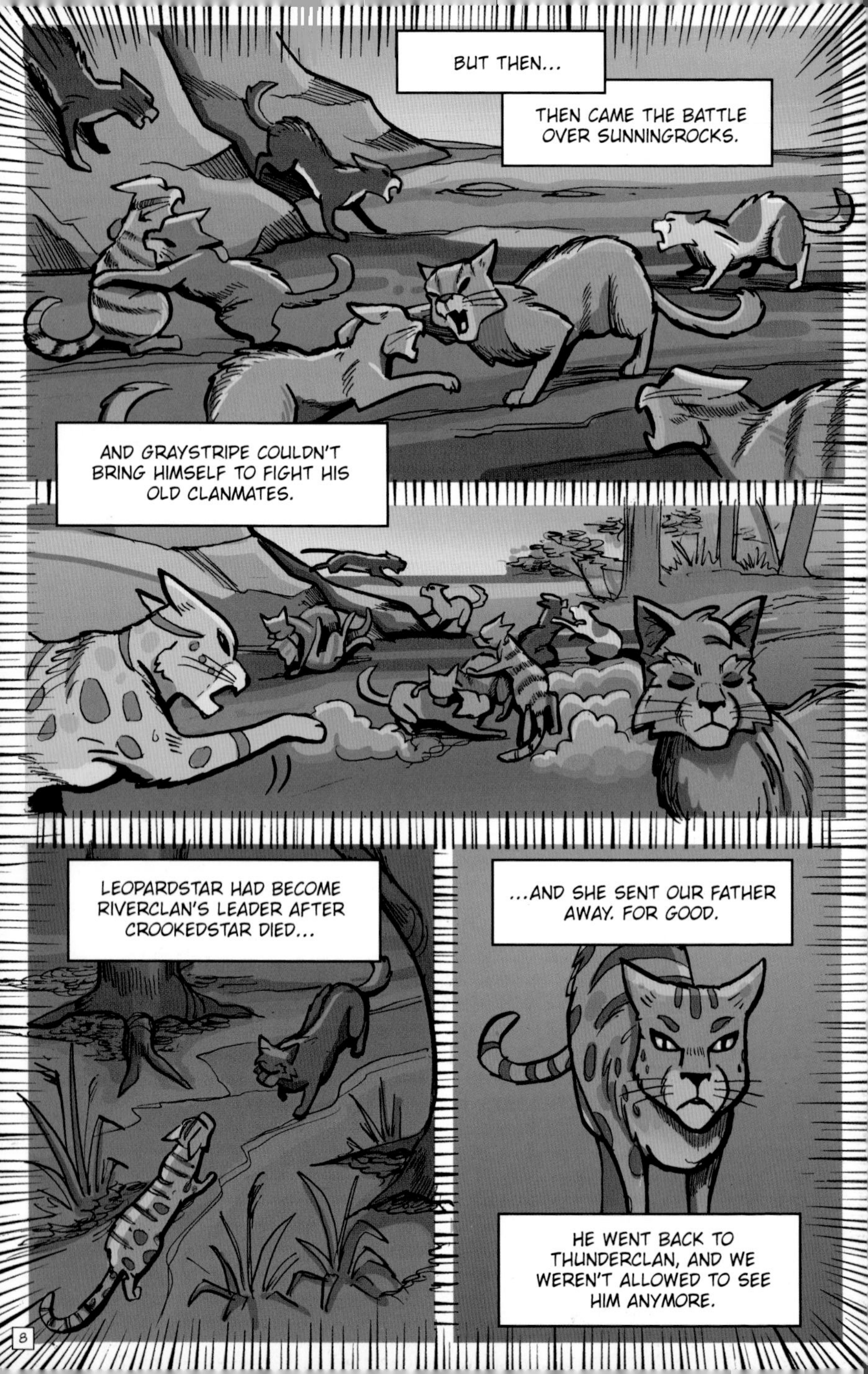
BUT THEN...
THEN CAME THE BATTLE OVER SUNNINGROCKS.
AND GRAYSTRIPE COULDN'T BRING HIMSELF TO FIGHT HIS OLD CLANMATES.
LEOPARDSTAR HAD BECOME RIVERCLAN'S LEADER AFTER CROOKEDSTAR DIED...
...AND SHE SENT OUR FATHER AWAY. FOR GOOD.
HE WENT BACK TO THUNDERCLAN, AND WE WEREN'T ALLOWED TO SEE HIM ANYMORE.

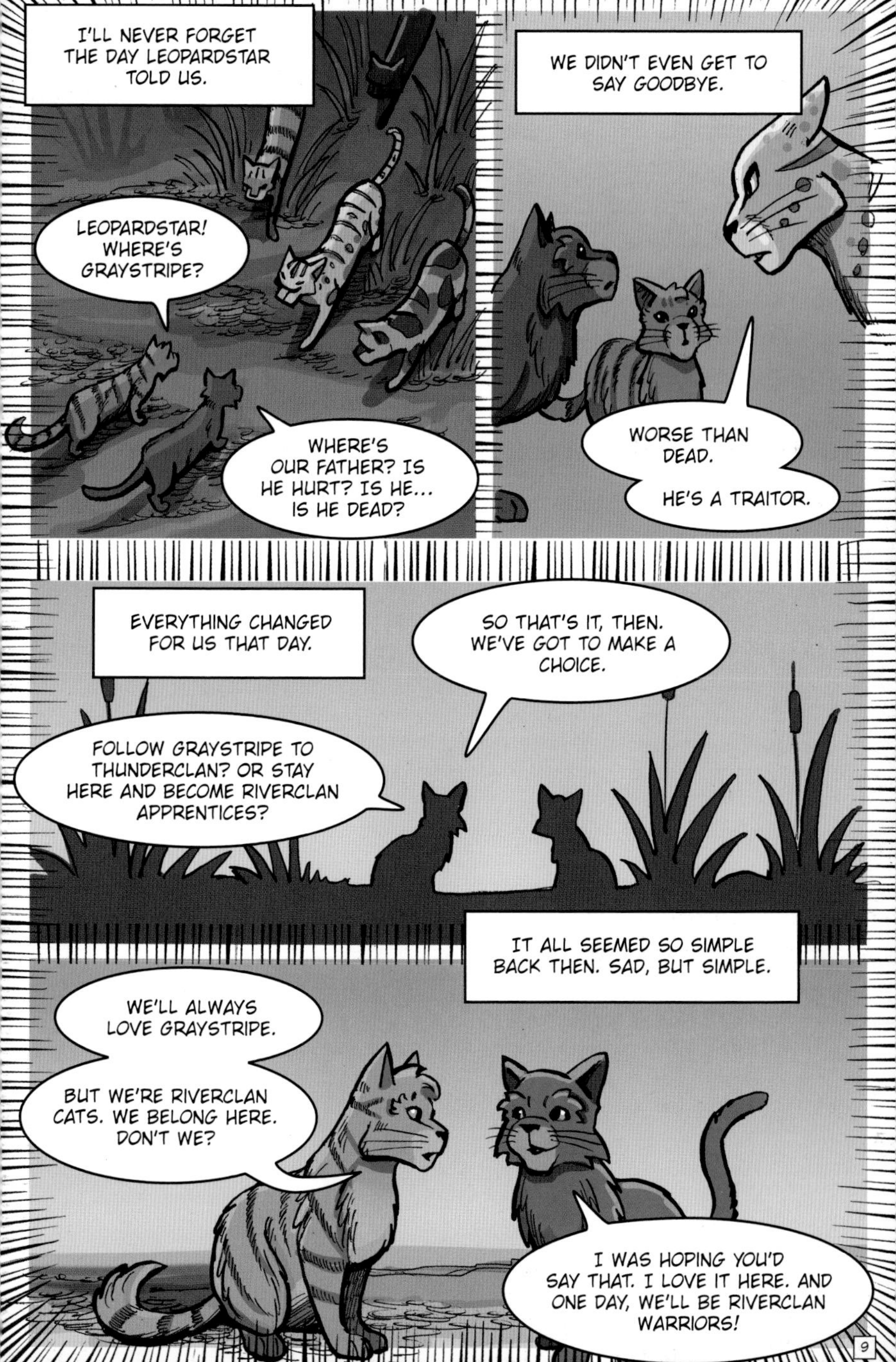
I'LL NEVER FORGET THE DAY LEOPARDSTAR TOLD US.
LEOPARDSTAR! WHERE'S GRAYSTRIPE?
WHERE'S OUR FATHER? IS HE HURT? IS HE... IS HE DEAD?
WE DIDN'T EVEN GET TO SAY GOODBYE.
WORSE THAN DEAD.
HE'S A TRAITOR.
EVERYTHING CHANGED FOR US THAT DAY.
SO THAT'S IT, THEN. WE'VE GOT TO MAKE A CHOICE.
FOLLOW GRAYSTRIPE TO THUNDERCLAN? OR STAY HERE AND BECOME RIVERCLAN APPRENTICES?
IT ALL SEEMED SO SIMPLE BACK THEN. SAD, BUT SIMPLE.
WE'LL ALWAYS LOVE GRAYSTRIPE.
BUT WE'RE RIVERCLAN CATS. WE BELONG HERE. DON'T WE?
I WAS HOPING YOU'D SAY THAT. I LOVE IT HERE. AND ONE DAY, WE'LL BE RIVERCLAN WARRIORS!

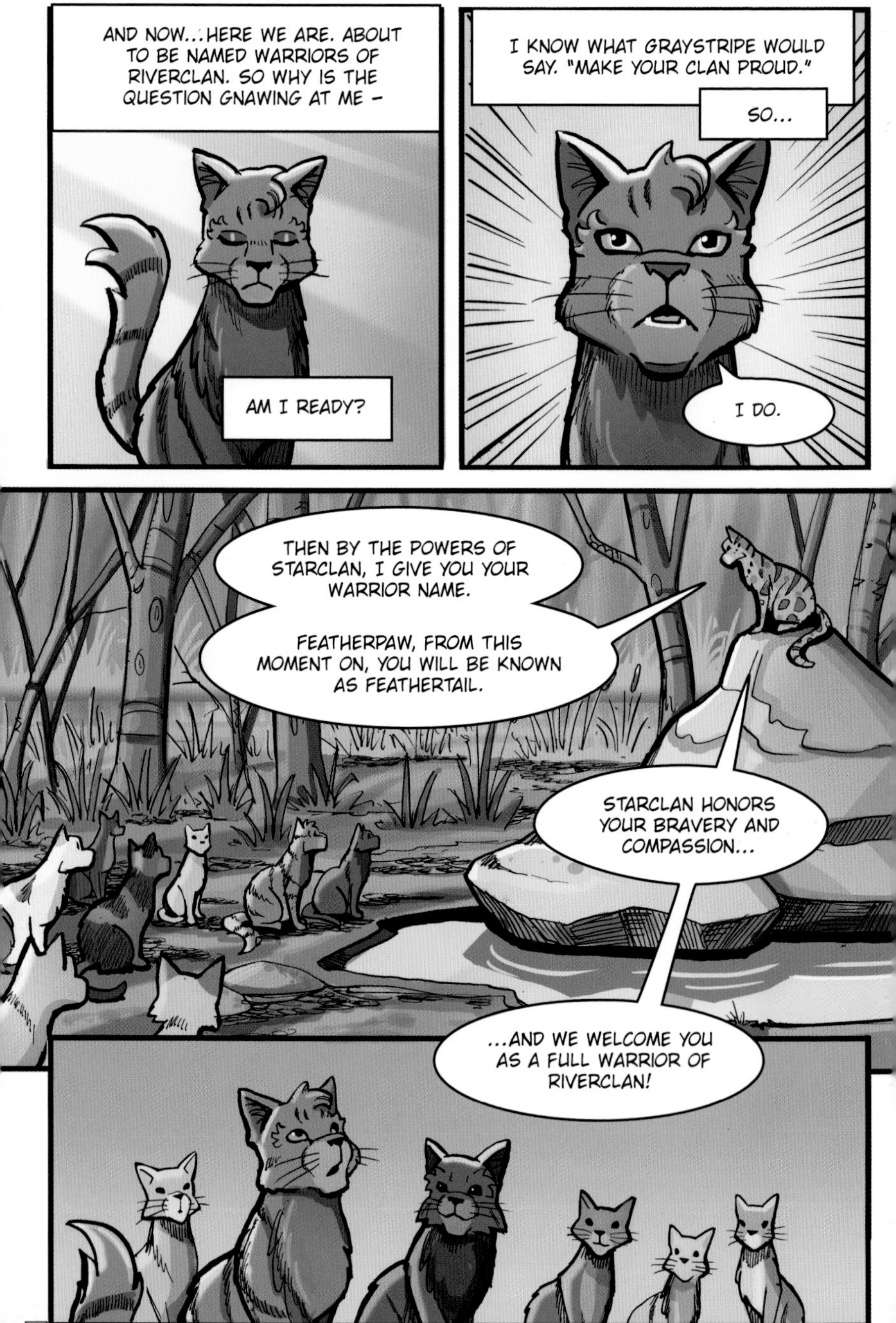
AND NOW...HERE WE ARE. ABOUT TO BE NAMED WARRIORS OF RIVERCLAN. SO WHY IS THE QUESTION GNAWING AT ME –
AM I READY?
I KNOW WHAT GRAYSTRIPE WOULD SAY. "MAKE YOUR CLAN PROUD."
SO...
I DO.
THEN BY THE POWERS OF STARCLAN, I GIVE YOU YOUR WARRIOR NAME.
FEATHERPAW, FROM THIS MOMENT ON, YOU WILL BE KNOWN AS FEATHERTAIL.
STARCLAN HONORS YOUR BRAVERY AND COMPASSION...
...AND WE WELCOME YOU AS A FULL WARRIOR OF RIVERCLAN!

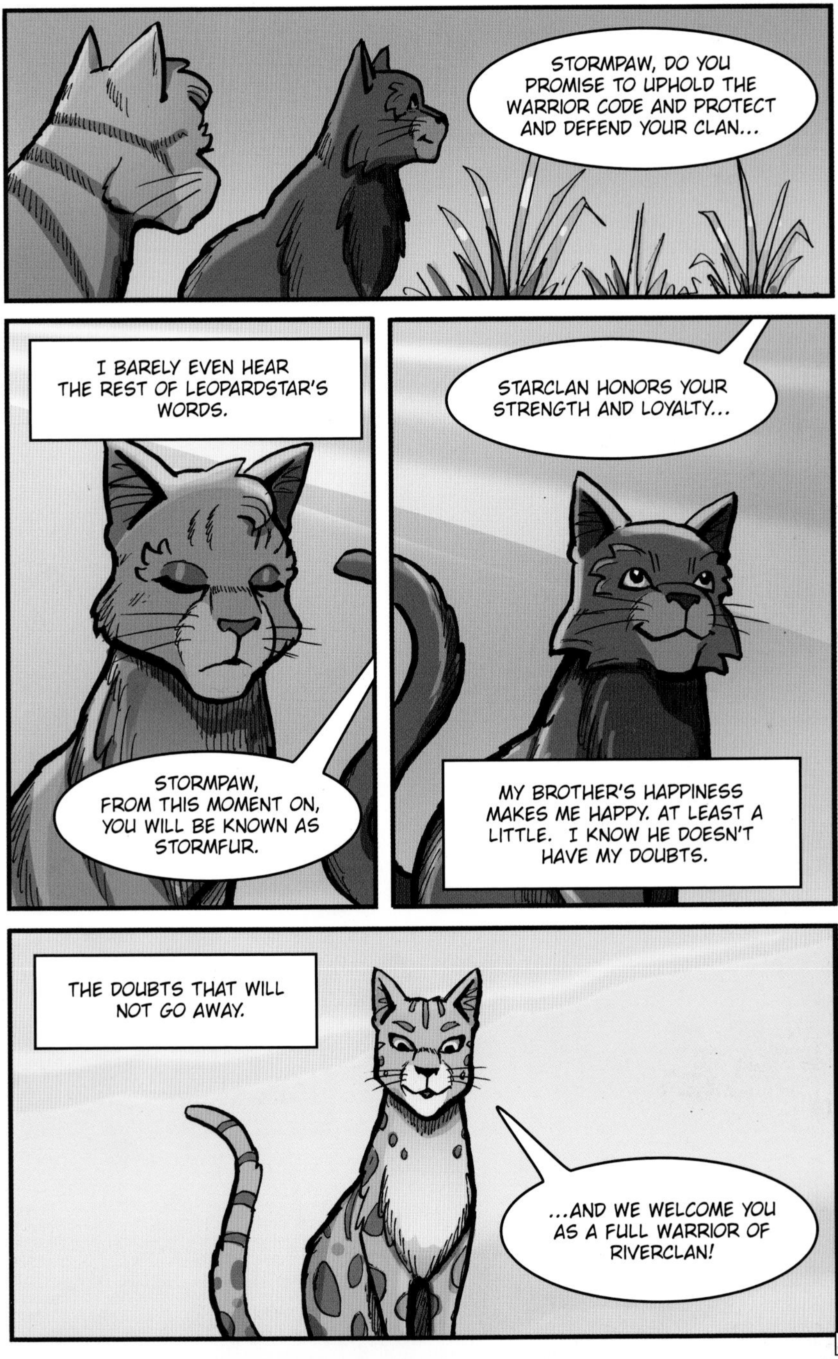
STORMPAW, DO YOU PROMISE TO UPHOLD THE WARRIOR CODE AND PROTECT AND DEFEND YOUR CLAN...
I BARELY EVEN HEAR THE REST OF LEOPARDSTAR'S WORDS.
STORMPAW, FROM THIS MOMENT ON, YOU WILL BE KNOWN AS STORMFUR.
STARCLAN HONORS YOUR STRENGTH AND LOYALTY...
MY BROTHER'S HAPPINESS MAKES ME HAPPY. AT LEAST A LITTLE. I KNOW HE DOESN'T HAVE MY DOUBTS.
THE DOUBTS THAT WILL NOT GO AWAY.
...AND WE WELCOME YOU AS A FULL WARRIOR OF RIVERCLAN!

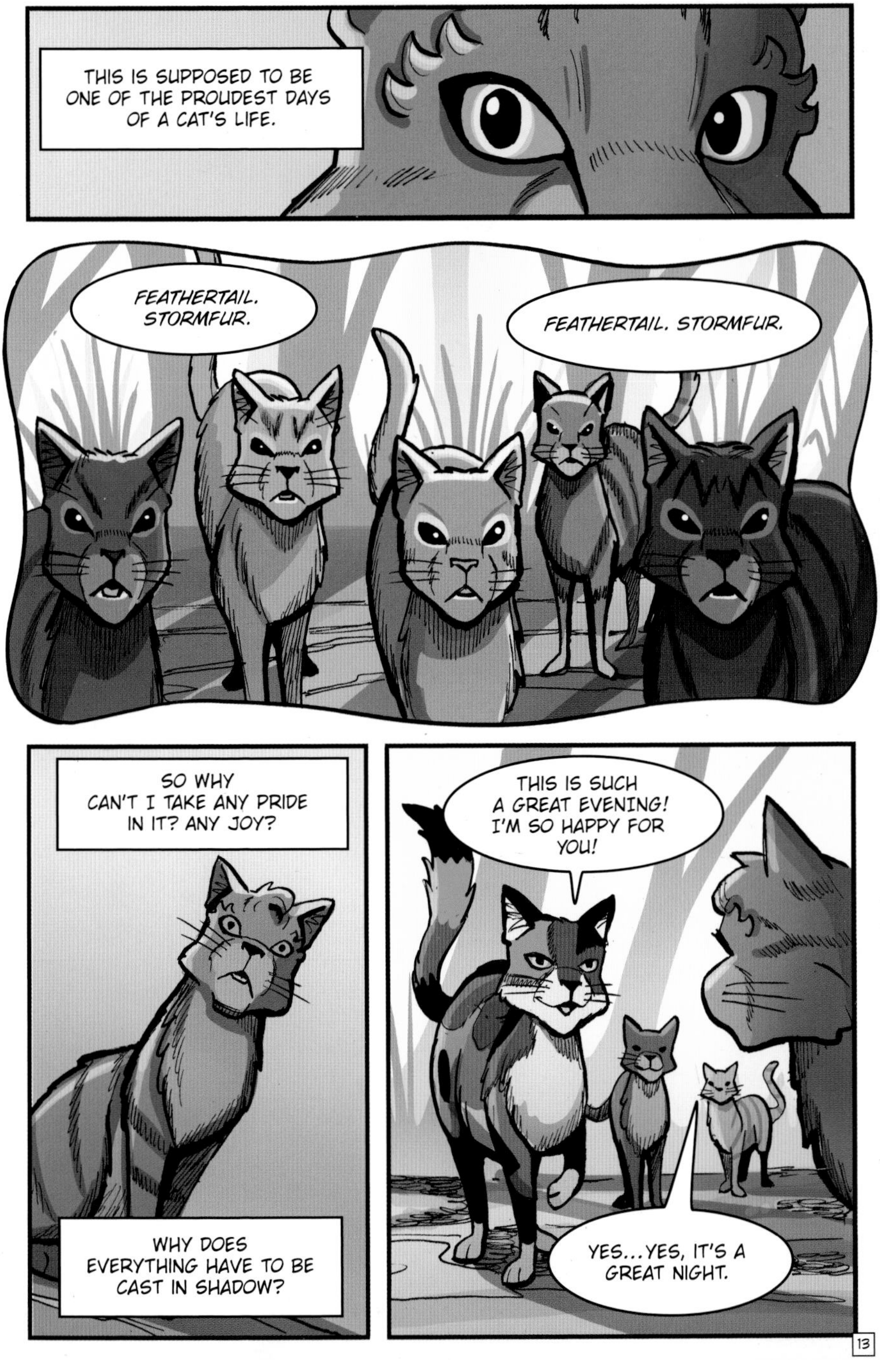
THIS IS SUPPOSED TO BE ONE OF THE PROUDEST DAYS OF A CAT'S LIFE.
FEATHERTAIL. STORMFUR.
FEATHERTAIL. STORMFUR.
SO WHY CAN'T I TAKE ANY PRIDE IN IT? ANY JOY?
WHY DOES EVERYTHING HAVE TO BE CAST IN SHADOW?
THIS IS SUCH A GREAT EVENING! I'M SO HAPPY FOR YOU!
YES...YES, IT'S A GREAT NIGHT.

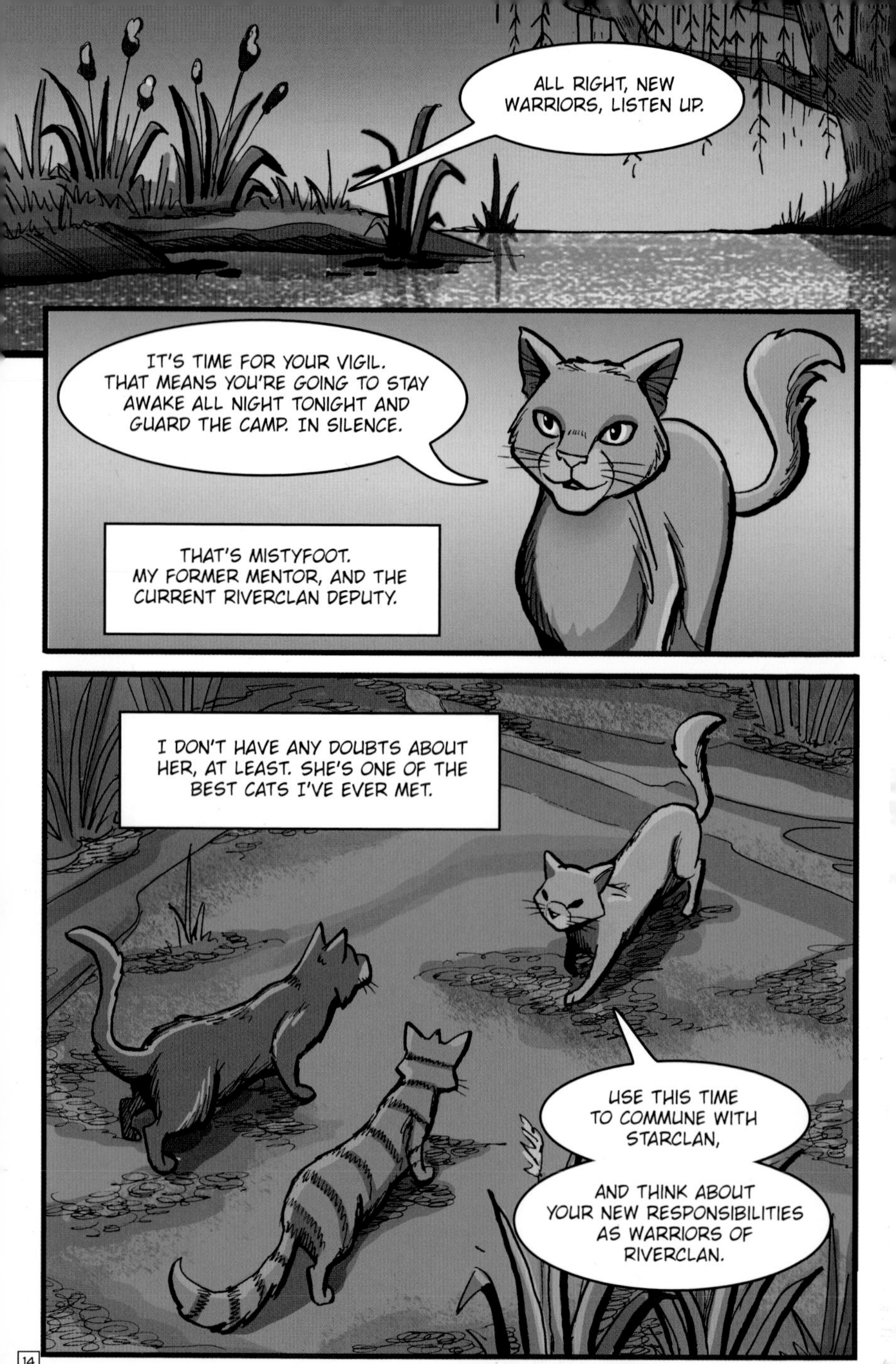
ALL RIGHT, NEW WARRIORS, LISTEN UP.
IT'S TIME FOR YOUR VIGIL. THAT MEANS YOU'RE GOING TO STAY AWAKE ALL NIGHT TONIGHT AND GUARD THE CAMP. IN SILENCE.
THAT'S MISTYFOOT. MY FORMER MENTOR, AND THE CURRENT RIVERCLAN DEPUTY.
I DON'T HAVE ANY DOUBTS ABOUT HER, AT LEAST. SHE'S ONE OF THE BEST CATS I'VE EVER MET.
USE THIS TIME TO COMMUNE WITH STARCLAN,
AND THINK ABOUT YOUR NEW RESPONSIBILITIES AS WARRIORS OF RIVERCLAN.

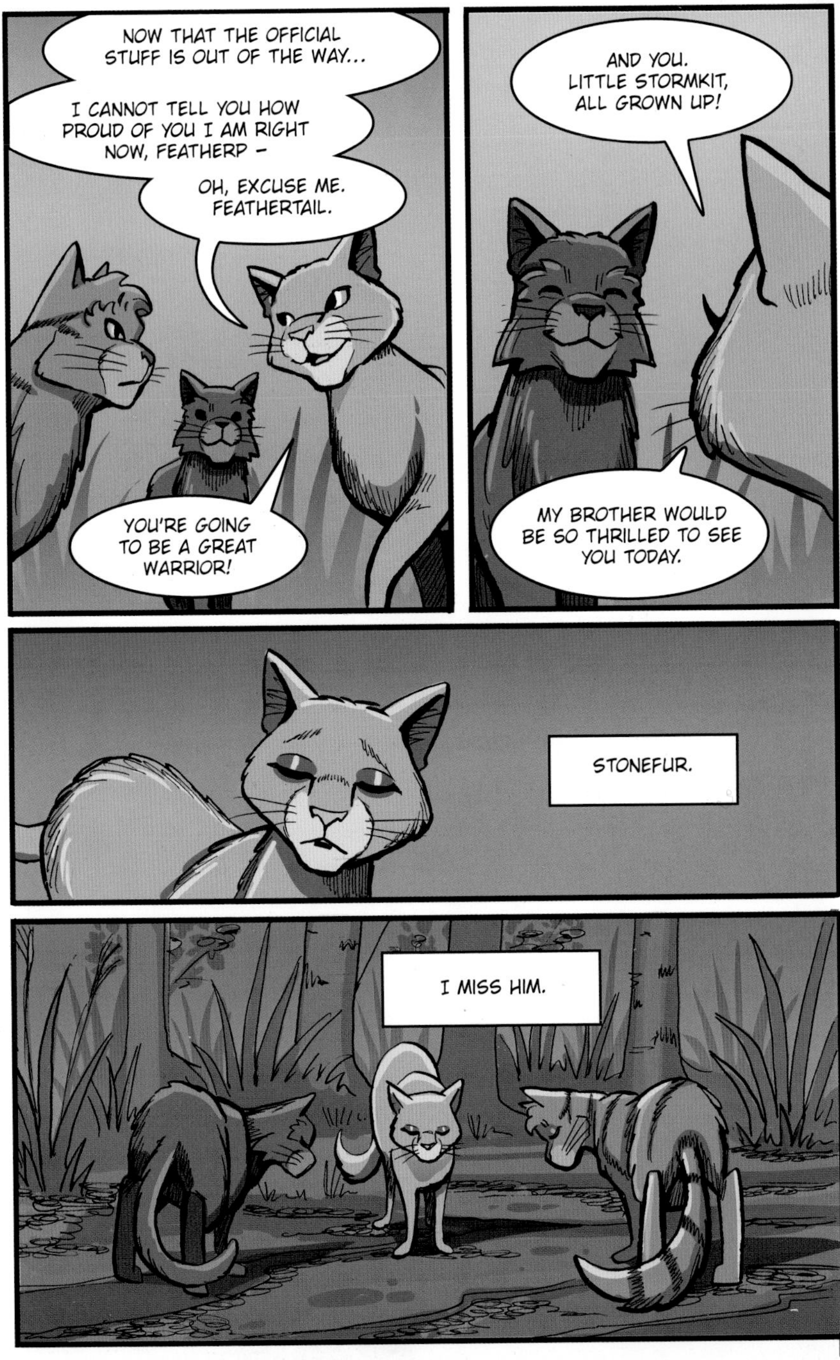
NOW THAT THE OFFICIAL STUFF IS OUT OF THE WAY...
I CANNOT TELL YOU HOW PROUD OF YOU I AM RIGHT NOW, FEATHERP –
OH, EXCUSE ME. FEATHERTAIL.
YOU'RE GOING TO BE A GREAT WARRIOR!
AND YOU. LITTLE STORMKIT, ALL GROWN UP!
MY BROTHER WOULD BE SO THRILLED TO SEE YOU TODAY.
STONEFUR.
I MISS HIM.

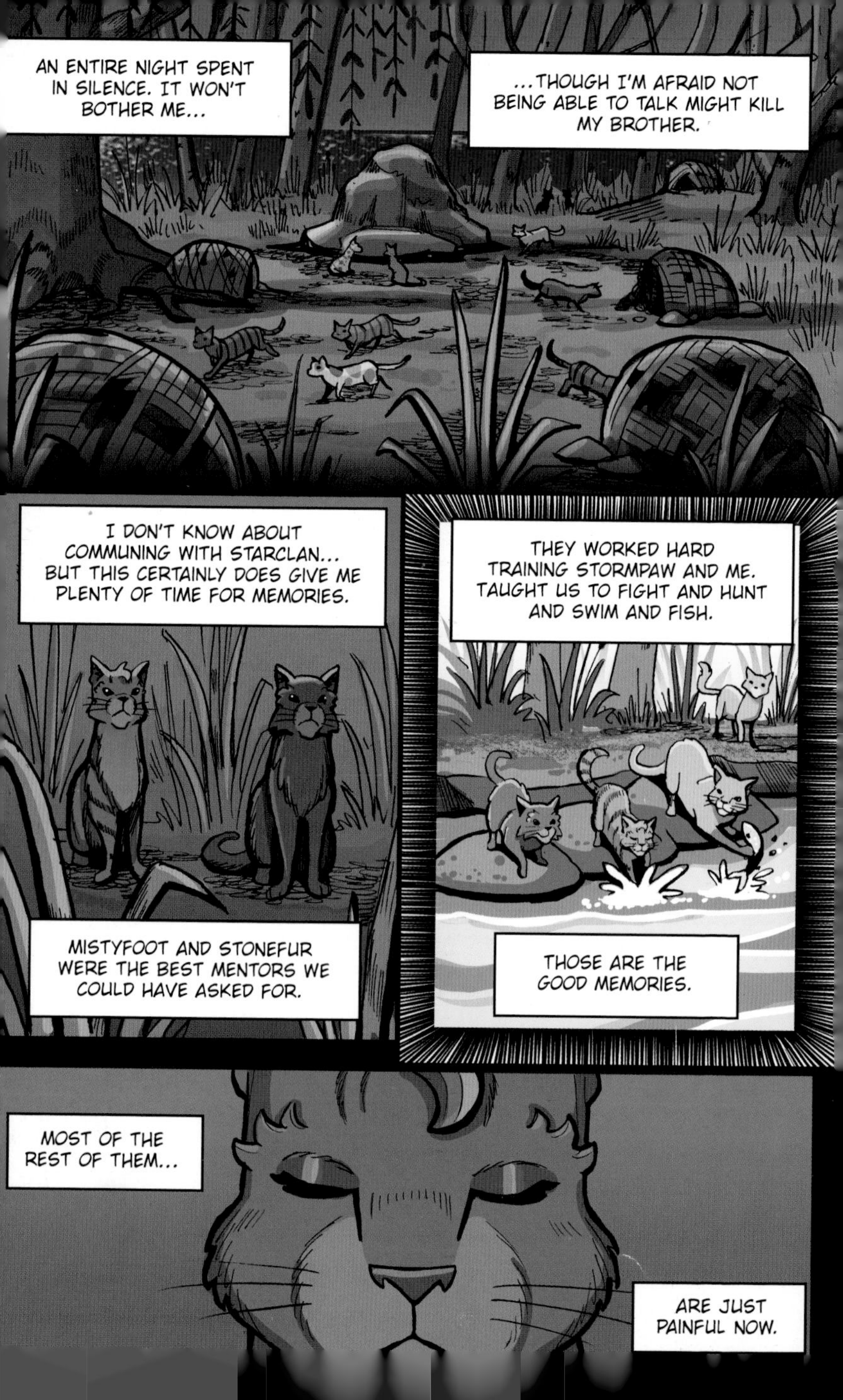
AN ENTIRE NIGHT SPENT IN SILENCE. IT WON'T BOTHER ME...
...THOUGH I'M AFRAID NOT BEING ABLE TO TALK MIGHT KILL MY BROTHER.
I DON'T KNOW ABOUT COMMUNING WITH STARCLAN... BUT THIS CERTAINLY DOES GIVE ME PLENTY OF TIME FOR MEMORIES.
MISTYFOOT AND STONEFUR WERE THE BEST MENTORS WE COULD HAVE ASKED FOR.
THEY WORKED HARD TRAINING STORMPAW AND ME. TAUGHT US TO FIGHT AND HUNT AND SWIM AND FISH.
THOSE ARE THE GOOD MEMORIES.
MOST OF THE REST OF THEM...
ARE JUST PAINFUL NOW.

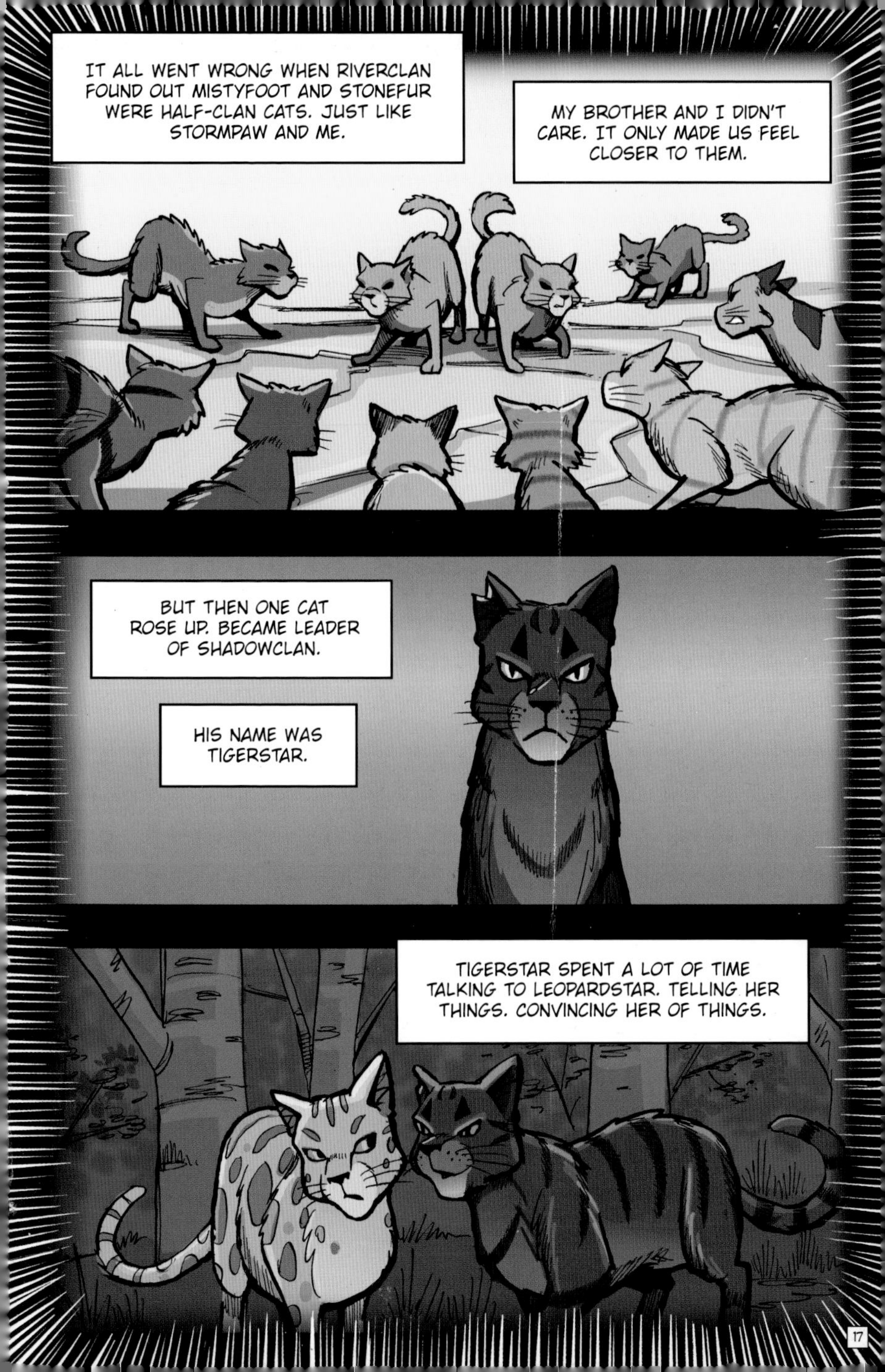
IT ALL WENT WRONG WHEN RIVERCLAN FOUND OUT MISTYFOOT AND STONEFUR WERE HALF-CLAN CATS. JUST LIKE STORMPAW AND ME.
MY BROTHER AND I DIDN'T CARE. IT ONLY MADE US FEEL CLOSER TO THEM.
BUT THEN ONE CAT ROSE UP. BECAME LEADER OF SHADOWCLAN.
HIS NAME WAS TIGERSTAR.
TIGERSTAR SPENT A LOT OF TIME TALKING TO LEOPARDSTAR. TELLING HER THINGS. CONVINCING HER OF THINGS.

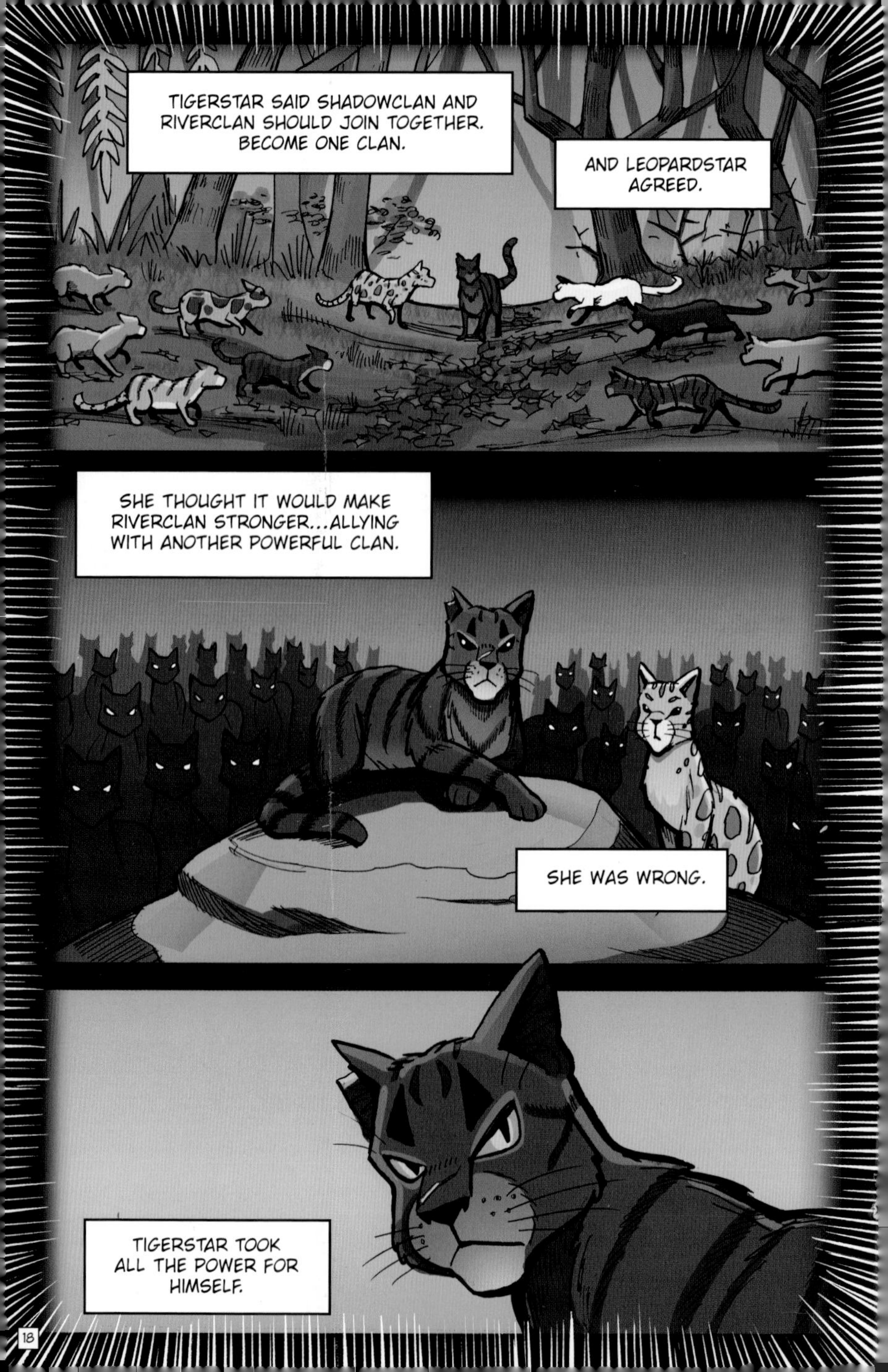
TIGERSTAR SAID SHADOWCLAN AND RIVERCLAN SHOULD JOIN TOGETHER. BECOME ONE CLAN.
AND LEOPARDSTAR AGREED.
SHE THOUGHT IT WOULD MAKE RIVERCLAN STRONGER...ALLYING WITH ANOTHER POWERFUL CLAN.
SHE WAS WRONG.
TIGERSTAR TOOK ALL THE POWER FOR HIMSELF.

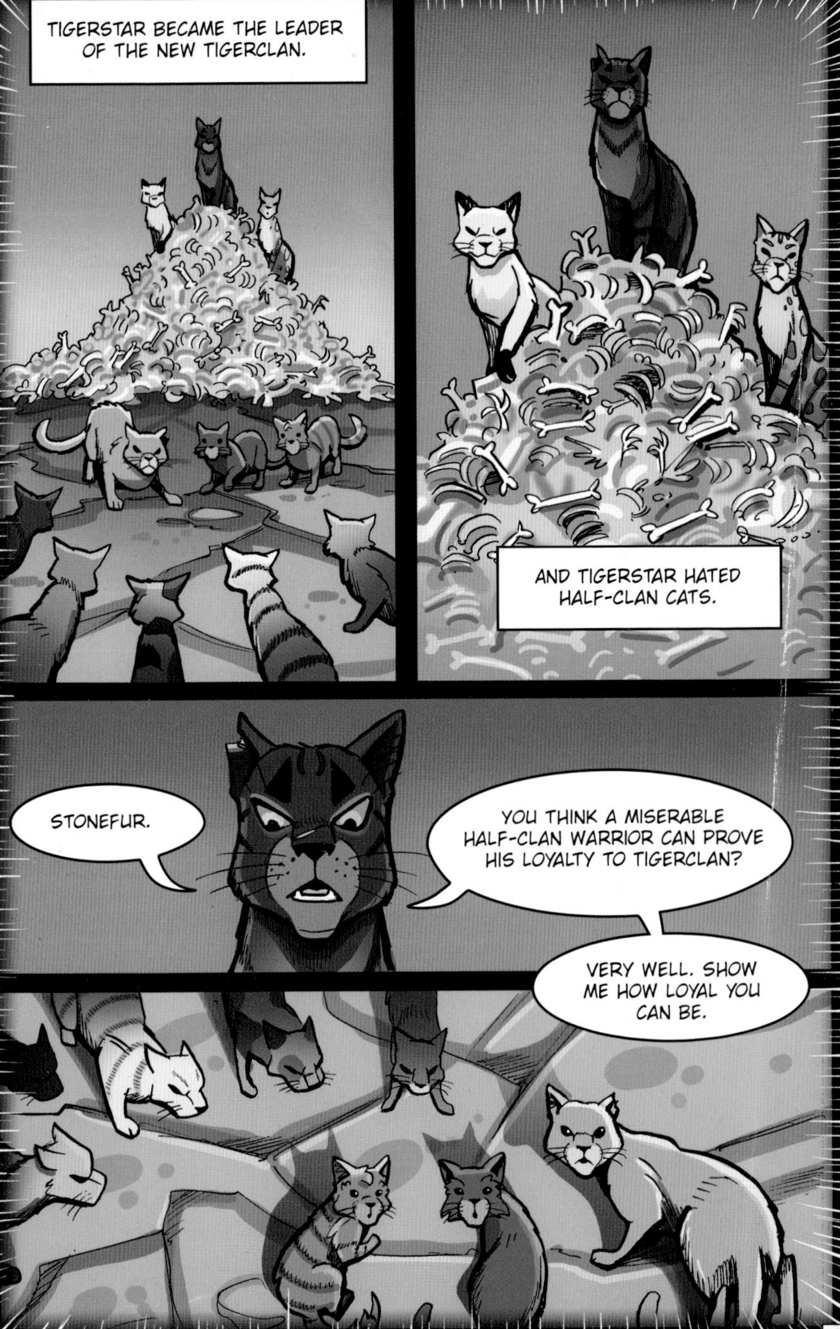

TIGERSTAR BECAME THE LEADER OF THE NEW TIGERCLAN.
AND TIGERSTAR HATED HALF-CLAN CATS.
STONEFUR.
YOU THINK A MISERABLE HALF-CLAN WARRIOR CAN PROVE HIS LOYALTY TO TIGERCLAN?
VERY WELL. SHOW ME HOW LOYAL YOU CAN BE.

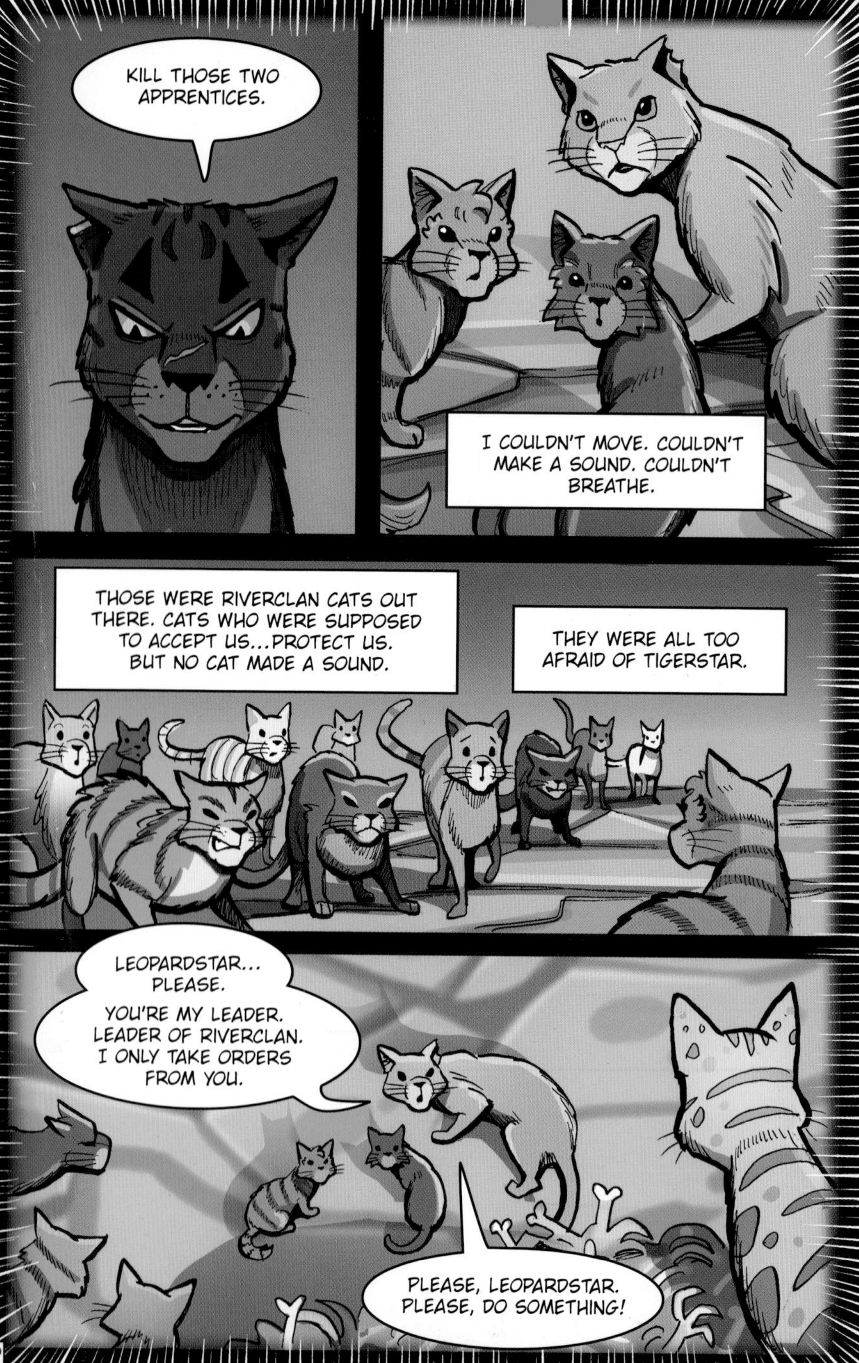
KILL THOSE TWO APPRENTICES.
I COULDN'T MOVE. COULDN'T MAKE A SOUND. COULDN'T BREATHE.
THOSE WERE RIVERCLAN CATS OUT THERE. CATS WHO WERE SUPPOSED TO ACCEPT US...PROTECT US. BUT NO CAT MADE A SOUND.
THEY WERE ALL TOO AFRAID OF TIGERSTAR.
LEOPARDSTAR... PLEASE.
YOU'RE MY LEADER. LEADER OF RIVERCLAN. I ONLY TAKE ORDERS FROM YOU.
PLEASE, LEOPARDSTAR. PLEASE, DO SOMETHING!

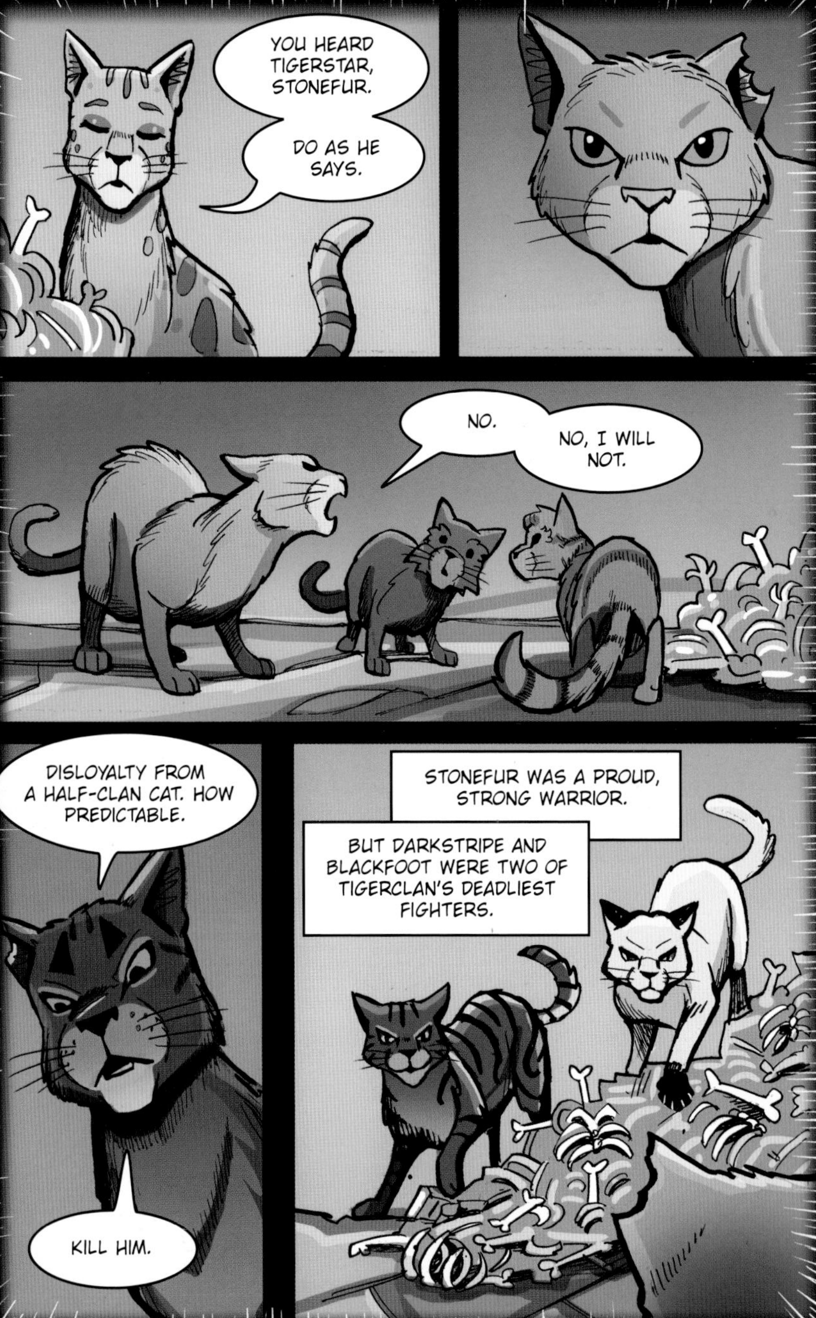
YOU HEARD TIGERSTAR, STONEFUR.
DO AS HE SAYS.
NO.
NO, I WILL NOT.
DISLOYALTY FROM A HALF-CLAN CAT. HOW PREDICTABLE.
KILL HIM.
STONEFUR WAS A PROUD, STRONG WARRIOR.
BUT DARKSTRIPE AND BLACKFOOT WERE TWO OF TIGERCLAN'S DEADLIEST FIGHTERS.

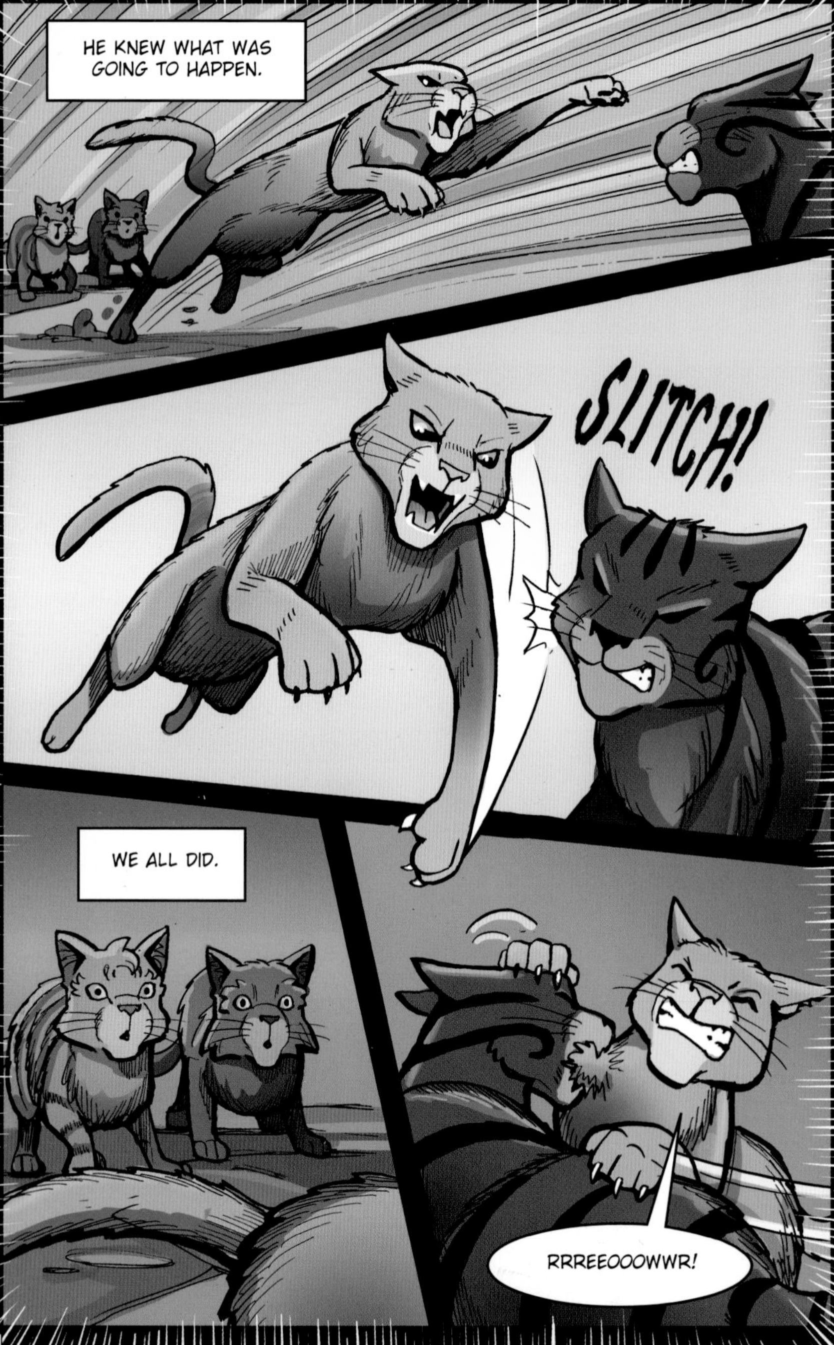
HE KNEW WHAT WAS GOING TO HAPPEN.
SLITCH!
WE ALL DID.
RRREEOOOWWR!

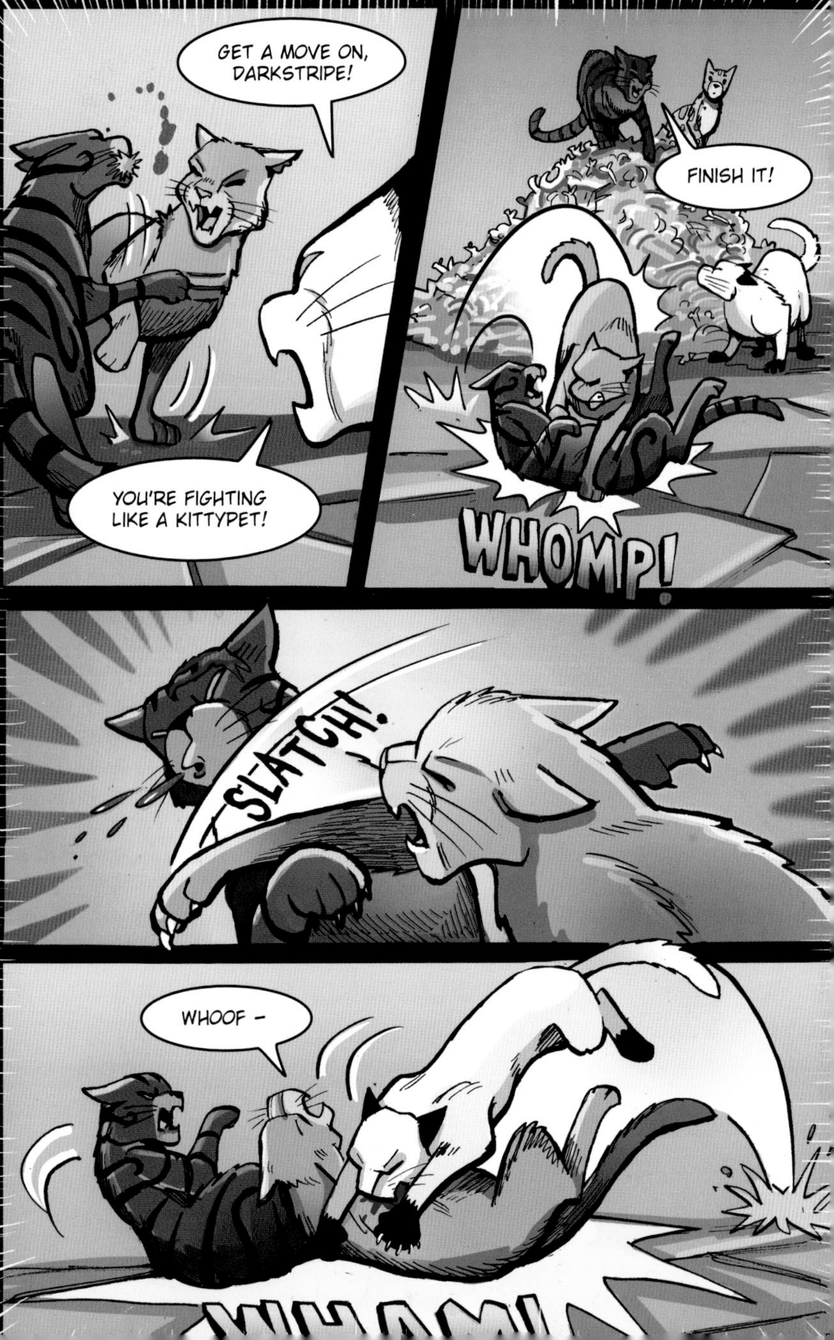
GET A MOVE ON, DARKSTRIPE!
YOU'RE FIGHTING LIKE A KITTYPET!
FINISH IT!
WHOMP!
SLATCH!
WHOOF –

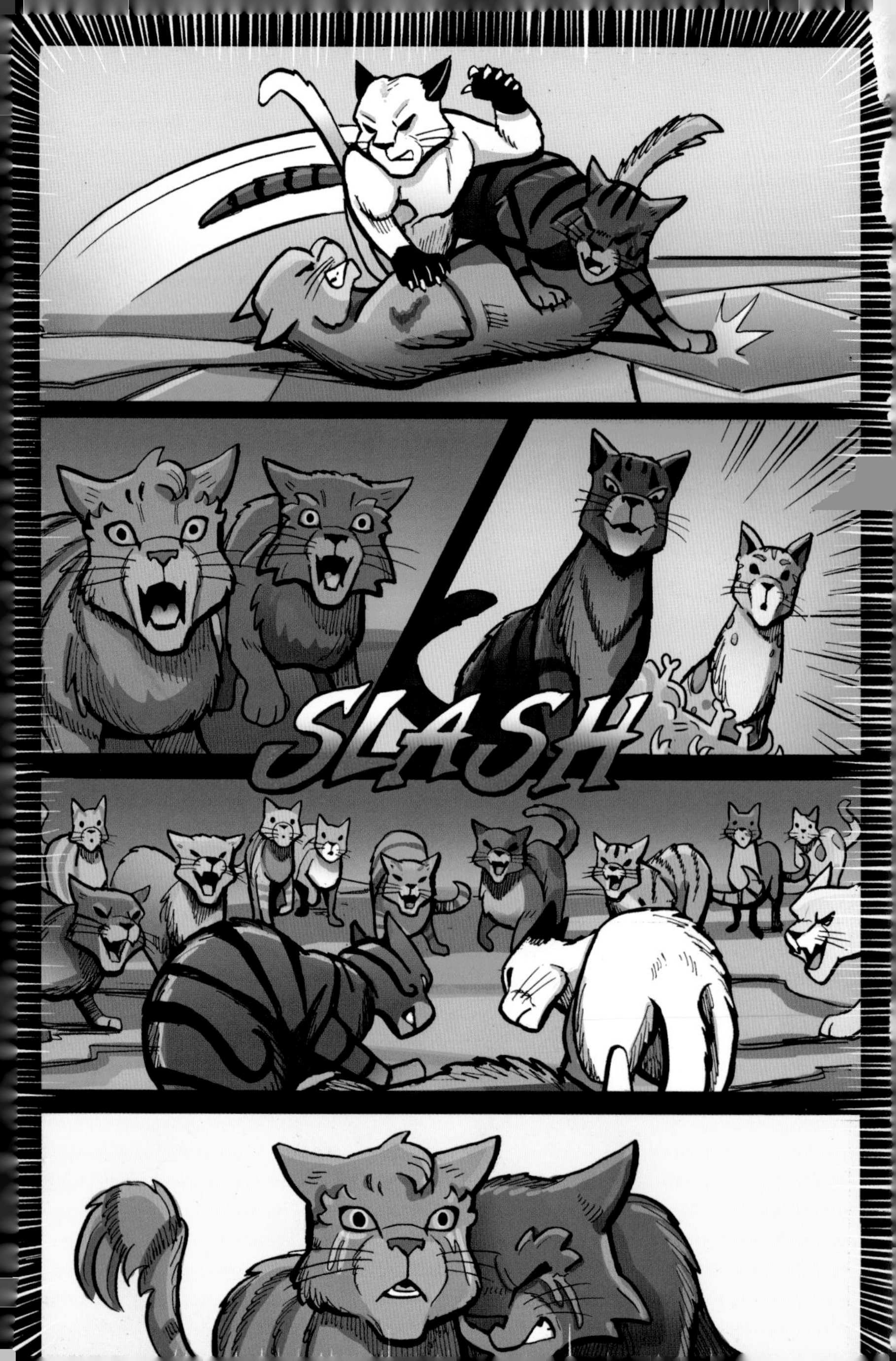
SLASH

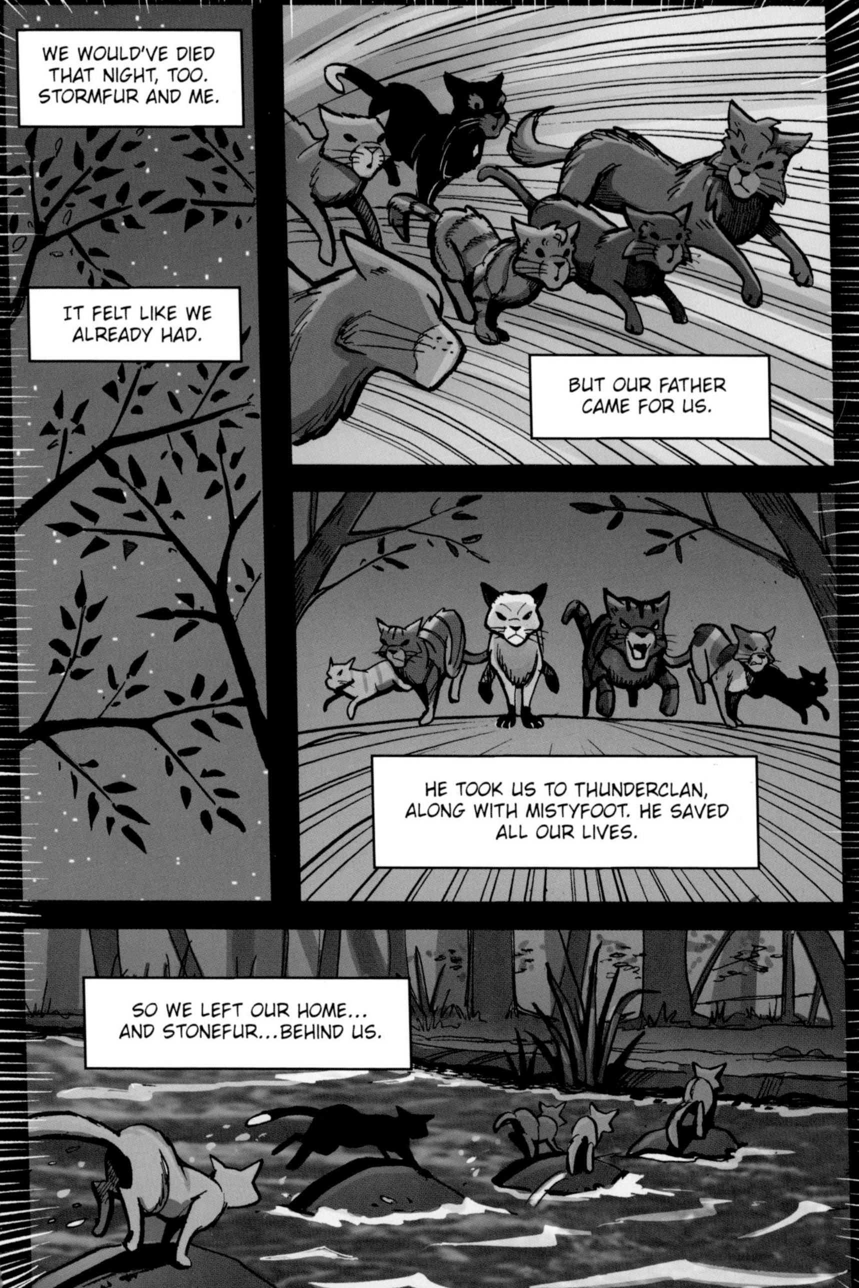
WE WOULD'VE DIED THAT NIGHT, TOO. STORMFUR AND ME.
IT FELT LIKE WE ALREADY HAD.
BUT OUR FATHER CAME FOR US.
HE TOOK US TO THUNDERCLAN, ALONG WITH MISTYFOOT. HE SAVED ALL OUR LIVES.
SO WE LEFT OUR HOME... AND STONEFUR...BEHIND US.

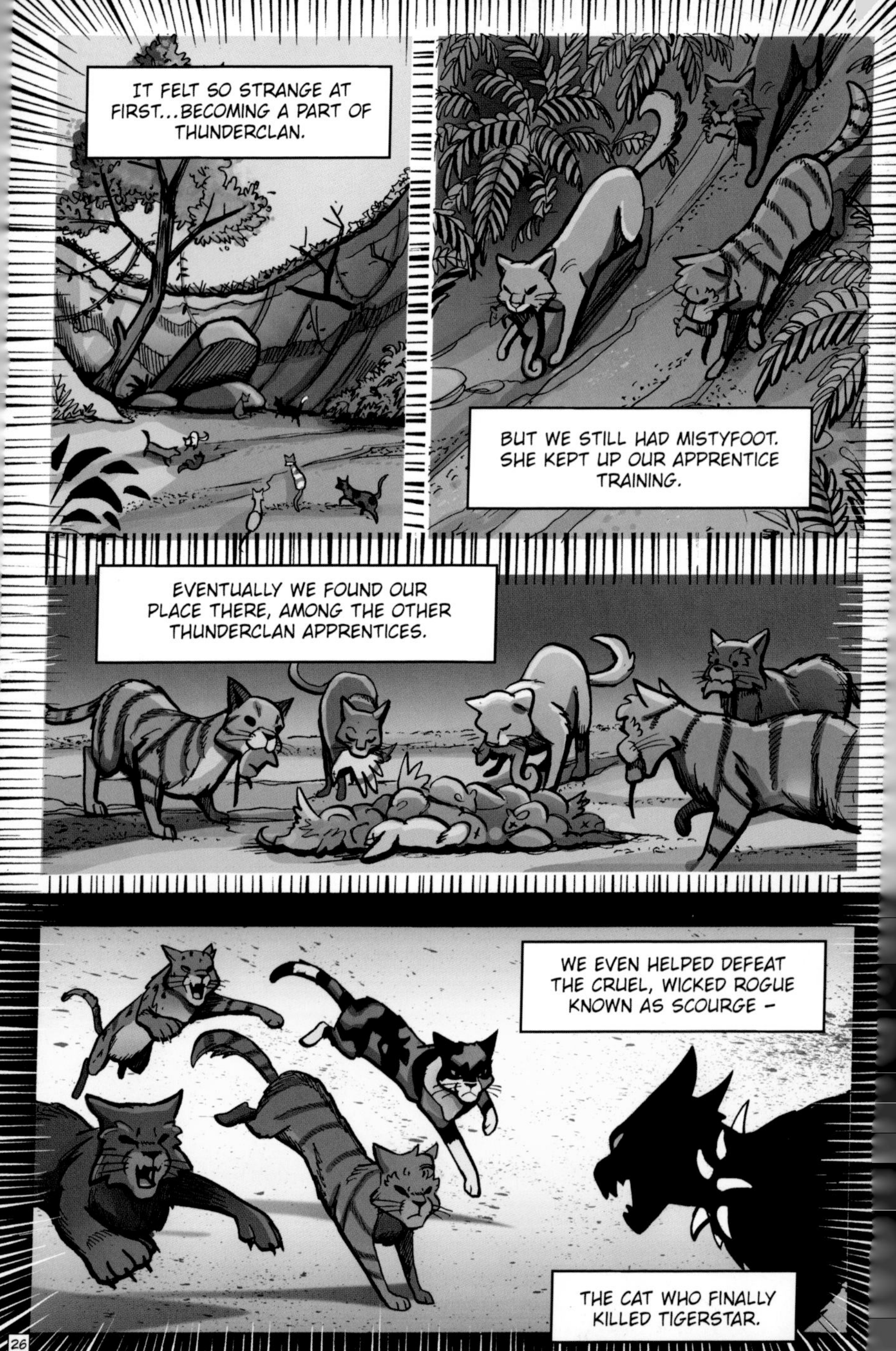
IT FELT SO STRANGE AT FIRST...BECOMING A PART OF THUNDERCLAN.
BUT WE STILL HAD MISTYFOOT. SHE KEPT UP OUR APPRENTICE TRAINING.
EVENTUALLY WE FOUND OUR PLACE THERE, AMONG THE OTHER THUNDERCLAN APPRENTICES.
WE EVEN HELPED DEFEAT THE CRUEL, WICKED ROGUE KNOWN AS SCOURGE –
THE CAT WHO FINALLY KILLED TIGERSTAR.

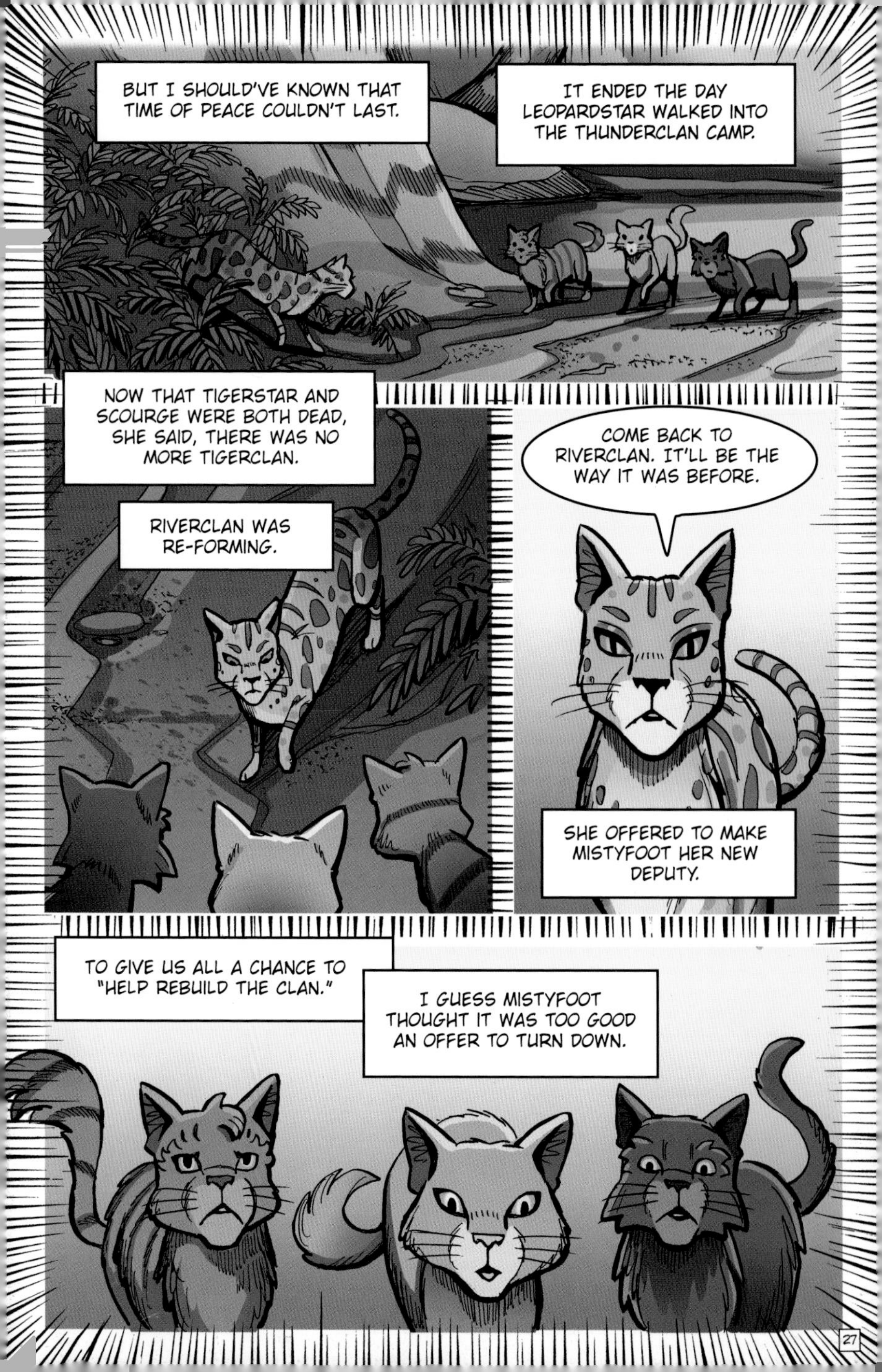
BUT I SHOULD'VE KNOWN THAT TIME OF PEACE COULDN'T LAST.
IT ENDED THE DAY LEOPARDSTAR WALKED INTO THE THUNDERCLAN CAMP.
NOW THAT TIGERSTAR AND SCOURGE WERE BOTH DEAD, SHE SAID, THERE WAS NO MORE TIGERCLAN.
RIVERCLAN WAS RE-FORMING.
COME BACK TO RIVERCLAN. IT'LL BE THE WAY IT WAS BEFORE.
SHE OFFERED TO MAKE MISTYFOOT HER NEW DEPUTY.
TO GIVE US ALL A CHANCE TO "HELP REBUILD THE CLAN."
I GUESS MISTYFOOT THOUGHT IT WAS TOO GOOD AN OFFER TO TURN DOWN.

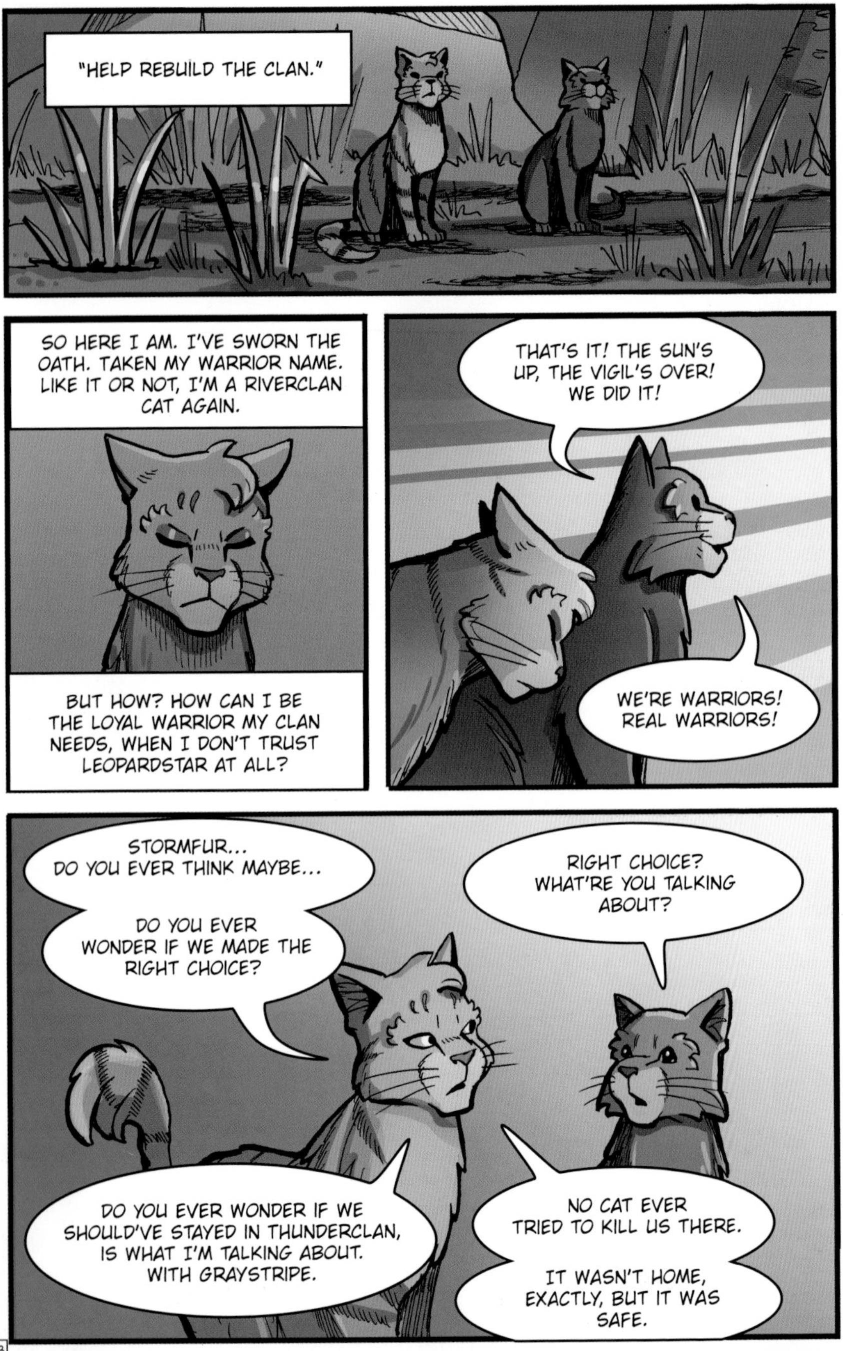
"HELP REBUILD THE CLAN."
SO HERE I AM. I'VE SWORN THE OATH. TAKEN MY WARRIOR NAME. LIKE IT OR NOT, I'M A RIVERCLAN CAT AGAIN.
BUT HOW? HOW CAN I BE THE LOYAL WARRIOR MY CLAN NEEDS, WHEN I DON'T TRUST LEOPARDSTAR AT ALL?
THAT'S IT! THE SUN'S UP, THE VIGIL'S OVER! WE DID IT!
WE'RE WARRIORS! REAL WARRIORS!
STORMFUR... DO YOU EVER THINK MAYBE...
DO YOU EVER WONDER IF WE MADE THE RIGHT CHOICE?
RIGHT CHOICE? WHAT'RE YOU TALKING ABOUT?
DO YOU EVER WONDER IF WE SHOULD'VE STAYED IN THUNDERCLAN, IS WHAT I'M TALKING ABOUT. WITH GRAYSTRIPE.
NO CAT EVER TRIED TO KILL US THERE.
IT WASN'T HOME, EXACTLY, BUT IT WAS SAFE.

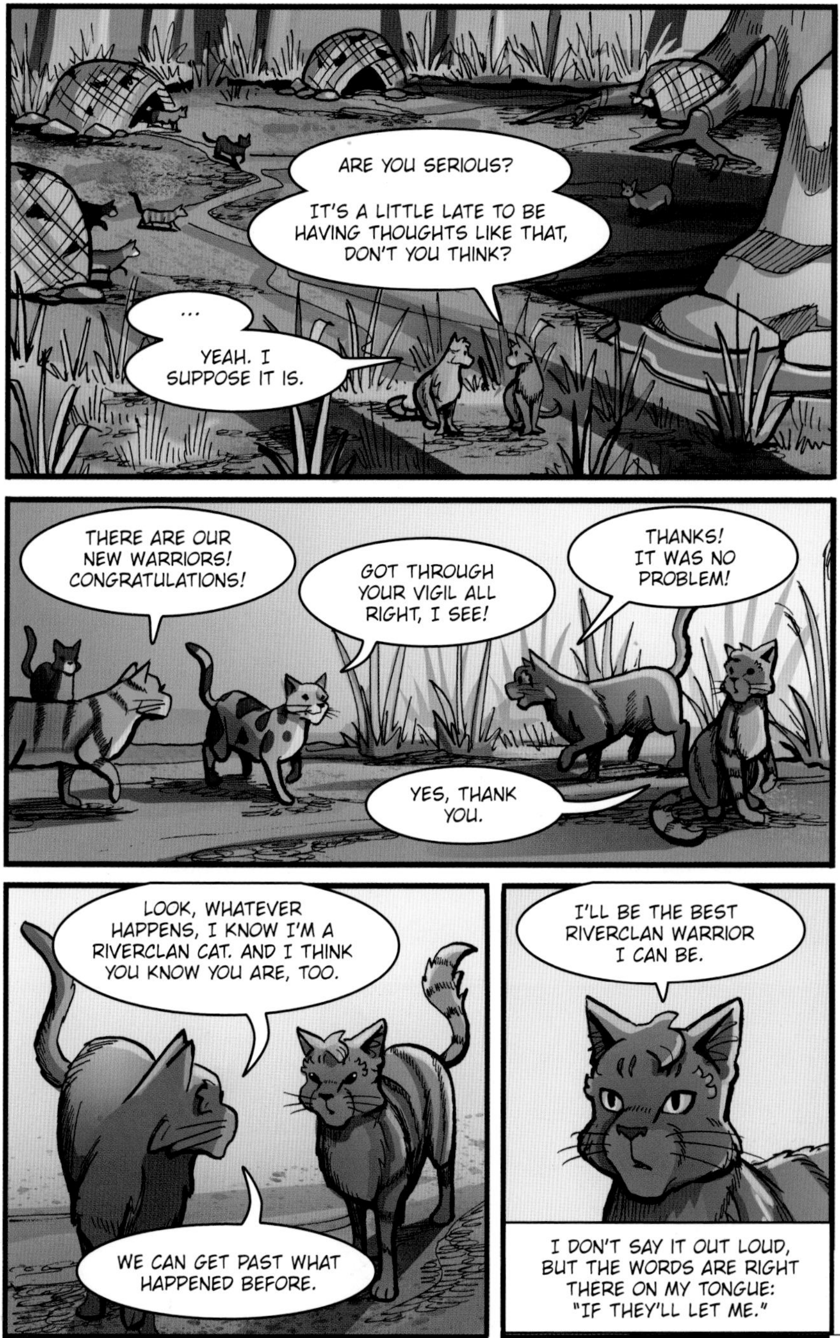
ARE YOU SERIOUS?
IT'S A LITTLE LATE TO BE HAVING THOUGHTS LIKE THAT, DON'T YOU THINK?
...
YEAH. I SUPPOSE IT IS.
THERE ARE OUR NEW WARRIORS! CONGRATULATIONS!
GOT THROUGH YOUR VIGIL ALL RIGHT, I SEE!
THANKS! IT WAS NO PROBLEM!
YES, THANK YOU.
LOOK, WHATEVER HAPPENS, I KNOW I'M A RIVERCLAN CAT. AND I THINK YOU KNOW YOU ARE, TOO.
WE CAN GET PAST WHAT HAPPENED BEFORE.
I'LL BE THE BEST RIVERCLAN WARRIOR I CAN BE.
I DON'T SAY IT OUT LOUD, BUT THE WORDS ARE RIGHT THERE ON MY TONGUE: "IF THEY'LL LET ME."

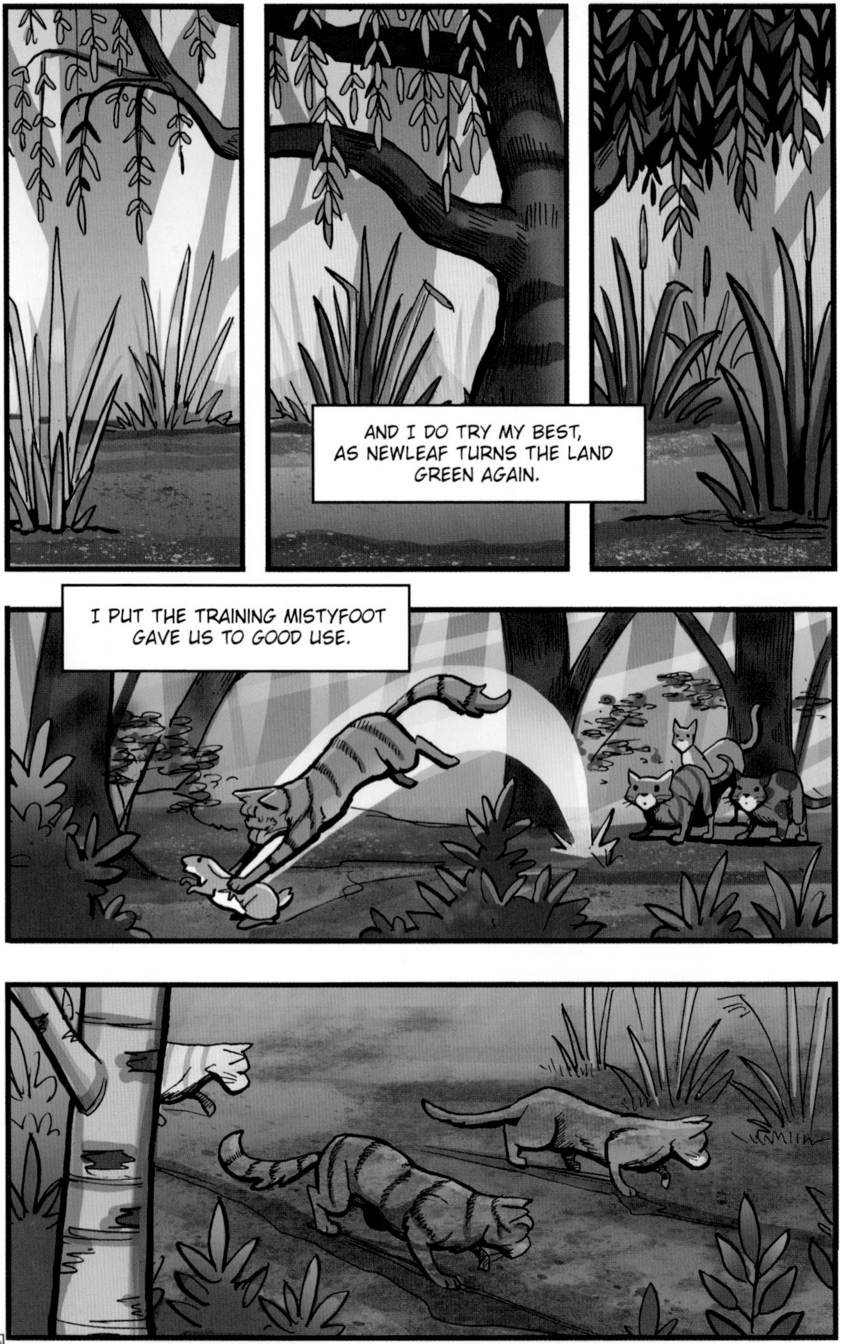
AND I DO TRY MY BEST, AS NEWLEAF TURNS THE LAND GREEN AGAIN.
I PUT THE TRAINING MISTYFOOT GAVE US TO GOOD USE.

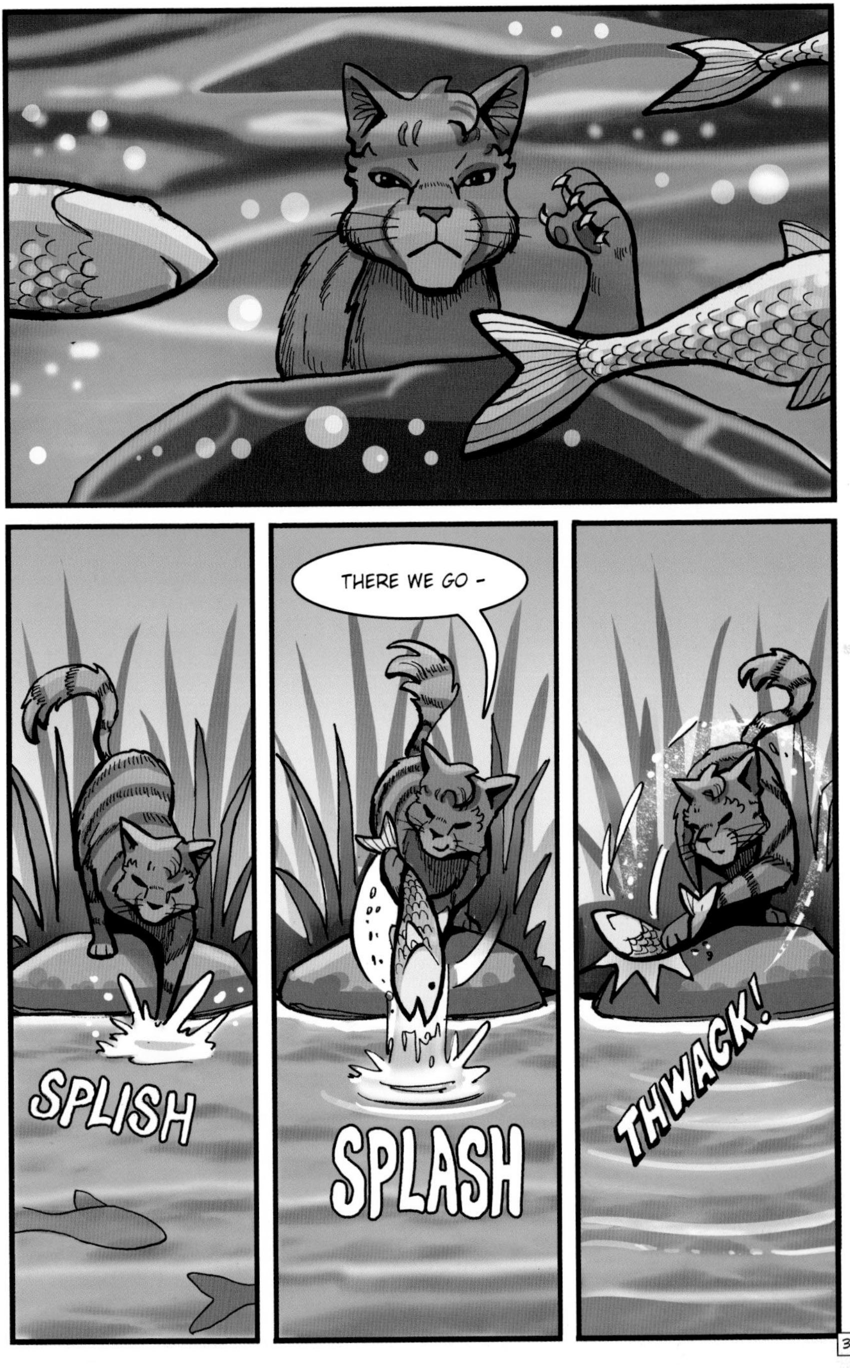
THERE WE GO -
SPLISH
SPLASH
THWACK!

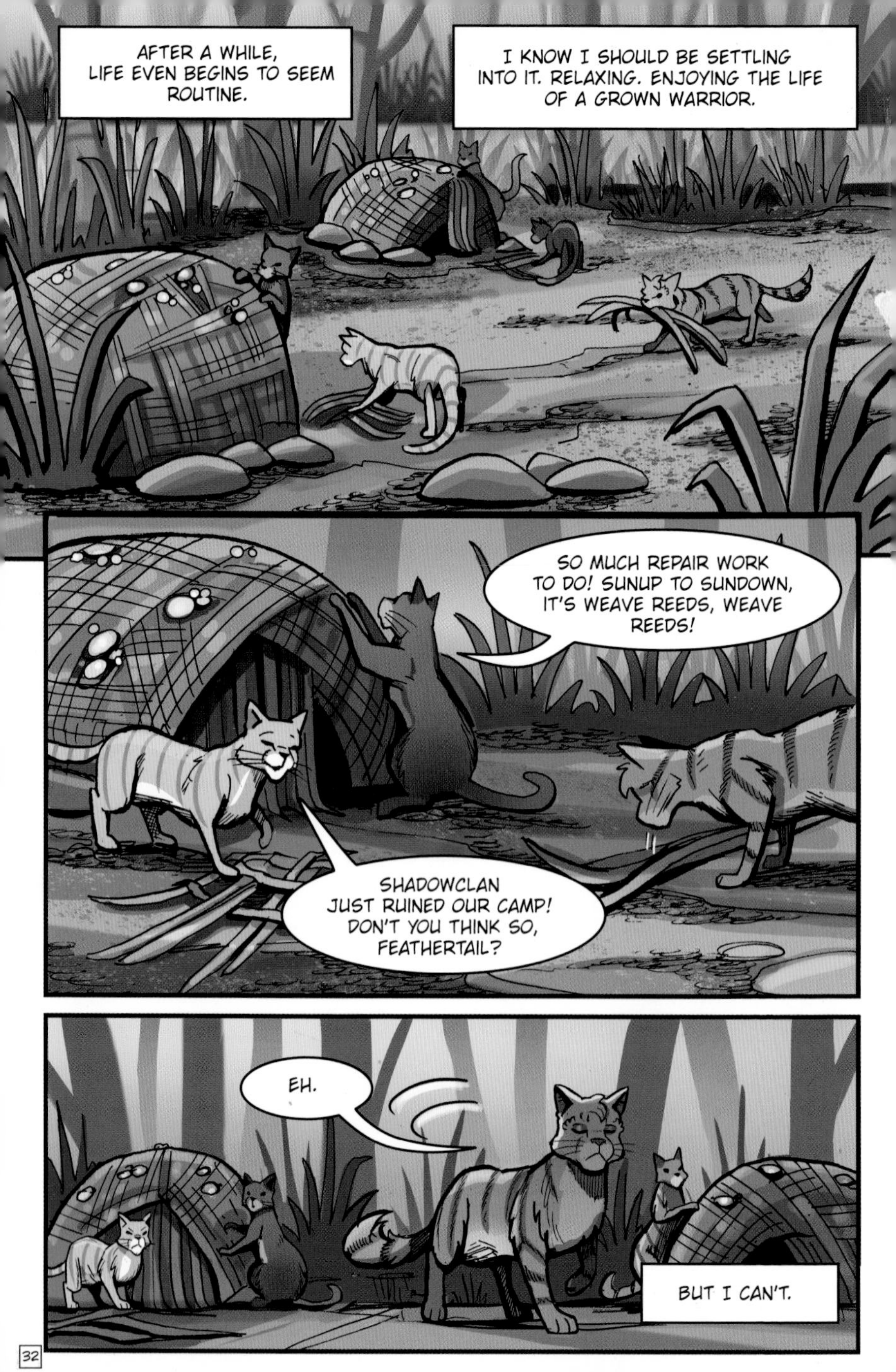
AFTER A WHILE, LIFE EVEN BEGINS TO SEEM ROUTINE.
I KNOW I SHOULD BE SETTLING INTO IT. RELAXING. ENJOYING THE LIFE OF A GROWN WARRIOR.
SO MUCH REPAIR WORK TO DO! SUNUP TO SUNDOWN, IT'S WEAVE REEDS, WEAVE REEDS!
SHADOWCLAN JUST RUINED OUR CAMP! DON'T YOU THINK SO, FEATHERTAIL?
EH.
BUT I CAN'T.

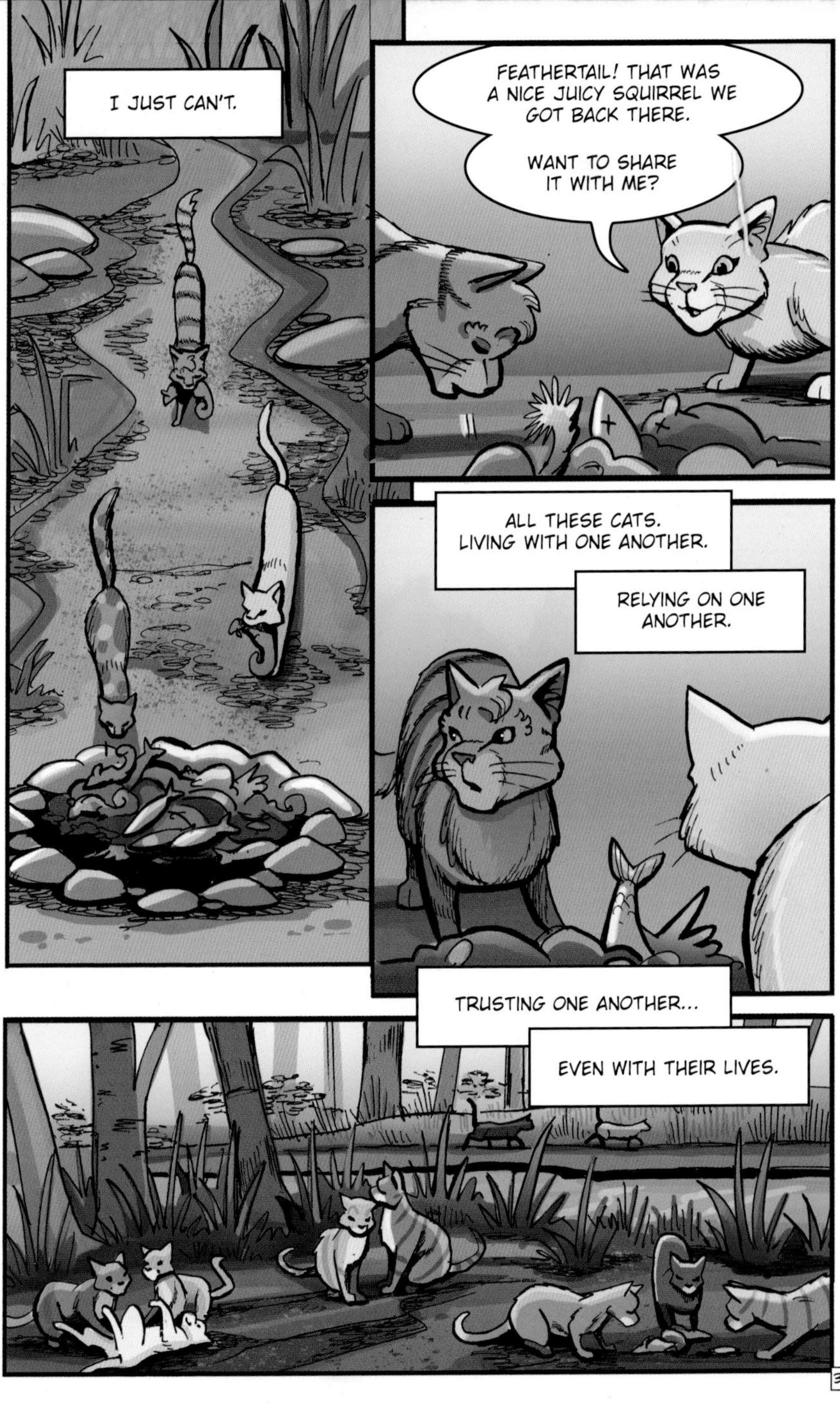
I JUST CAN'T.
FEATHERTAIL! THAT WAS A NICE JUICY SQUIRREL WE GOT BACK THERE.
WANT TO SHARE IT WITH ME?
ALL THESE CATS. LIVING WITH ONE ANOTHER.
RELYING ON ONE ANOTHER.
TRUSTING ONE ANOTHER...
EVEN WITH THEIR LIVES.

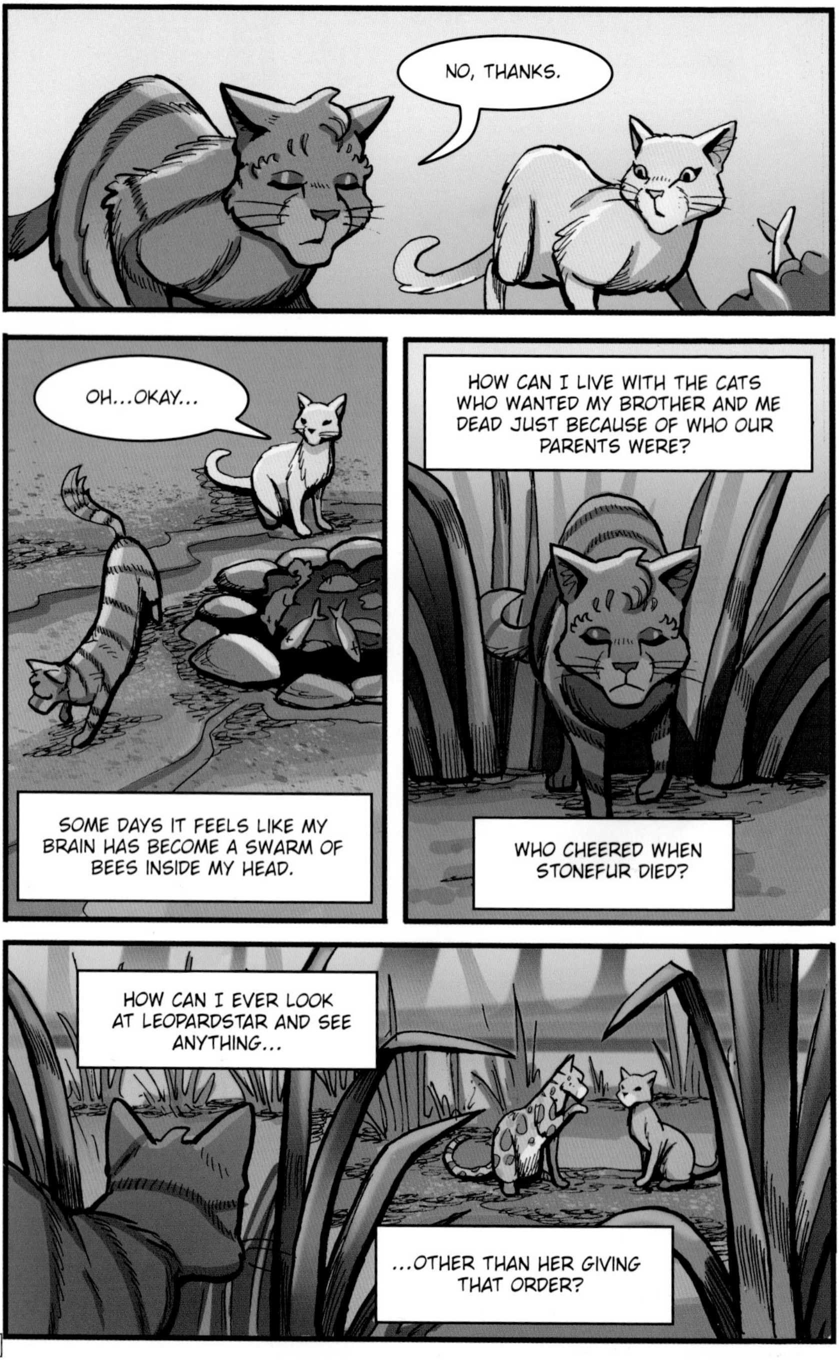

NO, THANKS.
OH...OKAY...
SOME DAYS IT FEELS LIKE MY BRAIN HAS BECOME A SWARM OF BEES INSIDE MY HEAD.
HOW CAN I LIVE WITH THE CATS WHO WANTED MY BROTHER AND ME DEAD JUST BECAUSE OF WHO OUR PARENTS WERE?
WHO CHEERED WHEN STONEFUR DIED?
HOW CAN I EVER LOOK AT LEOPARDSTAR AND SEE ANYTHING...
...OTHER THAN HER GIVING THAT ORDER?

THE DISTANCE STARTS SMALL...

...BUT IT GROWS EVERY DAY.

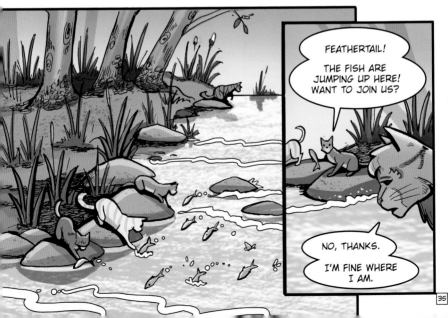

FEATHERTAIL!

THE FISH ARE JUMPING UP HERE! WANT TO JOIN US?

NO, THANKS.

I'M FINE WHERE I AM.

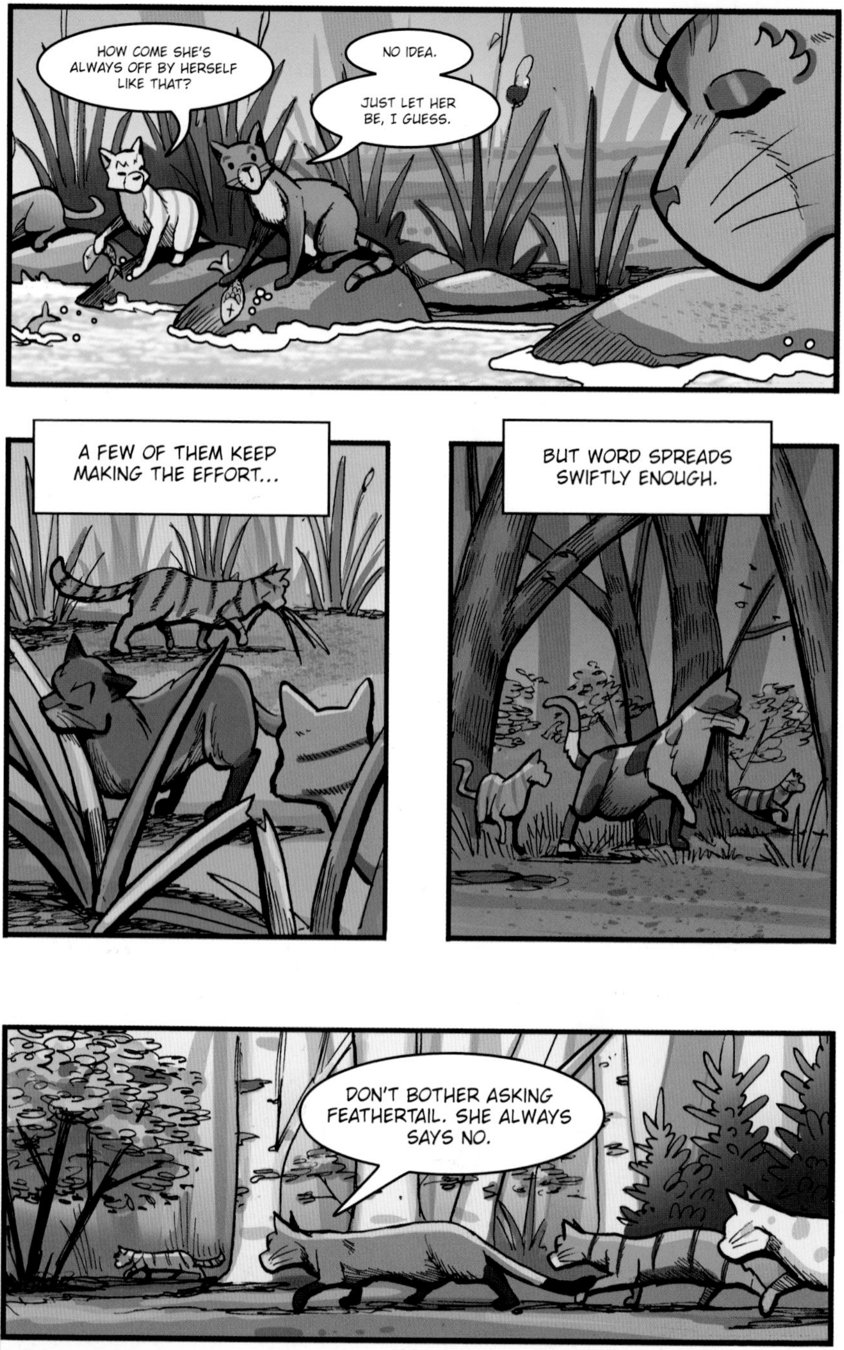
HOW COME SHE'S ALWAYS OFF BY HERSELF LIKE THAT?
NO IDEA.
JUST LET HER BE, I GUESS.
A FEW OF THEM KEEP MAKING THE EFFORT...
BUT WORD SPREADS SWIFTLY ENOUGH.
DON'T BOTHER ASKING FEATHERTAIL. SHE ALWAYS SAYS NO.

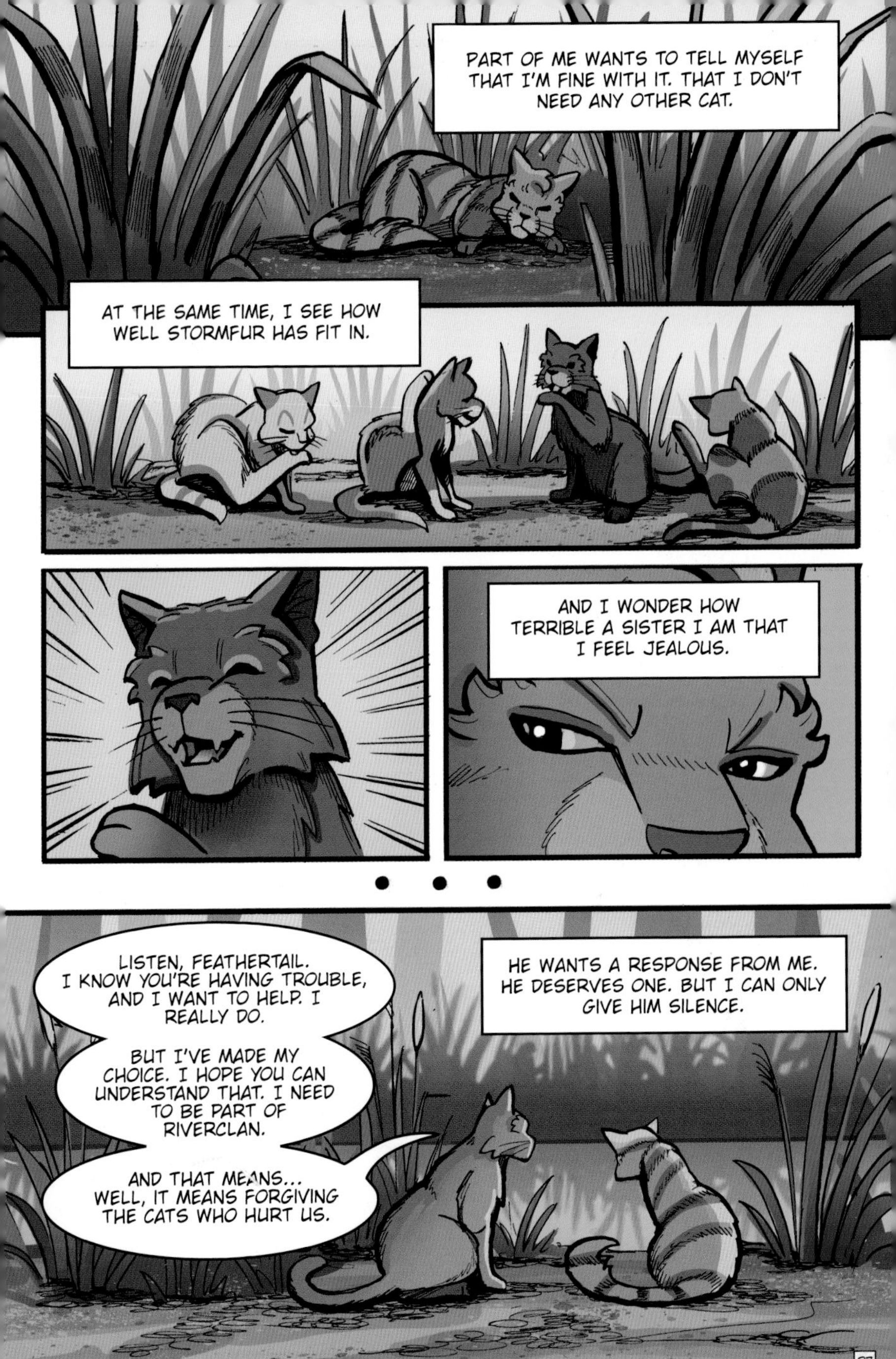
PART OF ME WANTS TO TELL MYSELF THAT I'M FINE WITH IT. THAT I DON'T NEED ANY OTHER CAT.
AT THE SAME TIME, I SEE HOW WELL STORMFUR HAS FIT IN.
AND I WONDER HOW TERRIBLE A SISTER I AM THAT I FEEL JEALOUS.
LISTEN, FEATHERTAIL. I KNOW YOU'RE HAVING TROUBLE, AND I WANT TO HELP. I REALLY DO.
BUT I'VE MADE MY CHOICE. I HOPE YOU CAN UNDERSTAND THAT. I NEED TO BE PART OF RIVERCLAN.
AND THAT MEANS... WELL, IT MEANS FORGIVING THE CATS WHO HURT US.
HE WANTS A RESPONSE FROM ME. HE DESERVES ONE. BUT I CAN ONLY GIVE HIM SILENCE.

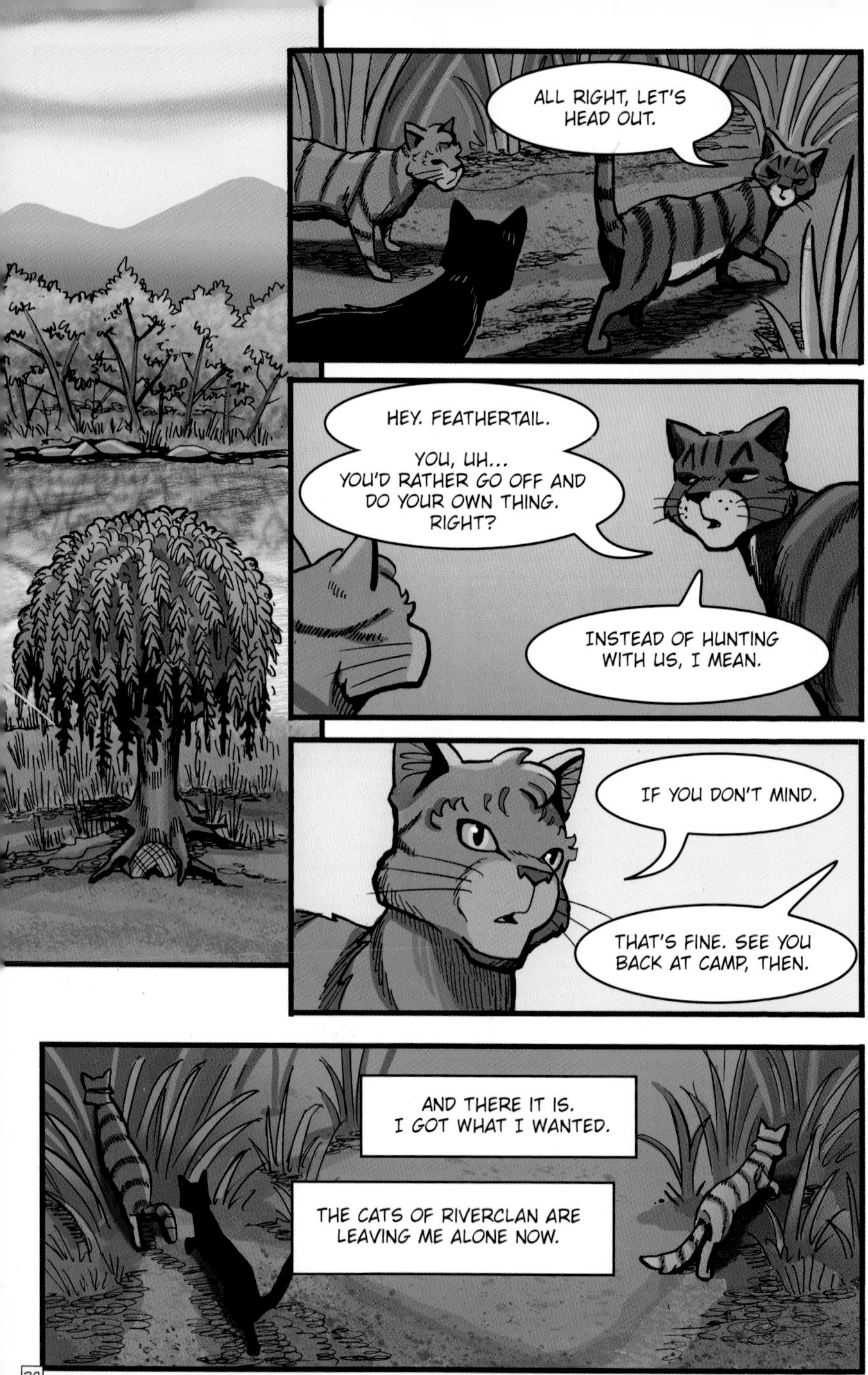
ALL RIGHT, LET'S HEAD OUT.
HEY. FEATHERTAIL.
YOU, UH... YOU'D RATHER GO OFF AND DO YOUR OWN THING. RIGHT?
INSTEAD OF HUNTING WITH US, I MEAN.
IF YOU DON'T MIND.
THAT'S FINE. SEE YOU BACK AT CAMP, THEN.
AND THERE IT IS. I GOT WHAT I WANTED.
THE CATS OF RIVERCLAN ARE LEAVING ME ALONE NOW.

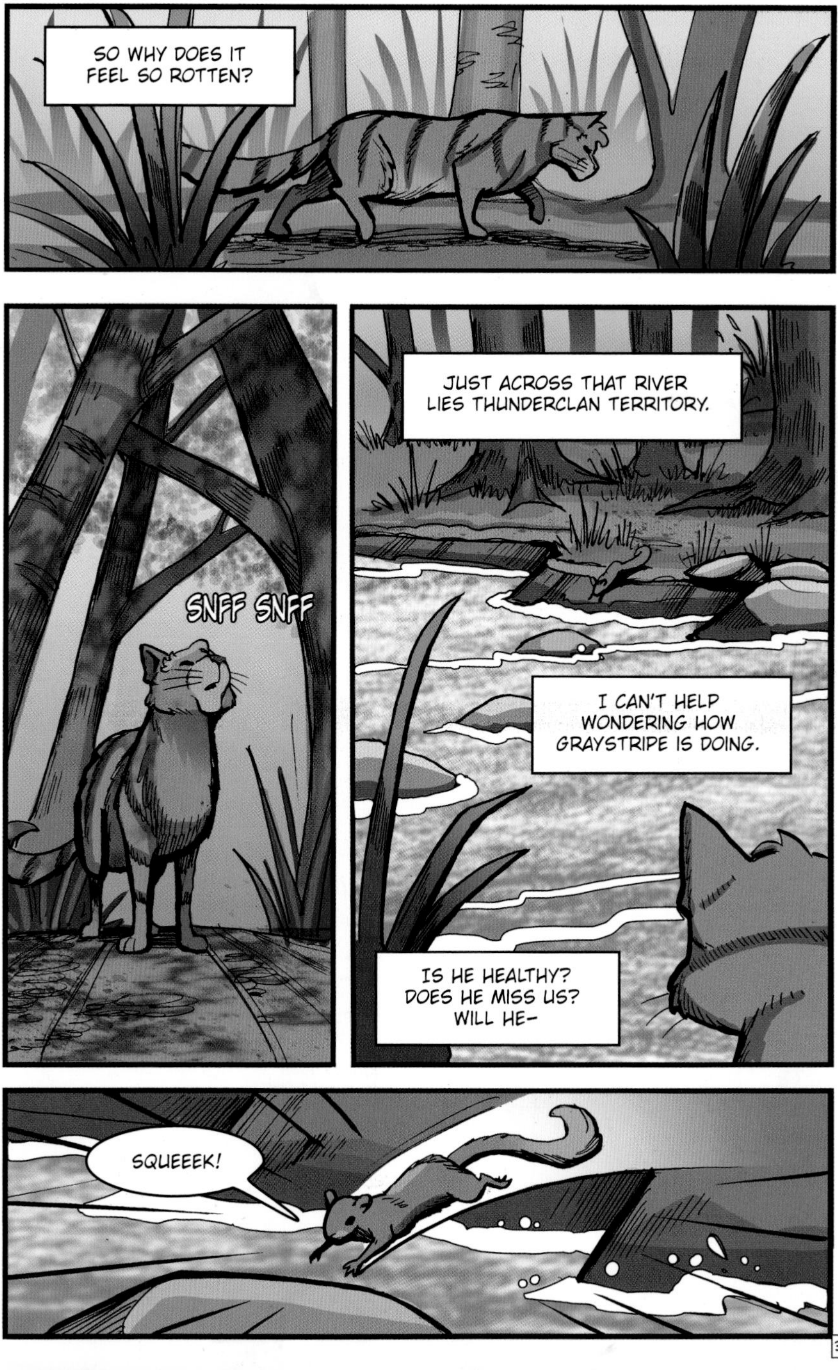
SO WHY DOES IT FEEL SO ROTTEN?
SNFF SNFF
JUST ACROSS THAT RIVER LIES THUNDERCLAN TERRITORY.
I CAN'T HELP WONDERING HOW GRAYSTRIPE IS DOING.
IS HE HEALTHY? DOES HE MISS US? WILL HE-
SQUEEEK!

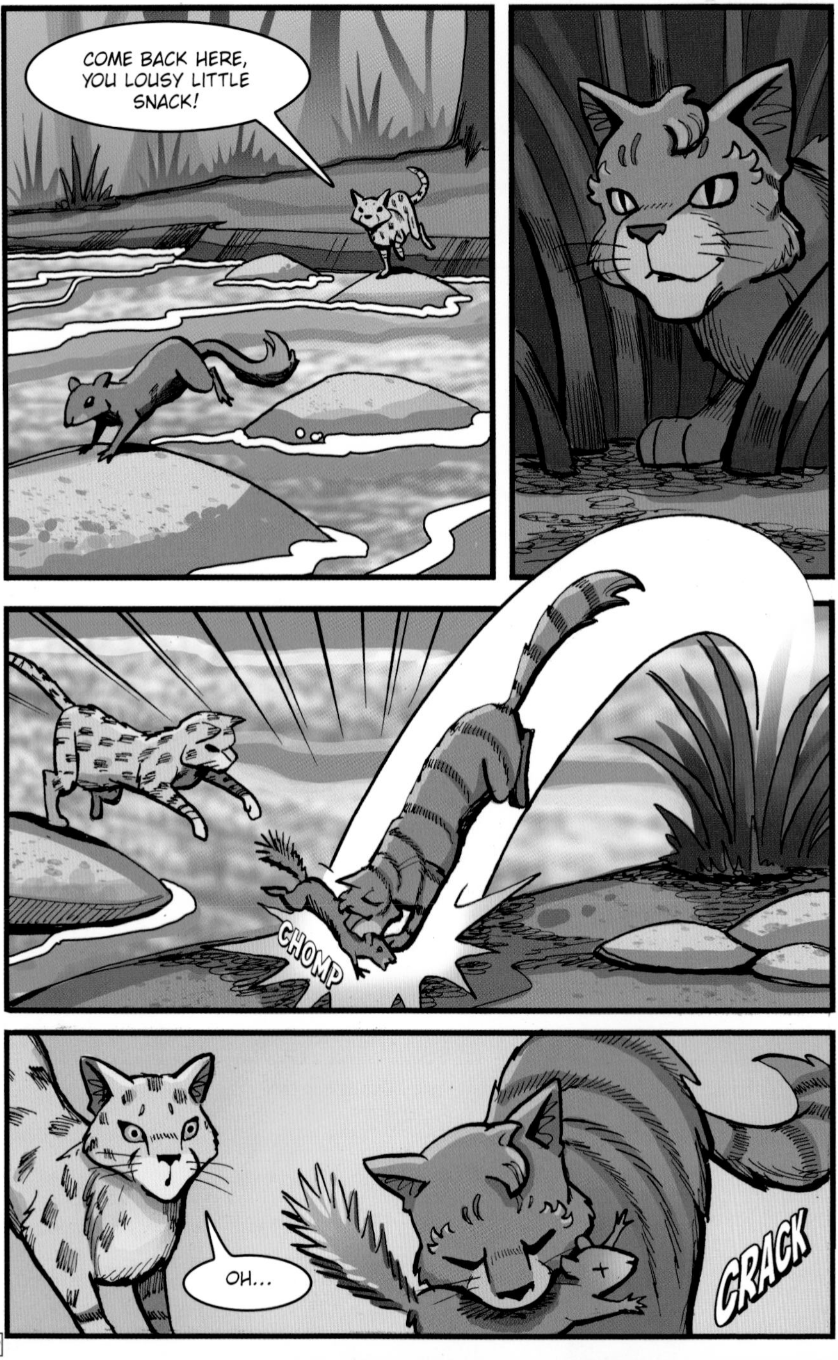
COME BACK HERE, YOU LOUSY LITTLE SNACK!
CHOMP
OH...
CRACK

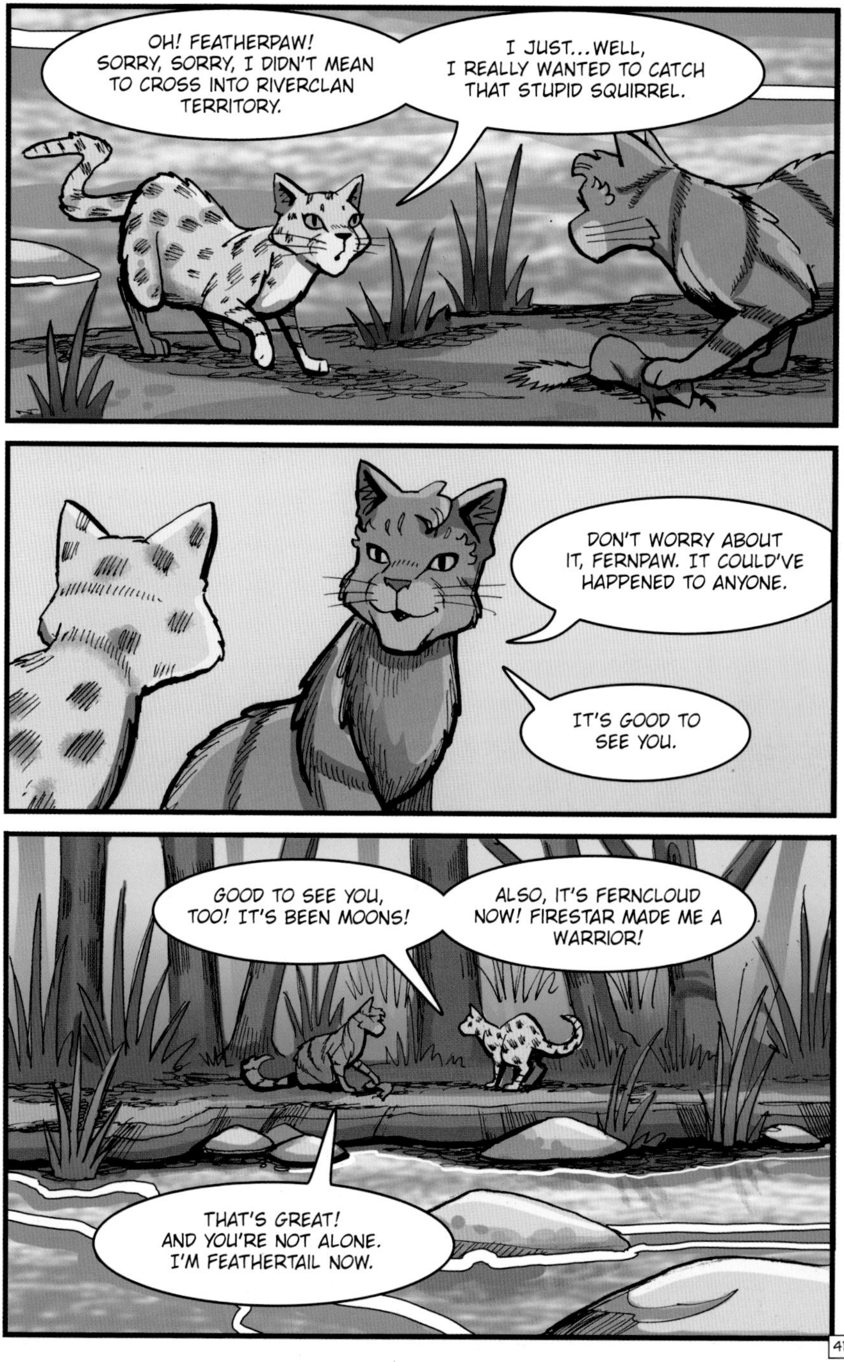
OH! FEATHERPAW! SORRY, SORRY, I DIDN'T MEAN TO CROSS INTO RIVERCLAN TERRITORY.
I JUST...WELL, I REALLY WANTED TO CATCH THAT STUPID SQUIRREL.
DON'T WORRY ABOUT IT, FERNPAW. IT COULD'VE HAPPENED TO ANYONE.
IT'S GOOD TO SEE YOU.
GOOD TO SEE YOU, TOO! IT'S BEEN MOONS!
ALSO, IT'S FERNCLOUD NOW! FIRESTAR MADE ME A WARRIOR!
THAT'S GREAT! AND YOU'RE NOT ALONE. I'M FEATHERTAIL NOW.

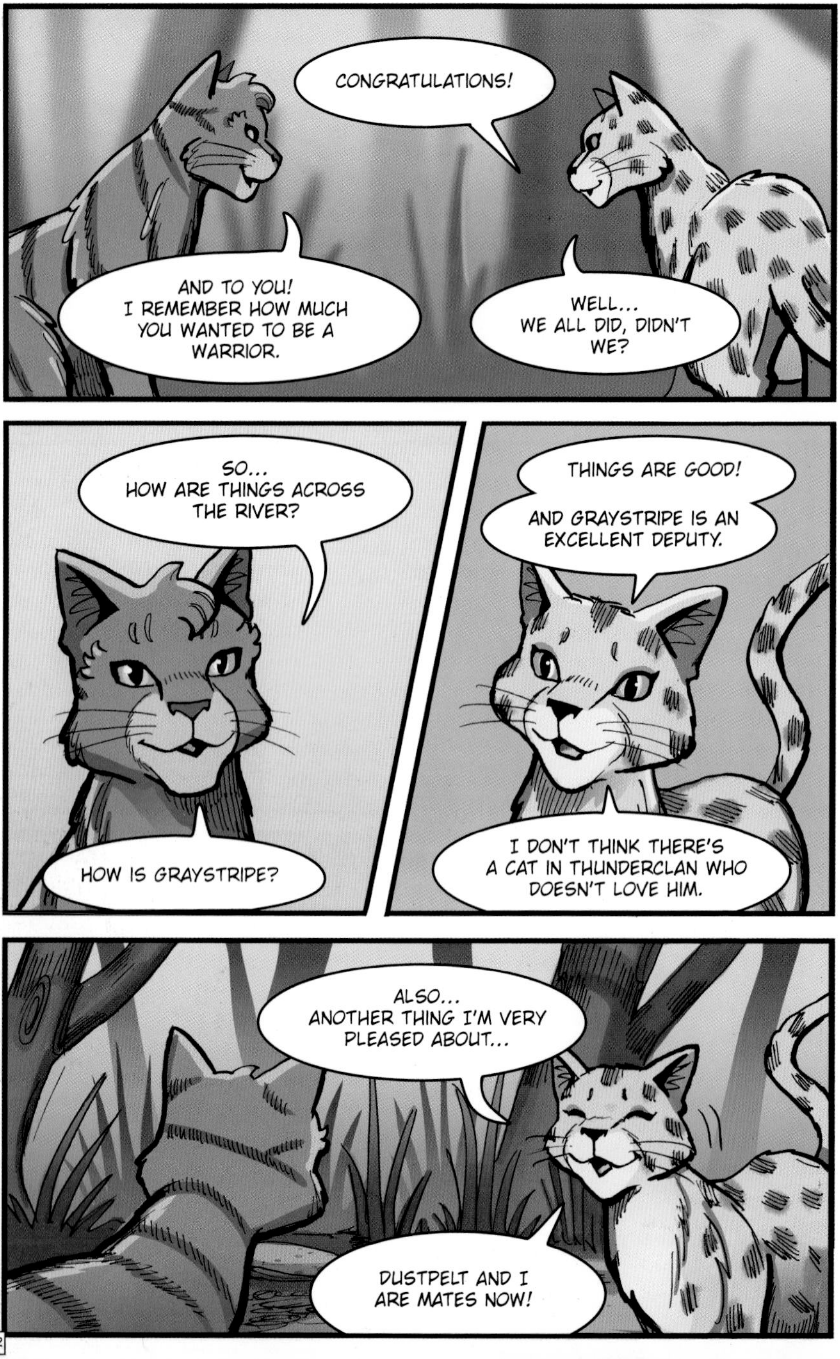
CONGRATULATIONS!
AND TO YOU! I REMEMBER HOW MUCH YOU WANTED TO BE A WARRIOR.
WELL... WE ALL DID, DIDN'T WE?
SO... HOW ARE THINGS ACROSS THE RIVER?
HOW IS GRAYSTRIPE?
THINGS ARE GOOD!
AND GRAYSTRIPE IS AN EXCELLENT DEPUTY.
I DON'T THINK THERE'S A CAT IN THUNDERCLAN WHO DOESN'T LOVE HIM.
ALSO... ANOTHER THING I'M VERY PLEASED ABOUT...
DUSTPELT AND I ARE MATES NOW!

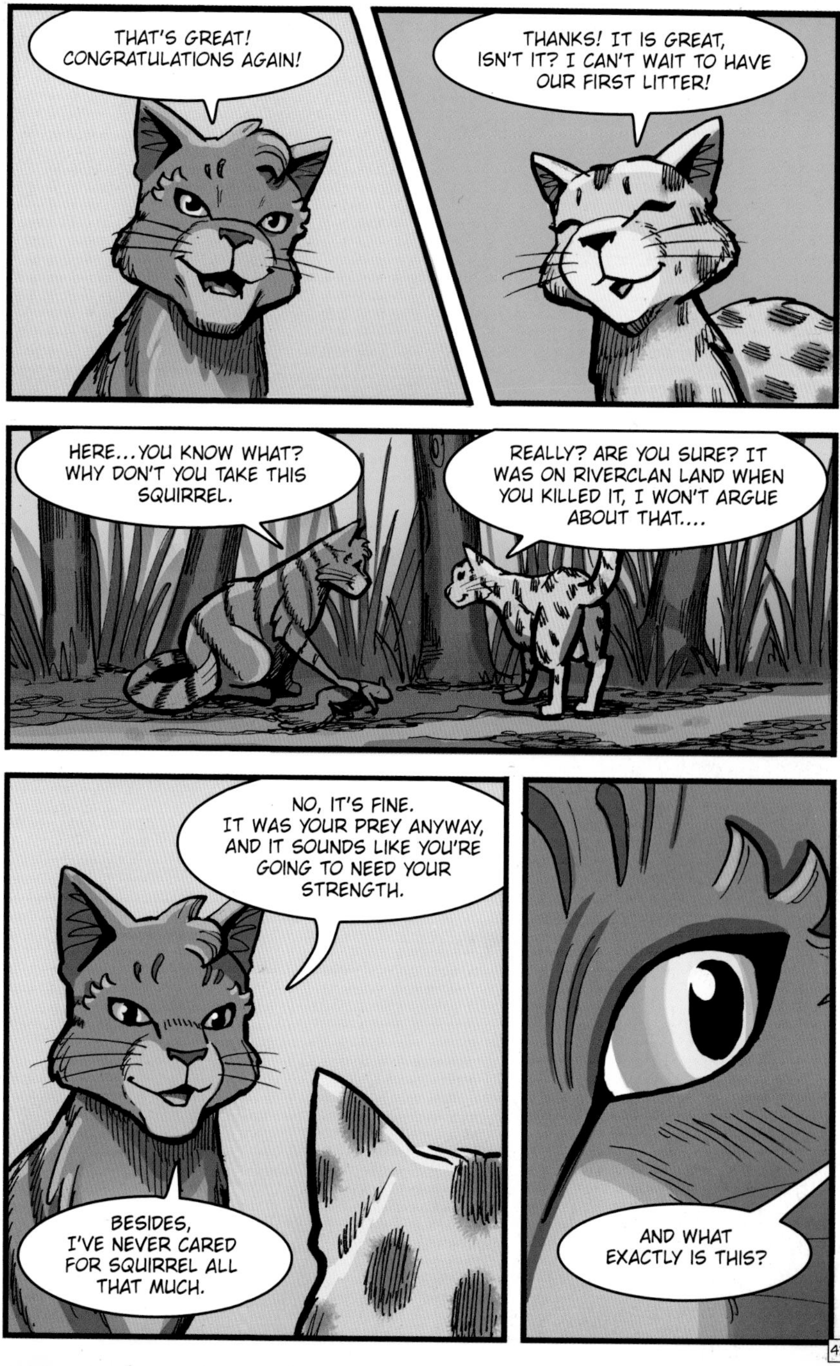
THAT'S GREAT! CONGRATULATIONS AGAIN!
THANKS! IT IS GREAT, ISN'T IT? I CAN'T WAIT TO HAVE OUR FIRST LITTER!
HERE...YOU KNOW WHAT? WHY DON'T YOU TAKE THIS SQUIRREL.
REALLY? ARE YOU SURE? IT WAS ON RIVERCLAN LAND WHEN YOU KILLED IT, I WON'T ARGUE ABOUT THAT....
NO, IT'S FINE. IT WAS YOUR PREY ANYWAY, AND IT SOUNDS LIKE YOU'RE GOING TO NEED YOUR STRENGTH.
BESIDES, I'VE NEVER CARED FOR SQUIRREL ALL THAT MUCH.
AND WHAT EXACTLY IS THIS?

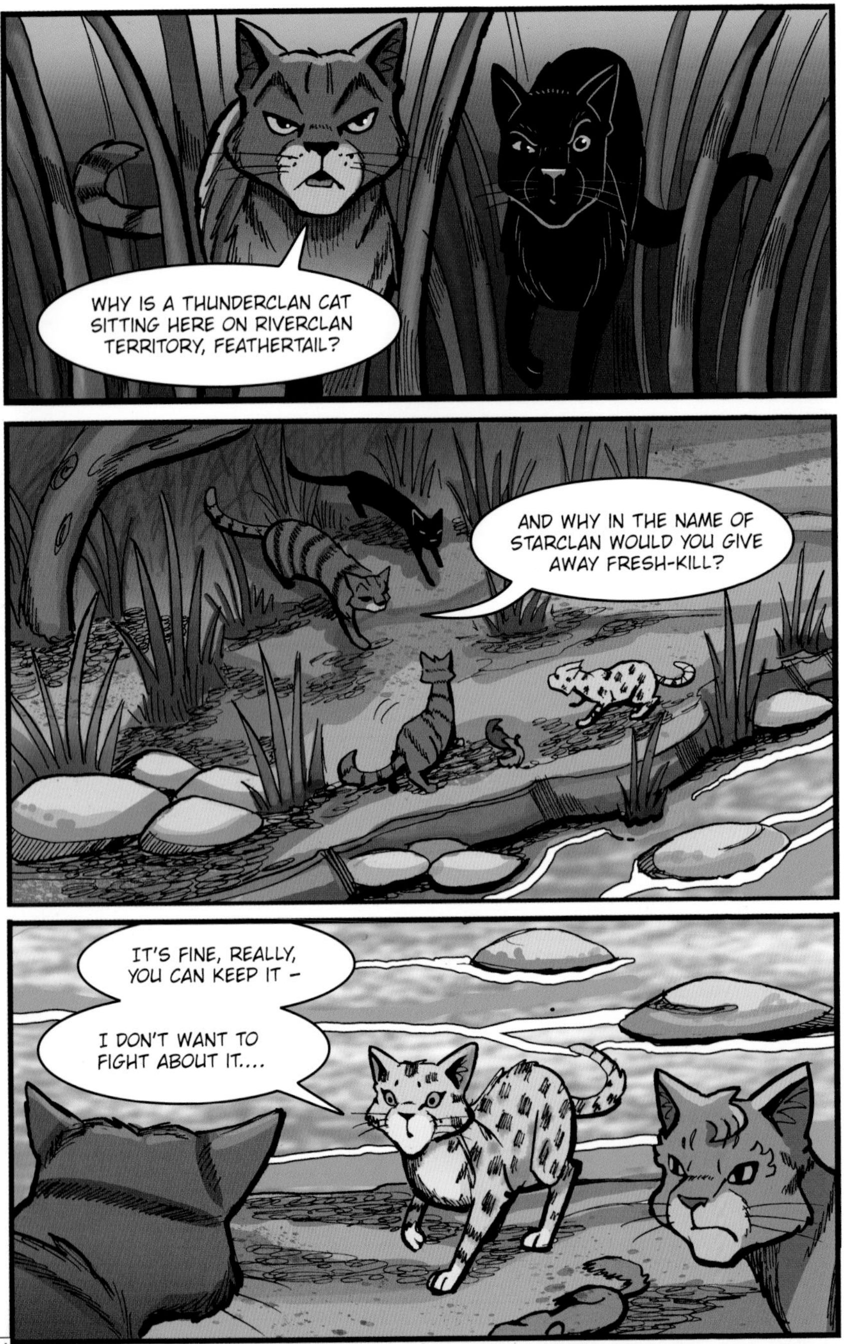
WHY IS A THUNDERCLAN CAT SITTING HERE ON RIVERCLAN TERRITORY, FEATHERTAIL?
AND WHY IN THE NAME OF STARCLAN WOULD YOU GIVE AWAY FRESH-KILL?
IT'S FINE, REALLY, YOU CAN KEEP IT –
I DON'T WANT TO FIGHT ABOUT IT....

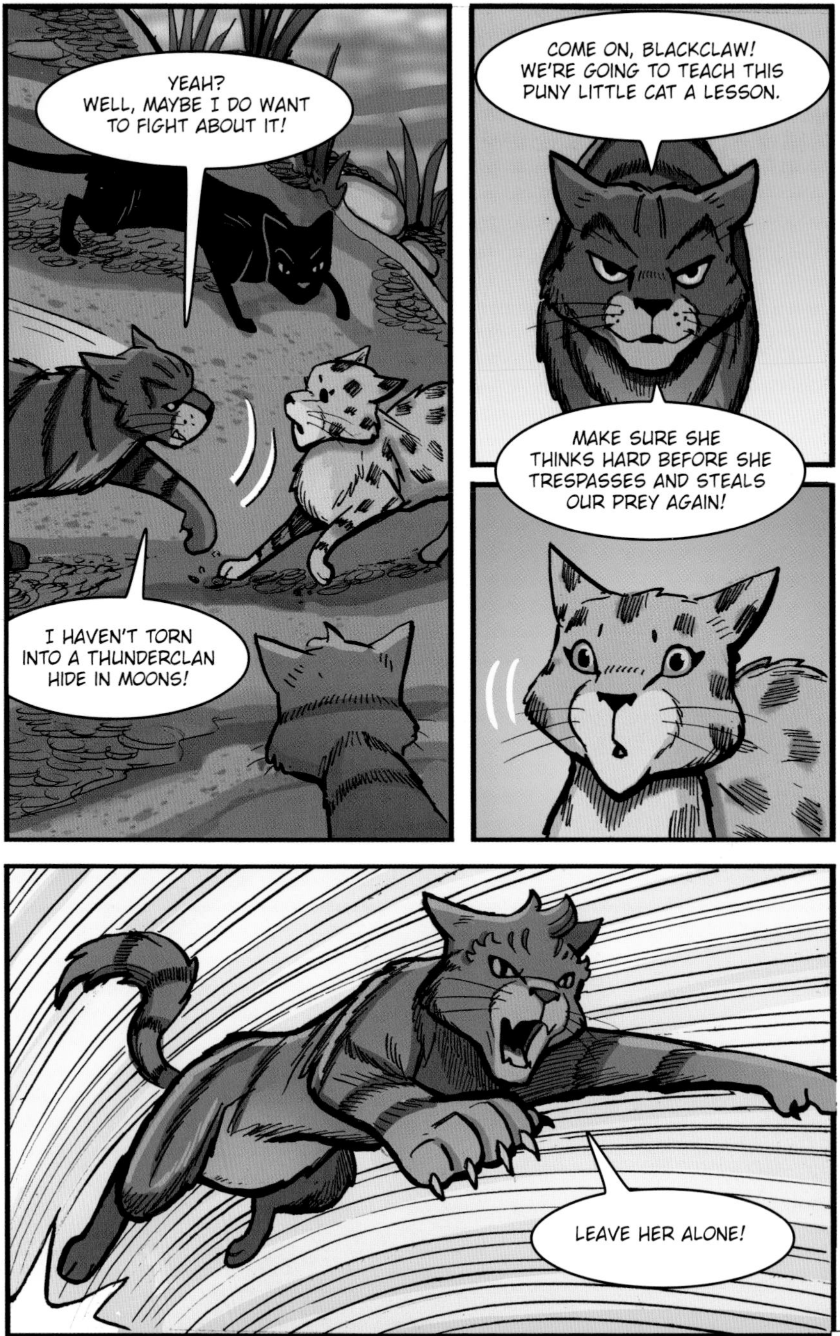
YEAH? WELL, MAYBE I DO WANT TO FIGHT ABOUT IT!
I HAVEN'T TORN INTO A THUNDERCLAN HIDE IN MOONS!
COME ON, BLACKCLAW! WE'RE GOING TO TEACH THIS PUNY LITTLE CAT A LESSON.
MAKE SURE SHE THINKS HARD BEFORE SHE TRESPASSES AND STEALS OUR PREY AGAIN!
LEAVE HER ALONE!

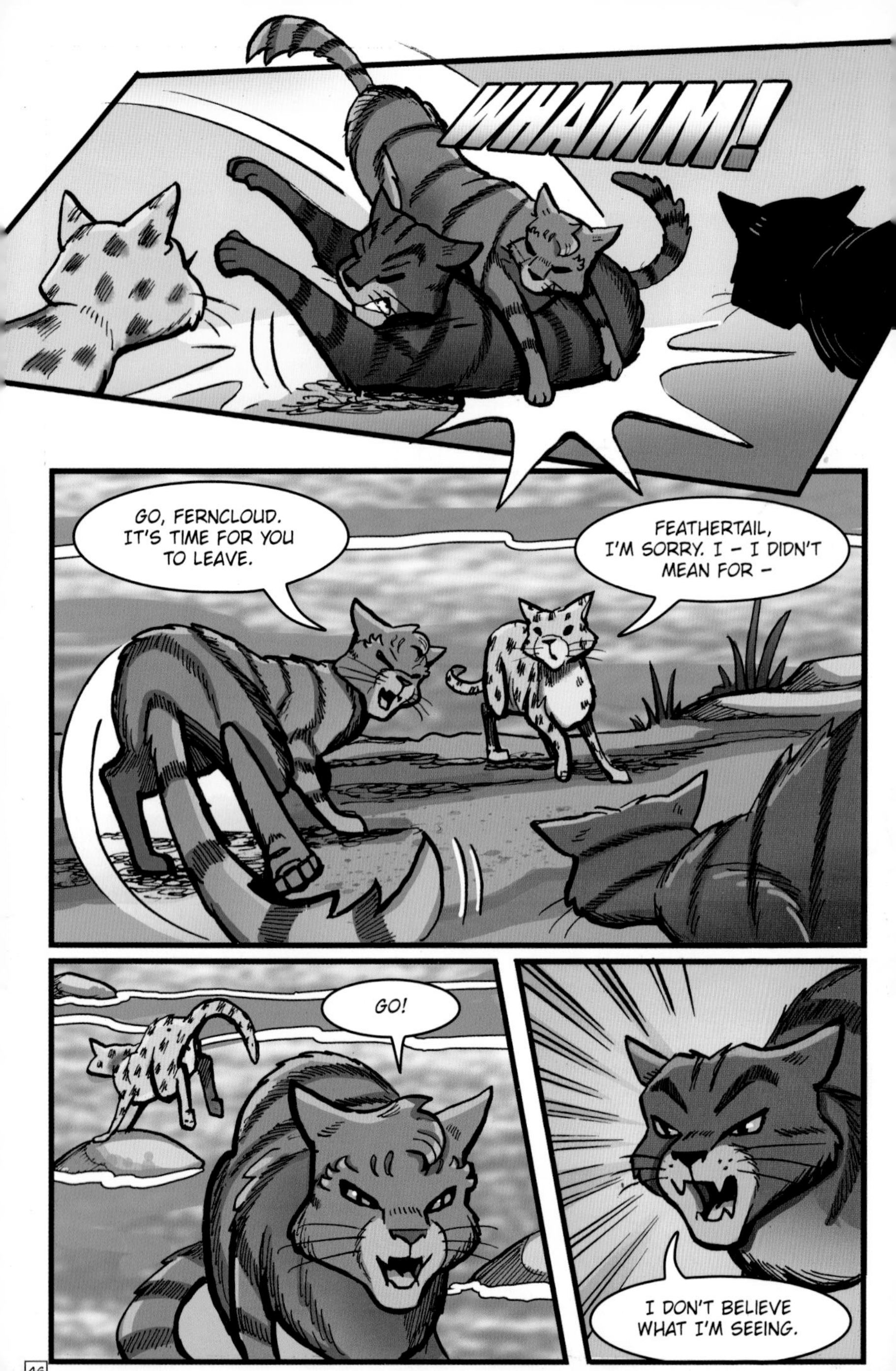
WHAMMM!
GO, FERNCLOUD. IT'S TIME FOR YOU TO LEAVE.
FEATHERTAIL, I'M SORRY. I – I DIDN'T MEAN FOR –
GO!
I DON'T BELIEVE WHAT I'M SEEING.

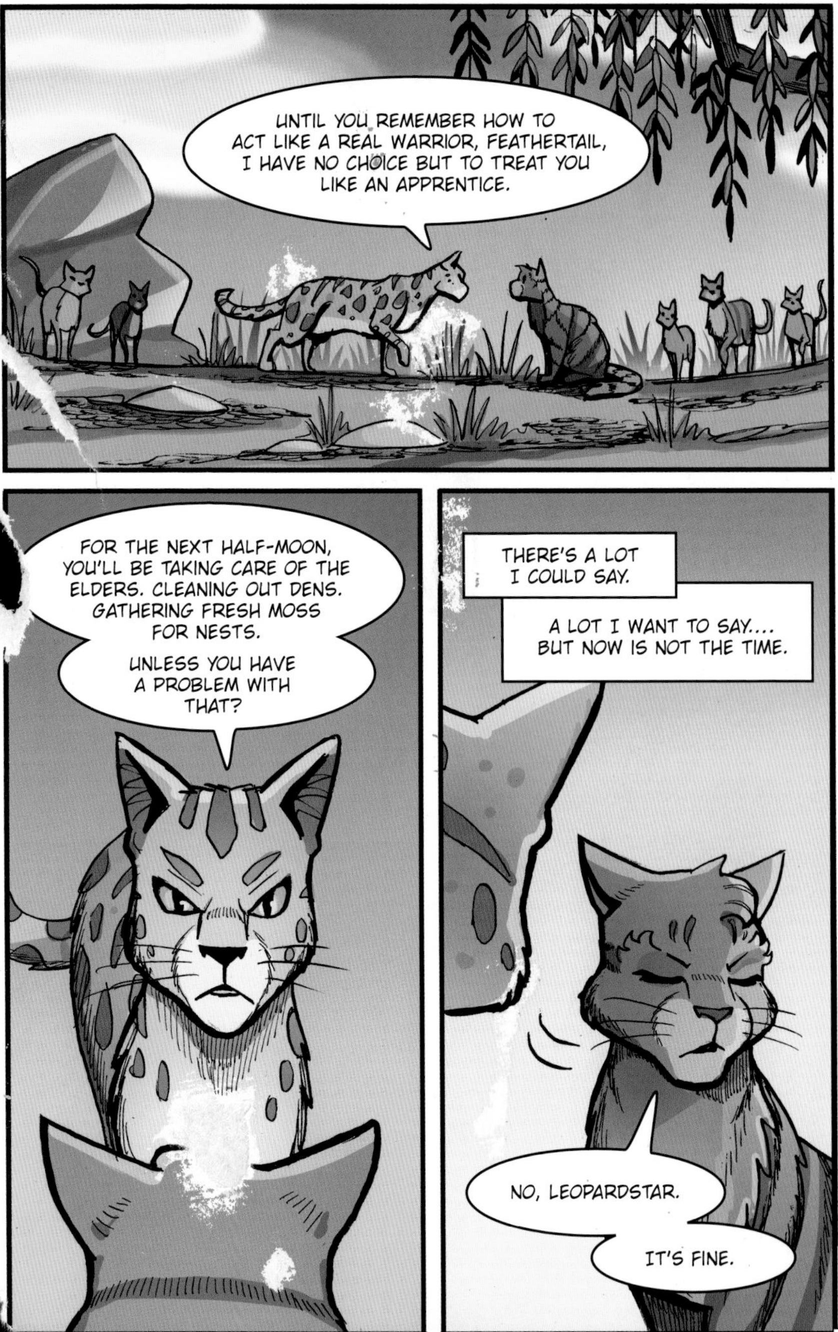
UNTIL YOU REMEMBER HOW TO ACT LIKE A REAL WARRIOR, FEATHERTAIL, I HAVE NO CHOICE BUT TO TREAT YOU LIKE AN APPRENTICE.
FOR THE NEXT HALF-MOON, YOU'LL BE TAKING CARE OF THE ELDERS. CLEANING OUT DENS. GATHERING FRESH MOSS FOR NESTS.
UNLESS YOU HAVE A PROBLEM WITH THAT?
THERE'S A LOT I COULD SAY.
A LOT I WANT TO SAY.... BUT NOW IS NOT THE TIME.
NO, LEOPARDSTAR.
IT'S FINE.

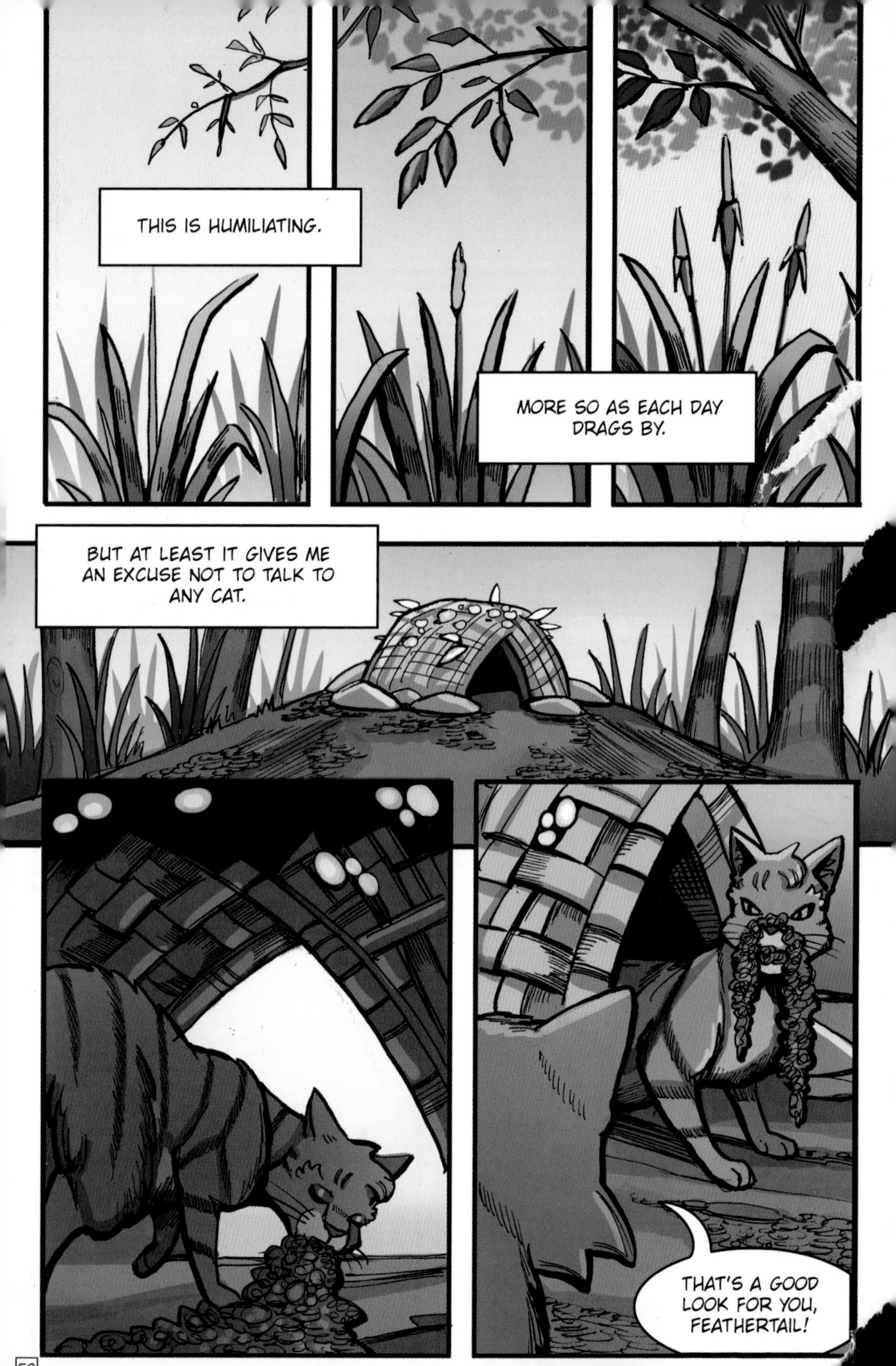
THIS IS HUMILIATING.
MORE SO AS EACH DAY DRAGS BY.
BUT AT LEAST IT GIVES ME AN EXCUSE NOT TO TALK TO ANY CAT.
THAT'S A GOOD LOOK FOR YOU, FEATHERTAIL!

YOU KNOW, THIS PUNISHMENT THING HAS WORKED OUT WELL FOR THE CLAN.

WE'RE A LITTLE SHORT ON YOUNG CATS, AFTER ALL. IT'S NICE TO HAVE SOME CAT TO DO THE APPRENTICE WORK.

HOW WOULD YOU LIKE TO EAT THIS MOSS?

HEY, EASY NOW, IT'S ONLY FOR ANOTHER COUPLE OF DAYS.

IT WOULDN'T BE SO BAD IF SOME OF THE OTHER WARRIORS WEREN'T SO FILTHY.

I THINK BLACKCLAW TEARS UP HIS NEST MOSS ON PURPOSE. HE'S TRYING TO MAKE THIS AS HARD FOR ME AS POSSIBLE.

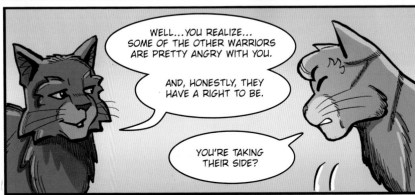

WELL...YOU REALIZE... SOME OF THE OTHER WARRIORS ARE PRETTY ANGRY WITH YOU.

AND, HONESTLY, THEY HAVE A RIGHT TO BE.

YOU'RE TAKING THEIR SIDE?

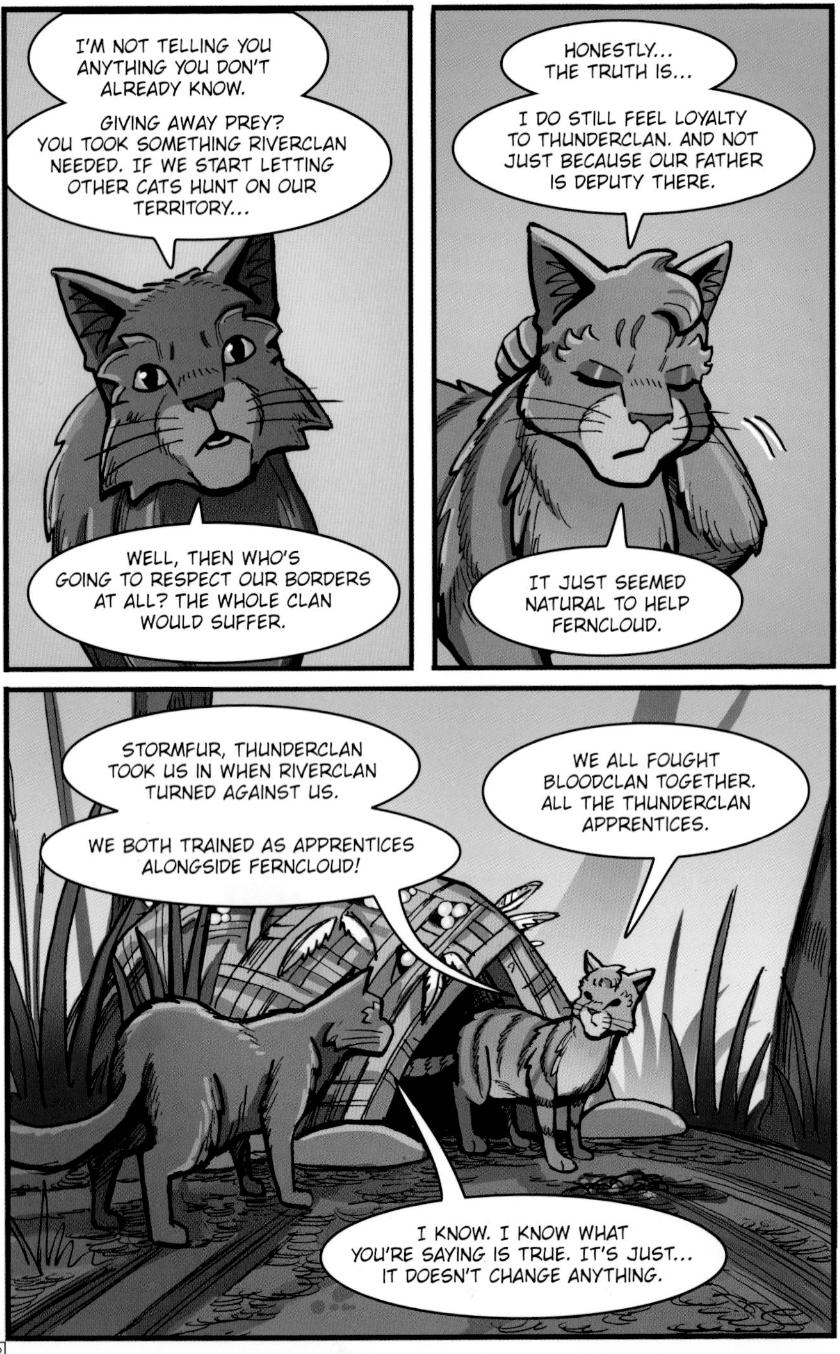
I'M NOT TELLING YOU ANYTHING YOU DON'T ALREADY KNOW.
GIVING AWAY PREY? YOU TOOK SOMETHING RIVERCLAN NEEDED. IF WE START LETTING OTHER CATS HUNT ON OUR TERRITORY...
WELL, THEN WHO'S GOING TO RESPECT OUR BORDERS AT ALL? THE WHOLE CLAN WOULD SUFFER.
HONESTLY... THE TRUTH IS...
I DO STILL FEEL LOYALTY TO THUNDERCLAN. AND NOT JUST BECAUSE OUR FATHER IS DEPUTY THERE.
IT JUST SEEMED NATURAL TO HELP FERNCLOUD.
STORMFUR, THUNDERCLAN TOOK US IN WHEN RIVERCLAN TURNED AGAINST US.
WE BOTH TRAINED AS APPRENTICES ALONGSIDE FERNCLOUD!
WE ALL FOUGHT BLOODCLAN TOGETHER. ALL THE THUNDERCLAN APPRENTICES.
I KNOW. I KNOW WHAT YOU'RE SAYING IS TRUE. IT'S JUST... IT DOESN'T CHANGE ANYTHING.

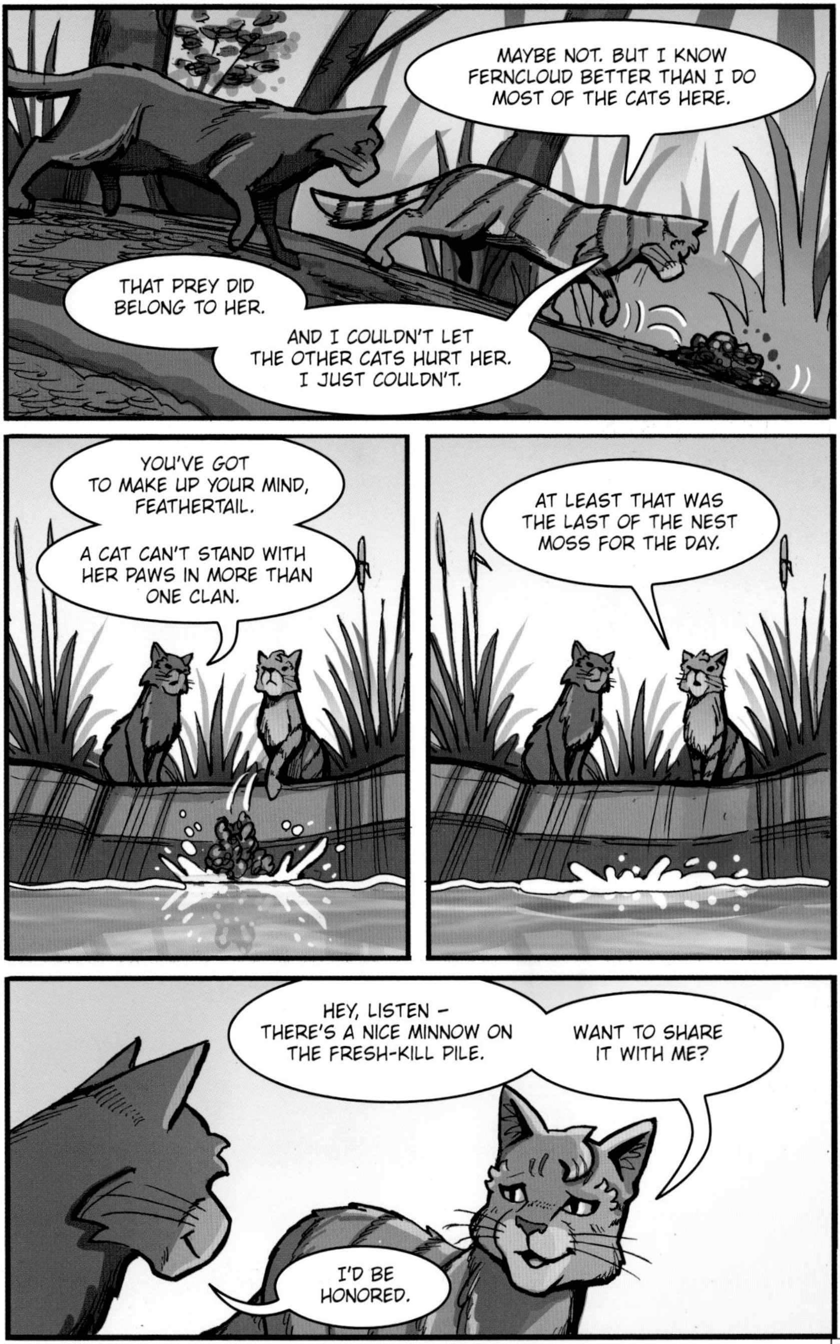
MAYBE NOT. BUT I KNOW FERNCLOUD BETTER THAN I DO MOST OF THE CATS HERE.
THAT PREY DID BELONG TO HER.
AND I COULDN'T LET THE OTHER CATS HURT HER. I JUST COULDN'T.
YOU'VE GOT TO MAKE UP YOUR MIND, FEATHERTAIL.
A CAT CAN'T STAND WITH HER PAWS IN MORE THAN ONE CLAN.
AT LEAST THAT WAS THE LAST OF THE NEST MOSS FOR THE DAY.
HEY, LISTEN – THERE'S A NICE MINNOW ON THE FRESH-KILL PILE.
WANT TO SHARE IT WITH ME?
I'D BE HONORED.

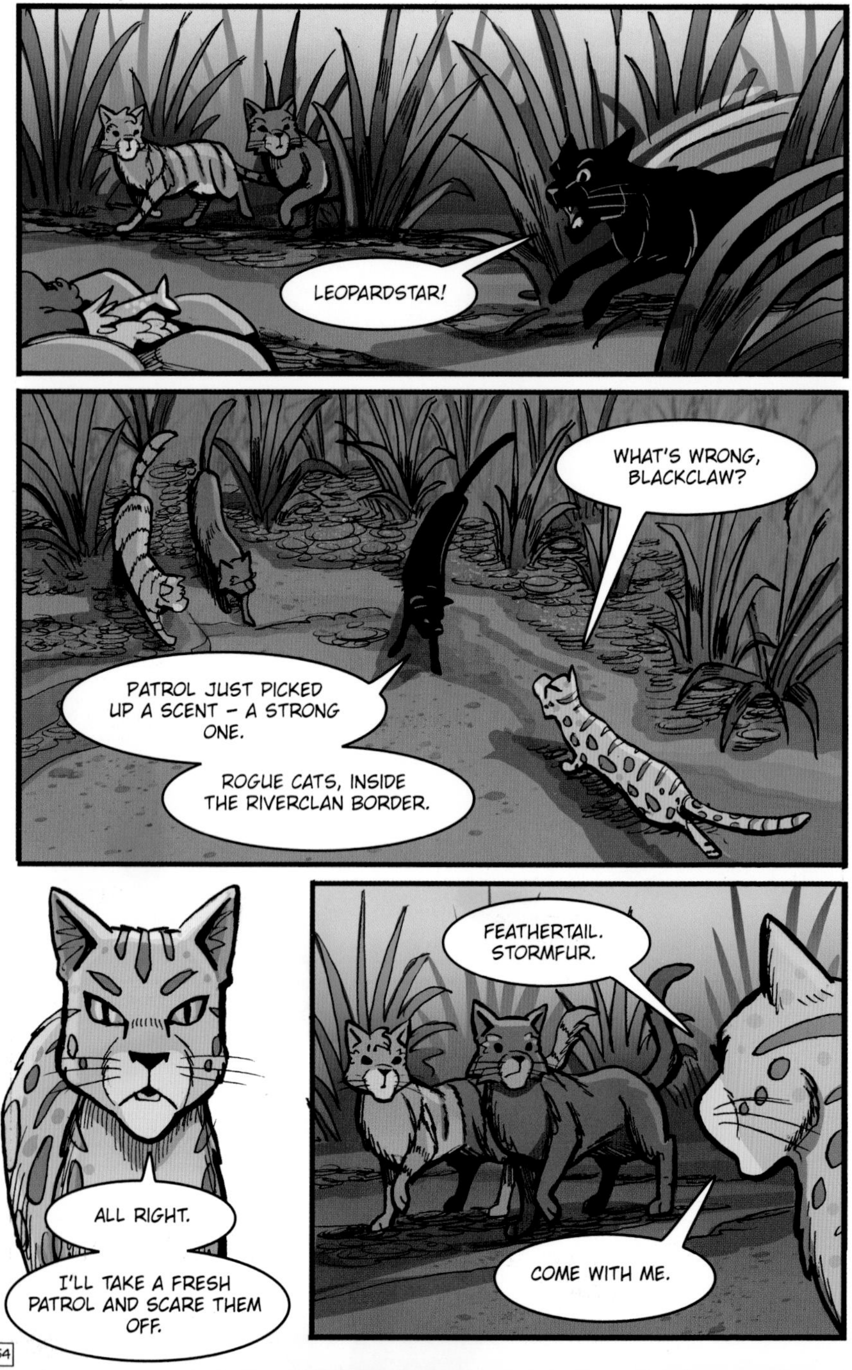
LEOPARDSTAR!
WHAT'S WRONG, BLACKCLAW?
PATROL JUST PICKED UP A SCENT – A STRONG ONE.
ROGUE CATS, INSIDE THE RIVERCLAN BORDER.
ALL RIGHT.
I'LL TAKE A FRESH PATROL AND SCARE THEM OFF.
FEATHERTAIL. STORMFUR.
COME WITH ME.

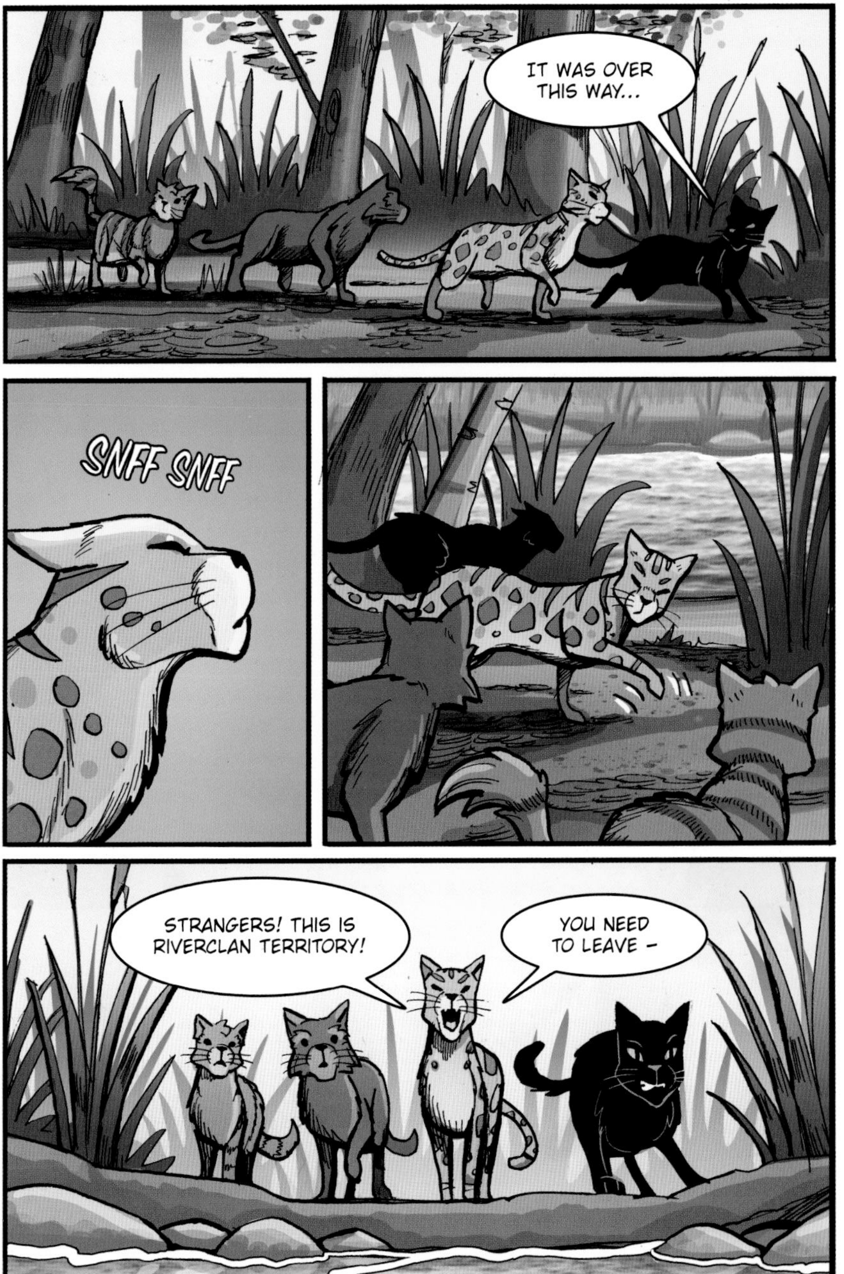
IT WAS OVER THIS WAY...
SNFF SNFF
STRANGERS! THIS IS RIVERCLAN TERRITORY!
YOU NEED TO LEAVE –

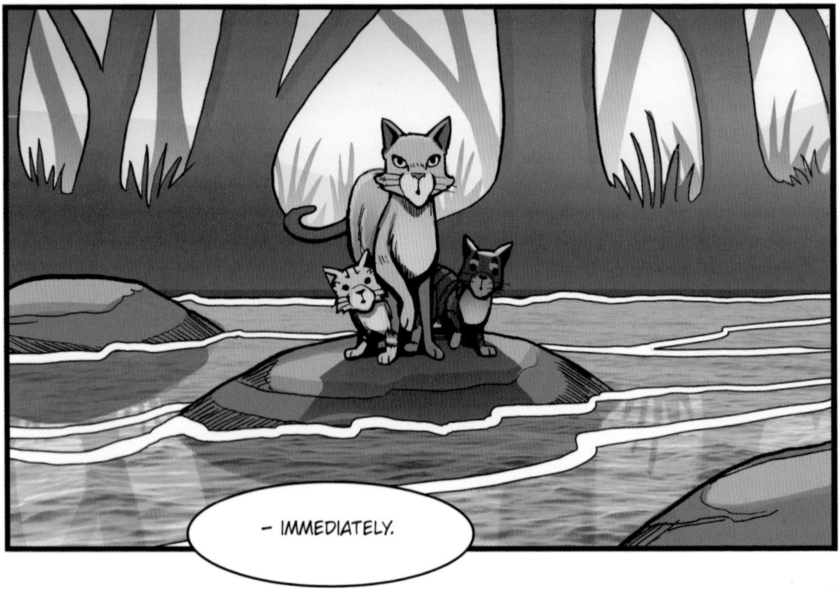
- IMMEDIATELY.

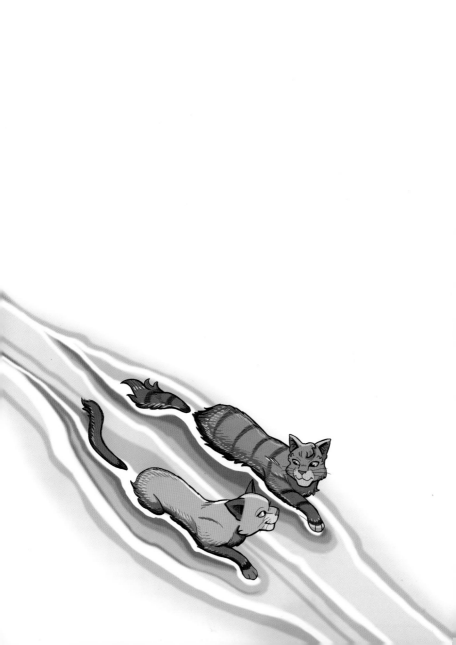

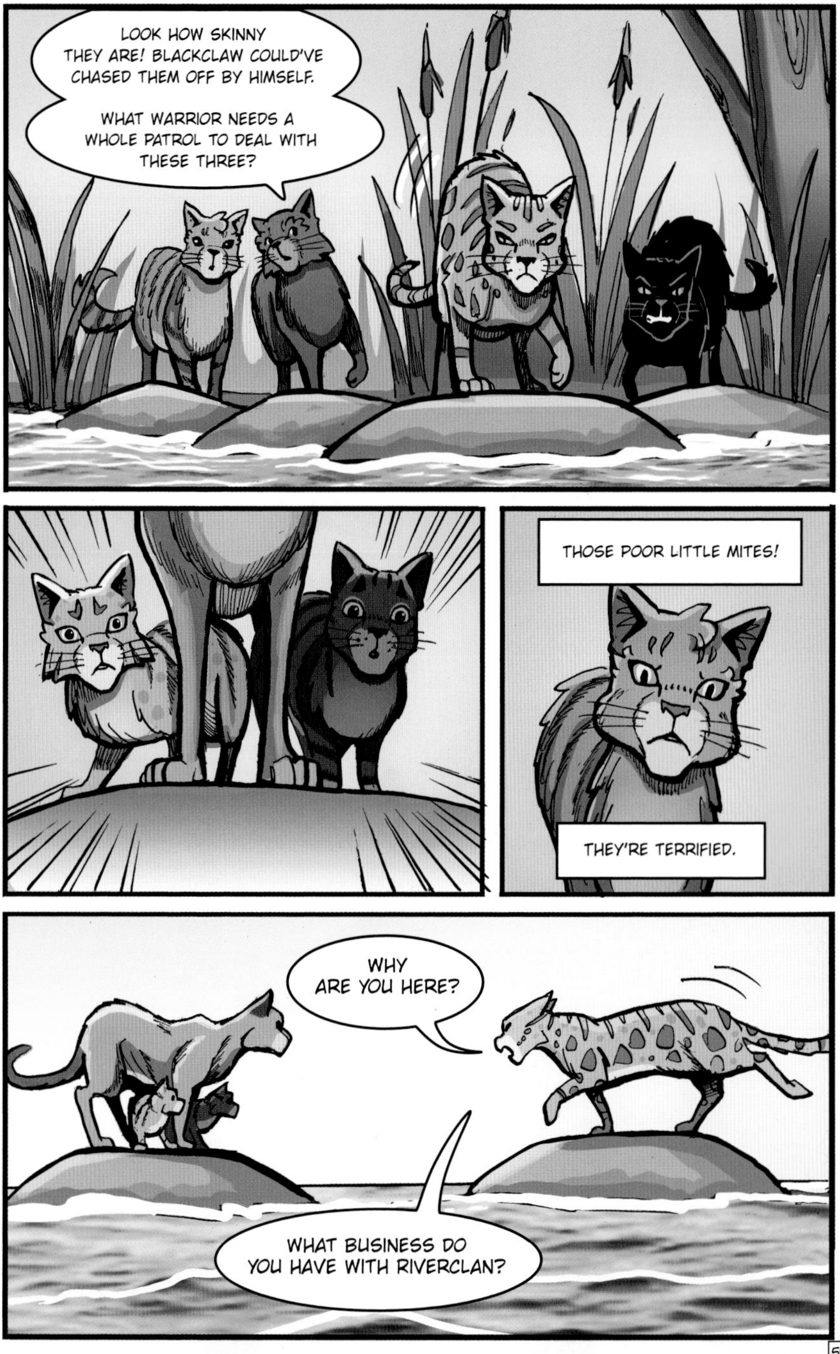
LOOK HOW SKINNY THEY ARE! BLACKCLAW COULD'VE CHASED THEM OFF BY HIMSELF.
WHAT WARRIOR NEEDS A WHOLE PATROL TO DEAL WITH THESE THREE?
THOSE POOR LITTLE MITES!
THEY'RE TERRIFIED.
WHY ARE YOU HERE?
WHAT BUSINESS DO YOU HAVE WITH RIVERCLAN?

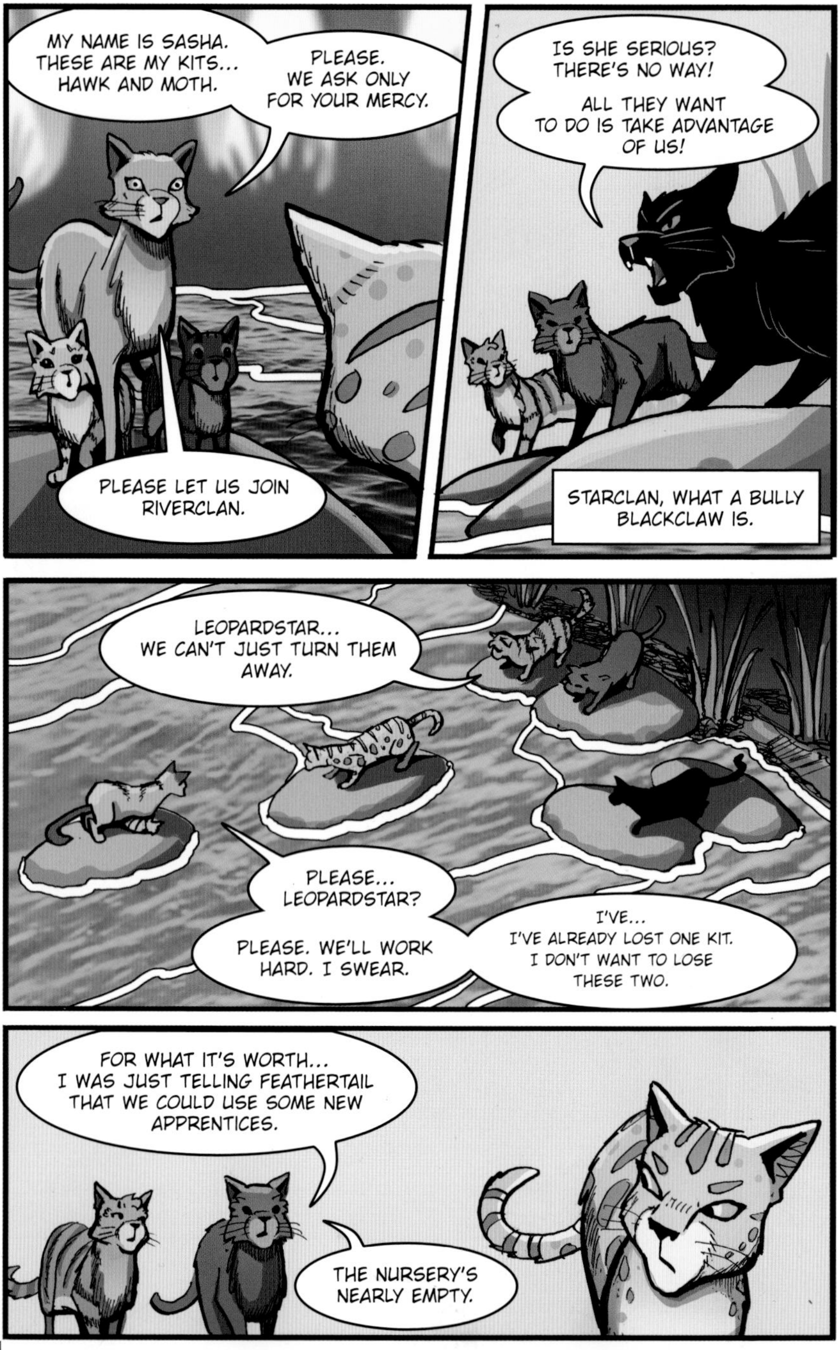
MY NAME IS SASHA. THESE ARE MY KITS... HAWK AND MOTH.
PLEASE. WE ASK ONLY FOR YOUR MERCY.
PLEASE LET US JOIN RIVERCLAN.
IS SHE SERIOUS? THERE'S NO WAY!
ALL THEY WANT TO DO IS TAKE ADVANTAGE OF US!
STARCLAN, WHAT A BULLY BLACKCLAW IS.
LEOPARDSTAR... WE CAN'T JUST TURN THEM AWAY.
PLEASE... LEOPARDSTAR?
PLEASE. WE'LL WORK HARD. I SWEAR.
I'VE... I'VE ALREADY LOST ONE KIT. I DON'T WANT TO LOSE THESE TWO.
FOR WHAT IT'S WORTH... I WAS JUST TELLING FEATHERTAIL THAT WE COULD USE SOME NEW APPRENTICES.
THE NURSERY'S NEARLY EMPTY.

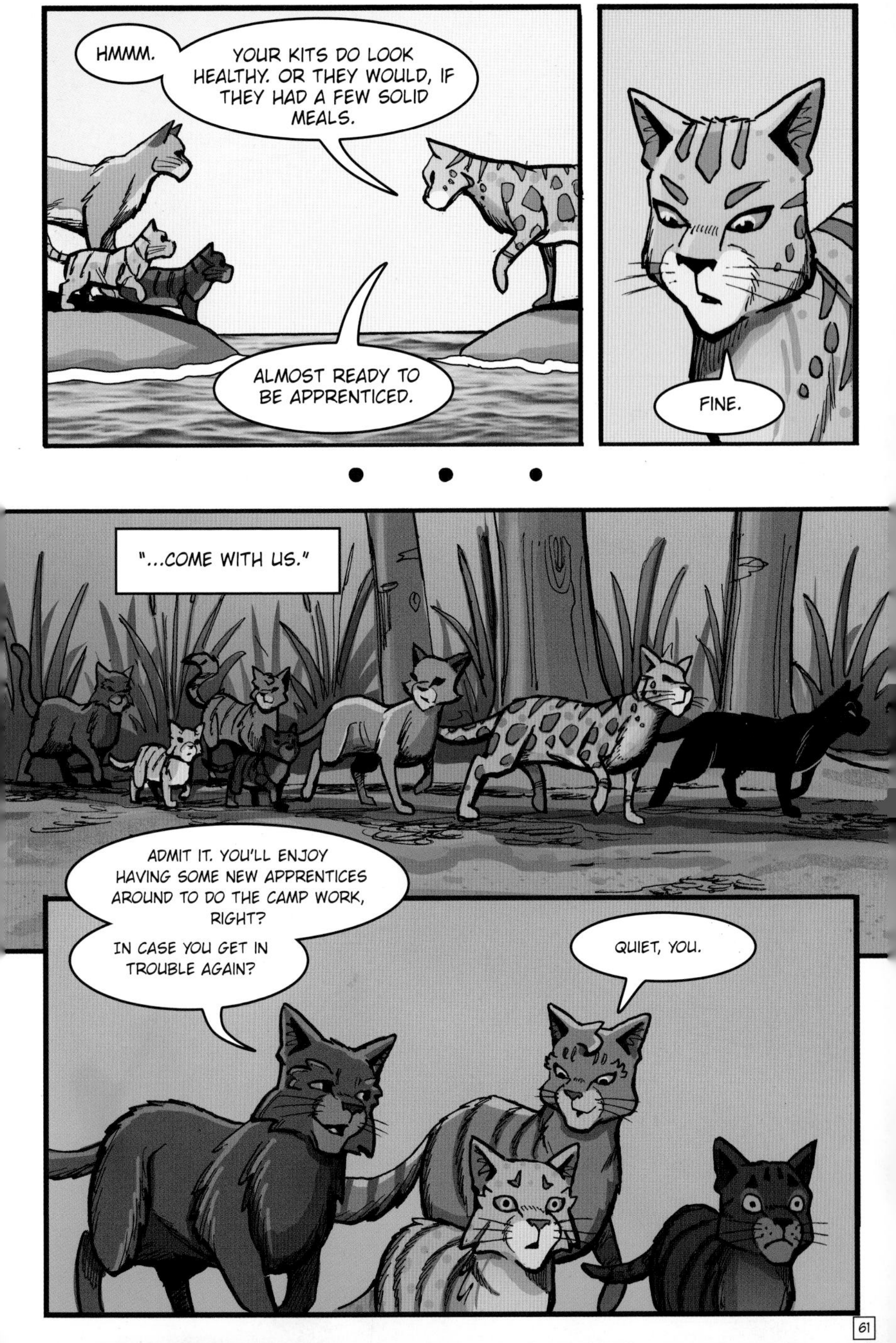
HMMM.
YOUR KITS DO LOOK HEALTHY. OR THEY WOULD, IF THEY HAD A FEW SOLID MEALS.
ALMOST READY TO BE APPRENTICED.
FINE.
"...COME WITH US."
ADMIT IT. YOU'LL ENJOY HAVING SOME NEW APPRENTICES AROUND TO DO THE CAMP WORK, RIGHT?
IN CASE YOU GET IN TROUBLE AGAIN?
QUIET, YOU.

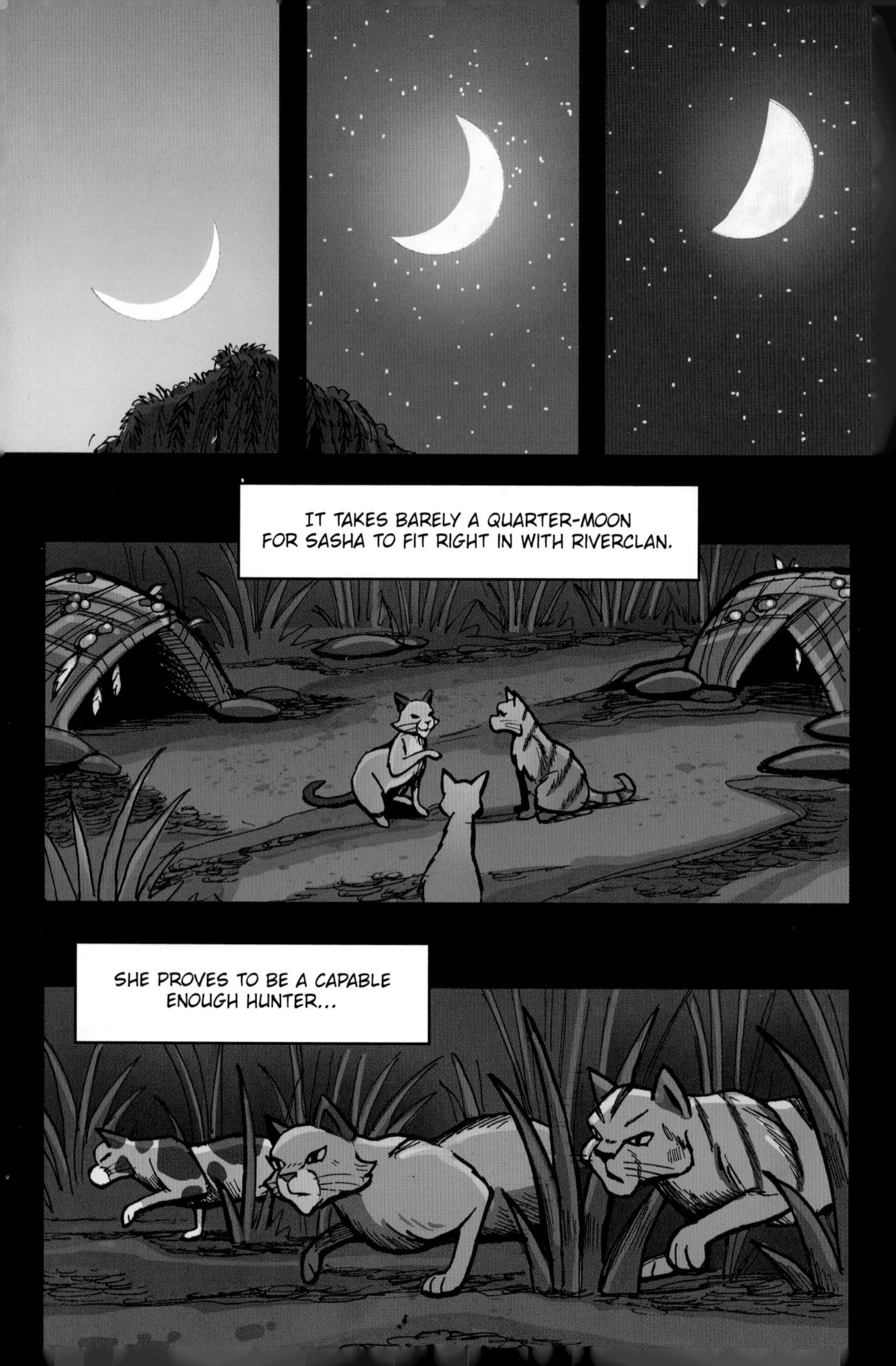
IT TAKES BARELY A QUARTER-MOON FOR SASHA TO FIT RIGHT IN WITH RIVERCLAN.
SHE PROVES TO BE A CAPABLE ENOUGH HUNTER...

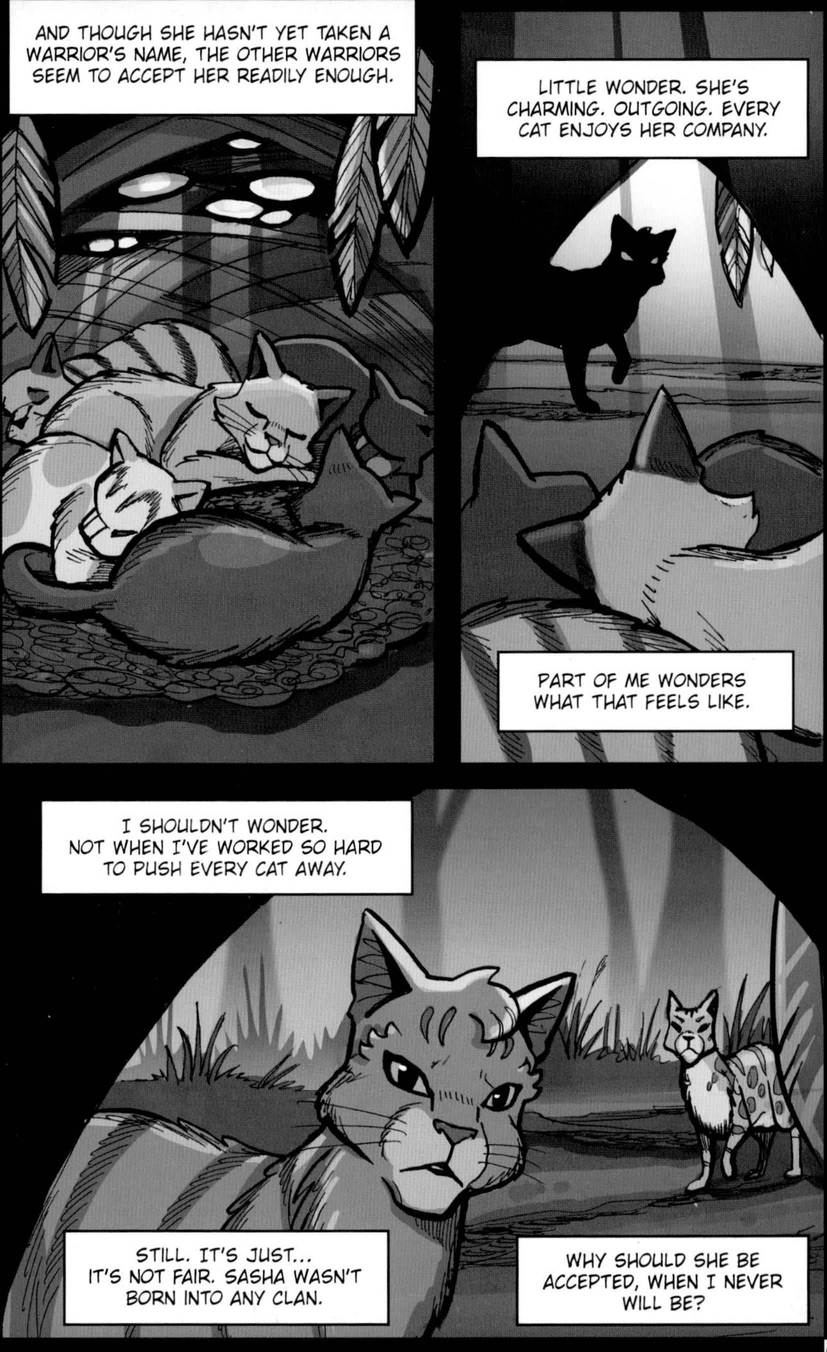
AND THOUGH SHE HASN'T YET TAKEN A WARRIOR'S NAME, THE OTHER WARRIORS SEEM TO ACCEPT HER READILY ENOUGH.
LITTLE WONDER. SHE'S CHARMING. OUTGOING. EVERY CAT ENJOYS HER COMPANY.
PART OF ME WONDERS WHAT THAT FEELS LIKE.
I SHOULDN'T WONDER. NOT WHEN I'VE WORKED SO HARD TO PUSH EVERY CAT AWAY.
STILL. IT'S JUST... IT'S NOT FAIR. SASHA WASN'T BORN INTO ANY CLAN.
WHY SHOULD SHE BE ACCEPTED, WHEN I NEVER WILL BE?

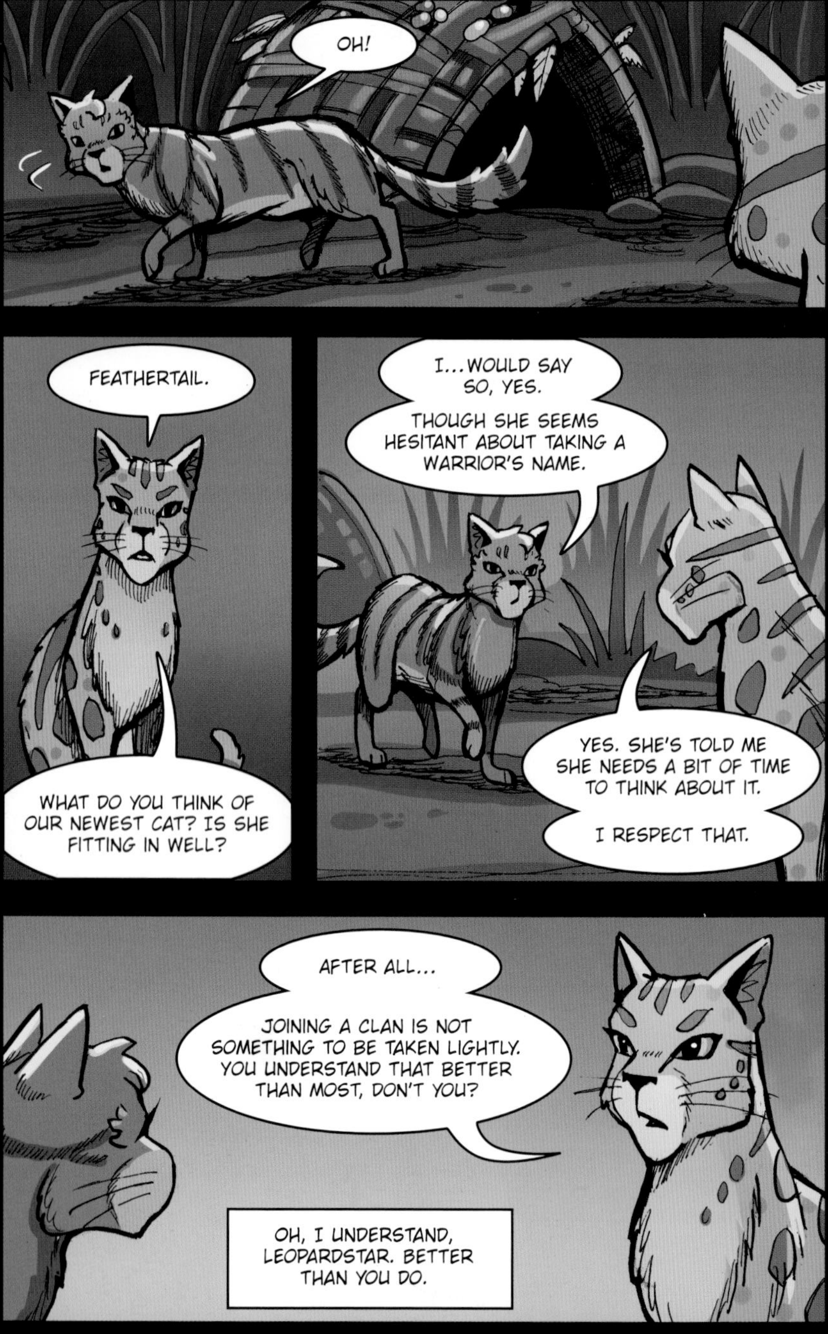
OH!
FEATHERTAIL.
WHAT DO YOU THINK OF OUR NEWEST CAT? IS SHE FITTING IN WELL?
I...WOULD SAY SO, YES.
THOUGH SHE SEEMS HESITANT ABOUT TAKING A WARRIOR'S NAME.
YES. SHE'S TOLD ME SHE NEEDS A BIT OF TIME TO THINK ABOUT IT.
I RESPECT THAT.
AFTER ALL...
JOINING A CLAN IS NOT SOMETHING TO BE TAKEN LIGHTLY. YOU UNDERSTAND THAT BETTER THAN MOST, DON'T YOU?
OH, I UNDERSTAND, LEOPARDSTAR. BETTER THAN YOU DO.

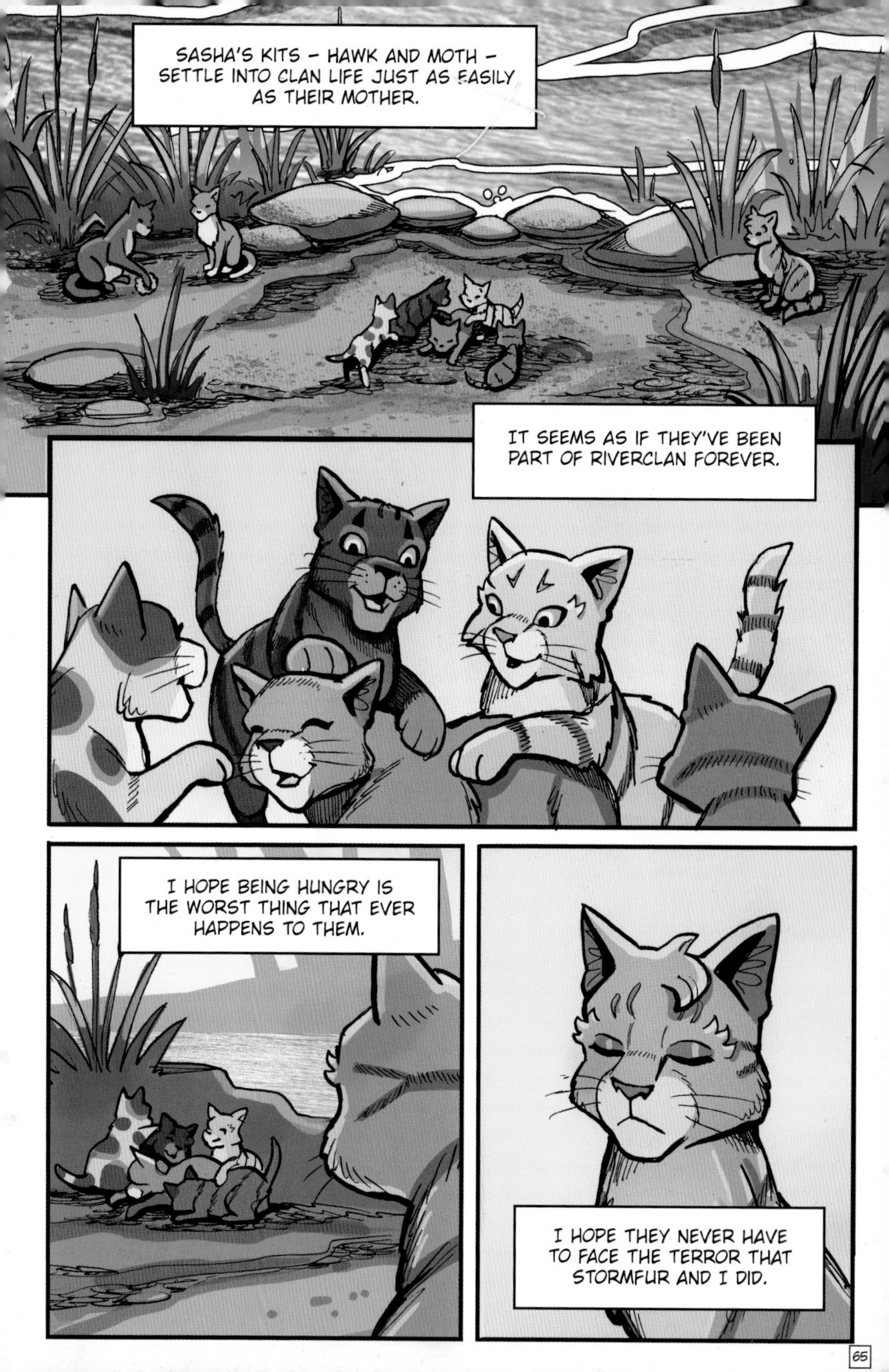
SASHA'S KITS – HAWK AND MOTH – SETTLE INTO CLAN LIFE JUST AS EASILY AS THEIR MOTHER.
IT SEEMS AS IF THEY'VE BEEN PART OF RIVERCLAN FOREVER.
I HOPE BEING HUNGRY IS THE WORST THING THAT EVER HAPPENS TO THEM.
I HOPE THEY NEVER HAVE TO FACE THE TERROR THAT STORMFUR AND I DID.

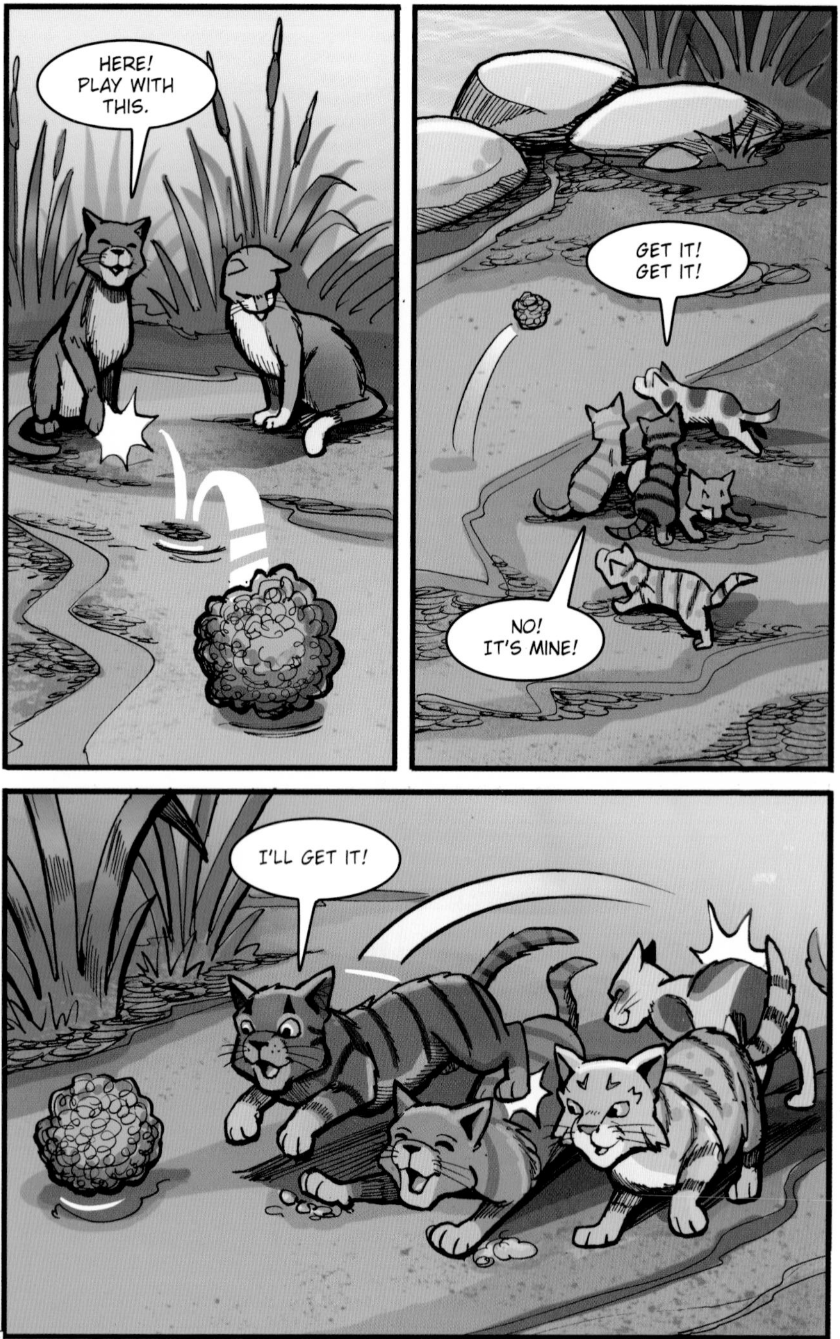
HERE! PLAY WITH THIS.
GET IT! GET IT!
NO! IT'S MINE!
I'LL GET IT!

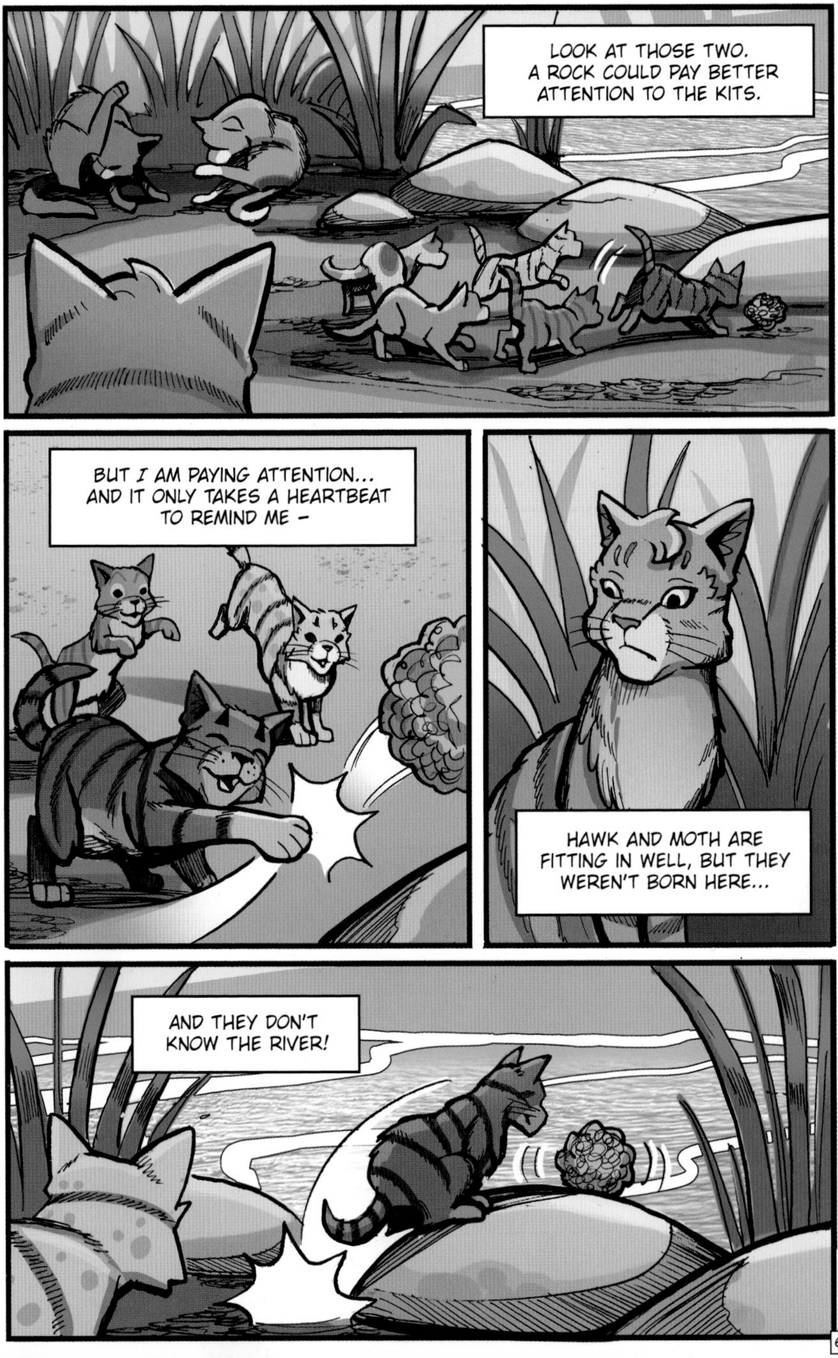
LOOK AT THOSE TWO.
A ROCK COULD PAY BETTER
ATTENTION TO THE KITS.
BUT *I* AM PAYING ATTENTION...
AND IT ONLY TAKES A HEARTBEAT
TO REMIND ME –
HAWK AND MOTH ARE
FITTING IN WELL, BUT THEY
WEREN'T BORN HERE...
AND THEY DON'T
KNOW THE RIVER!

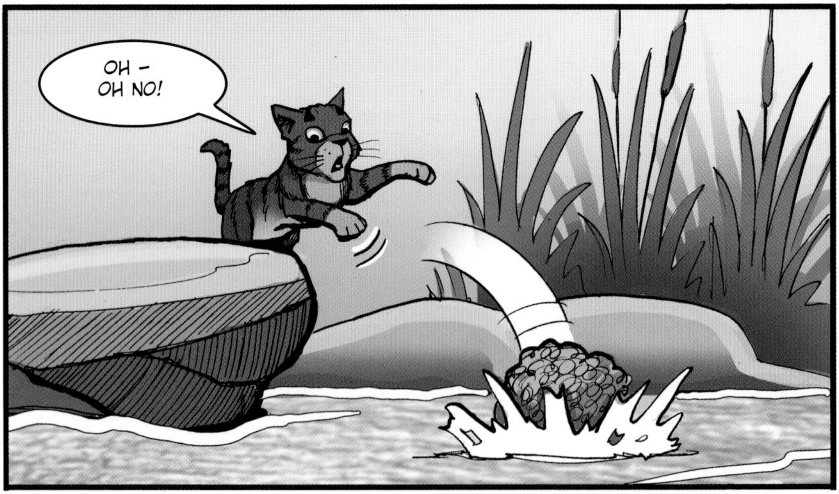
OH -
OH NO!

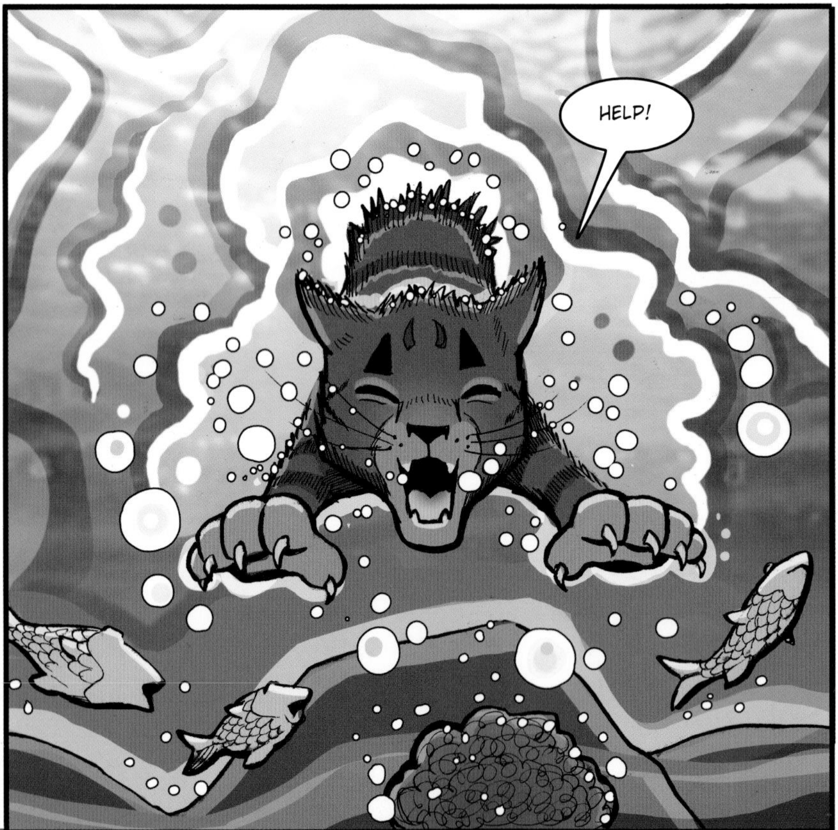
HELP!

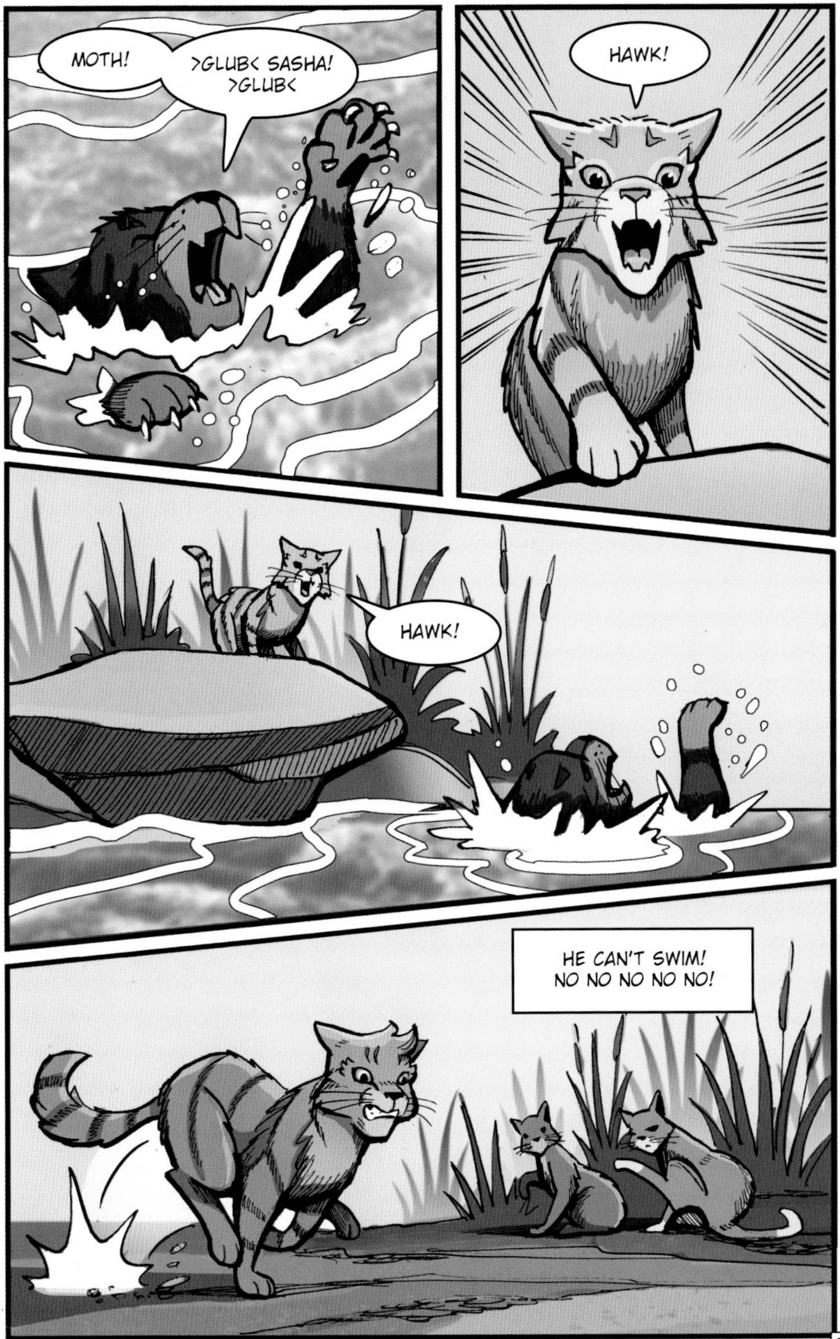
MOTH!
>GLUB< SASHA! >GLUB<
HAWK!
HAWK!
HE CAN'T SWIM! NO NO NO NO NO!

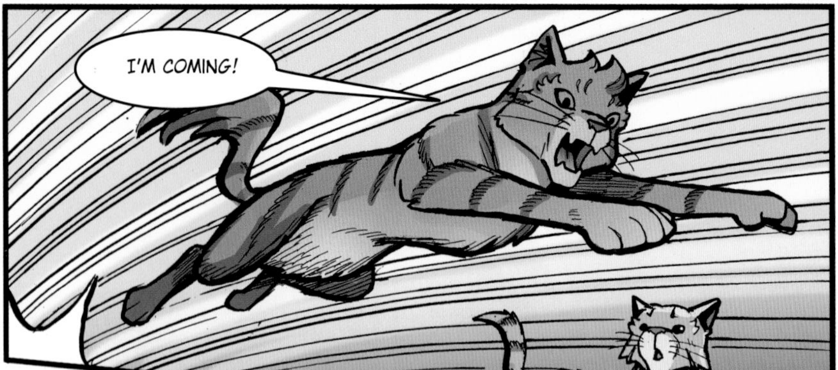
I'M COMING!

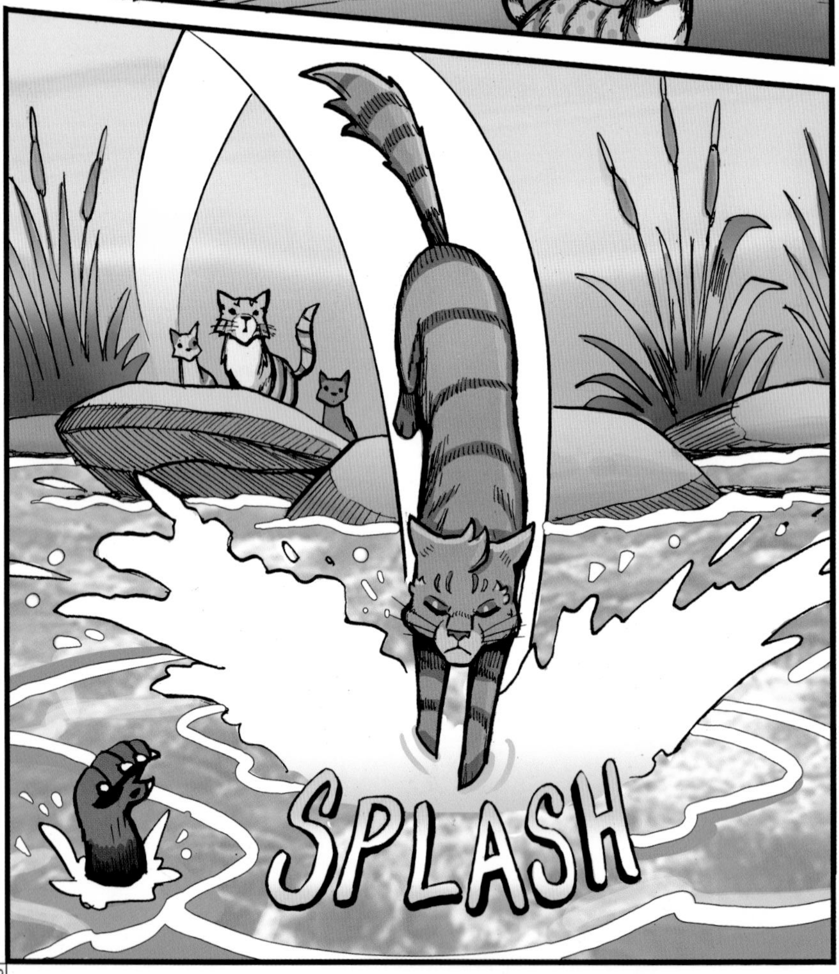
SPLASH

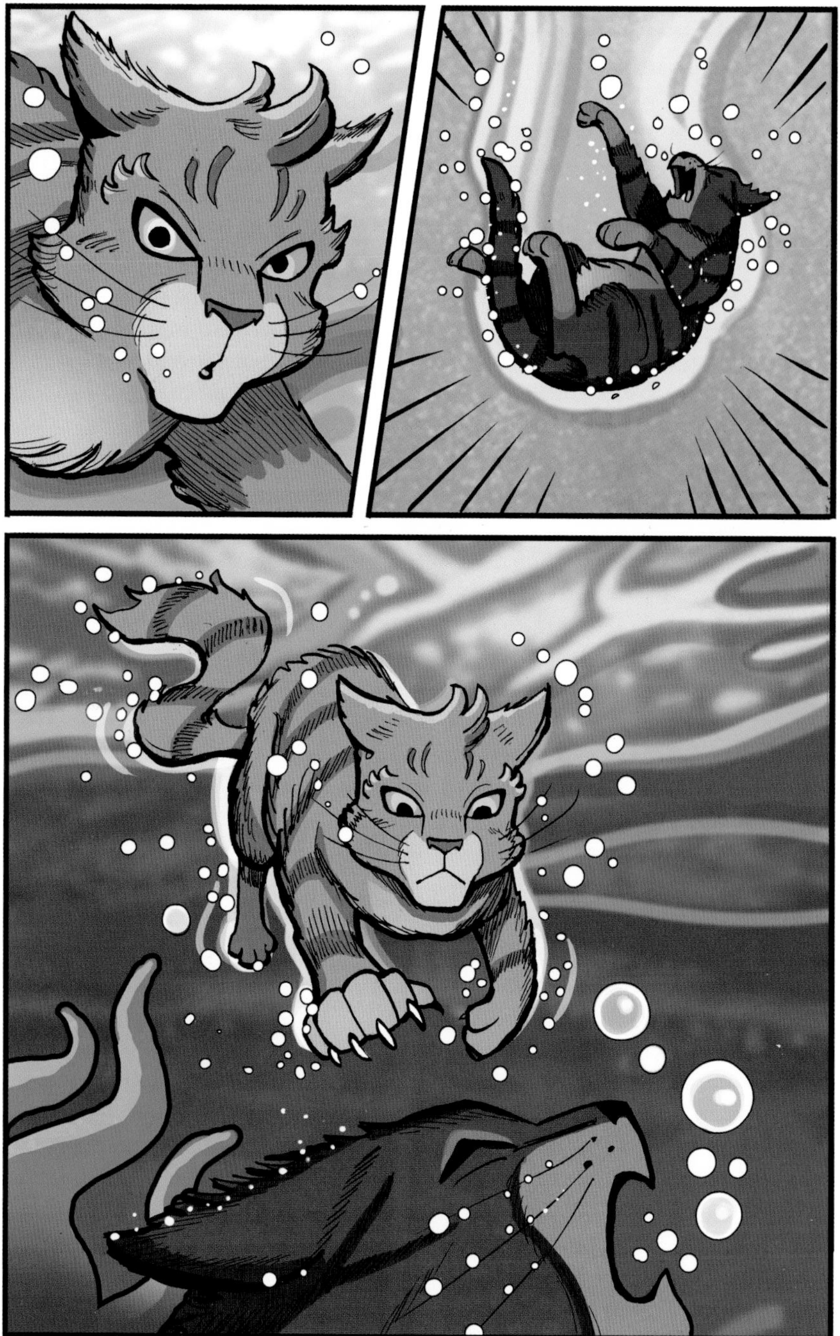

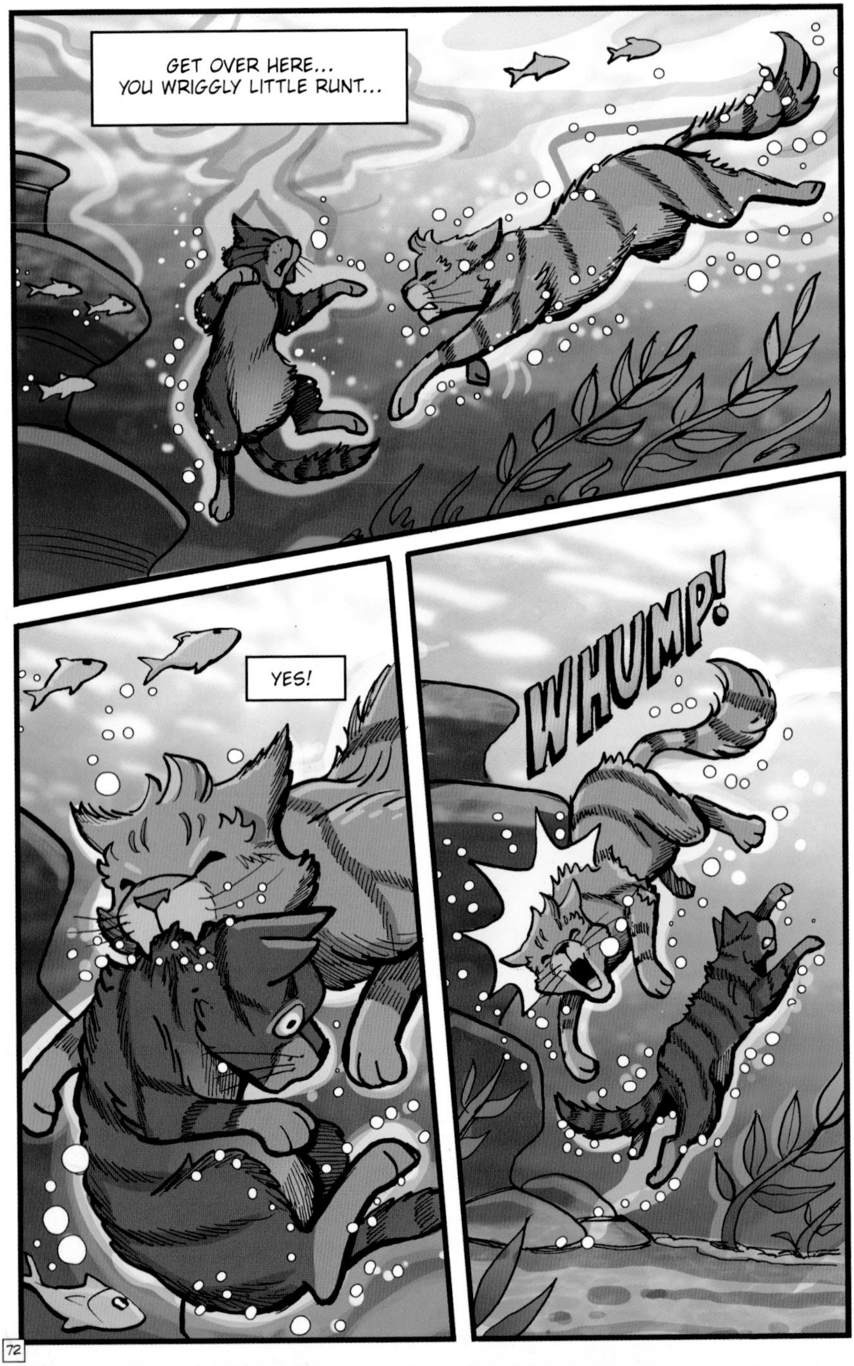
GET OVER HERE...
YOU WRIGGLY LITTLE RUNT...
YES!
WHUMP!

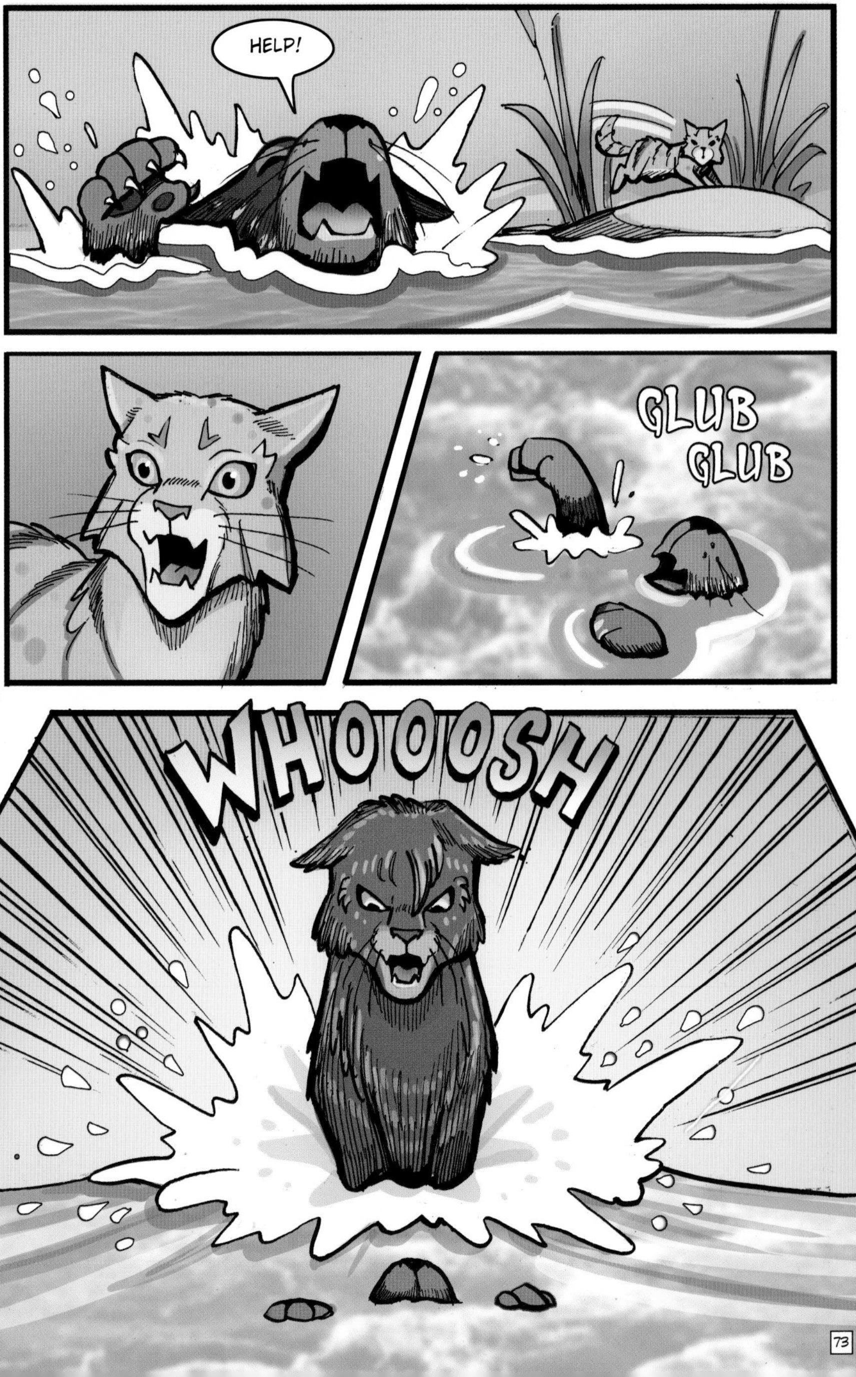
HELP!
GLUB
GLUB
!
WHOOOSH

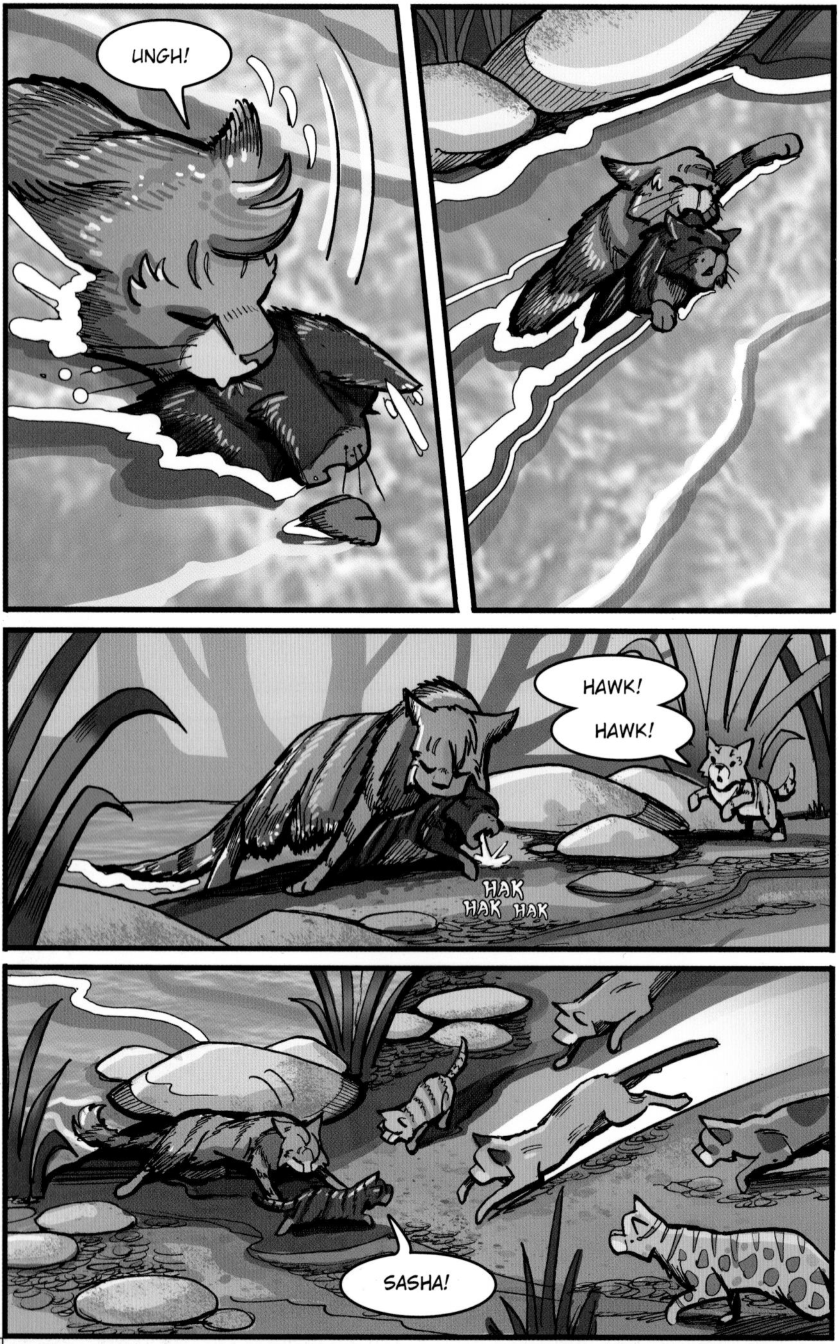

UNGH!
HAWK!
HAWK!
HAK
HAK HAK
SASHA!

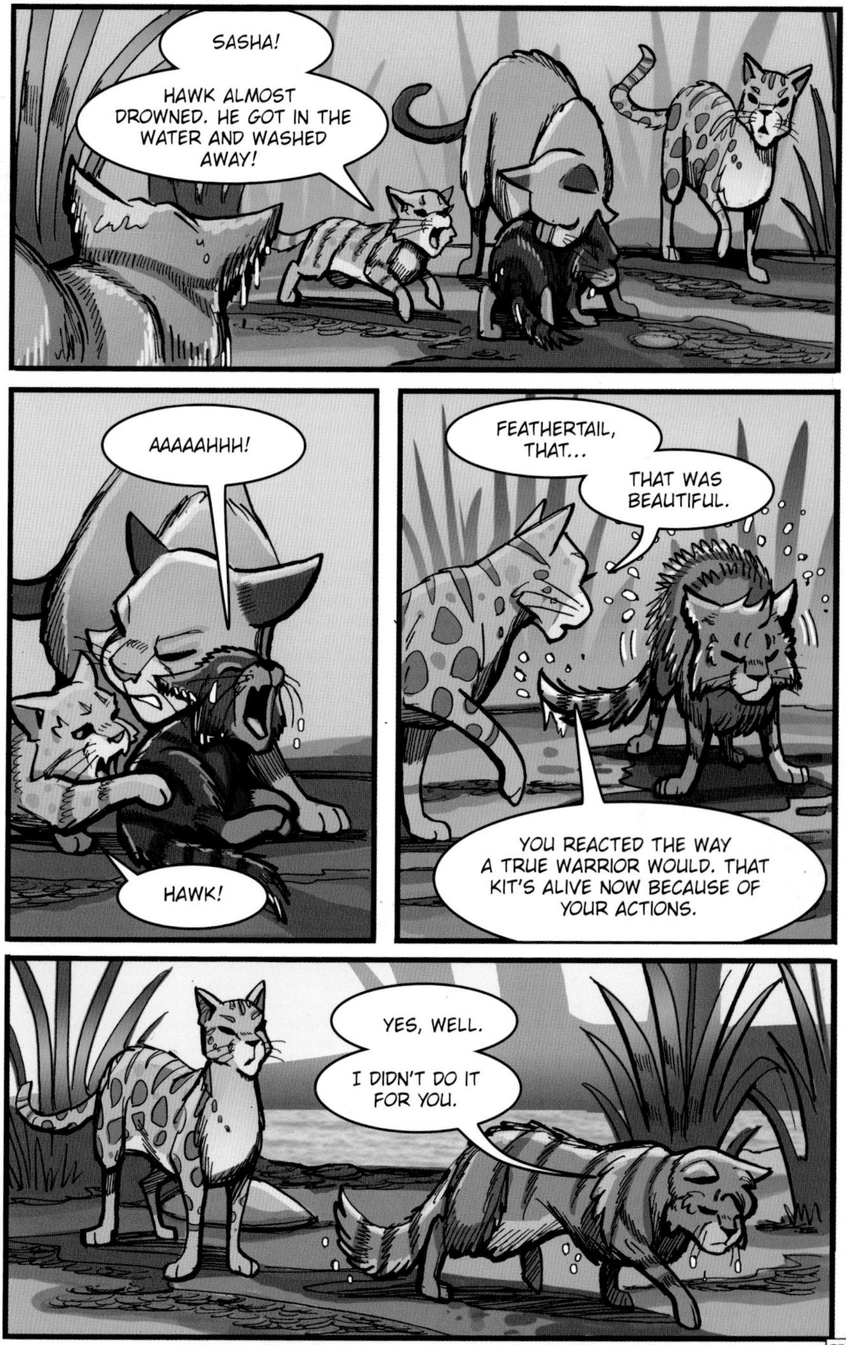
SASHA!
HAWK ALMOST DROWNED. HE GOT IN THE WATER AND WASHED AWAY!
AAAAAHHH!
HAWK!
FEATHERTAIL, THAT...
THAT WAS BEAUTIFUL.
YOU REACTED THE WAY A TRUE WARRIOR WOULD. THAT KIT'S ALIVE NOW BECAUSE OF YOUR ACTIONS.
YES, WELL.
I DIDN'T DO IT FOR YOU.

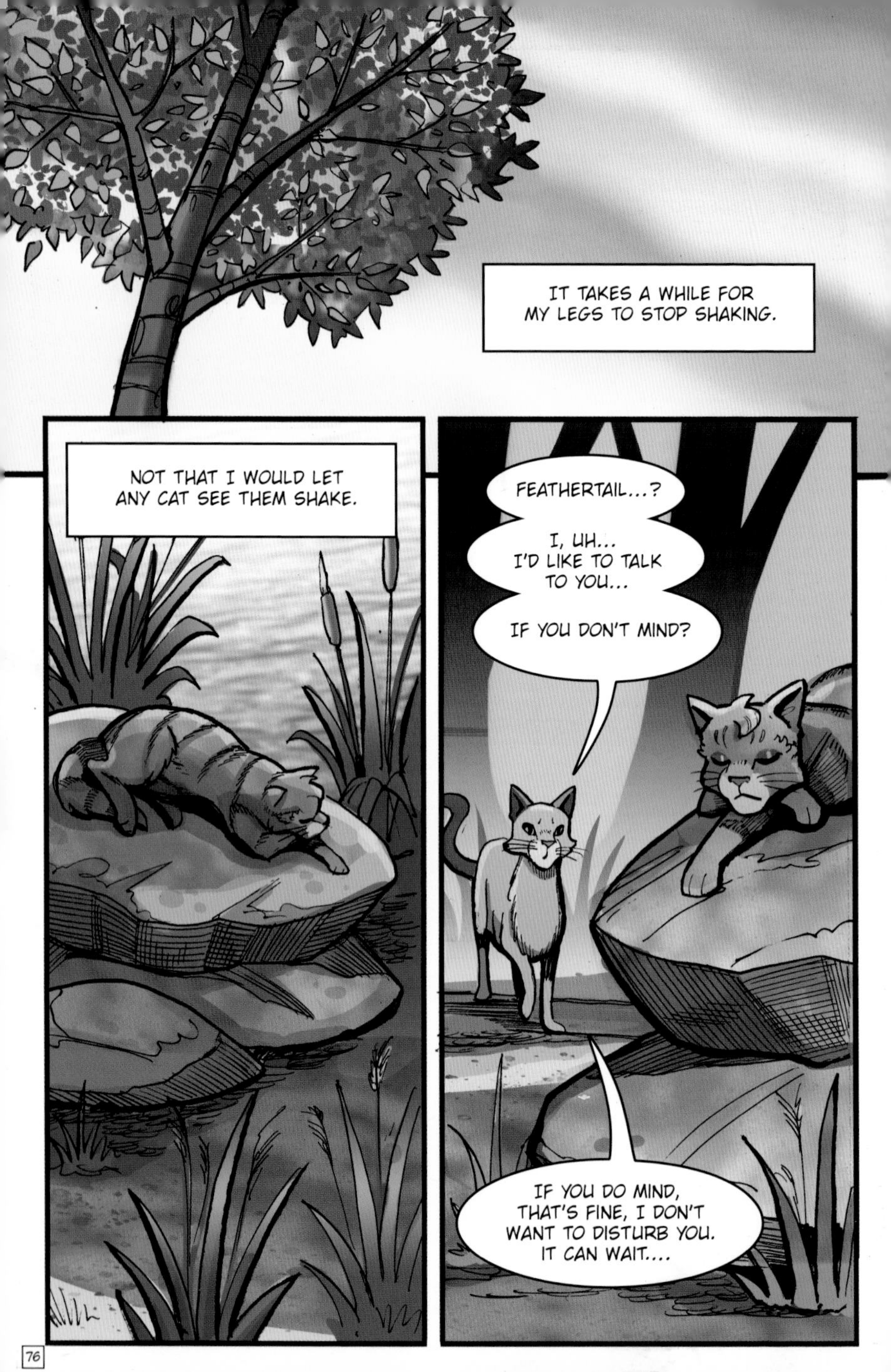
IT TAKES A WHILE FOR MY LEGS TO STOP SHAKING.
NOT THAT I WOULD LET ANY CAT SEE THEM SHAKE.
FEATHERTAIL...?
I, UH... I'D LIKE TO TALK TO YOU...
IF YOU DON'T MIND?
IF YOU DO MIND, THAT'S FINE, I DON'T WANT TO DISTURB YOU. IT CAN WAIT....

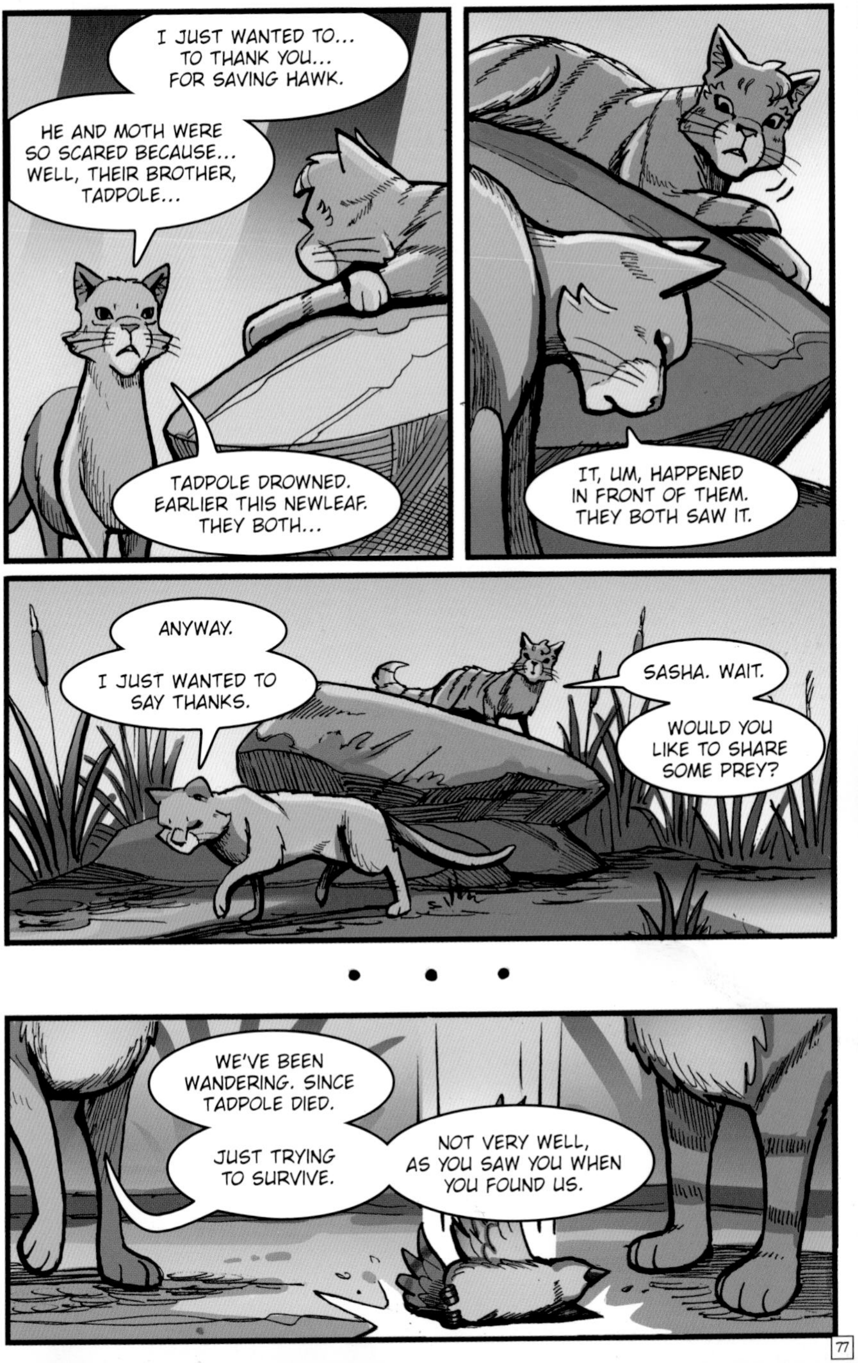
I JUST WANTED TO... TO THANK YOU... FOR SAVING HAWK.
HE AND MOTH WERE SO SCARED BECAUSE... WELL, THEIR BROTHER, TADPOLE...
TADPOLE DROWNED. EARLIER THIS NEWLEAF. THEY BOTH...
IT, UM, HAPPENED IN FRONT OF THEM. THEY BOTH SAW IT.
ANYWAY.
I JUST WANTED TO SAY THANKS.
SASHA. WAIT.
WOULD YOU LIKE TO SHARE SOME PREY?
WE'VE BEEN WANDERING. SINCE TADPOLE DIED.
JUST TRYING TO SURVIVE.
NOT VERY WELL, AS YOU SAW YOU WHEN YOU FOUND US.

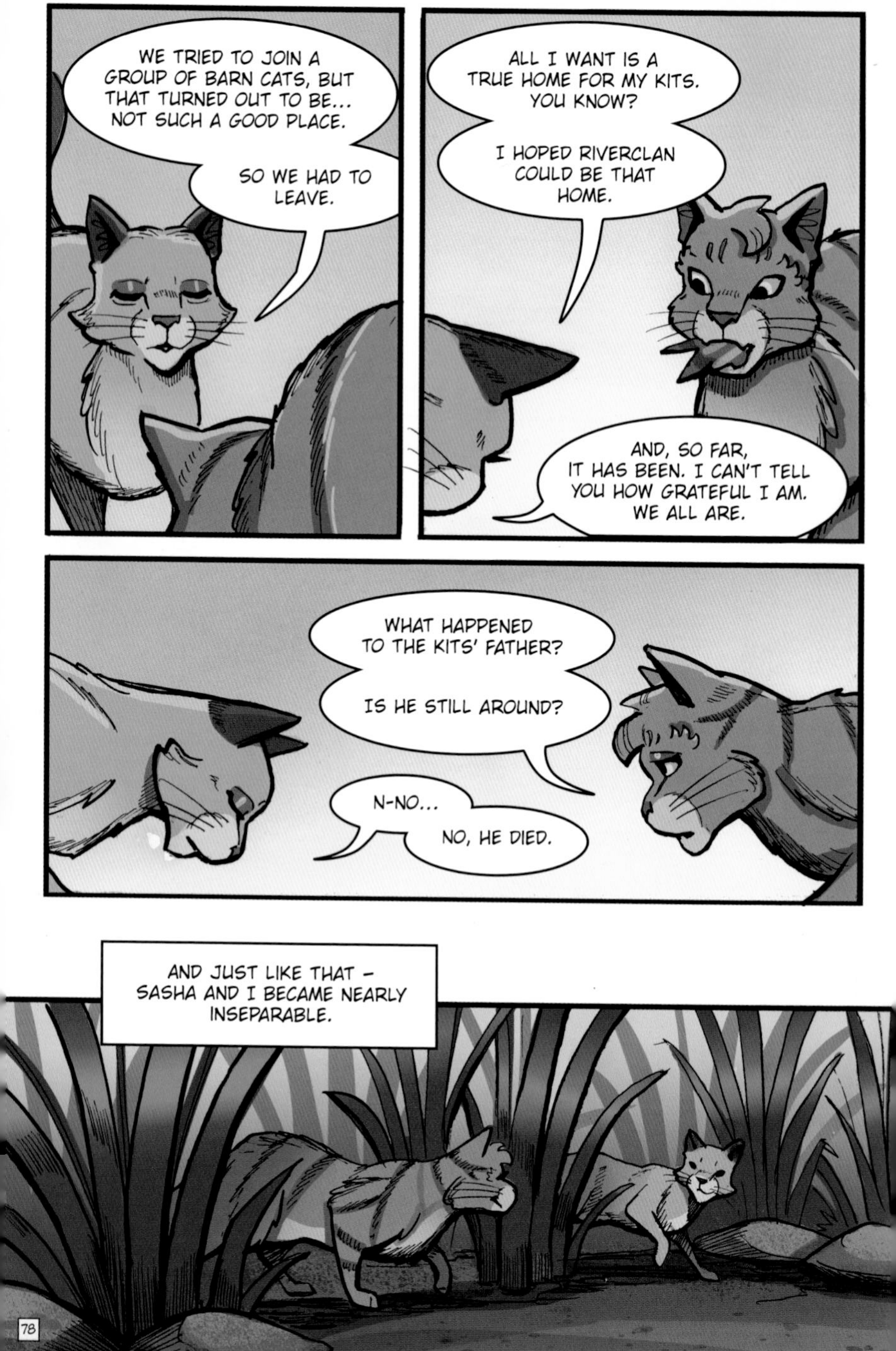

WE TRIED TO JOIN A GROUP OF BARN CATS, BUT THAT TURNED OUT TO BE... NOT SUCH A GOOD PLACE.
SO WE HAD TO LEAVE.
ALL I WANT IS A TRUE HOME FOR MY KITS. YOU KNOW?
I HOPED RIVERCLAN COULD BE THAT HOME.
AND, SO FAR, IT HAS BEEN. I CAN'T TELL YOU HOW GRATEFUL I AM. WE ALL ARE.
WHAT HAPPENED TO THE KITS' FATHER?
IS HE STILL AROUND?
N-NO...
NO, HE DIED.
AND JUST LIKE THAT – SASHA AND I BECAME NEARLY INSEPARABLE.

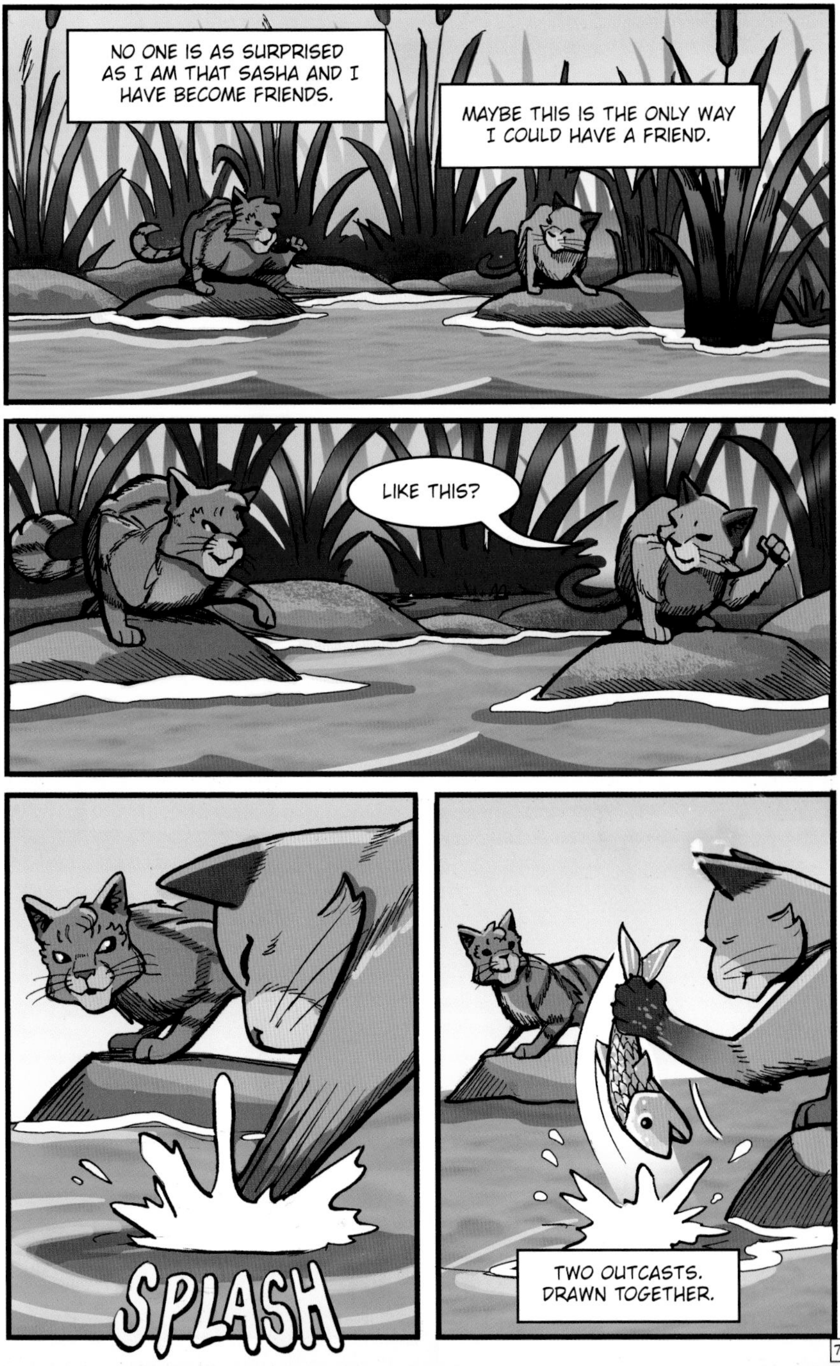
NO ONE IS AS SURPRISED AS I AM THAT SASHA AND I HAVE BECOME FRIENDS.
MAYBE THIS IS THE ONLY WAY I COULD HAVE A FRIEND.
LIKE THIS?
SPLASH
TWO OUTCASTS. DRAWN TOGETHER.

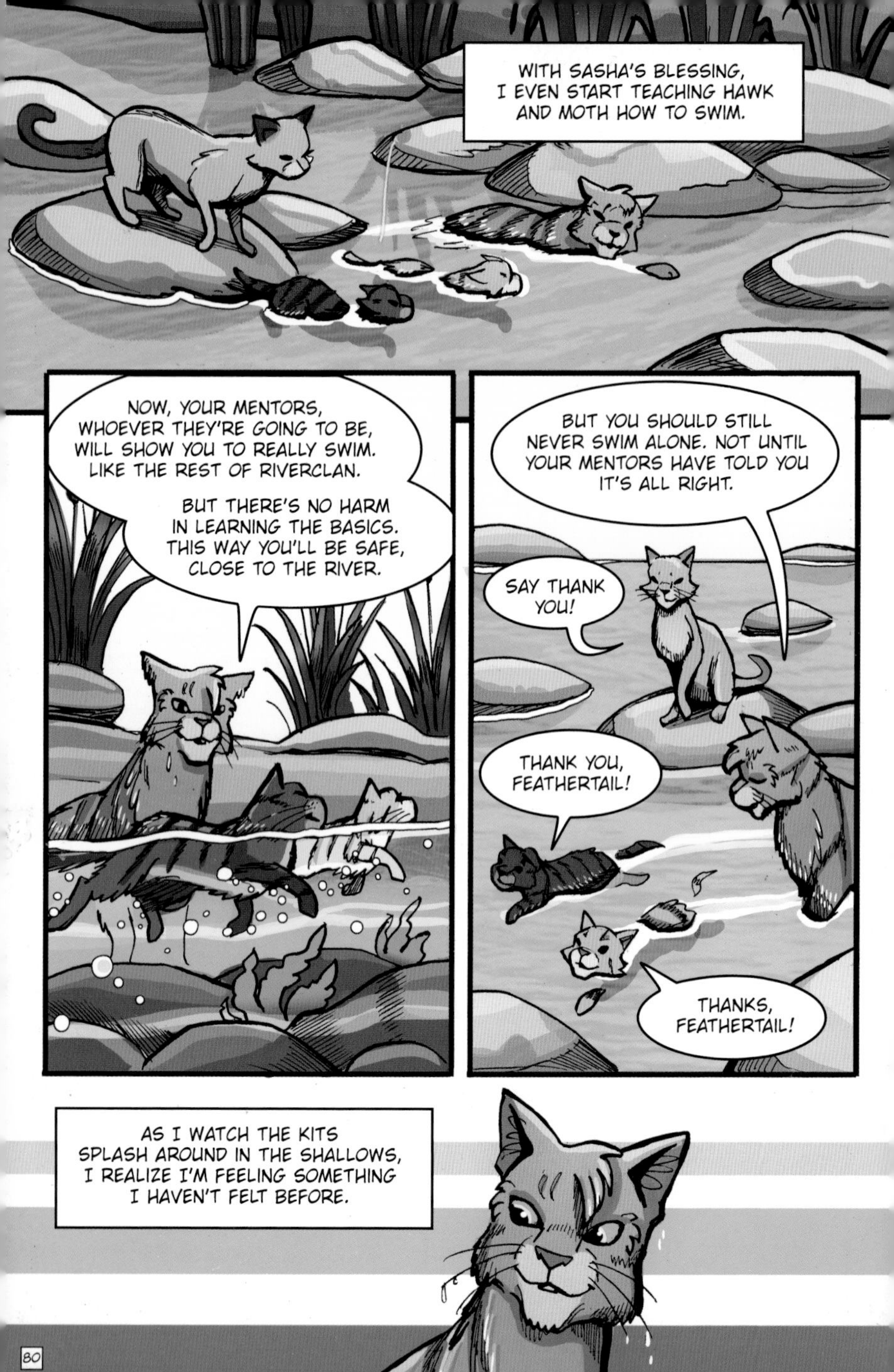
WITH SASHA'S BLESSING, I EVEN START TEACHING HAWK AND MOTH HOW TO SWIM.
NOW, YOUR MENTORS, WHOEVER THEY'RE GOING TO BE, WILL SHOW YOU TO REALLY SWIM. LIKE THE REST OF RIVERCLAN.
BUT THERE'S NO HARM IN LEARNING THE BASICS. THIS WAY YOU'LL BE SAFE, CLOSE TO THE RIVER.
BUT YOU SHOULD STILL NEVER SWIM ALONE. NOT UNTIL YOUR MENTORS HAVE TOLD YOU IT'S ALL RIGHT.
SAY THANK YOU!
THANK YOU, FEATHERTAIL!
THANKS, FEATHERTAIL!
AS I WATCH THE KITS SPLASH AROUND IN THE SHALLOWS, I REALIZE I'M FEELING SOMETHING I HAVEN'T FELT BEFORE.

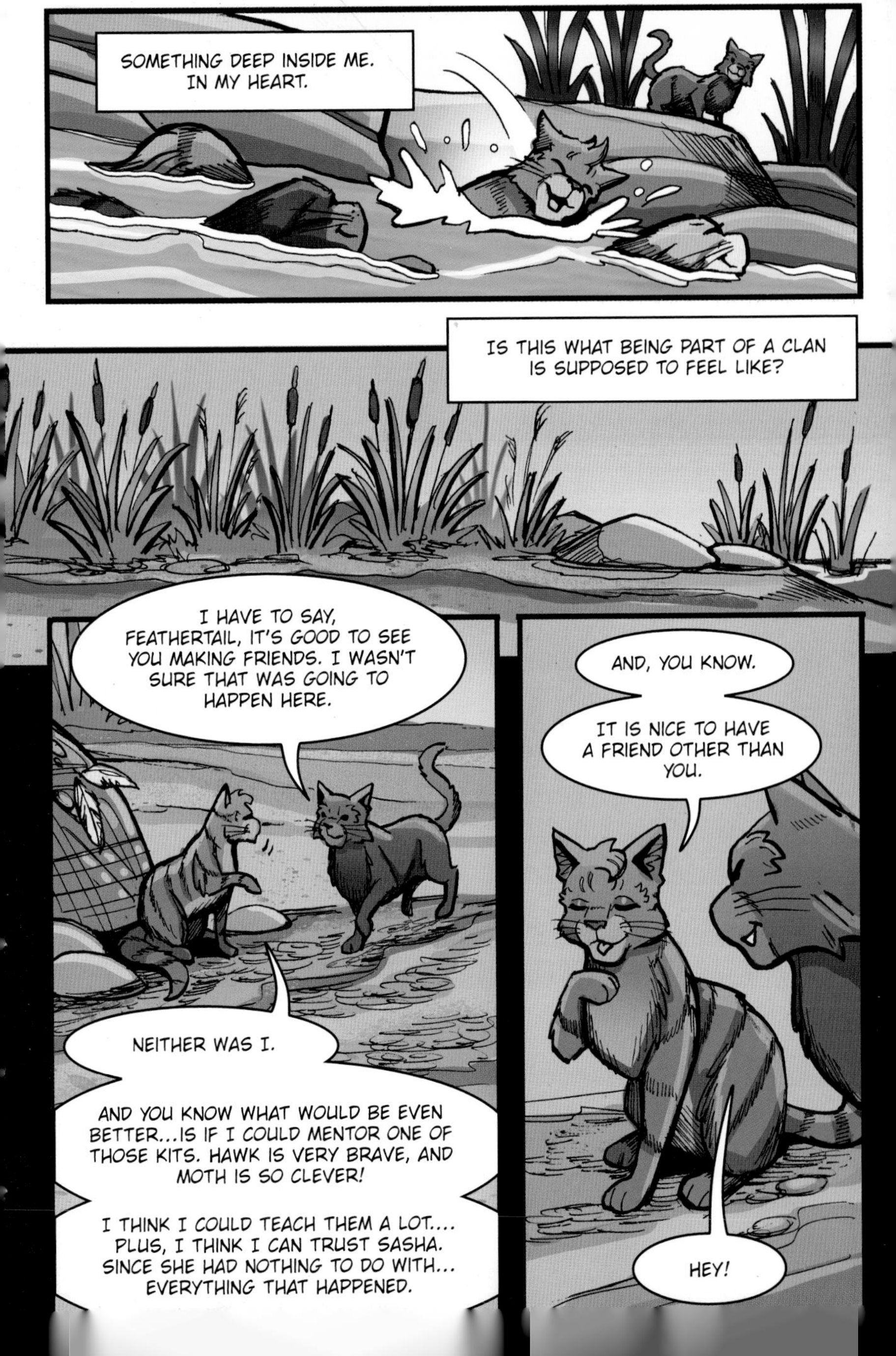
SOMETHING DEEP INSIDE ME. IN MY HEART.
IS THIS WHAT BEING PART OF A CLAN IS SUPPOSED TO FEEL LIKE?
I HAVE TO SAY, FEATHERTAIL, IT'S GOOD TO SEE YOU MAKING FRIENDS. I WASN'T SURE THAT WAS GOING TO HAPPEN HERE.
NEITHER WAS I.
AND YOU KNOW WHAT WOULD BE EVEN BETTER...IS IF I COULD MENTOR ONE OF THOSE KITS. HAWK IS VERY BRAVE, AND MOTH IS SO CLEVER!
I THINK I COULD TEACH THEM A LOT.... PLUS, I THINK I CAN TRUST SASHA. SINCE SHE HAD NOTHING TO DO WITH... EVERYTHING THAT HAPPENED.
AND, YOU KNOW.
IT IS NICE TO HAVE A FRIEND OTHER THAN YOU.
HEY!

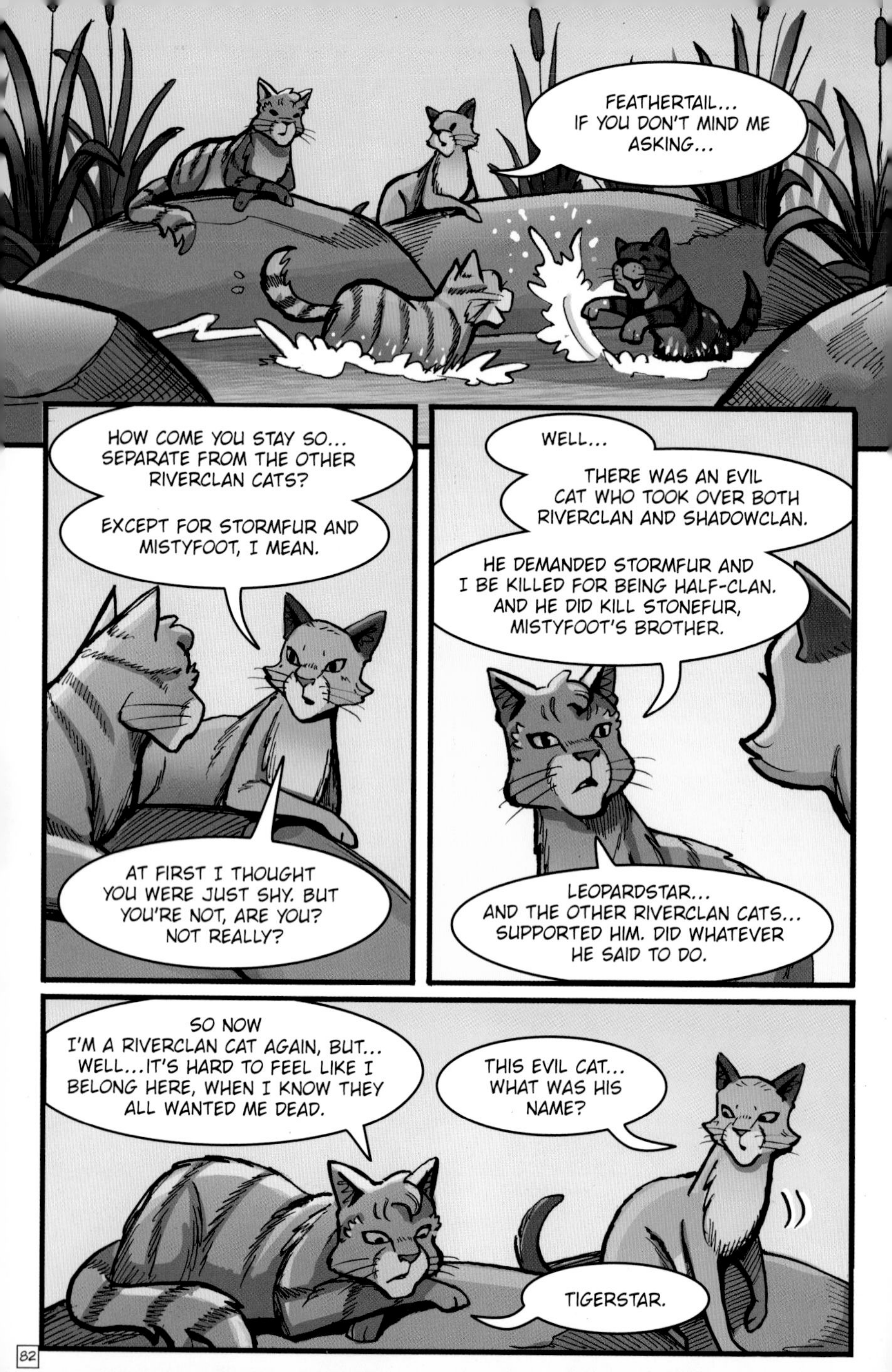
FEATHERTAIL... IF YOU DON'T MIND ME ASKING...
HOW COME YOU STAY SO... SEPARATE FROM THE OTHER RIVERCLAN CATS?
EXCEPT FOR STORMFUR AND MISTYFOOT, I MEAN.
AT FIRST I THOUGHT YOU WERE JUST SHY. BUT YOU'RE NOT, ARE YOU? NOT REALLY?
WELL...
THERE WAS AN EVIL CAT WHO TOOK OVER BOTH RIVERCLAN AND SHADOWCLAN.
HE DEMANDED STORMFUR AND I BE KILLED FOR BEING HALF-CLAN. AND HE DID KILL STONEFUR, MISTYFOOT'S BROTHER.
LEOPARDSTAR... AND THE OTHER RIVERCLAN CATS... SUPPORTED HIM. DID WHATEVER HE SAID TO DO.
SO NOW I'M A RIVERCLAN CAT AGAIN, BUT... WELL...IT'S HARD TO FEEL LIKE I BELONG HERE, WHEN I KNOW THEY ALL WANTED ME DEAD.
THIS EVIL CAT... WHAT WAS HIS NAME?
TIGERSTAR.

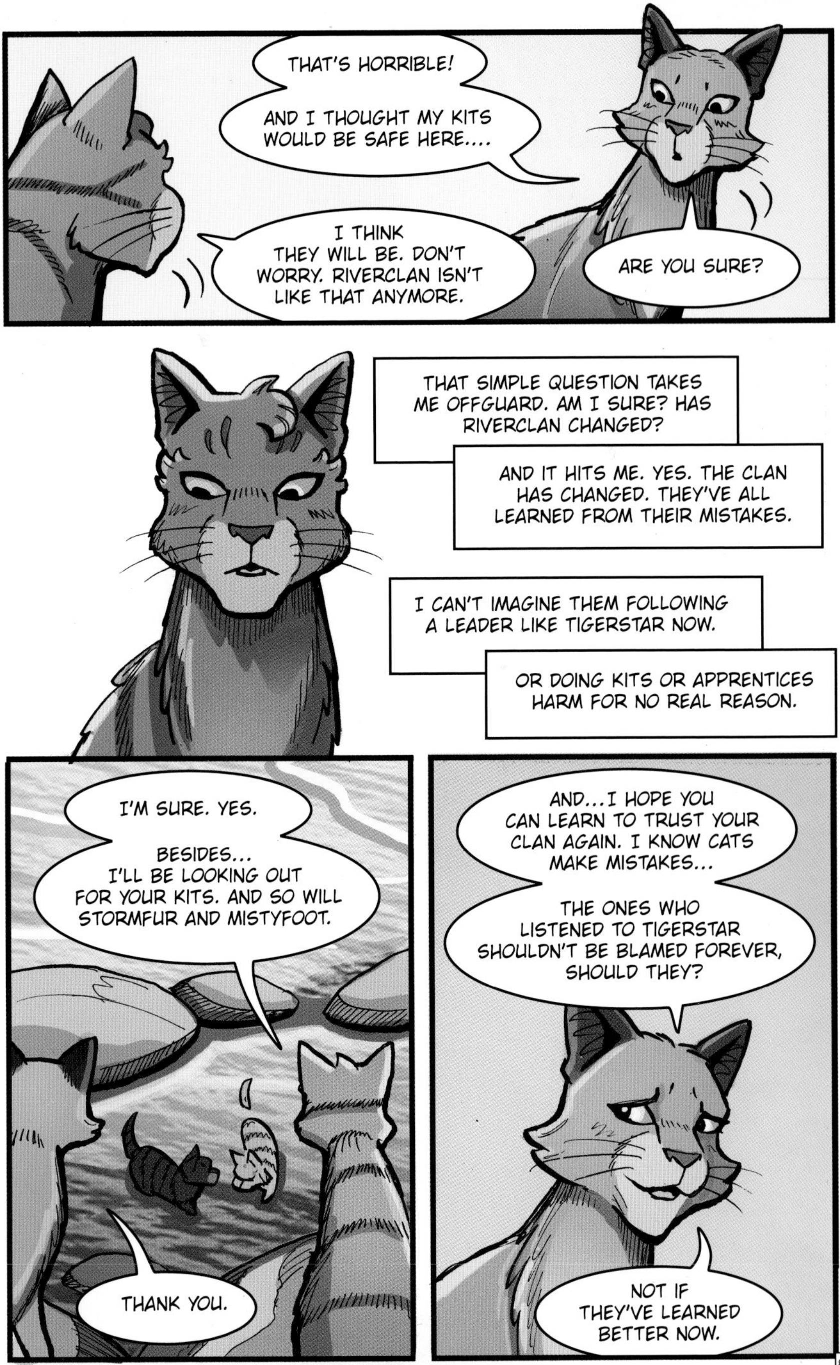
THAT'S HORRIBLE!
AND I THOUGHT MY KITS WOULD BE SAFE HERE....
I THINK THEY WILL BE. DON'T WORRY. RIVERCLAN ISN'T LIKE THAT ANYMORE.
ARE YOU SURE?
THAT SIMPLE QUESTION TAKES ME OFFGUARD. AM I SURE? HAS RIVERCLAN CHANGED?
AND IT HITS ME. YES. THE CLAN HAS CHANGED. THEY'VE ALL LEARNED FROM THEIR MISTAKES.
I CAN'T IMAGINE THEM FOLLOWING A LEADER LIKE TIGERSTAR NOW.
OR DOING KITS OR APPRENTICES HARM FOR NO REAL REASON.
I'M SURE. YES.
BESIDES... I'LL BE LOOKING OUT FOR YOUR KITS. AND SO WILL STORMFUR AND MISTYFOOT.
THANK YOU.
AND...I HOPE YOU CAN LEARN TO TRUST YOUR CLAN AGAIN. I KNOW CATS MAKE MISTAKES...
THE ONES WHO LISTENED TO TIGERSTAR SHOULDN'T BE BLAMED FOREVER, SHOULD THEY?
NOT IF THEY'VE LEARNED BETTER NOW.

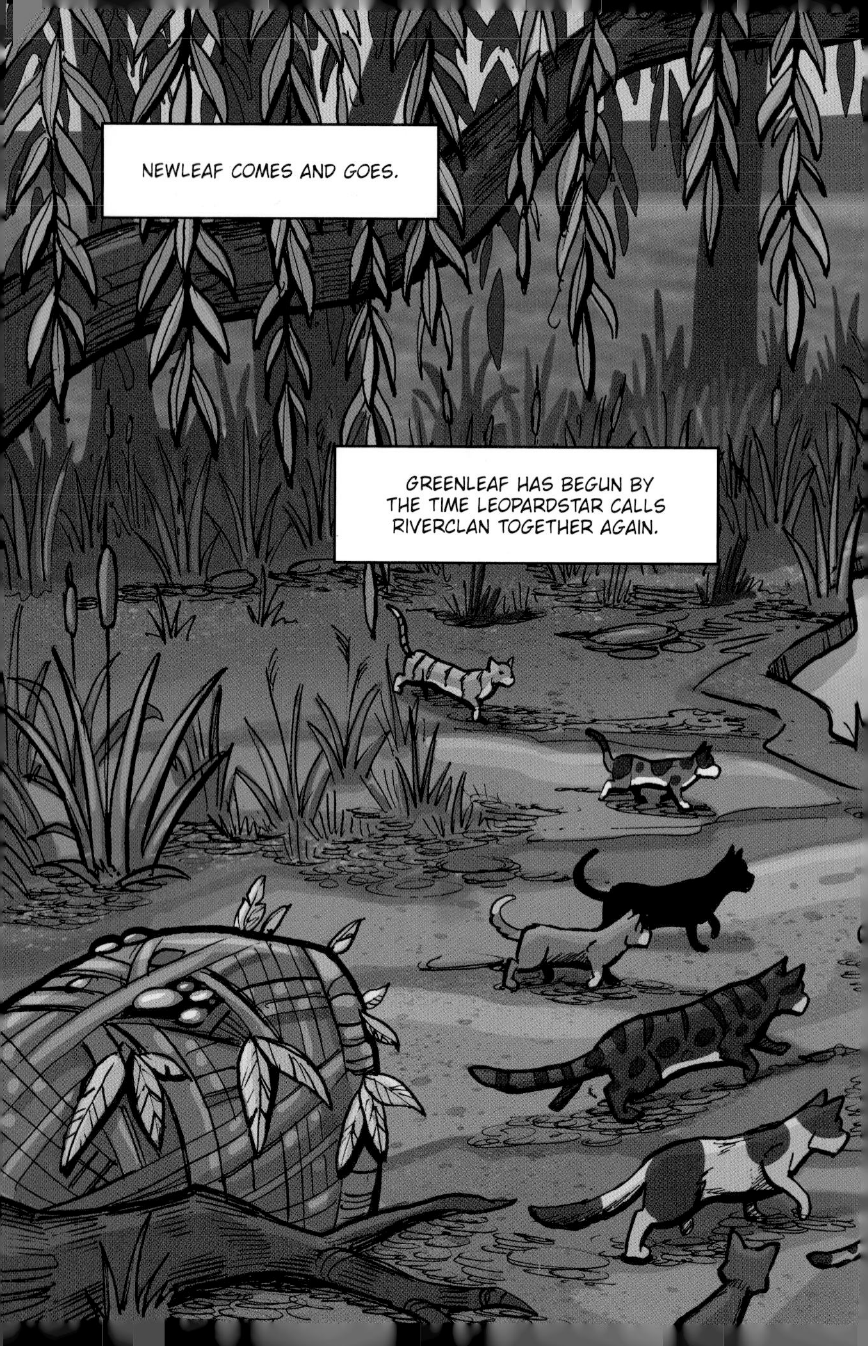
NEWLEAF COMES AND GOES.
GREENLEAF HAS BEGUN BY THE TIME LEOPARDSTAR CALLS RIVERCLAN TOGETHER AGAIN.

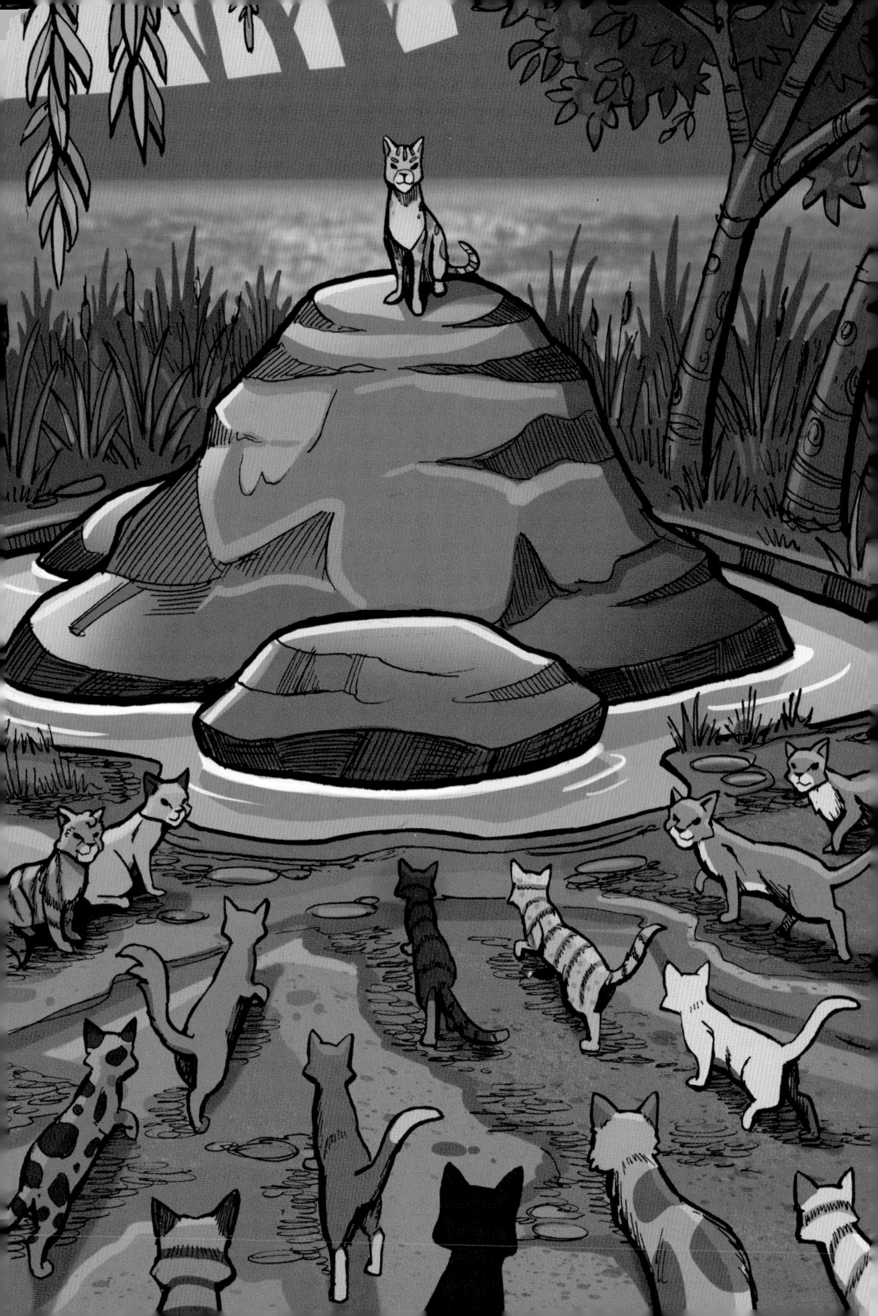

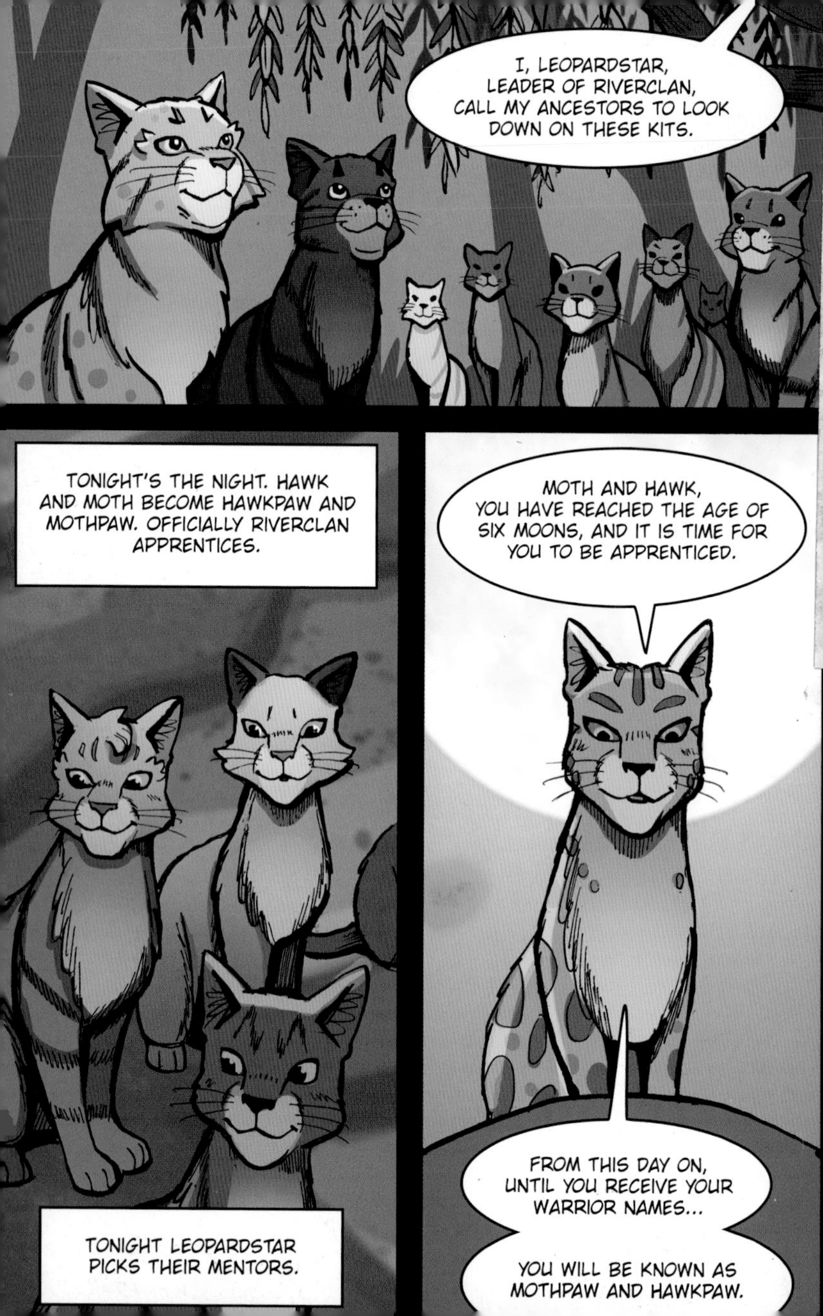
I, LEOPARDSTAR, LEADER OF RIVERCLAN, CALL MY ANCESTORS TO LOOK DOWN ON THESE KITS.
TONIGHT'S THE NIGHT. HAWK AND MOTH BECOME HAWKPAW AND MOTHPAW. OFFICIALLY RIVERCLAN APPRENTICES.
TONIGHT LEOPARDSTAR PICKS THEIR MENTORS.
MOTH AND HAWK, YOU HAVE REACHED THE AGE OF SIX MOONS, AND IT IS TIME FOR YOU TO BE APPRENTICED.
FROM THIS DAY ON, UNTIL YOU RECEIVE YOUR WARRIOR NAMES...
YOU WILL BE KNOWN AS MOTHPAW AND HAWKPAW.

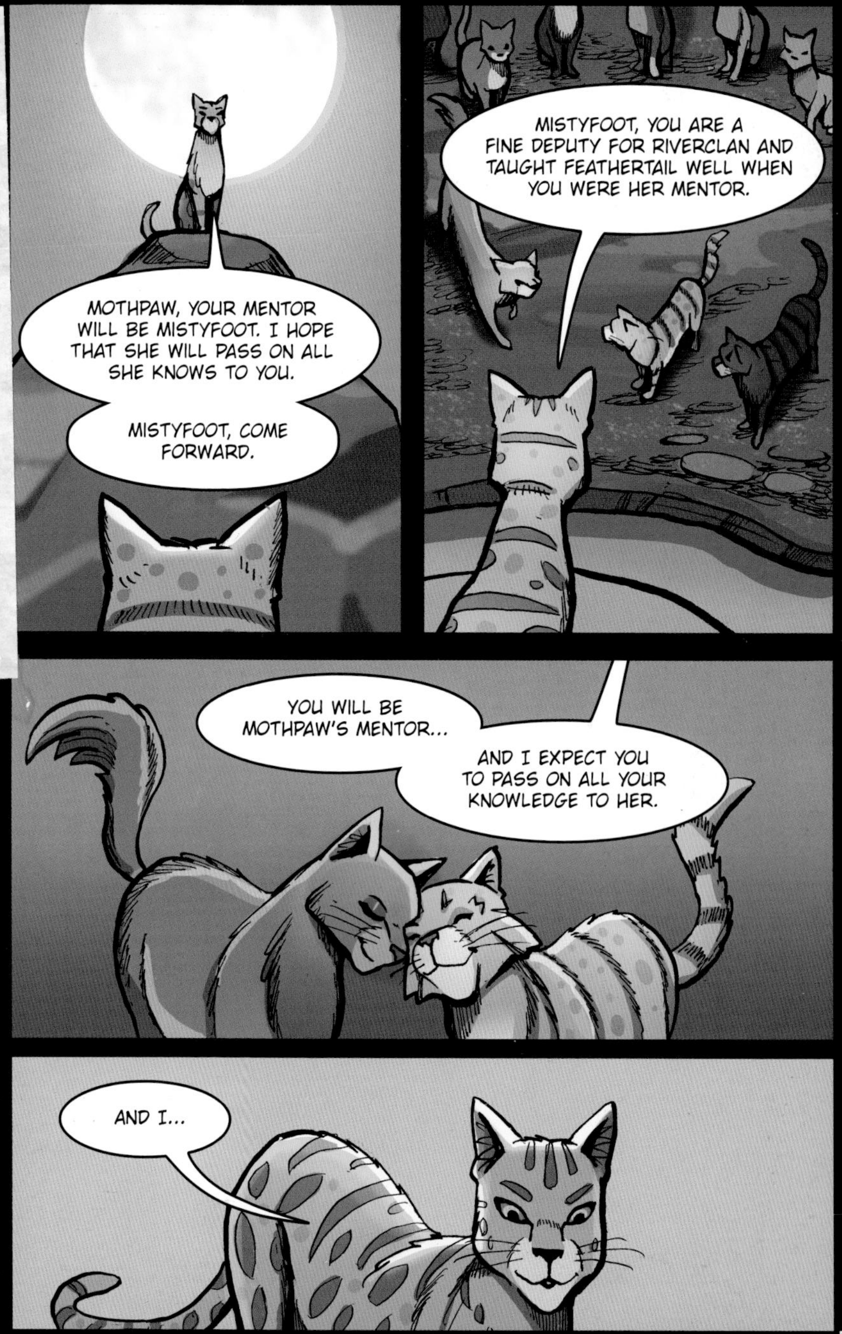
MOTHPAW, YOUR MENTOR WILL BE MISTYFOOT. I HOPE THAT SHE WILL PASS ON ALL SHE KNOWS TO YOU.
MISTYFOOT, COME FORWARD.
MISTYFOOT, YOU ARE A FINE DEPUTY FOR RIVERCLAN AND TAUGHT FEATHERTAIL WELL WHEN YOU WERE HER MENTOR.
YOU WILL BE MOTHPAW'S MENTOR...
AND I EXPECT YOU TO PASS ON ALL YOUR KNOWLEDGE TO HER.
AND I...

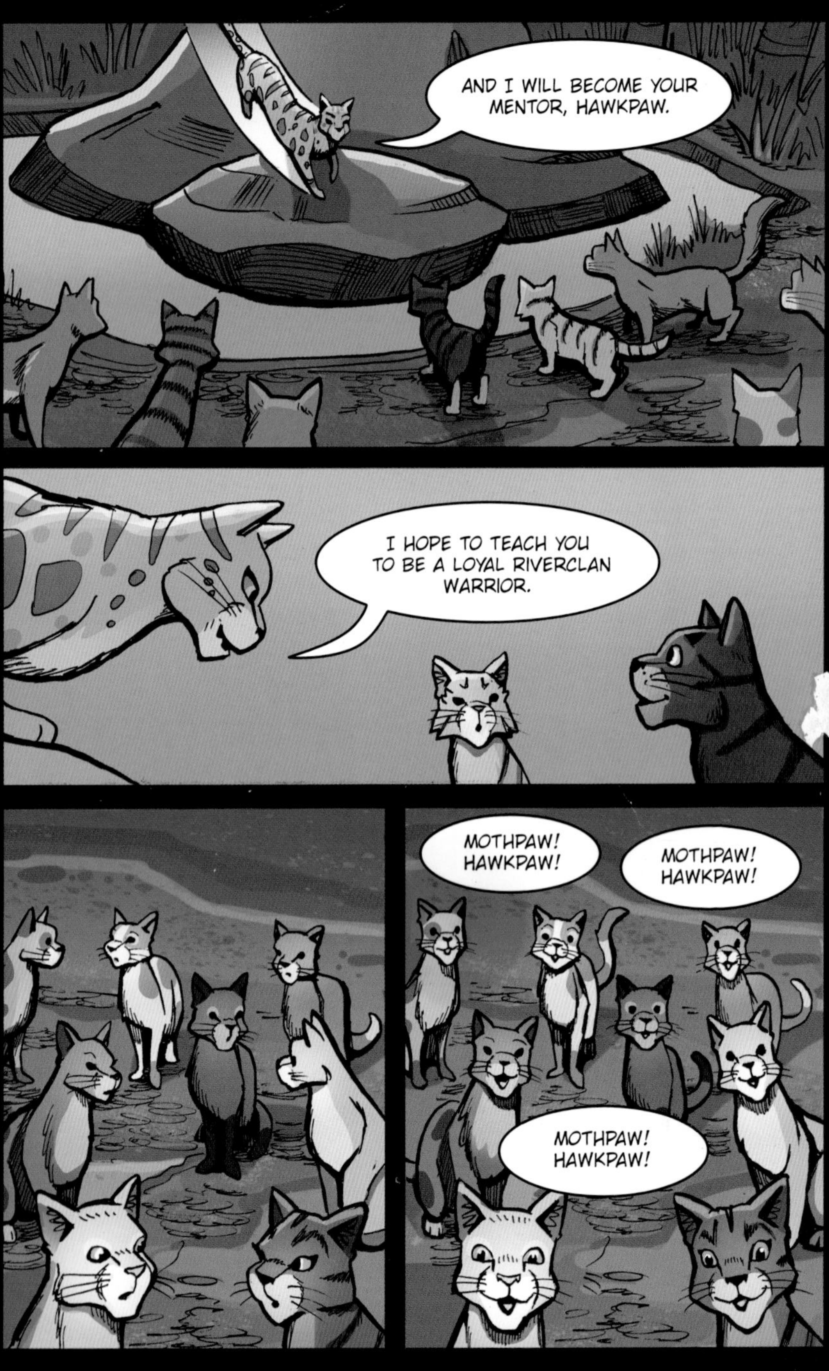
AND I WILL BECOME YOUR MENTOR, HAWKPAW.
I HOPE TO TEACH YOU TO BE A LOYAL RIVERCLAN WARRIOR.
MOTHPAW! HAWKPAW!
MOTHPAW! HAWKPAW!
MOTHPAW! HAWKPAW!

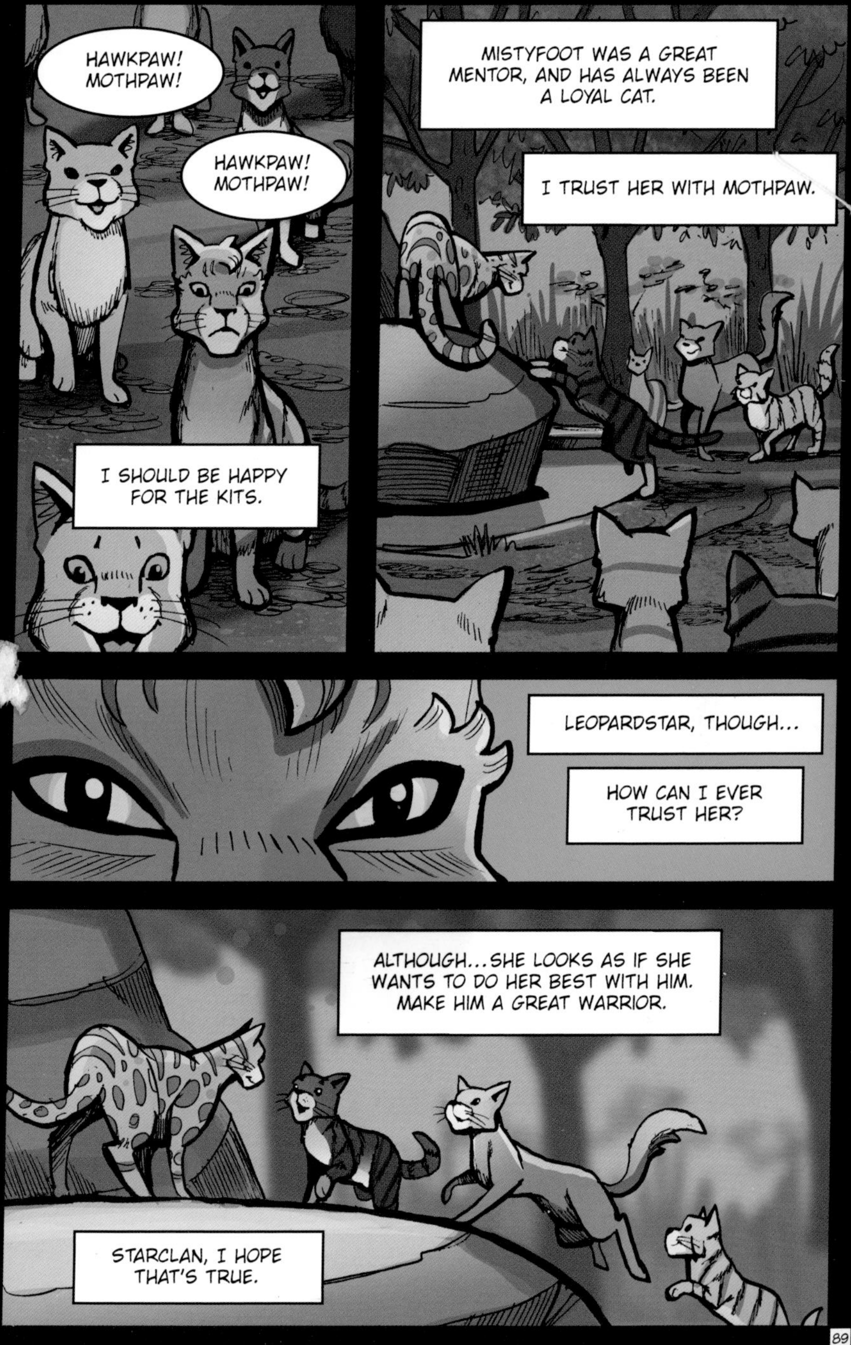
HAWKPAW! MOTHPAW!
HAWKPAW! MOTHPAW!
I SHOULD BE HAPPY FOR THE KITS.
MISTYFOOT WAS A GREAT MENTOR, AND HAS ALWAYS BEEN A LOYAL CAT.
I TRUST HER WITH MOTHPAW.
LEOPARDSTAR, THOUGH...
HOW CAN I EVER TRUST HER?
ALTHOUGH...SHE LOOKS AS IF SHE WANTS TO DO HER BEST WITH HIM. MAKE HIM A GREAT WARRIOR.
STARCLAN, I HOPE THAT'S TRUE.

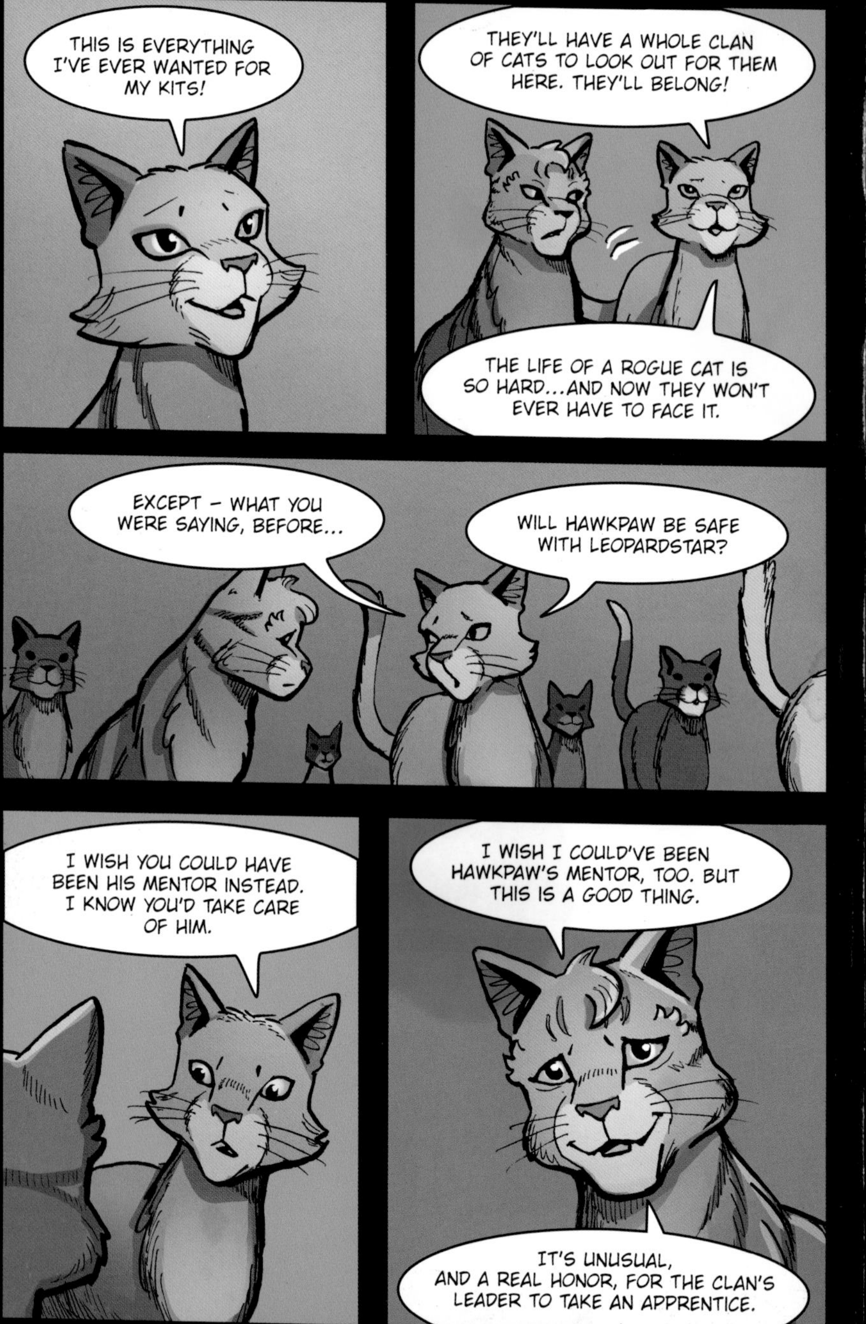
THIS IS EVERYTHING I'VE EVER WANTED FOR MY KITS!
THEY'LL HAVE A WHOLE CLAN OF CATS TO LOOK OUT FOR THEM HERE. THEY'LL BELONG!
THE LIFE OF A ROGUE CAT IS SO HARD...AND NOW THEY WON'T EVER HAVE TO FACE IT.
EXCEPT – WHAT YOU WERE SAYING, BEFORE...
WILL HAWKPAW BE SAFE WITH LEOPARDSTAR?
I WISH YOU COULD HAVE BEEN HIS MENTOR INSTEAD. I KNOW YOU'D TAKE CARE OF HIM.
I WISH I COULD'VE BEEN HAWKPAW'S MENTOR, TOO. BUT THIS IS A GOOD THING.
IT'S UNUSUAL, AND A REAL HONOR, FOR THE CLAN'S LEADER TO TAKE AN APPRENTICE.

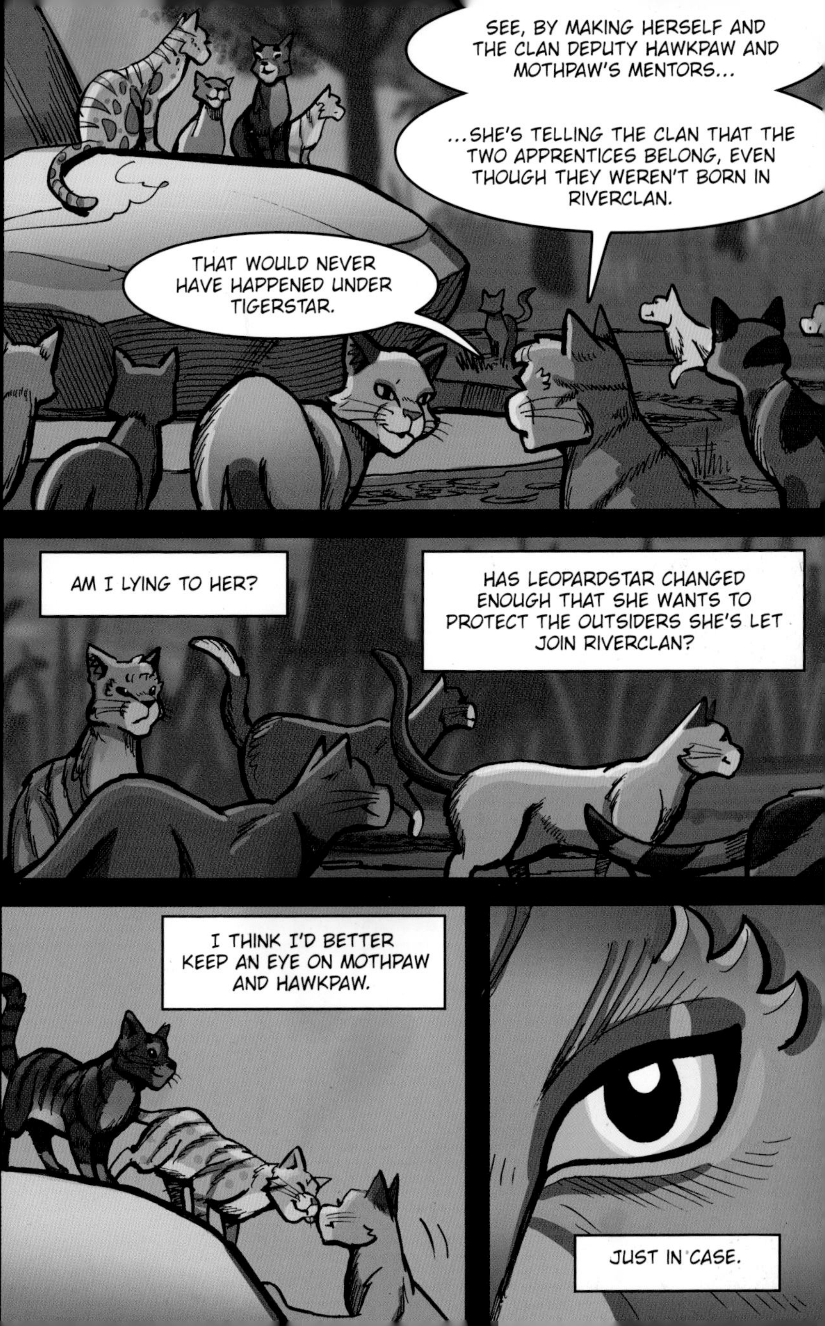
SEE, BY MAKING HERSELF AND THE CLAN DEPUTY HAWKPAW AND MOTHPAW'S MENTORS...
...SHE'S TELLING THE CLAN THAT THE TWO APPRENTICES BELONG, EVEN THOUGH THEY WEREN'T BORN IN RIVERCLAN.
THAT WOULD NEVER HAVE HAPPENED UNDER TIGERSTAR.
AM I LYING TO HER?
HAS LEOPARDSTAR CHANGED ENOUGH THAT SHE WANTS TO PROTECT THE OUTSIDERS SHE'S LET JOIN RIVERCLAN?
I THINK I'D BETTER KEEP AN EYE ON MOTHPAW AND HAWKPAW.
JUST IN CASE.

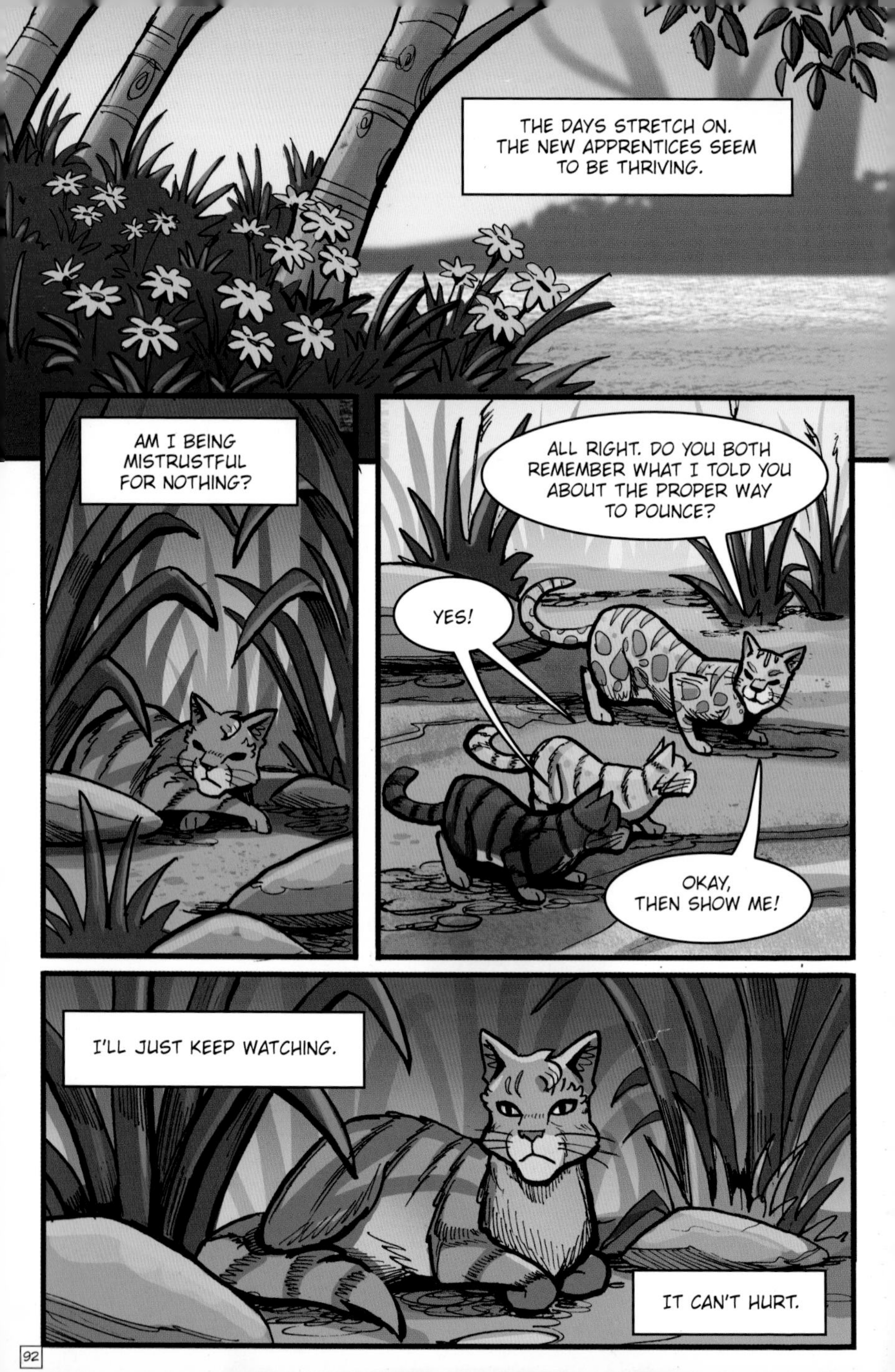
THE DAYS STRETCH ON. THE NEW APPRENTICES SEEM TO BE THRIVING.
AM I BEING MISTRUSTFUL FOR NOTHING?
ALL RIGHT. DO YOU BOTH REMEMBER WHAT I TOLD YOU ABOUT THE PROPER WAY TO POUNCE?
YES!
OKAY, THEN SHOW ME!
I'LL JUST KEEP WATCHING.
IT CAN'T HURT.

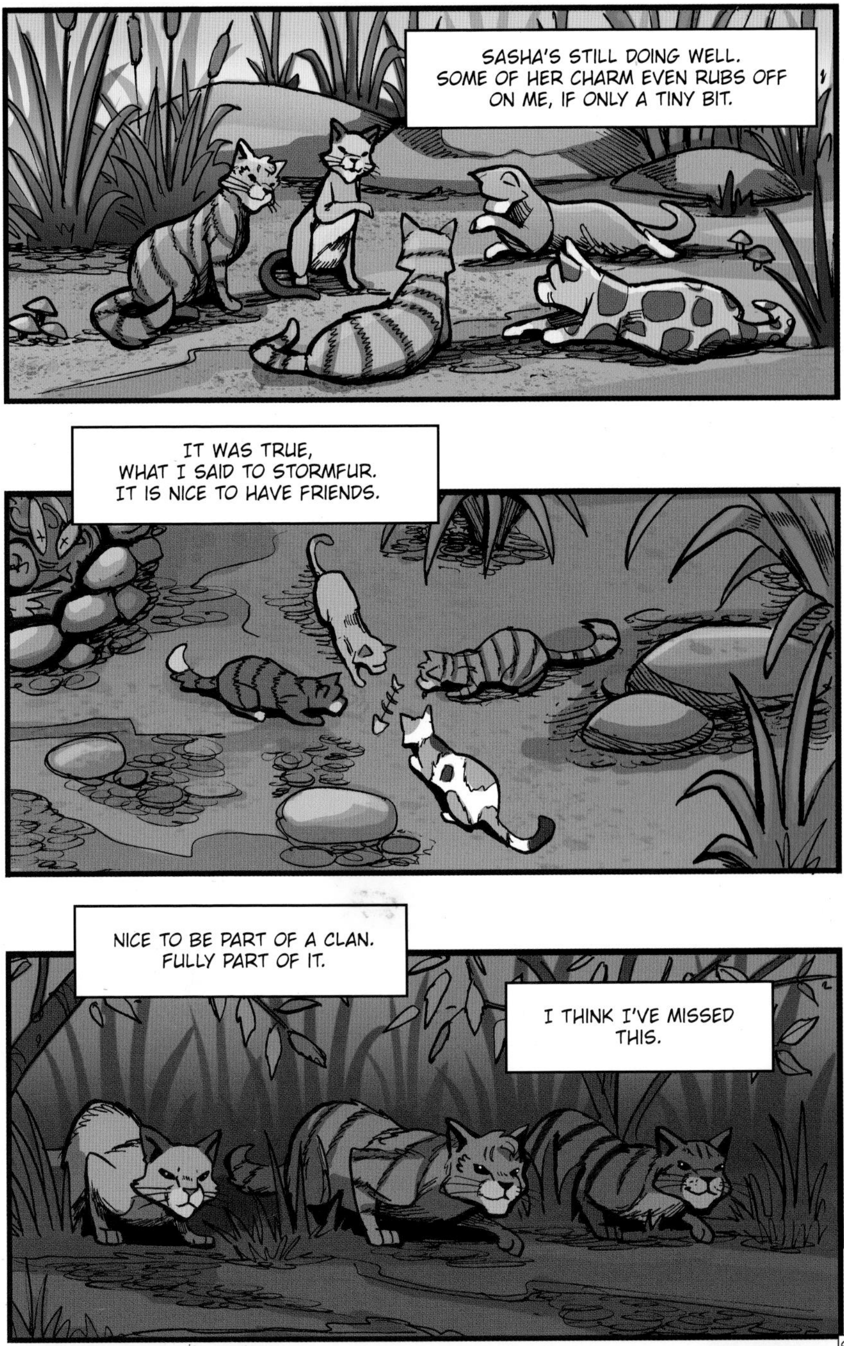
SASHA'S STILL DOING WELL. SOME OF HER CHARM EVEN RUBS OFF ON ME, IF ONLY A TINY BIT.
IT WAS TRUE, WHAT I SAID TO STORMFUR. IT IS NICE TO HAVE FRIENDS.
NICE TO BE PART OF A CLAN. FULLY PART OF IT.
I THINK I'VE MISSED THIS.

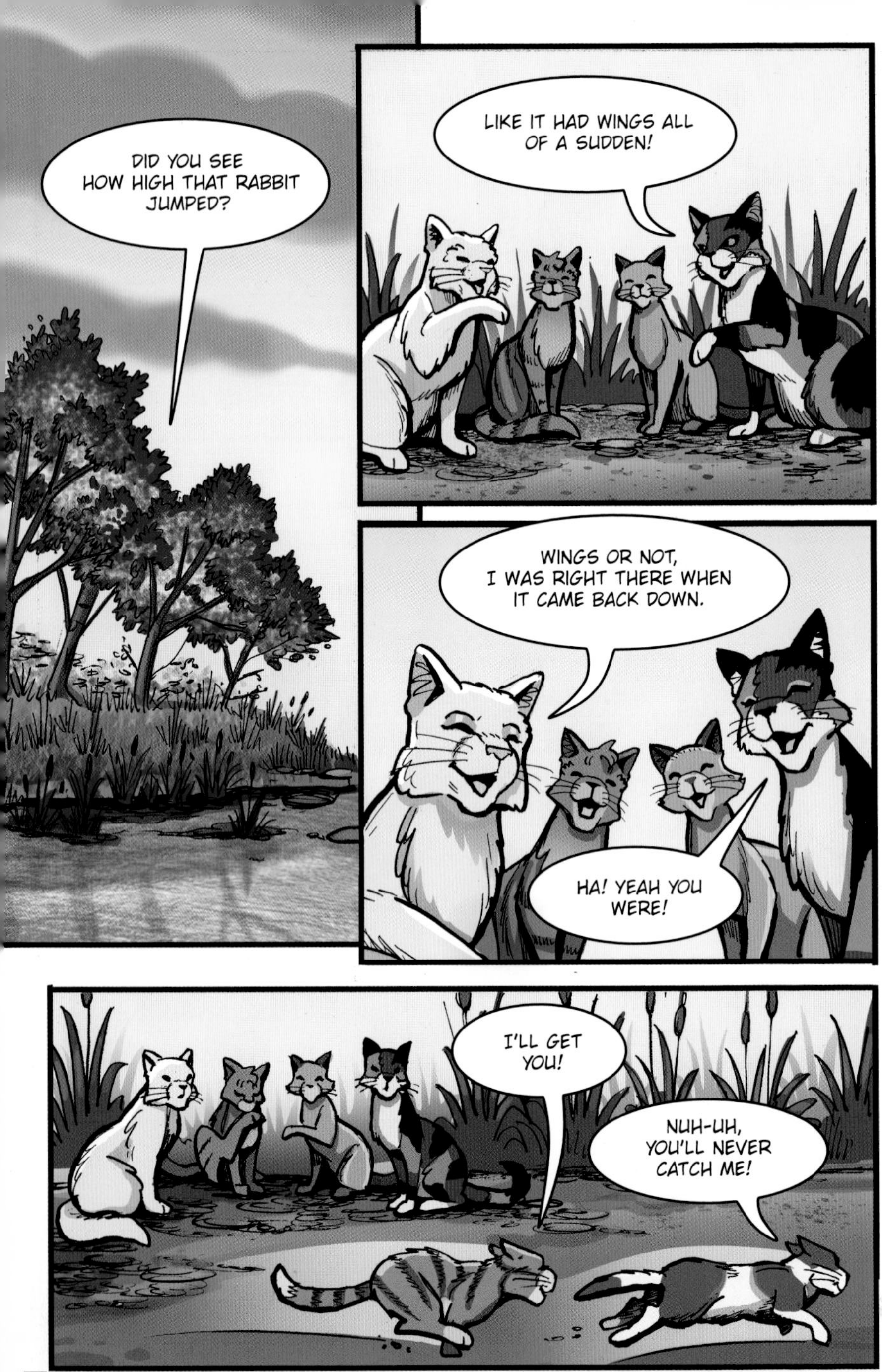
DID YOU SEE HOW HIGH THAT RABBIT JUMPED?
LIKE IT HAD WINGS ALL OF A SUDDEN!
WINGS OR NOT, I WAS RIGHT THERE WHEN IT CAME BACK DOWN.
HA! YEAH YOU WERE!
I'LL GET YOU!
NUH-UH, YOU'LL NEVER CATCH ME!

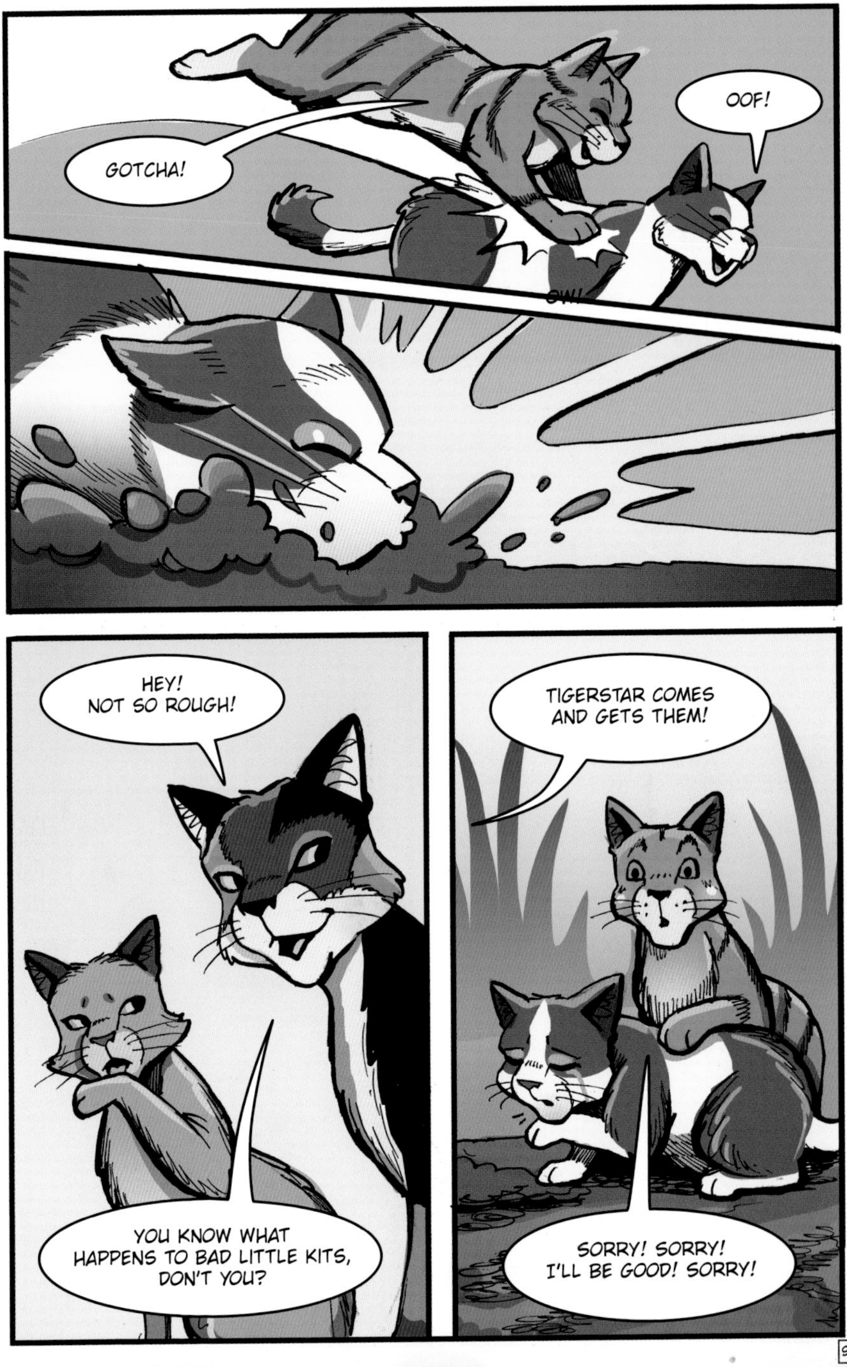
GOTCHA!
OOF!
OW!
HEY! NOT SO ROUGH!
YOU KNOW WHAT HAPPENS TO BAD LITTLE KITS, DON'T YOU?
TIGERSTAR COMES AND GETS THEM!
SORRY! SORRY! I'LL BE GOOD! SORRY!

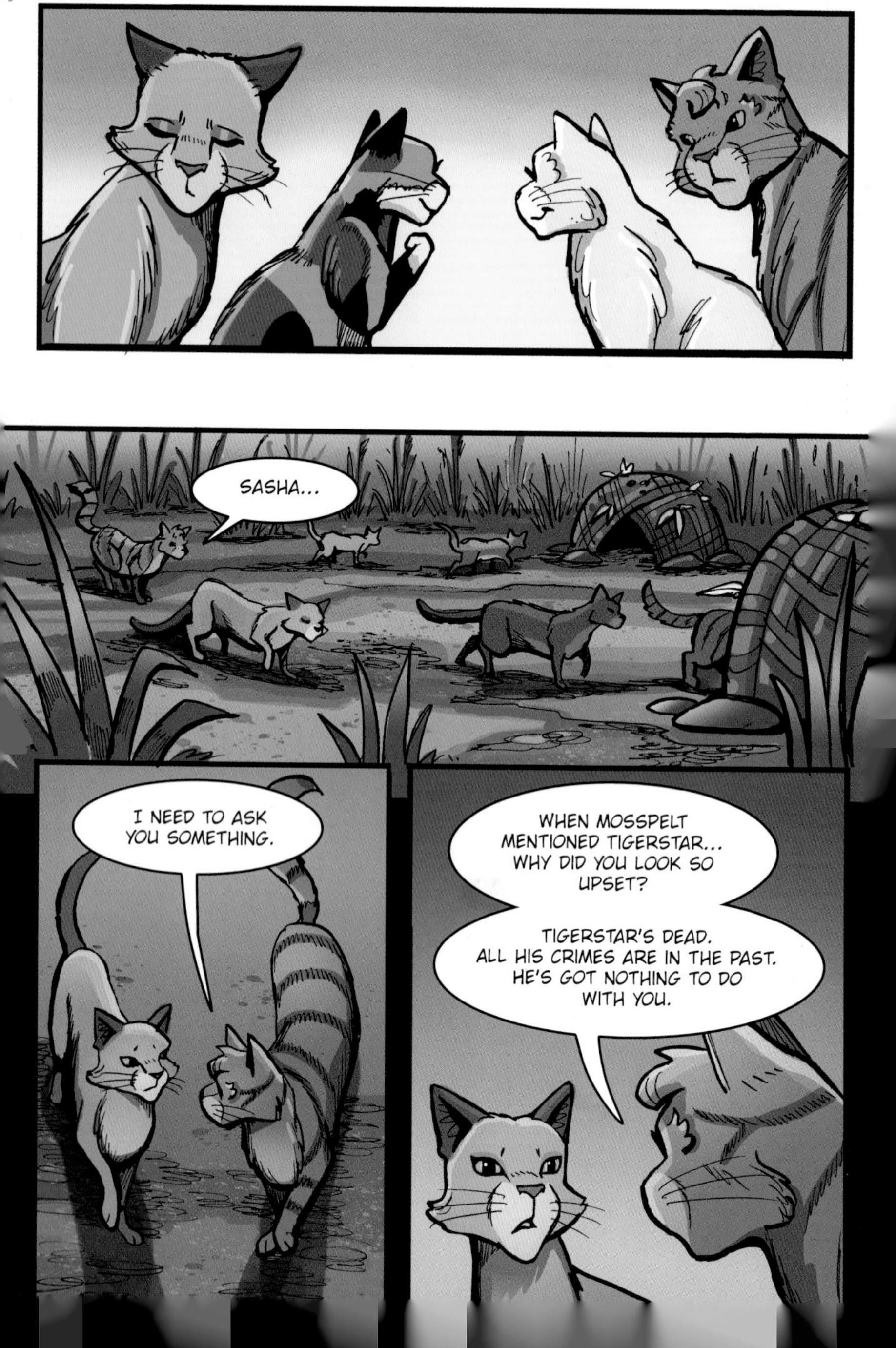
SASHA...
I NEED TO ASK YOU SOMETHING.
WHEN MOSSPELT MENTIONED TIGERSTAR... WHY DID YOU LOOK SO UPSET?
TIGERSTAR'S DEAD. ALL HIS CRIMES ARE IN THE PAST. HE'S GOT NOTHING TO DO WITH YOU.

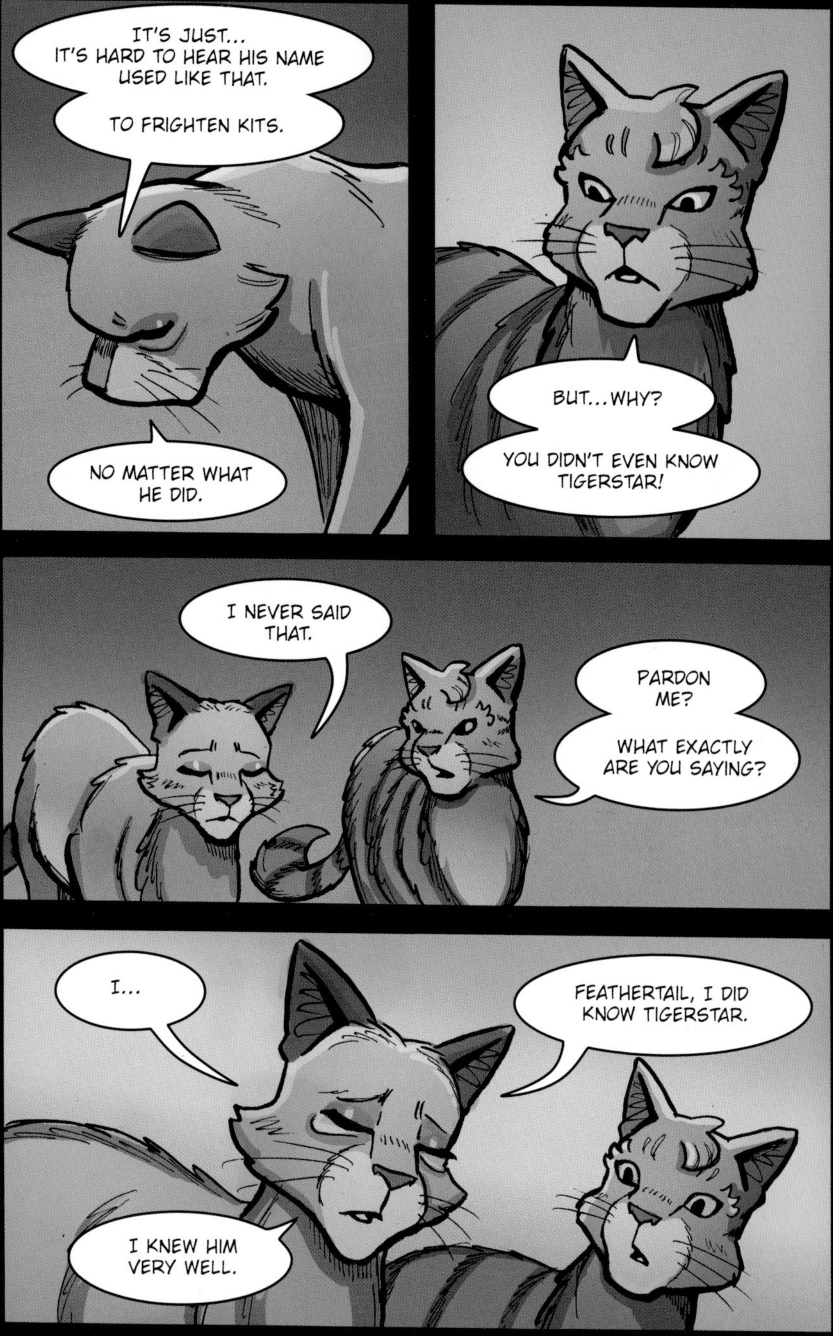
IT'S JUST...
IT'S HARD TO HEAR HIS NAME USED LIKE THAT.
TO FRIGHTEN KITS.
NO MATTER WHAT HE DID.
BUT...WHY?
YOU DIDN'T EVEN KNOW TIGERSTAR!
I NEVER SAID THAT.
PARDON ME?
WHAT EXACTLY ARE YOU SAYING?
I...
FEATHERTAIL, I DID KNOW TIGERSTAR.
I KNEW HIM VERY WELL.

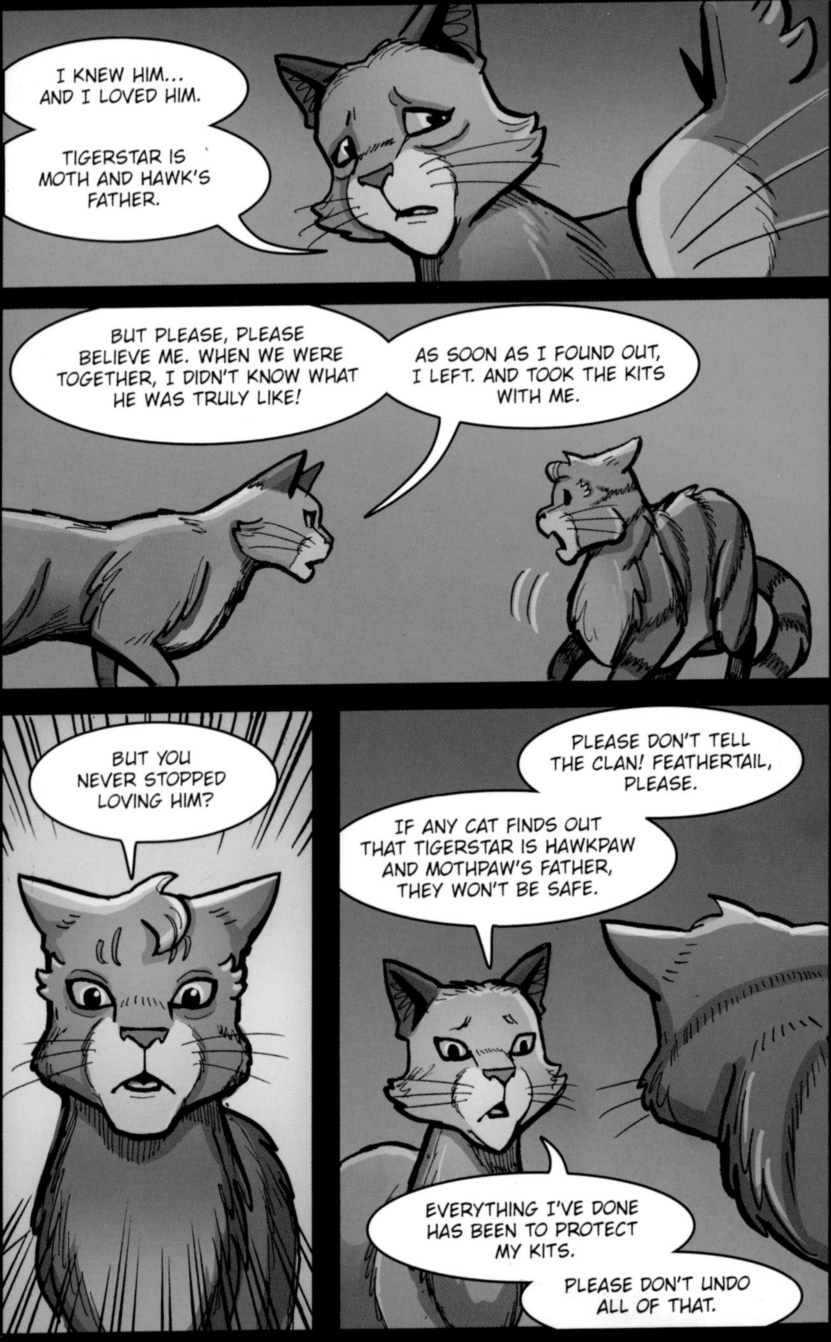
I KNEW HIM... AND I LOVED HIM.
TIGERSTAR IS MOTH AND HAWK'S FATHER.
BUT PLEASE, PLEASE BELIEVE ME. WHEN WE WERE TOGETHER, I DIDN'T KNOW WHAT HE WAS TRULY LIKE!
AS SOON AS I FOUND OUT, I LEFT. AND TOOK THE KITS WITH ME.
BUT YOU NEVER STOPPED LOVING HIM?
PLEASE DON'T TELL THE CLAN! FEATHERTAIL, PLEASE.
IF ANY CAT FINDS OUT THAT TIGERSTAR IS HAWKPAW AND MOTHPAW'S FATHER, THEY WON'T BE SAFE.
EVERYTHING I'VE DONE HAS BEEN TO PROTECT MY KITS.
PLEASE DON'T UNDO ALL OF THAT.

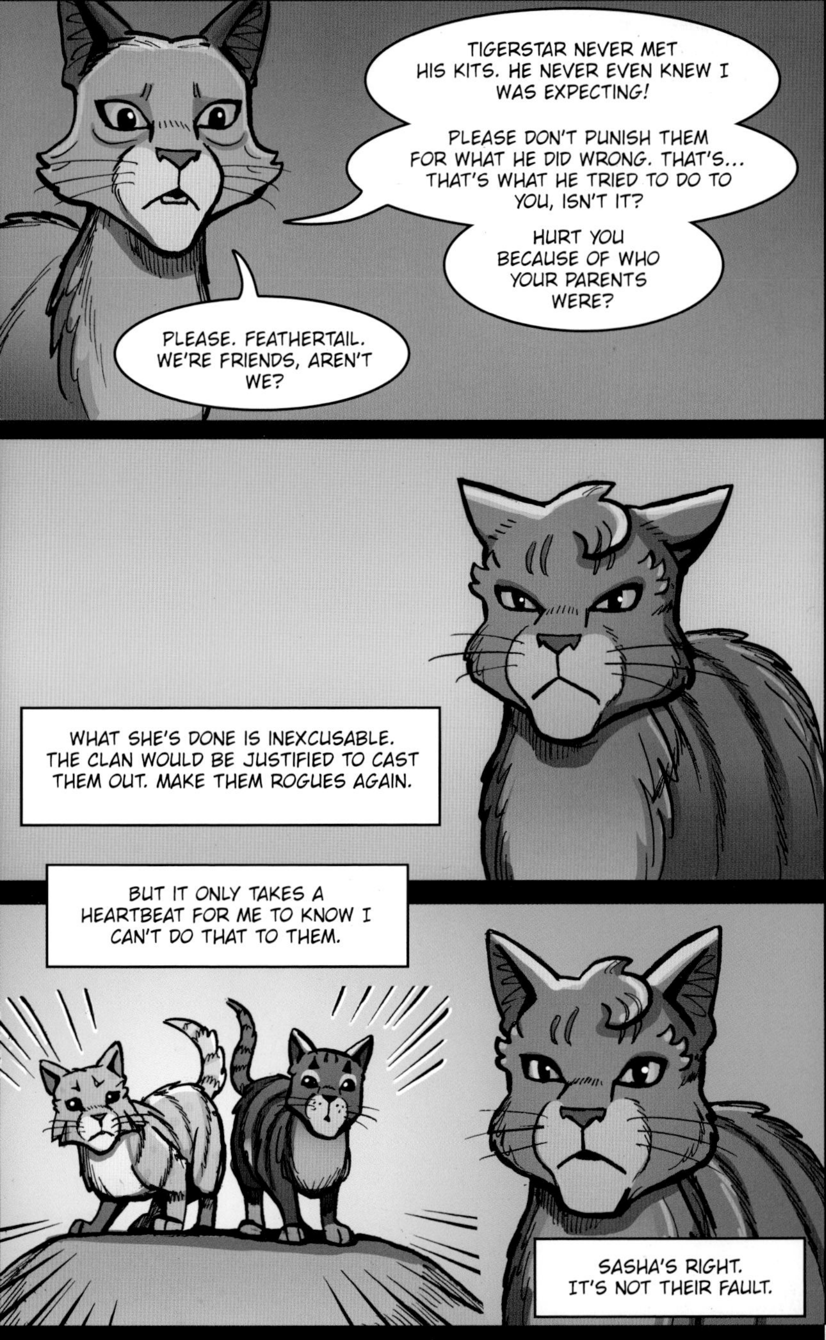
TIGERSTAR NEVER MET HIS KITS. HE NEVER EVEN KNEW I WAS EXPECTING!
PLEASE DON'T PUNISH THEM FOR WHAT HE DID WRONG. THAT'S... THAT'S WHAT HE TRIED TO DO TO YOU, ISN'T IT?
HURT YOU BECAUSE OF WHO YOUR PARENTS WERE?
PLEASE. FEATHERTAIL. WE'RE FRIENDS, AREN'T WE?
WHAT SHE'S DONE IS INEXCUSABLE. THE CLAN WOULD BE JUSTIFIED TO CAST THEM OUT. MAKE THEM ROGUES AGAIN.
BUT IT ONLY TAKES A HEARTBEAT FOR ME TO KNOW I CAN'T DO THAT TO THEM.
SASHA'S RIGHT. IT'S NOT THEIR FAULT.

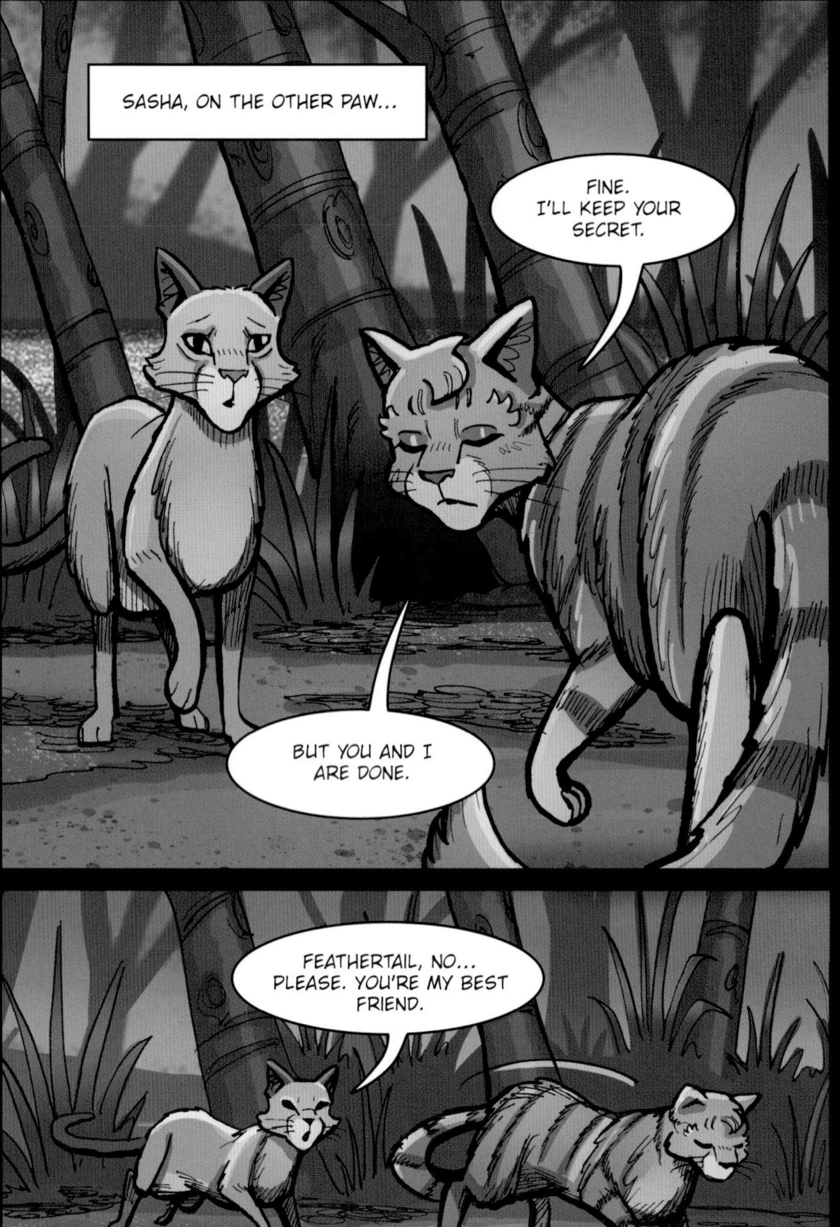
SASHA, ON THE OTHER PAW...
FINE. I'LL KEEP YOUR SECRET.
BUT YOU AND I ARE DONE.
FEATHERTAIL, NO... PLEASE. YOU'RE MY BEST FRIEND.

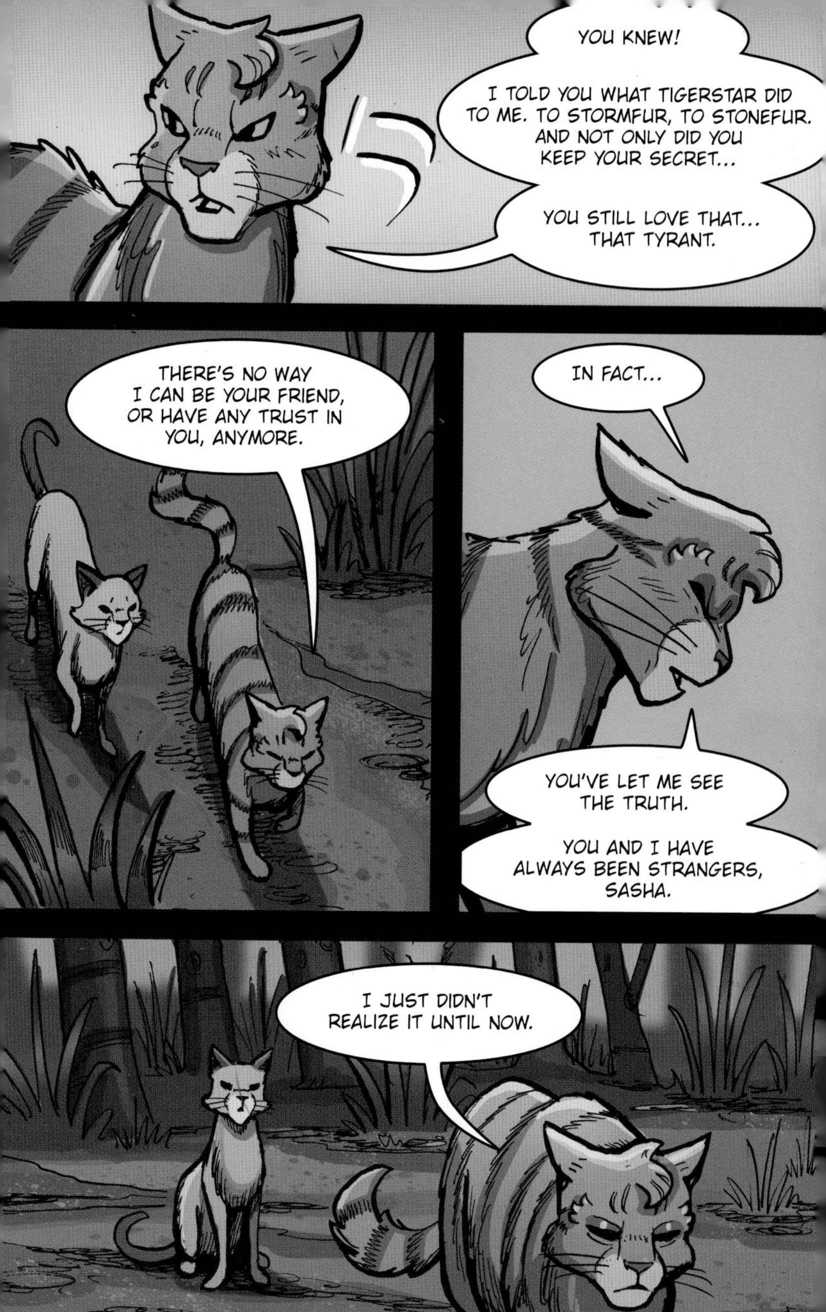
YOU KNEW!
I TOLD YOU WHAT TIGERSTAR DID TO ME. TO STORMFUR, TO STONEFUR. AND NOT ONLY DID YOU KEEP YOUR SECRET...
YOU STILL LOVE THAT... THAT TYRANT.
THERE'S NO WAY I CAN BE YOUR FRIEND, OR HAVE ANY TRUST IN YOU, ANYMORE.
IN FACT...
YOU'VE LET ME SEE THE TRUTH.
YOU AND I HAVE ALWAYS BEEN STRANGERS, SASHA.
I JUST DIDN'T REALIZE IT UNTIL NOW.

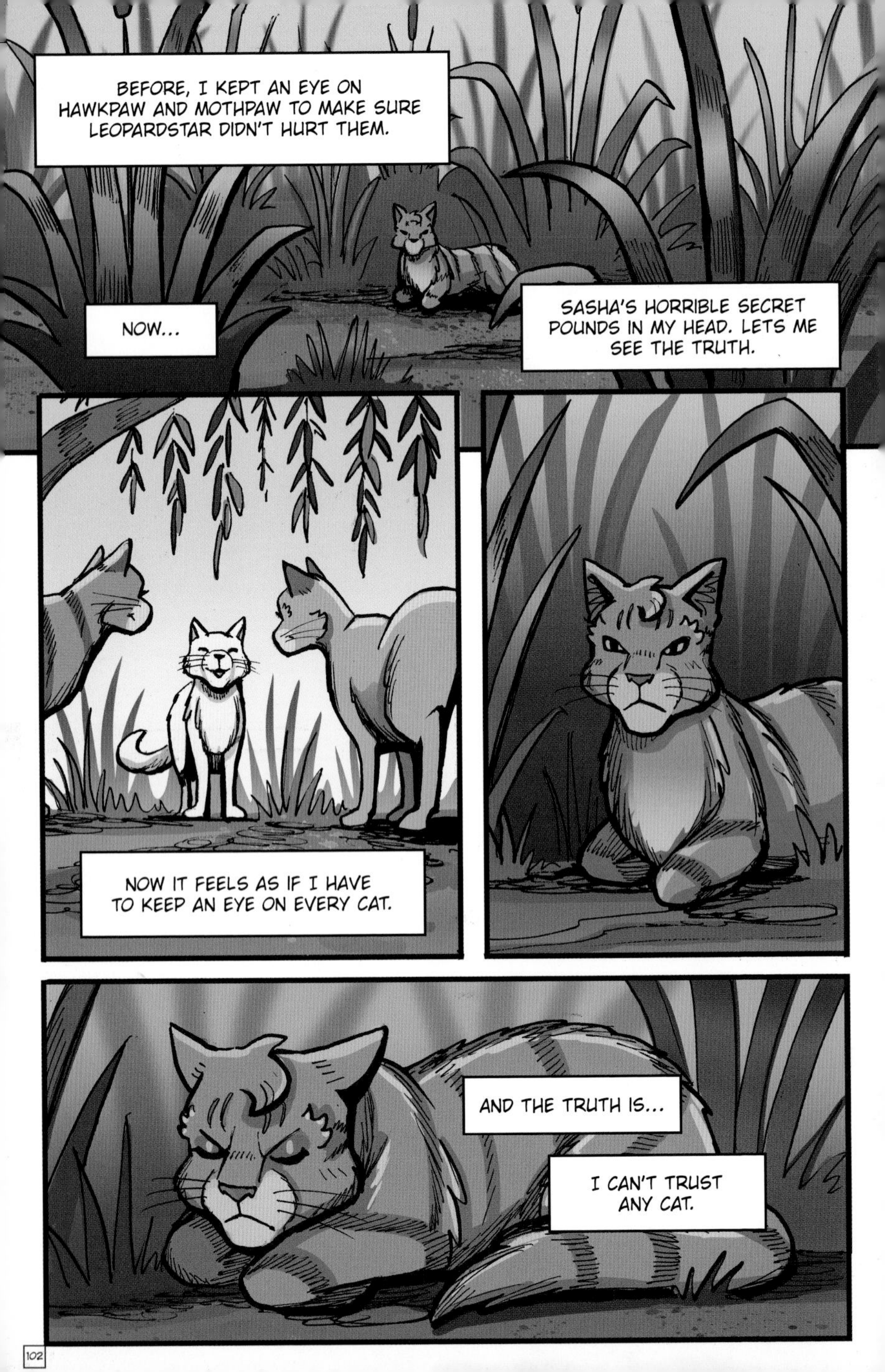
BEFORE, I KEPT AN EYE ON HAWKPAW AND MOTHPAW TO MAKE SURE LEOPARDSTAR DIDN'T HURT THEM.
NOW...
SASHA'S HORRIBLE SECRET POUNDS IN MY HEAD. LETS ME SEE THE TRUTH.
NOW IT FEELS AS IF I HAVE TO KEEP AN EYE ON EVERY CAT.
AND THE TRUTH IS...
I CAN'T TRUST ANY CAT.

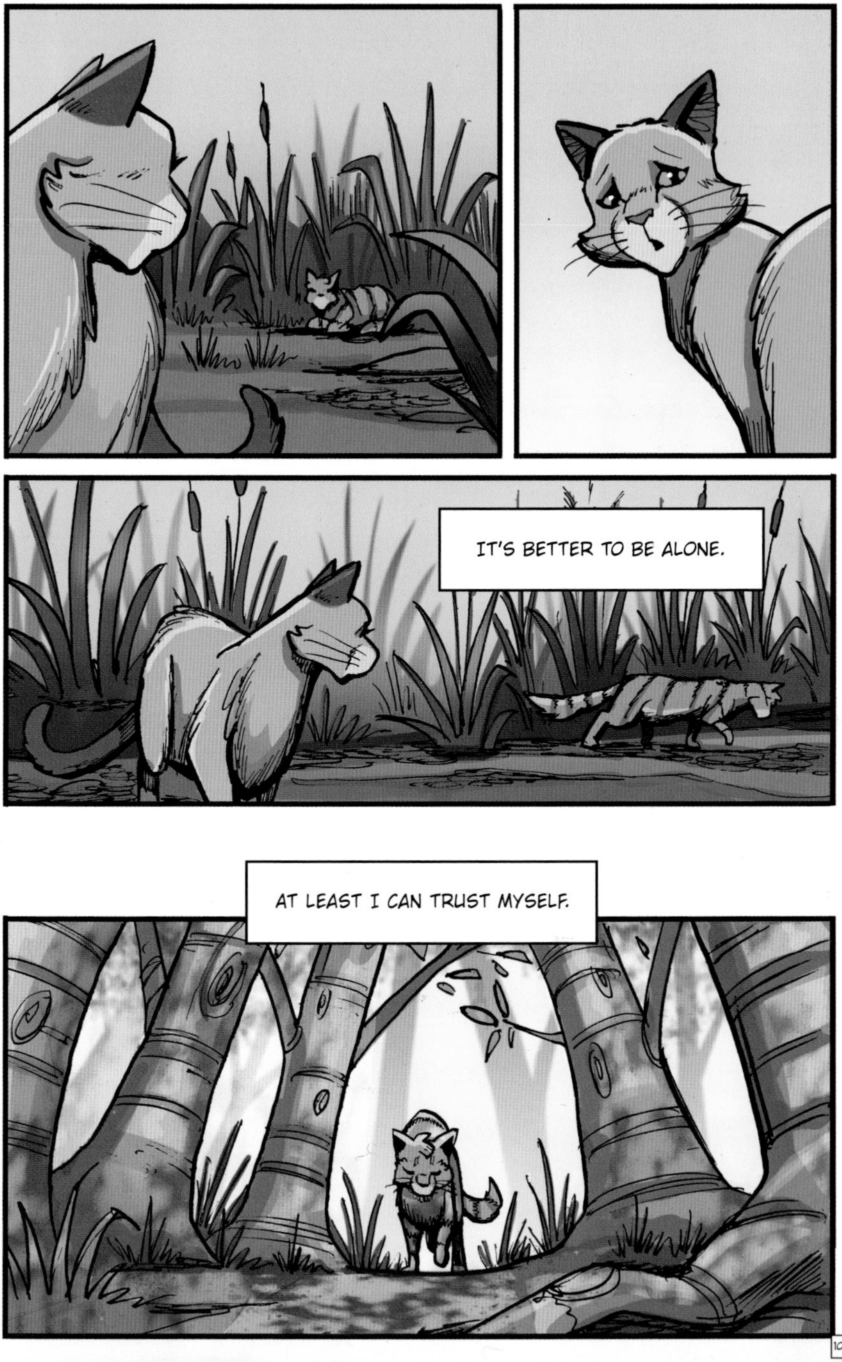
IT'S BETTER TO BE ALONE.
AT LEAST I CAN TRUST MYSELF.

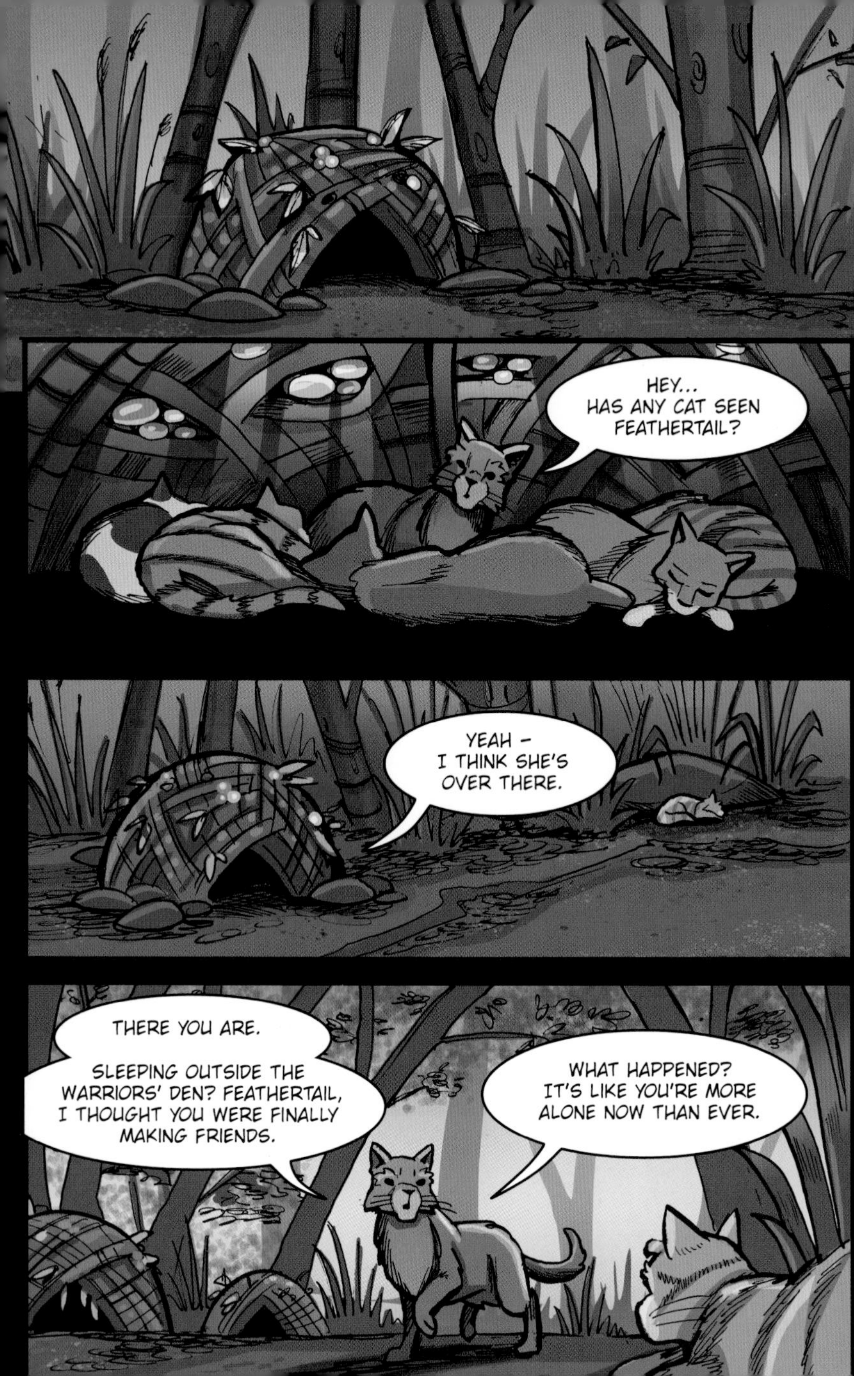
HEY... HAS ANY CAT SEEN FEATHERTAIL?
YEAH – I THINK SHE'S OVER THERE.
THERE YOU ARE.
SLEEPING OUTSIDE THE WARRIORS' DEN? FEATHERTAIL, I THOUGHT YOU WERE FINALLY MAKING FRIENDS.
WHAT HAPPENED? IT'S LIKE YOU'RE MORE ALONE NOW THAN EVER.

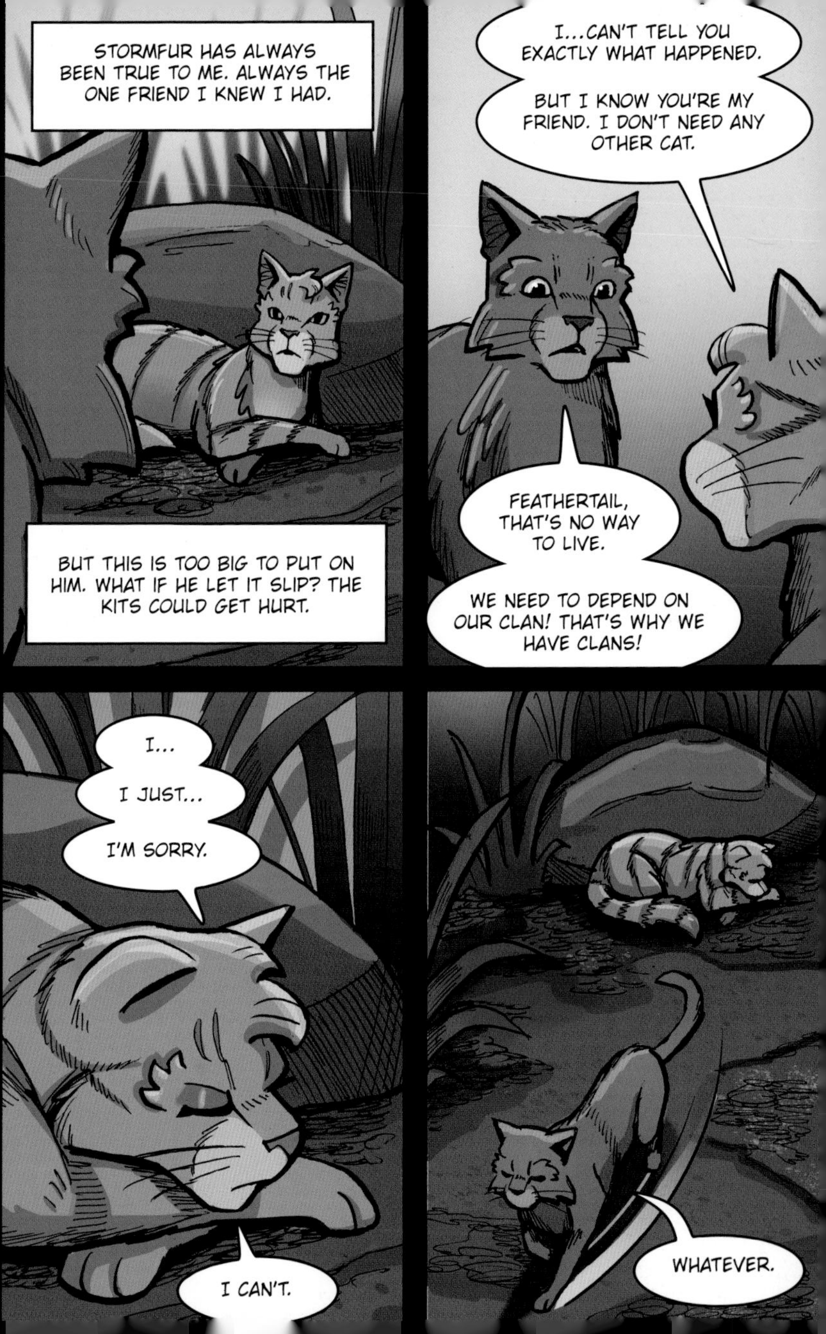
STORMFUR HAS ALWAYS BEEN TRUE TO ME. ALWAYS THE ONE FRIEND I KNEW I HAD.
BUT THIS IS TOO BIG TO PUT ON HIM. WHAT IF HE LET IT SLIP? THE KITS COULD GET HURT.
I...CAN'T TELL YOU EXACTLY WHAT HAPPENED.
BUT I KNOW YOU'RE MY FRIEND. I DON'T NEED ANY OTHER CAT.
FEATHERTAIL, THAT'S NO WAY TO LIVE.
WE NEED TO DEPEND ON OUR CLAN! THAT'S WHY WE HAVE CLANS!
I...
I JUST...
I'M SORRY.
I CAN'T.
WHATEVER.

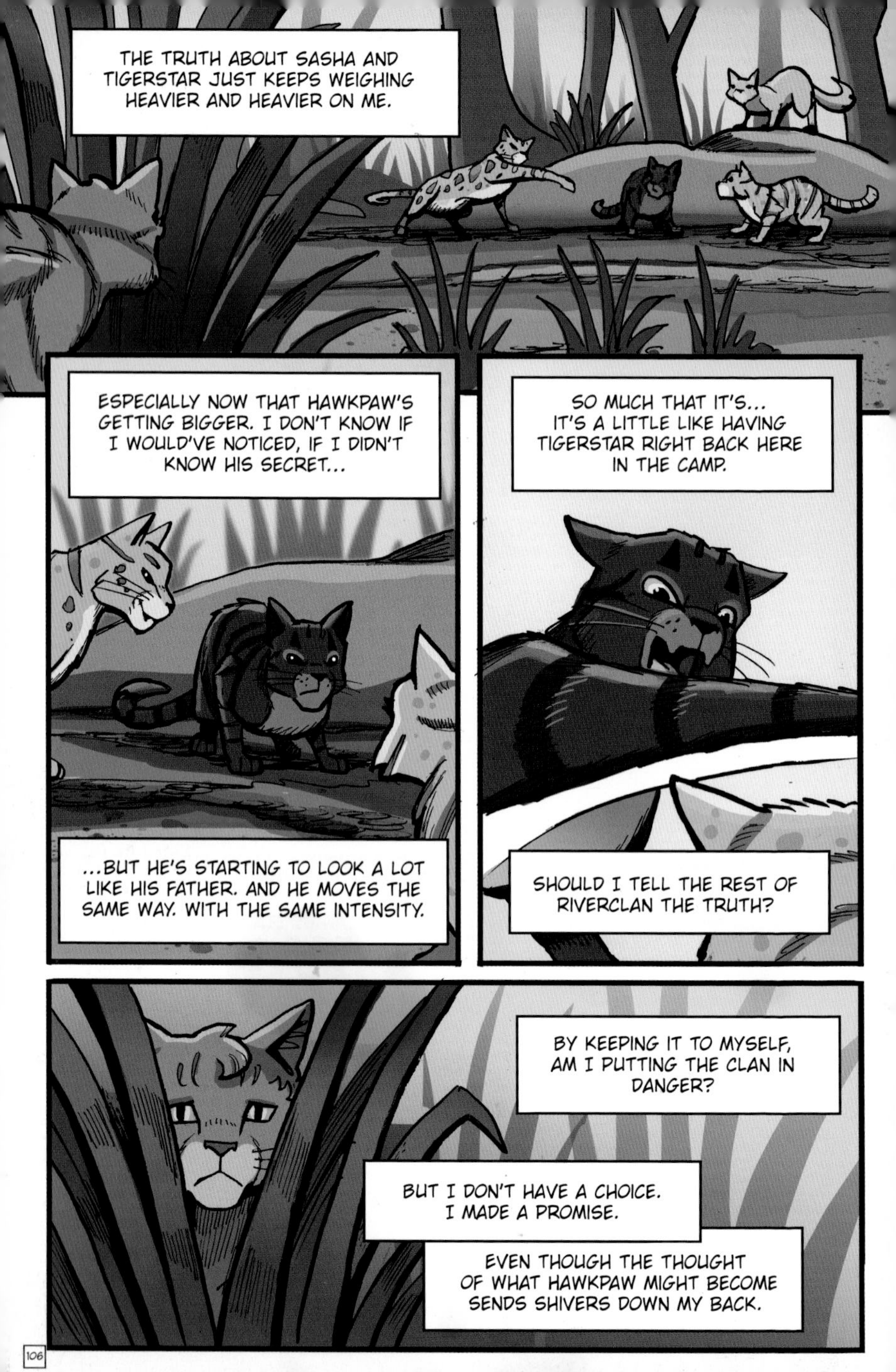
THE TRUTH ABOUT SASHA AND TIGERSTAR JUST KEEPS WEIGHING HEAVIER AND HEAVIER ON ME.
ESPECIALLY NOW THAT HAWKPAW'S GETTING BIGGER. I DON'T KNOW IF I WOULD'VE NOTICED, IF I DIDN'T KNOW HIS SECRET...
...BUT HE'S STARTING TO LOOK A LOT LIKE HIS FATHER. AND HE MOVES THE SAME WAY. WITH THE SAME INTENSITY.
SO MUCH THAT IT'S... IT'S A LITTLE LIKE HAVING TIGERSTAR RIGHT BACK HERE IN THE CAMP.
SHOULD I TELL THE REST OF RIVERCLAN THE TRUTH?
BY KEEPING IT TO MYSELF, AM I PUTTING THE CLAN IN DANGER?
BUT I DON'T HAVE A CHOICE. I MADE A PROMISE.
EVEN THOUGH THE THOUGHT OF WHAT HAWKPAW MIGHT BECOME SENDS SHIVERS DOWN MY BACK.

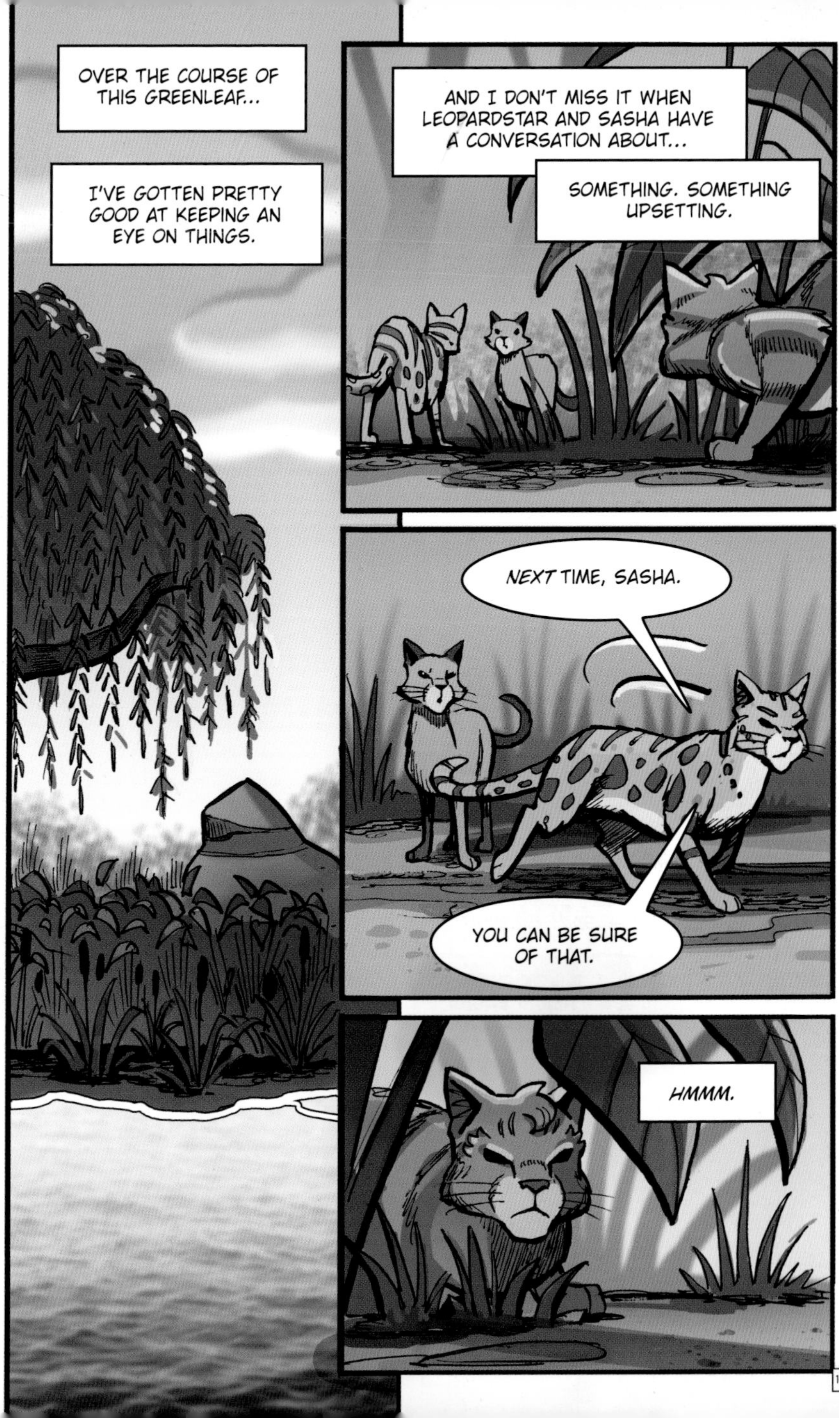
OVER THE COURSE OF THIS GREENLEAF...
I'VE GOTTEN PRETTY GOOD AT KEEPING AN EYE ON THINGS.
AND I DON'T MISS IT WHEN LEOPARDSTAR AND SASHA HAVE A CONVERSATION ABOUT...
SOMETHING. SOMETHING UPSETTING.
*NEXT* TIME, SASHA.
YOU CAN BE SURE OF THAT.
*HMMM.*

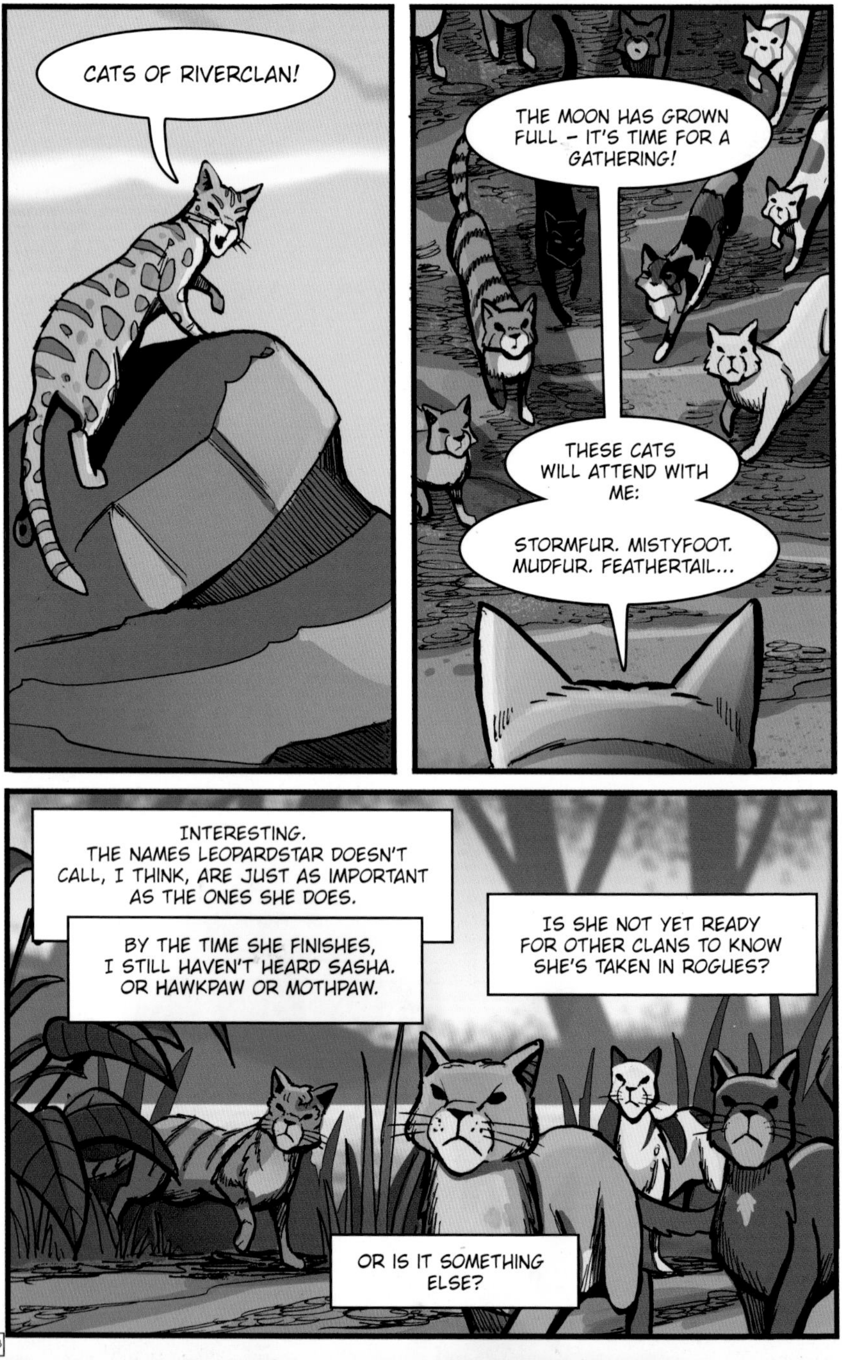
CATS OF RIVERCLAN!
THE MOON HAS GROWN FULL – IT'S TIME FOR A GATHERING!
THESE CATS WILL ATTEND WITH ME:
STORMFUR. MISTYFOOT. MUDFUR. FEATHERTAIL...
INTERESTING. THE NAMES LEOPARDSTAR DOESN'T CALL, I THINK, ARE JUST AS IMPORTANT AS THE ONES SHE DOES.
BY THE TIME SHE FINISHES, I STILL HAVEN'T HEARD SASHA. OR HAWKPAW OR MOTHPAW.
IS SHE NOT YET READY FOR OTHER CLANS TO KNOW SHE'S TAKEN IN ROGUES?
OR IS IT SOMETHING ELSE?

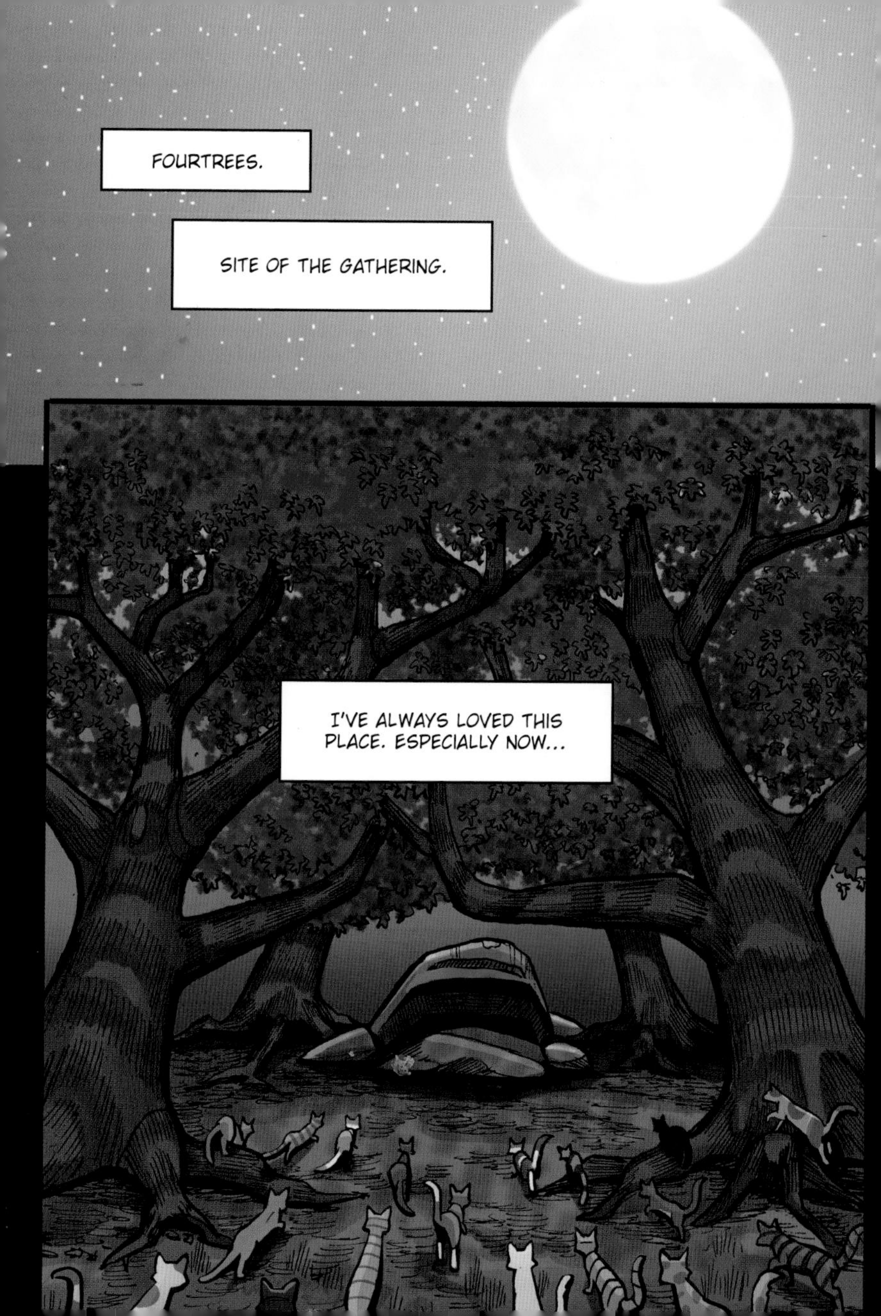
FOURTREES.
SITE OF THE GATHERING.
I'VE ALWAYS LOVED THIS PLACE. ESPECIALLY NOW...

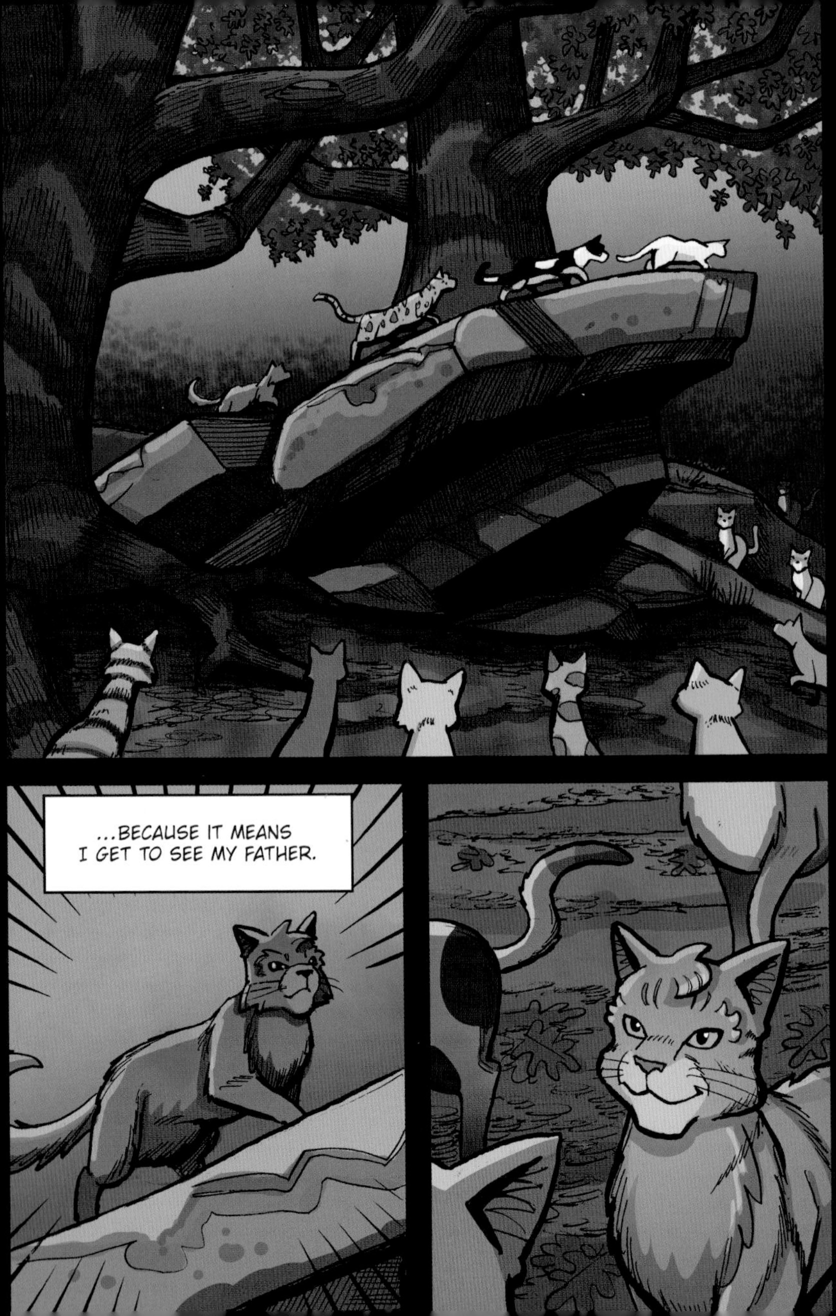
...BECAUSE IT MEANS
I GET TO SEE MY FATHER.

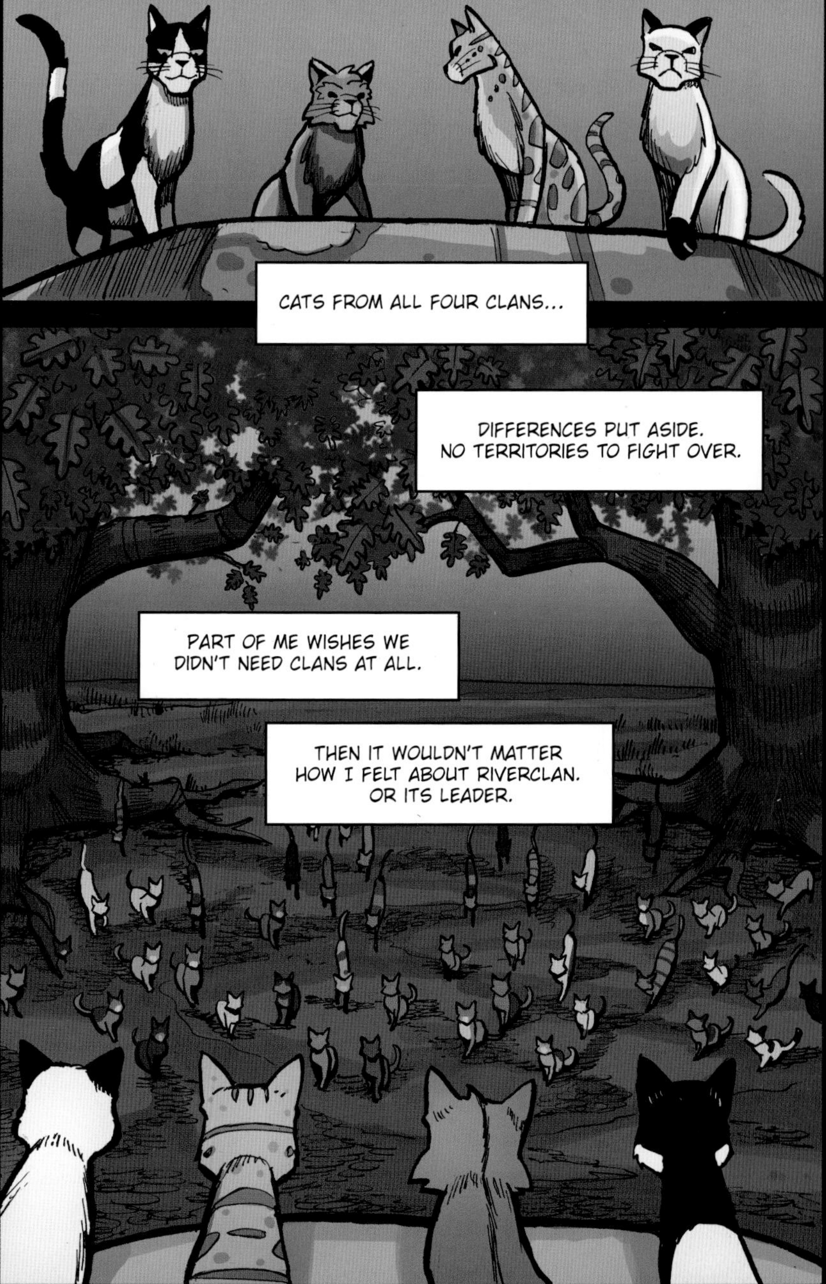
CATS FROM ALL FOUR CLANS...
DIFFERENCES PUT ASIDE. NO TERRITORIES TO FIGHT OVER.
PART OF ME WISHES WE DIDN'T NEED CLANS AT ALL.
THEN IT WOULDN'T MATTER HOW I FELT ABOUT RIVERCLAN. OR ITS LEADER.

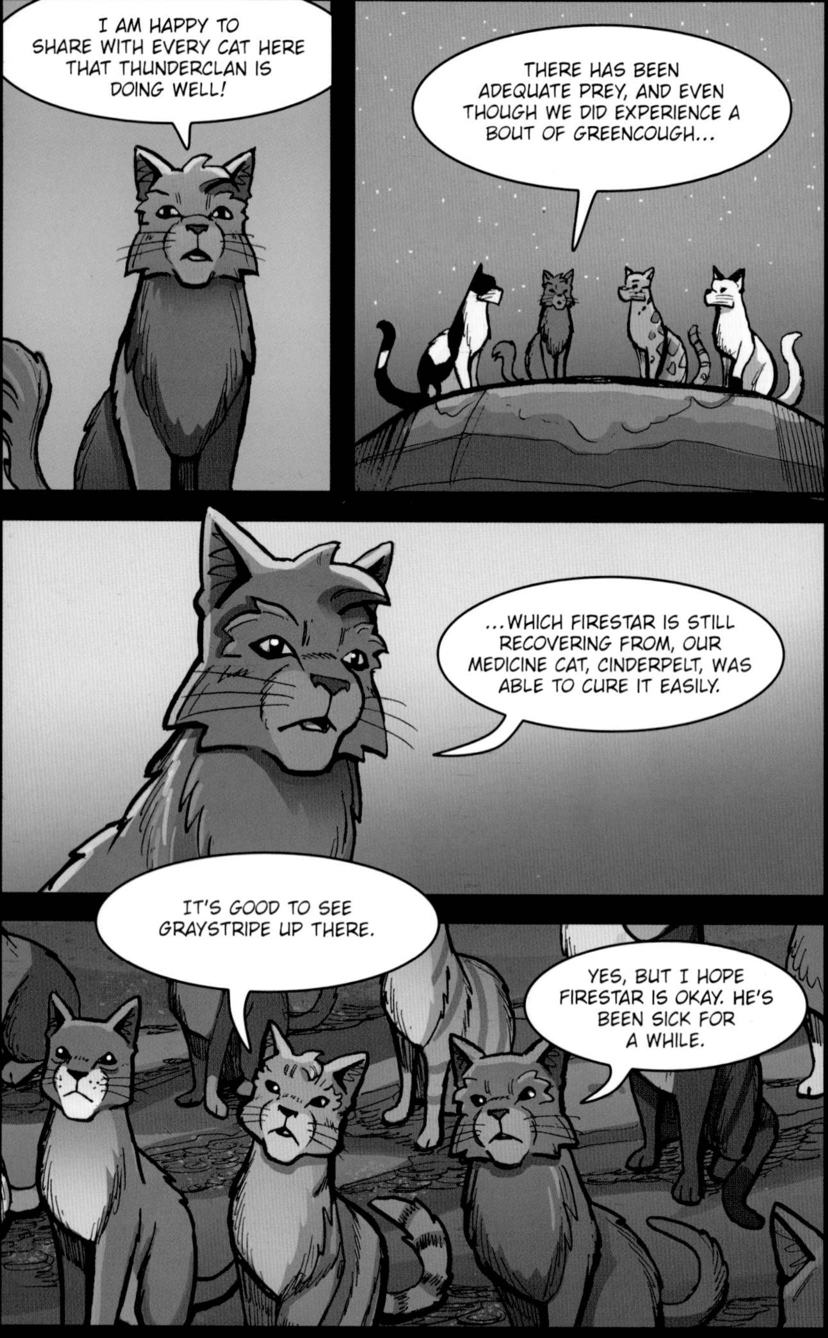
I AM HAPPY TO SHARE WITH EVERY CAT HERE THAT THUNDERCLAN IS DOING WELL!
THERE HAS BEEN ADEQUATE PREY, AND EVEN THOUGH WE DID EXPERIENCE A BOUT OF GREENCOUGH...
...WHICH FIRESTAR IS STILL RECOVERING FROM, OUR MEDICINE CAT, CINDERPELT, WAS ABLE TO CURE IT EASILY.
IT'S GOOD TO SEE GRAYSTRIPE UP THERE.
YES, BUT I HOPE FIRESTAR IS OKAY. HE'S BEEN SICK FOR A WHILE.

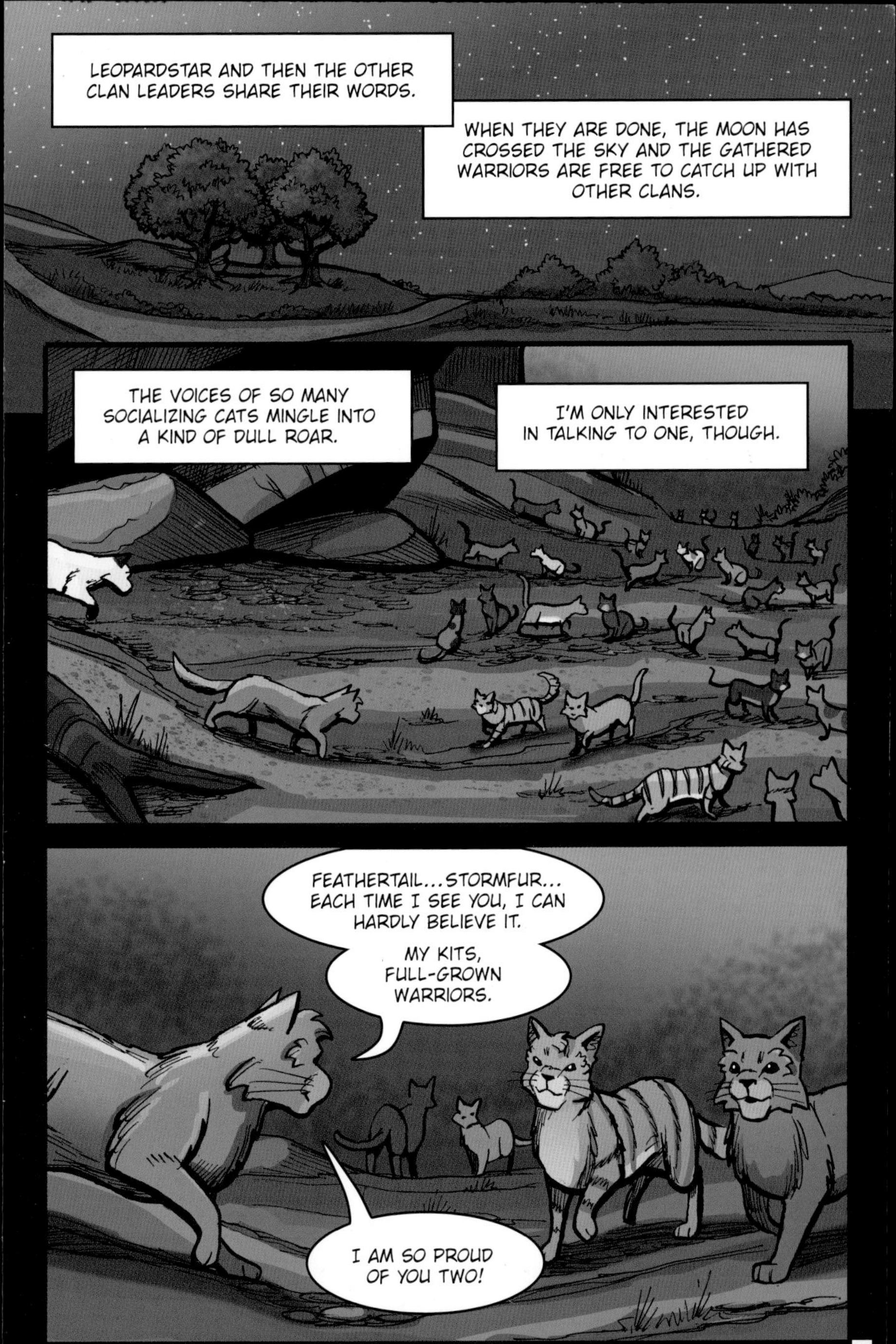
LEOPARDSTAR AND THEN THE OTHER CLAN LEADERS SHARE THEIR WORDS.
WHEN THEY ARE DONE, THE MOON HAS CROSSED THE SKY AND THE GATHERED WARRIORS ARE FREE TO CATCH UP WITH OTHER CLANS.
THE VOICES OF SO MANY SOCIALIZING CATS MINGLE INTO A KIND OF DULL ROAR.
I'M ONLY INTERESTED IN TALKING TO ONE, THOUGH.
FEATHERTAIL...STORMFUR... EACH TIME I SEE YOU, I CAN HARDLY BELIEVE IT.
MY KITS, FULL-GROWN WARRIORS.
I AM SO PROUD OF YOU TWO!

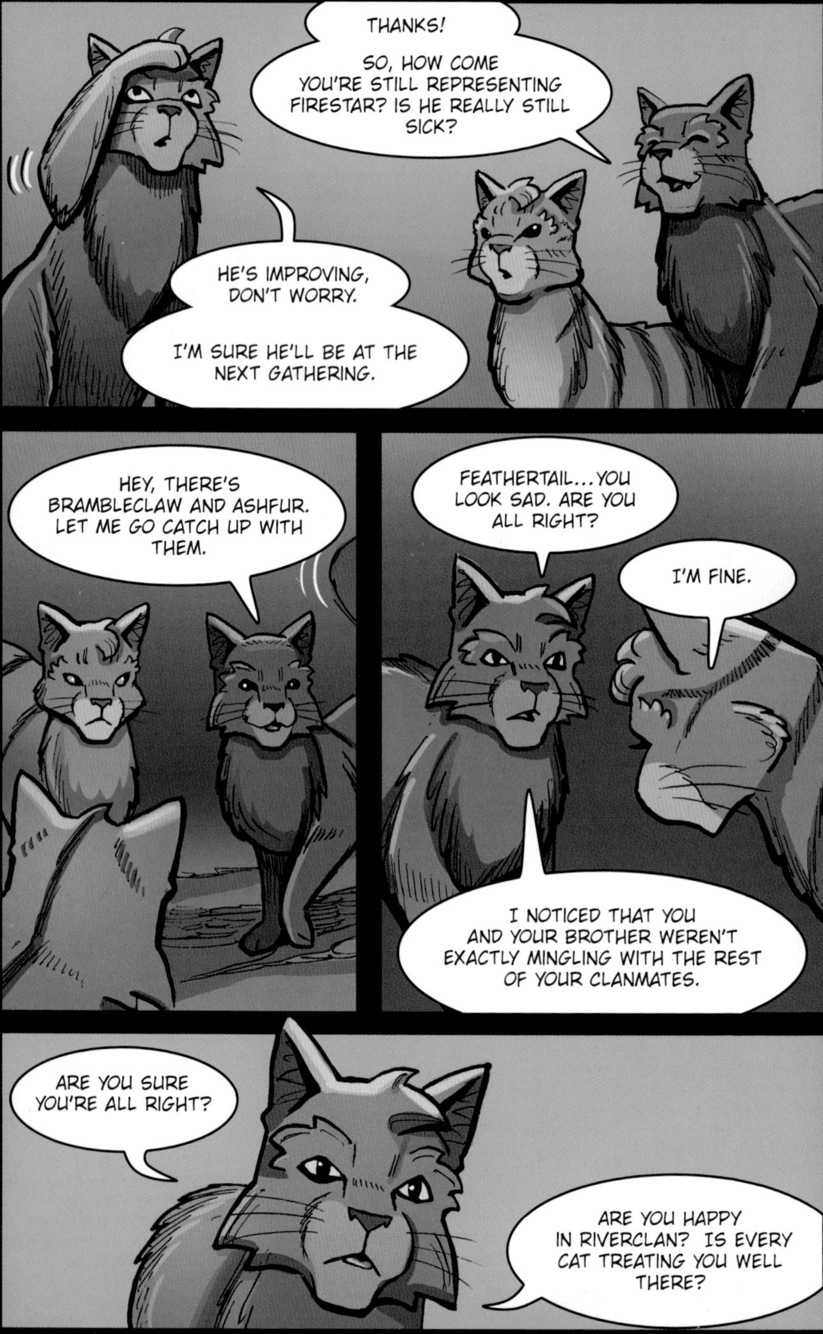
THANKS!
SO, HOW COME YOU'RE STILL REPRESENTING FIRESTAR? IS HE REALLY STILL SICK?
HE'S IMPROVING, DON'T WORRY.
I'M SURE HE'LL BE AT THE NEXT GATHERING.
HEY, THERE'S BRAMBLECLAW AND ASHFUR. LET ME GO CATCH UP WITH THEM.
FEATHERTAIL...YOU LOOK SAD. ARE YOU ALL RIGHT?
I'M FINE.
I NOTICED THAT YOU AND YOUR BROTHER WEREN'T EXACTLY MINGLING WITH THE REST OF YOUR CLANMATES.
ARE YOU SURE YOU'RE ALL RIGHT?
ARE YOU HAPPY IN RIVERCLAN? IS EVERY CAT TREATING YOU WELL THERE?

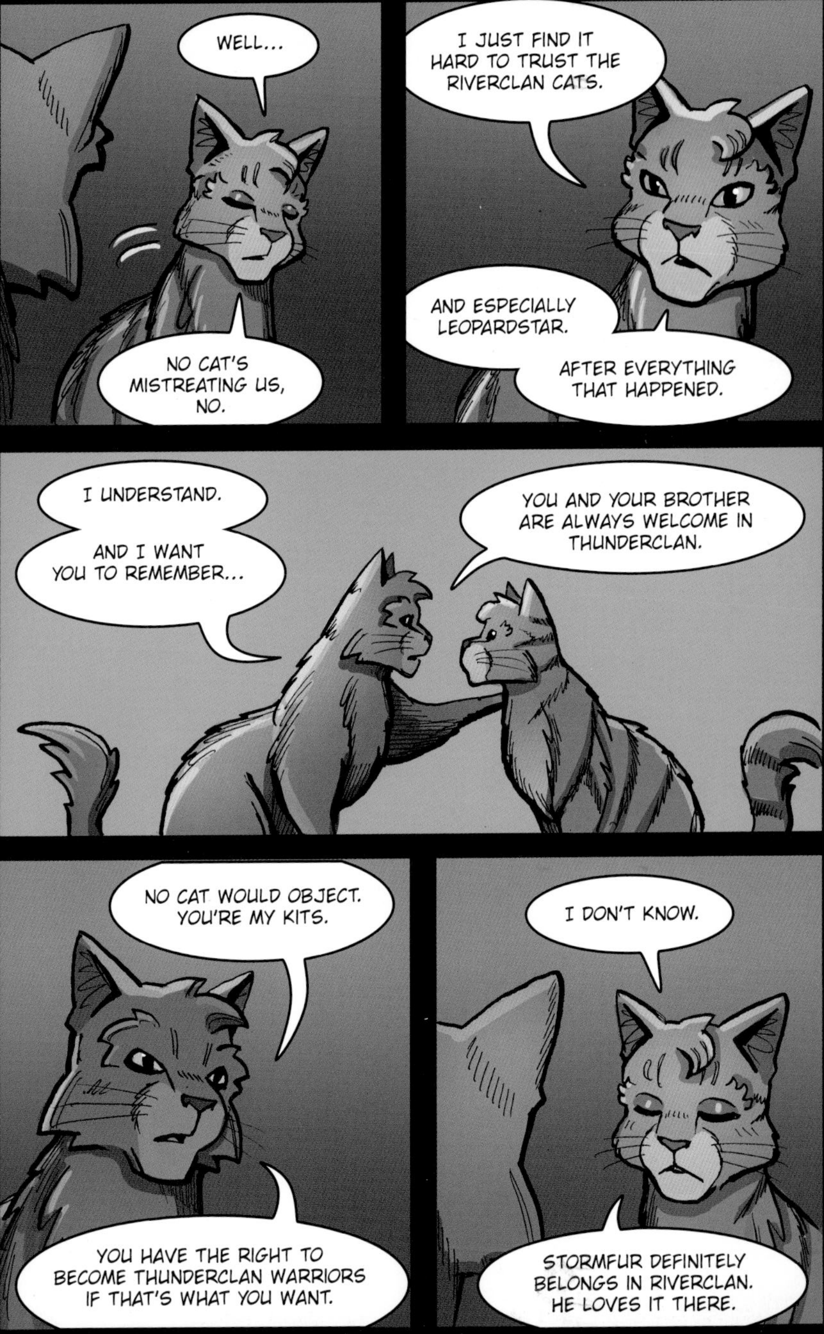
WELL...
NO CAT'S MISTREATING US, NO.
I JUST FIND IT HARD TO TRUST THE RIVERCLAN CATS.
AND ESPECIALLY LEOPARDSTAR.
AFTER EVERYTHING THAT HAPPENED.
I UNDERSTAND.
AND I WANT YOU TO REMEMBER...
YOU AND YOUR BROTHER ARE ALWAYS WELCOME IN THUNDERCLAN.
NO CAT WOULD OBJECT. YOU'RE MY KITS.
YOU HAVE THE RIGHT TO BECOME THUNDERCLAN WARRIORS IF THAT'S WHAT YOU WANT.
I DON'T KNOW.
STORMFUR DEFINITELY BELONGS IN RIVERCLAN. HE LOVES IT THERE.

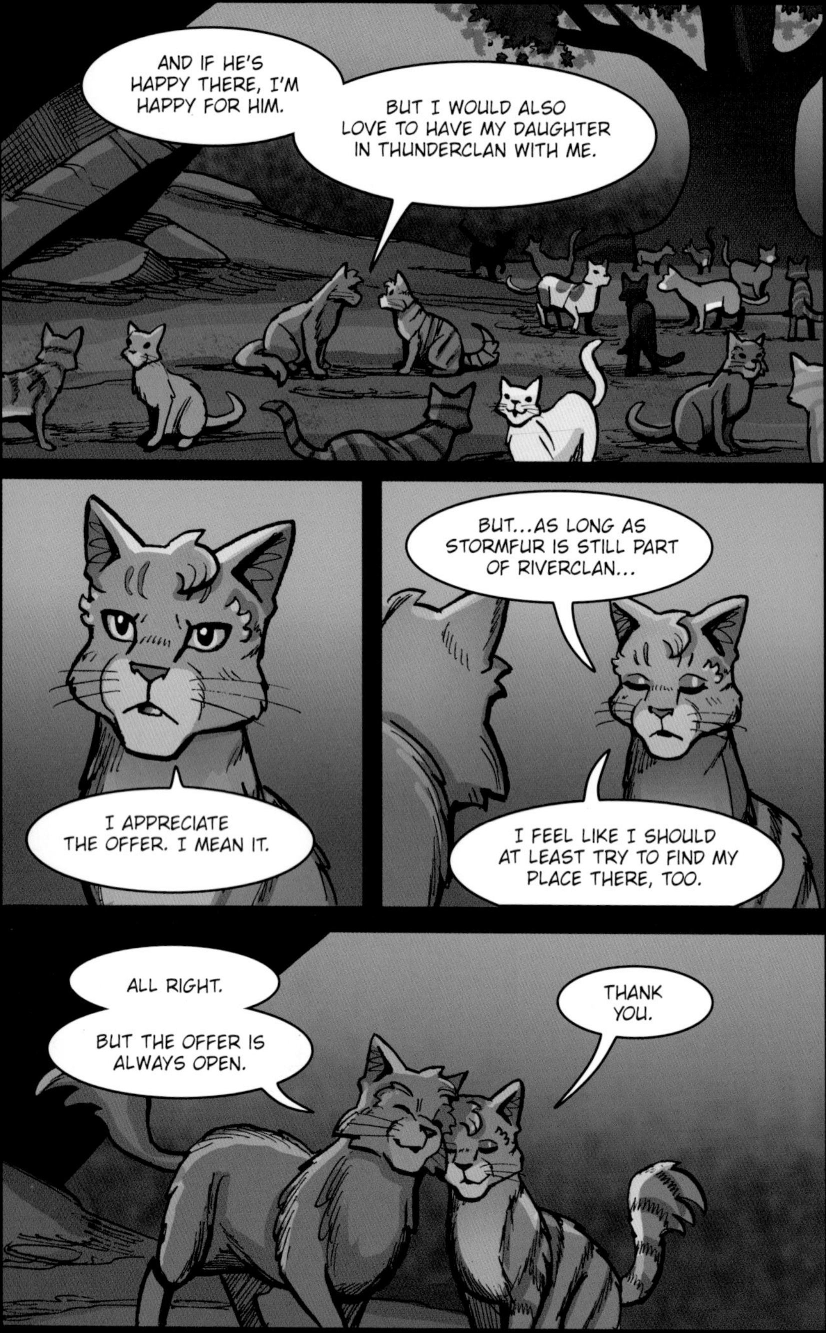
AND IF HE'S HAPPY THERE, I'M HAPPY FOR HIM.
BUT I WOULD ALSO LOVE TO HAVE MY DAUGHTER IN THUNDERCLAN WITH ME.
I APPRECIATE THE OFFER. I MEAN IT.
BUT...AS LONG AS STORMFUR IS STILL PART OF RIVERCLAN...
I FEEL LIKE I SHOULD AT LEAST TRY TO FIND MY PLACE THERE, TOO.
ALL RIGHT.
BUT THE OFFER IS ALWAYS OPEN.
THANK YOU.

I SPEND THE NIGHT WITH MY FATHER'S WORDS ECHOING IN MY HEAD.

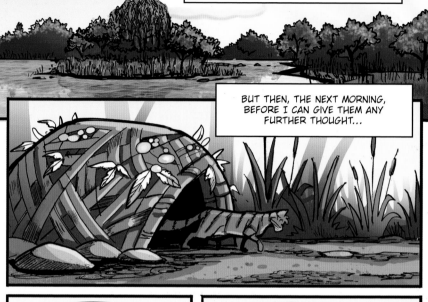

BUT THEN, THE NEXT MORNING, BEFORE I CAN GIVE THEM ANY FURTHER THOUGHT...

FEATHERTAIL. I NEED TO TALK TO YOU.

IN PRIVATE.

PLEASE.

WHAT DO YOU WANT, SASHA? I HAVE NOTHING TO SAY TO YOU.

MAYBE NOT, BUT I THINK YOU'LL WANT TO HEAR THIS.

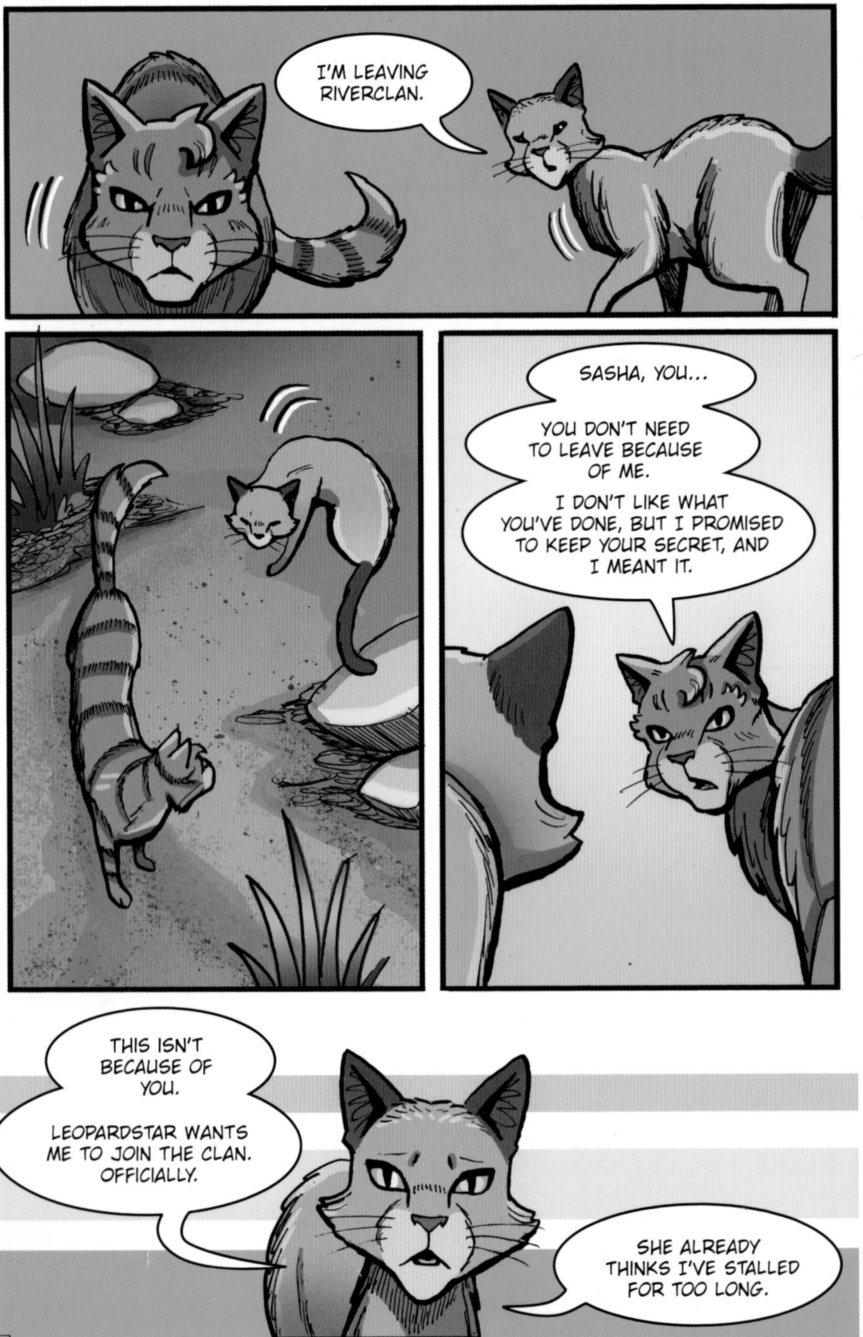
I'M LEAVING RIVERCLAN.
SASHA, YOU...
YOU DON'T NEED TO LEAVE BECAUSE OF ME.
I DON'T LIKE WHAT YOU'VE DONE, BUT I PROMISED TO KEEP YOUR SECRET, AND I MEANT IT.
THIS ISN'T BECAUSE OF YOU.
LEOPARDSTAR WANTS ME TO JOIN THE CLAN. OFFICIALLY.
SHE ALREADY THINKS I'VE STALLED FOR TOO LONG.

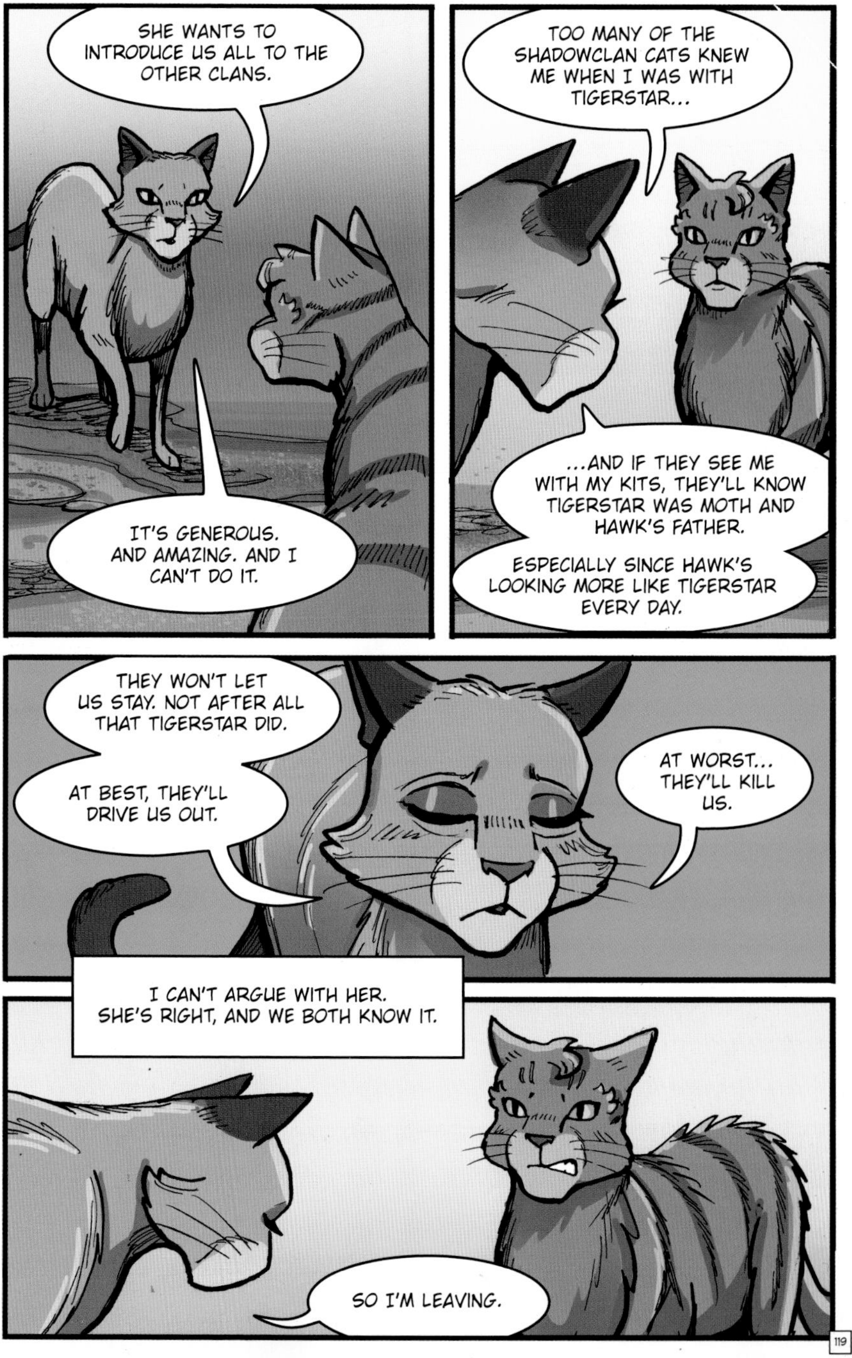
SHE WANTS TO INTRODUCE US ALL TO THE OTHER CLANS.
IT'S GENEROUS. AND AMAZING. AND I CAN'T DO IT.
TOO MANY OF THE SHADOWCLAN CATS KNEW ME WHEN I WAS WITH TIGERSTAR...
...AND IF THEY SEE ME WITH MY KITS, THEY'LL KNOW TIGERSTAR WAS MOTH AND HAWK'S FATHER.
ESPECIALLY SINCE HAWK'S LOOKING MORE LIKE TIGERSTAR EVERY DAY.
THEY WON'T LET US STAY. NOT AFTER ALL THAT TIGERSTAR DID.
AT BEST, THEY'LL DRIVE US OUT.
AT WORST... THEY'LL KILL US.
I CAN'T ARGUE WITH HER. SHE'S RIGHT, AND WE BOTH KNOW IT.
SO I'M LEAVING.

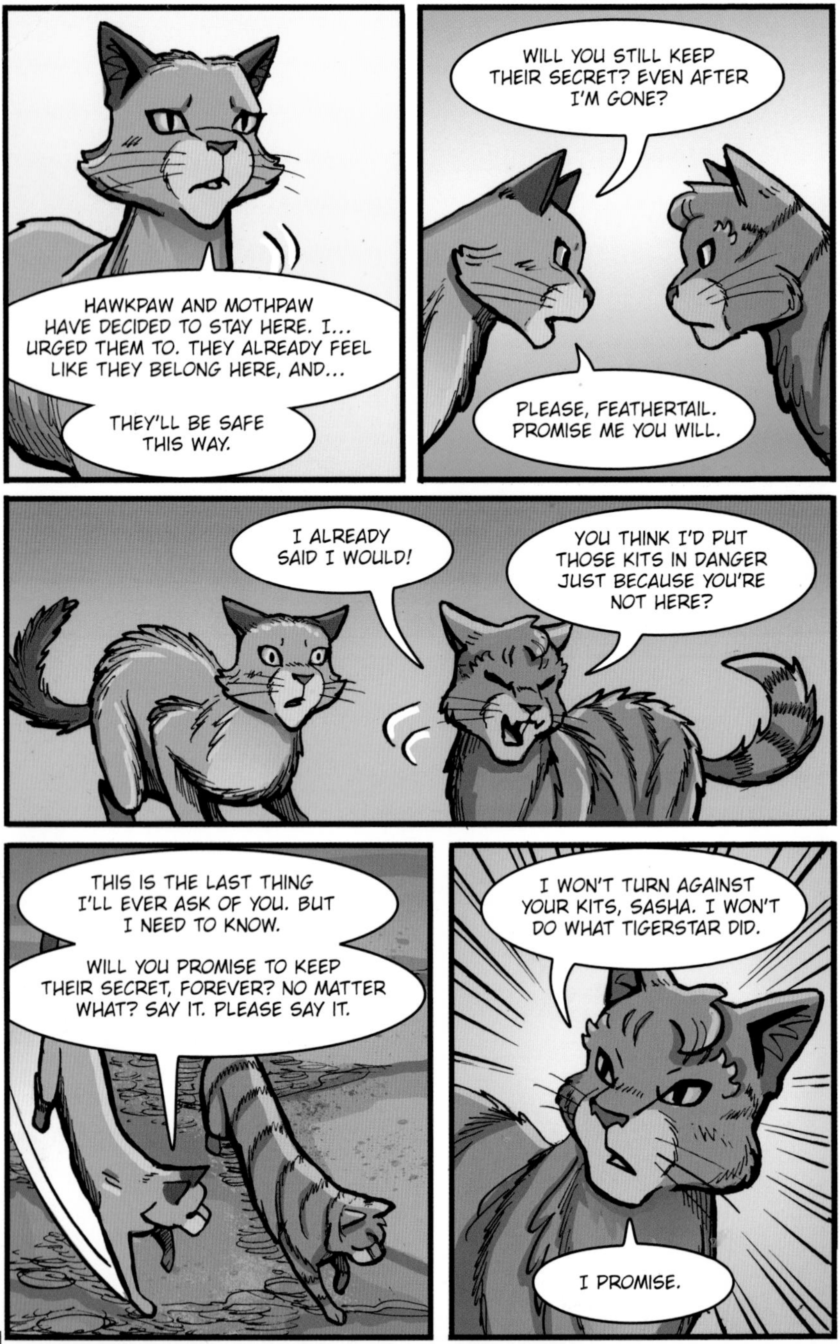
HAWKPAW AND MOTHPAW HAVE DECIDED TO STAY HERE. I... URGED THEM TO. THEY ALREADY FEEL LIKE THEY BELONG HERE, AND...
THEY'LL BE SAFE THIS WAY.
WILL YOU STILL KEEP THEIR SECRET? EVEN AFTER I'M GONE?
PLEASE, FEATHERTAIL. PROMISE ME YOU WILL.
I ALREADY SAID I WOULD!
YOU THINK I'D PUT THOSE KITS IN DANGER JUST BECAUSE YOU'RE NOT HERE?
THIS IS THE LAST THING I'LL EVER ASK OF YOU. BUT I NEED TO KNOW.
WILL YOU PROMISE TO KEEP THEIR SECRET, FOREVER? NO MATTER WHAT? SAY IT. PLEASE SAY IT.
I WON'T TURN AGAINST YOUR KITS, SASHA. I WON'T DO WHAT TIGERSTAR DID.
I PROMISE.

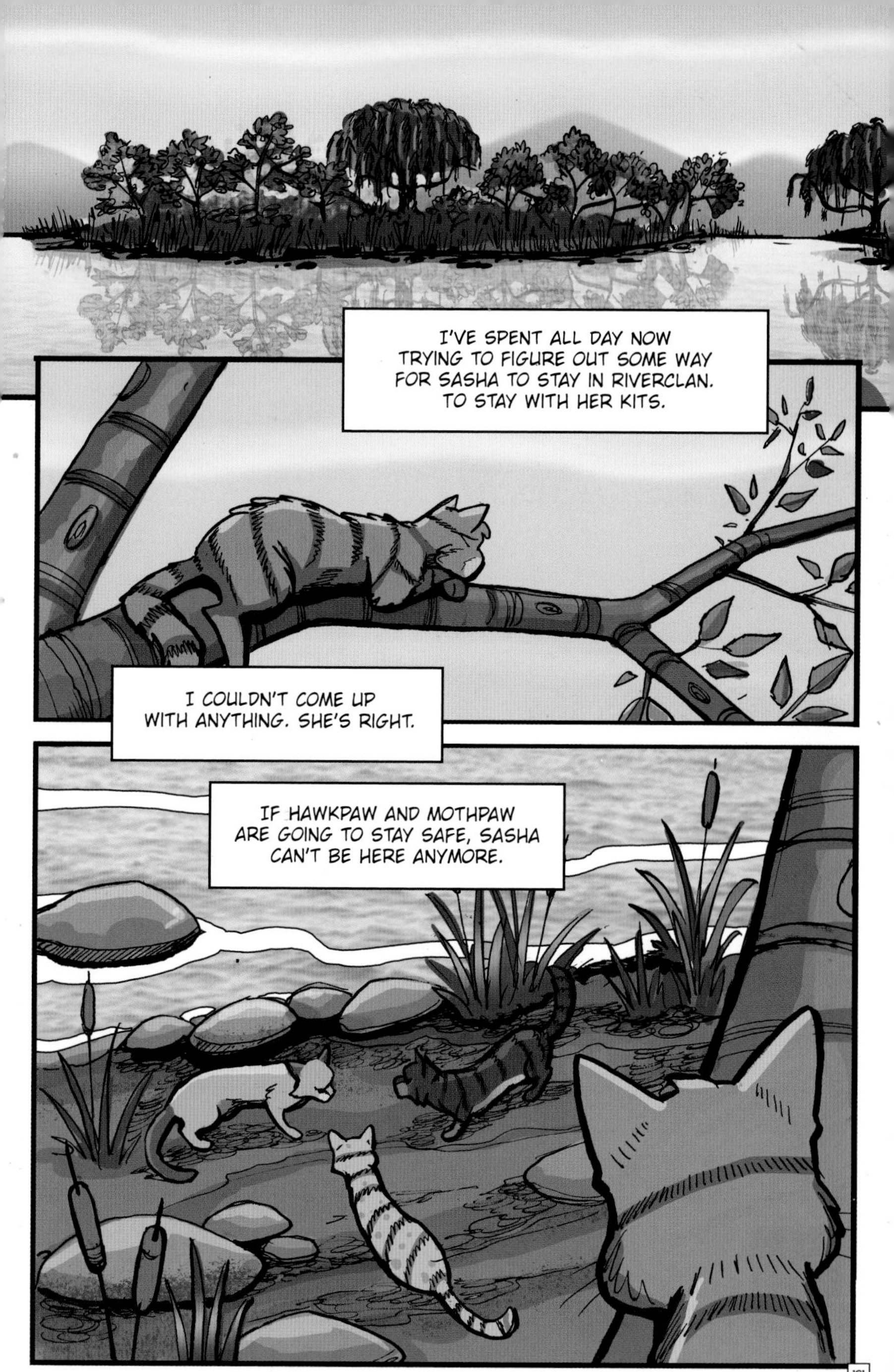
I'VE SPENT ALL DAY NOW TRYING TO FIGURE OUT SOME WAY FOR SASHA TO STAY IN RIVERCLAN. TO STAY WITH HER KITS.
I COULDN'T COME UP WITH ANYTHING. SHE'S RIGHT.
IF HAWKPAW AND MOTHPAW ARE GOING TO STAY SAFE, SASHA CAN'T BE HERE ANYMORE.

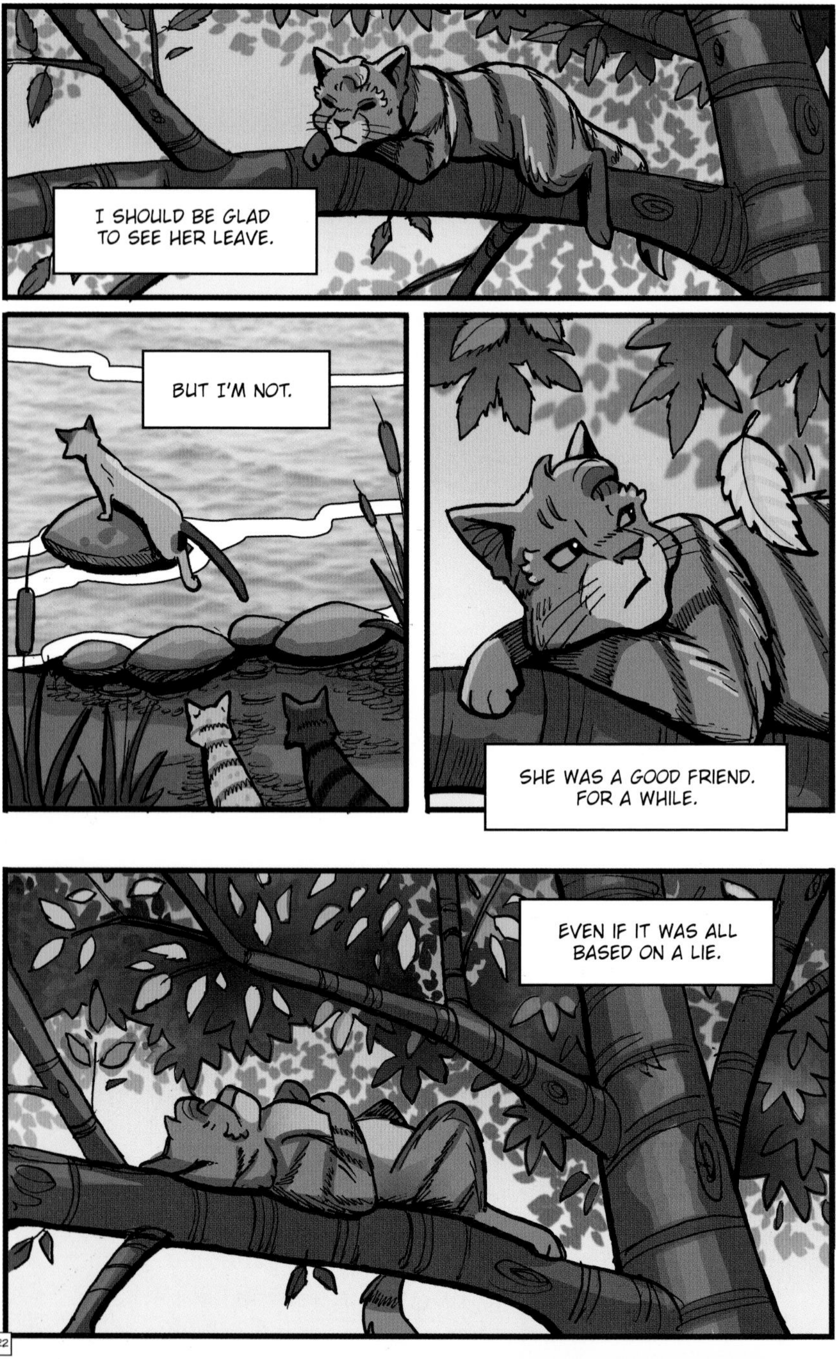
I SHOULD BE GLAD TO SEE HER LEAVE.
BUT I'M NOT.
SHE WAS A GOOD FRIEND. FOR A WHILE.
EVEN IF IT WAS ALL BASED ON A LIE.

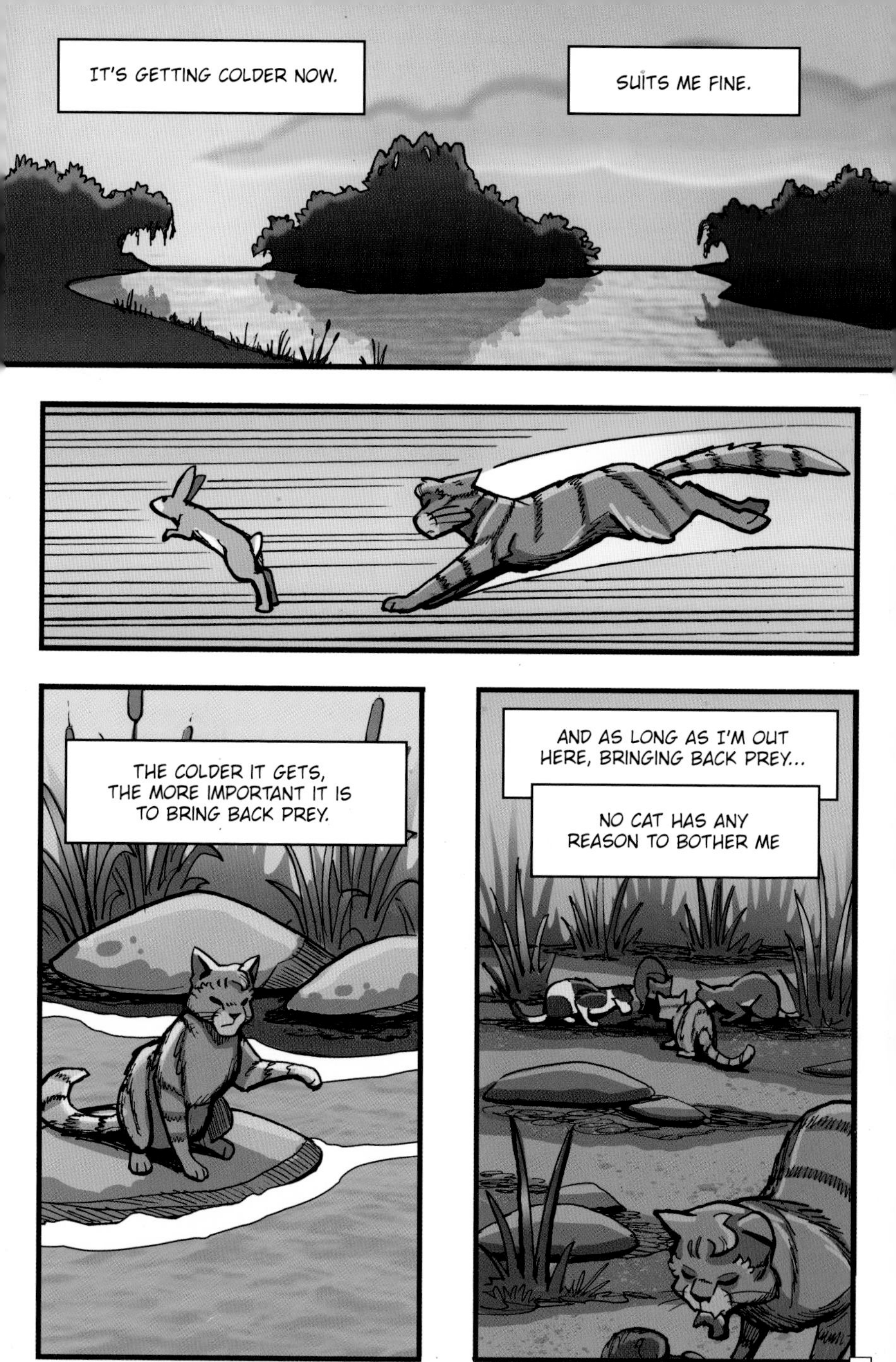
IT'S GETTING COLDER NOW.
SUITS ME FINE.
THE COLDER IT GETS, THE MORE IMPORTANT IT IS TO BRING BACK PREY.
AND AS LONG AS I'M OUT HERE, BRINGING BACK PREY...
NO CAT HAS ANY REASON TO BOTHER ME

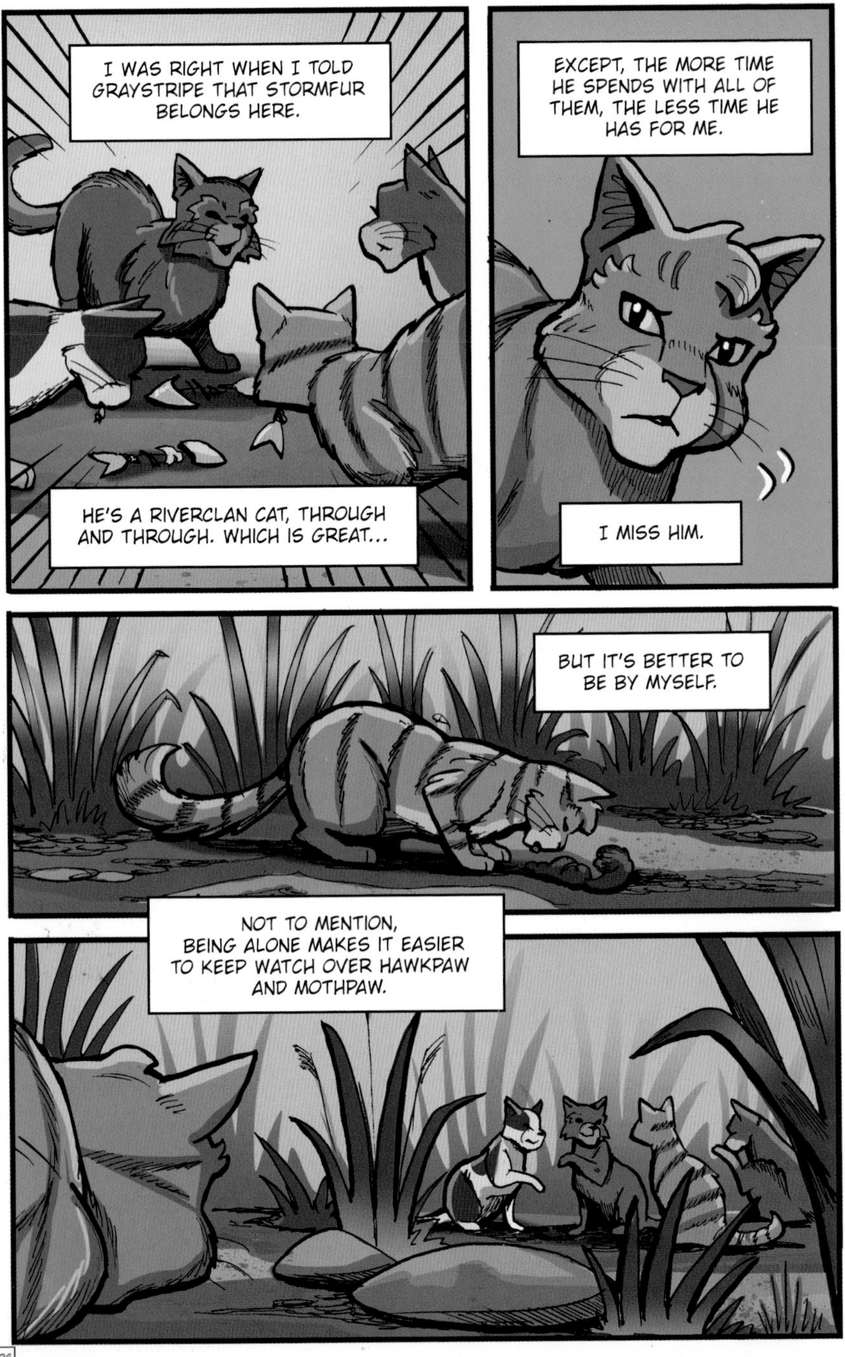
I WAS RIGHT WHEN I TOLD GRAYSTRIPE THAT STORMFUR BELONGS HERE.
HE'S A RIVERCLAN CAT, THROUGH AND THROUGH. WHICH IS GREAT...
EXCEPT, THE MORE TIME HE SPENDS WITH ALL OF THEM, THE LESS TIME HE HAS FOR ME.
I MISS HIM.
BUT IT'S BETTER TO BE BY MYSELF.
NOT TO MENTION, BEING ALONE MAKES IT EASIER TO KEEP WATCH OVER HAWKPAW AND MOTHPAW.

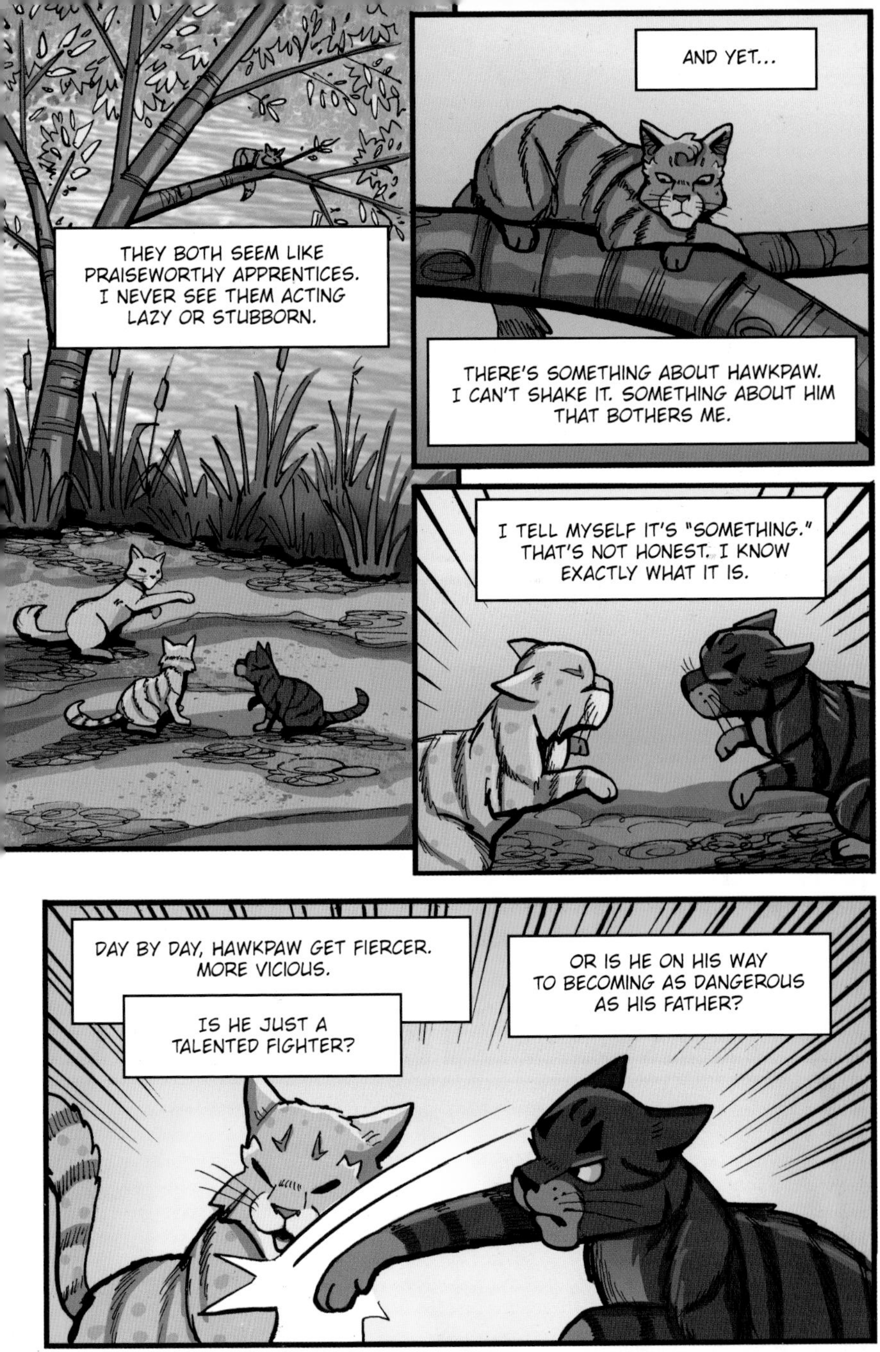
THEY BOTH SEEM LIKE PRAISEWORTHY APPRENTICES. I NEVER SEE THEM ACTING LAZY OR STUBBORN.
AND YET...
THERE'S SOMETHING ABOUT HAWKPAW. I CAN'T SHAKE IT. SOMETHING ABOUT HIM THAT BOTHERS ME.
I TELL MYSELF IT'S "SOMETHING." THAT'S NOT HONEST. I KNOW EXACTLY WHAT IT IS.
DAY BY DAY, HAWKPAW GET FIERCER. MORE VICIOUS.
IS HE JUST A TALENTED FIGHTER?
OR IS HE ON HIS WAY TO BECOMING AS DANGEROUS AS HIS FATHER?

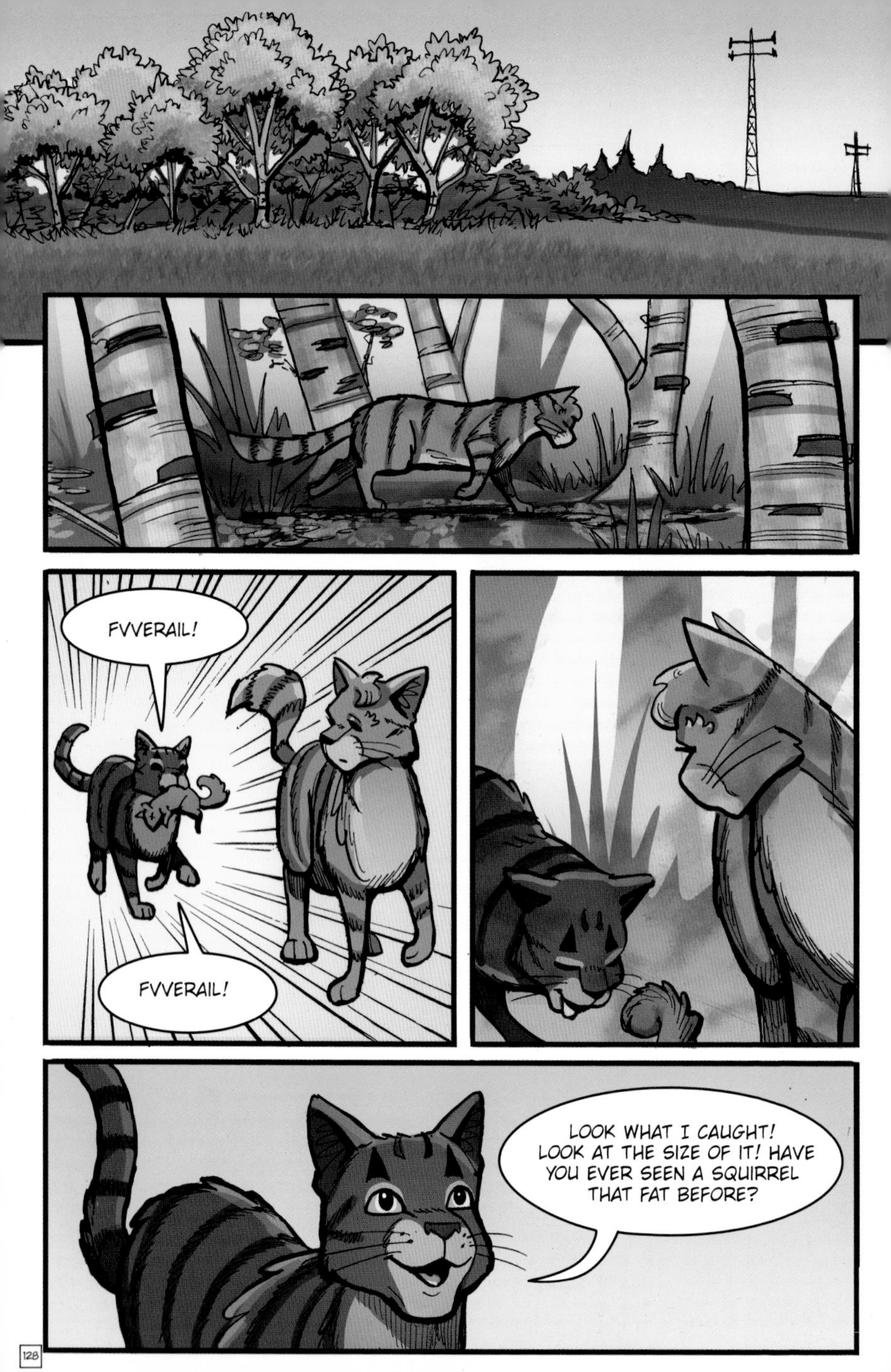
FVVERAIL!
FVVERAIL!
LOOK WHAT I CAUGHT! LOOK AT THE SIZE OF IT! HAVE YOU EVER SEEN A SQUIRREL THAT FAT BEFORE?

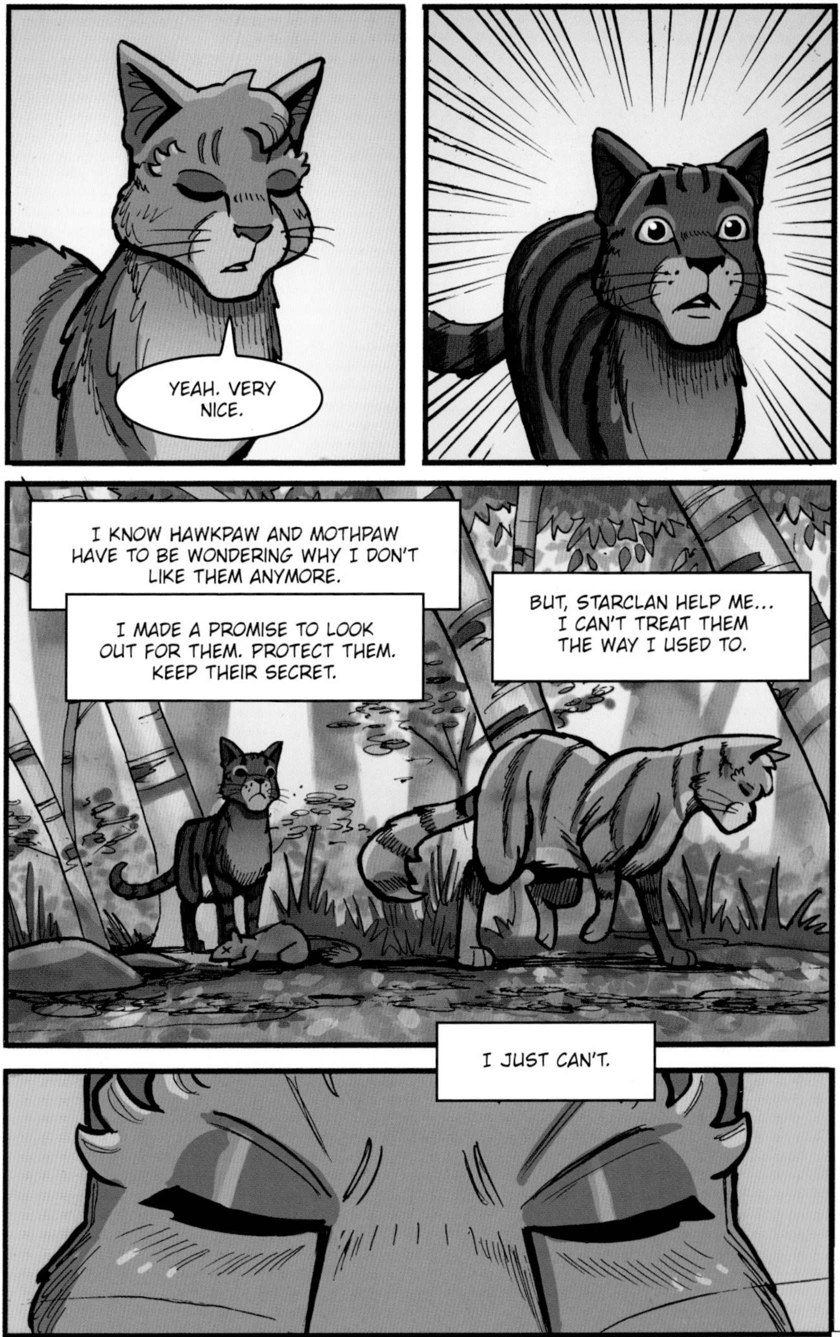
YEAH. VERY NICE.
I KNOW HAWKPAW AND MOTHPAW HAVE TO BE WONDERING WHY I DON'T LIKE THEM ANYMORE.
I MADE A PROMISE TO LOOK OUT FOR THEM. PROTECT THEM. KEEP THEIR SECRET.
BUT, STARCLAN HELP ME... I CAN'T TREAT THEM THE WAY I USED TO.
I JUST CAN'T.

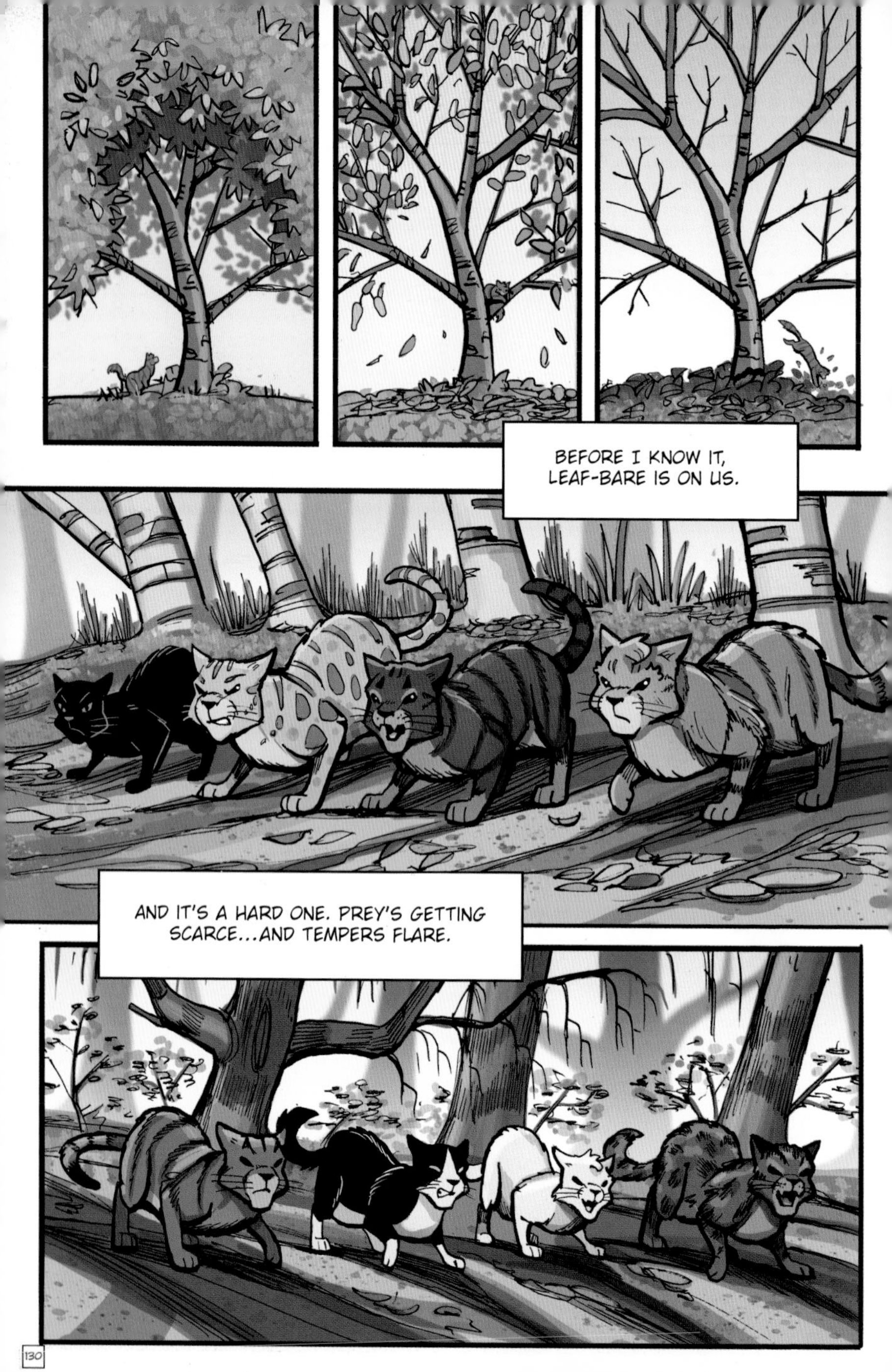
BEFORE I KNOW IT, LEAF-BARE IS ON US.
AND IT'S A HARD ONE. PREY'S GETTING SCARCE...AND TEMPERS FLARE.

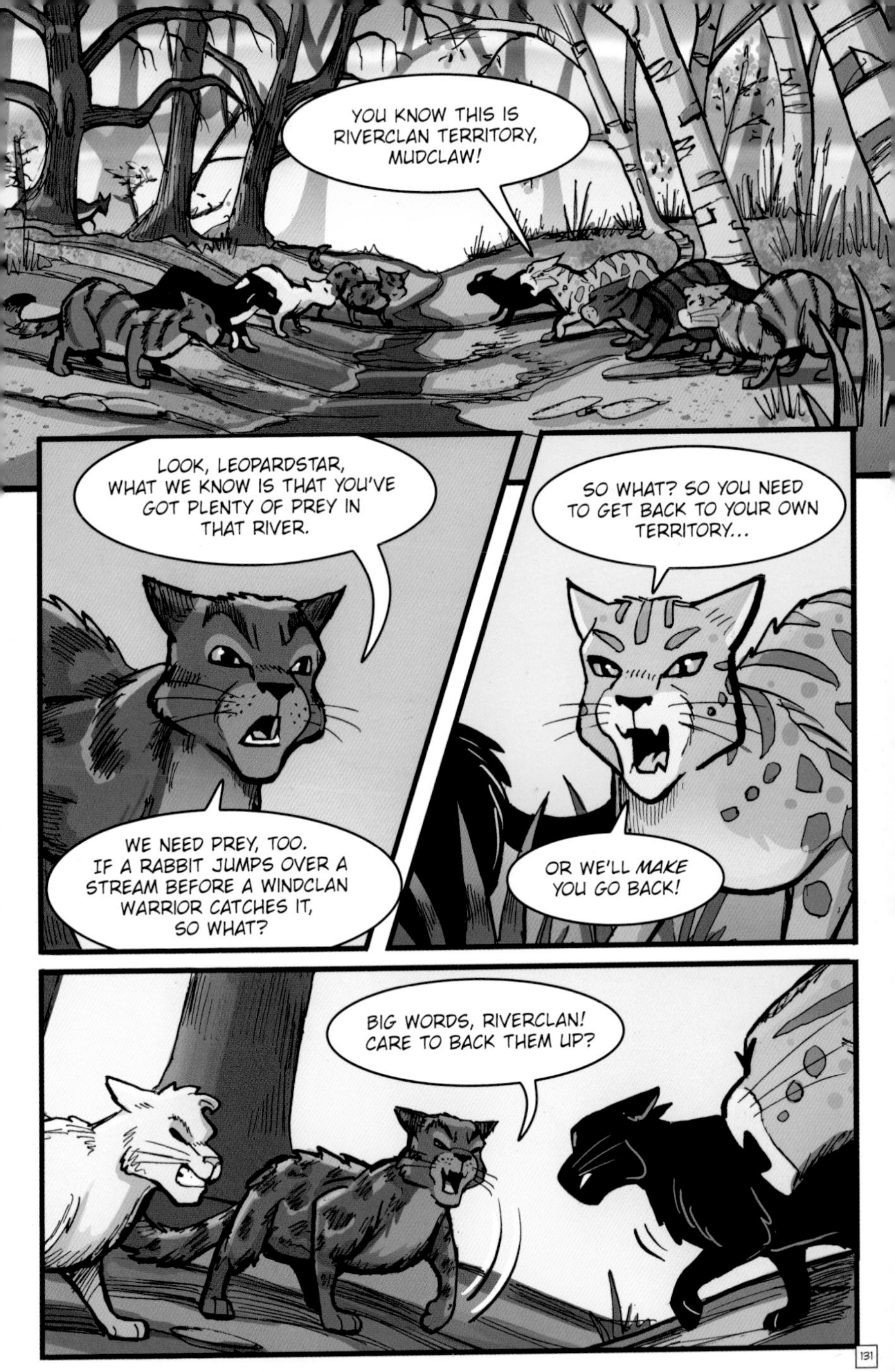
YOU KNOW THIS IS RIVERCLAN TERRITORY, MUDCLAW!
LOOK, LEOPARDSTAR, WHAT WE KNOW IS THAT YOU'VE GOT PLENTY OF PREY IN THAT RIVER.
WE NEED PREY, TOO. IF A RABBIT JUMPS OVER A STREAM BEFORE A WINDCLAN WARRIOR CATCHES IT, SO WHAT?
SO WHAT? SO YOU NEED TO GET BACK TO YOUR OWN TERRITORY...
OR WE'LL *MAKE* YOU GO BACK!
BIG WORDS, RIVERCLAN! CARE TO BACK THEM UP?

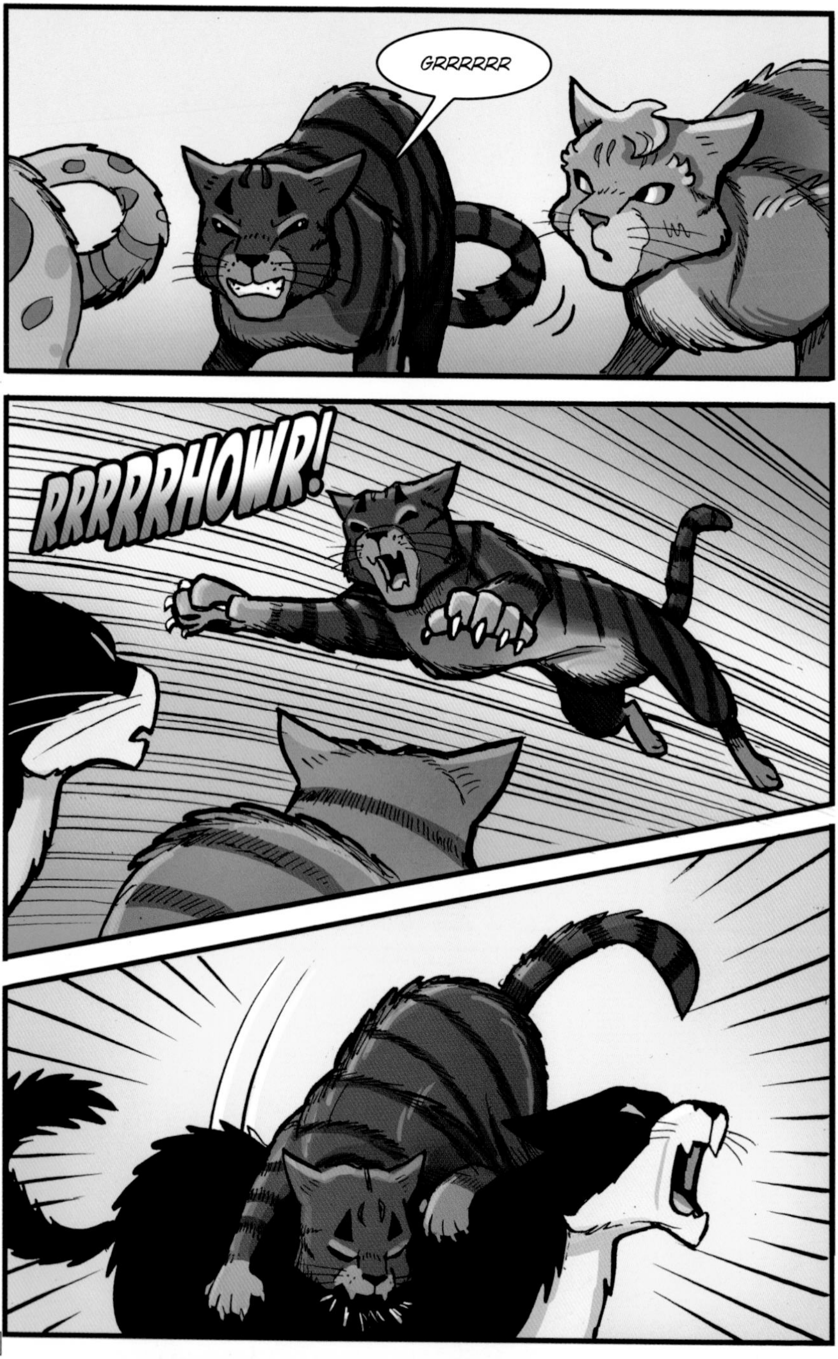
GRRRRRR
RRRRRHOWR!

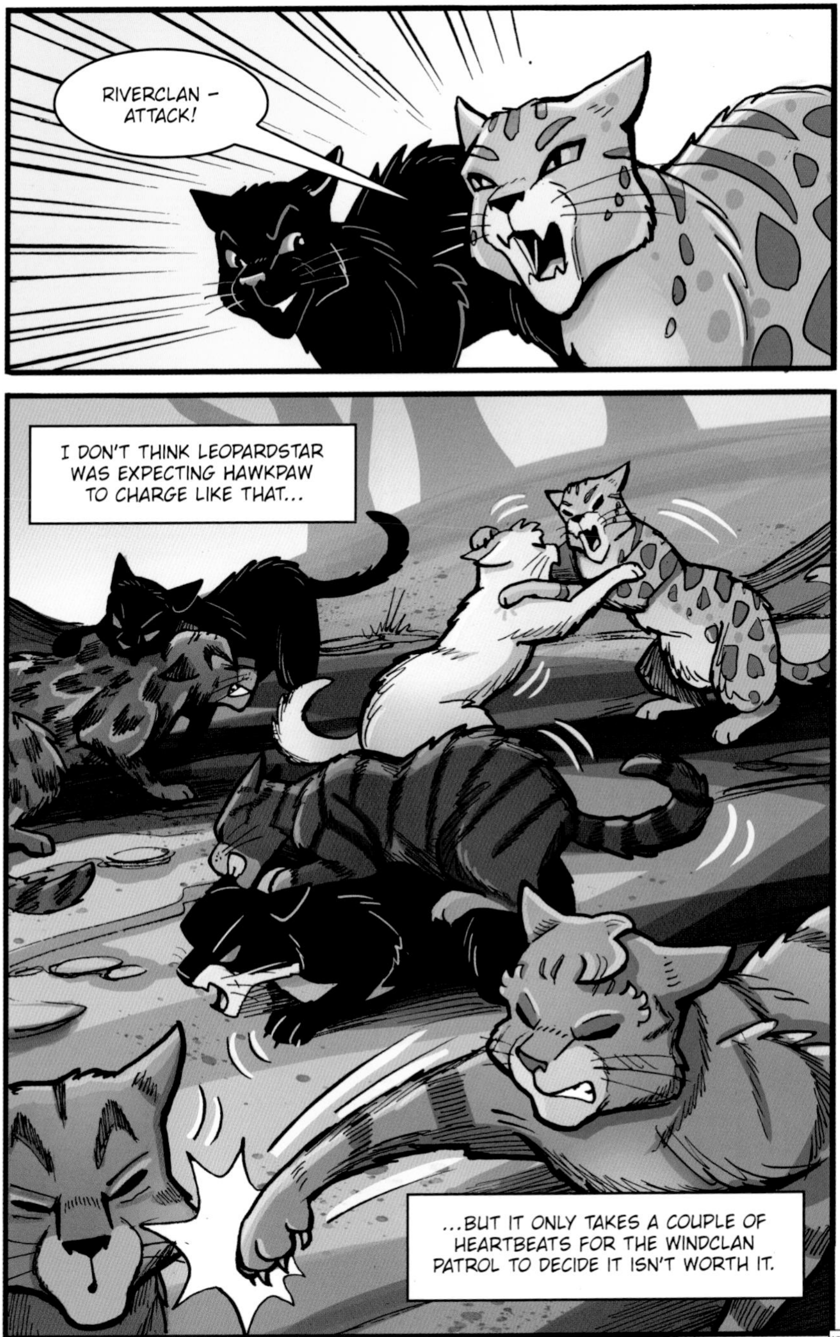
RIVERCLAN – ATTACK!
I DON'T THINK LEOPARDSTAR WAS EXPECTING HAWKPAW TO CHARGE LIKE THAT...
...BUT IT ONLY TAKES A COUPLE OF HEARTBEATS FOR THE WINDCLAN PATROL TO DECIDE IT ISN'T WORTH IT.

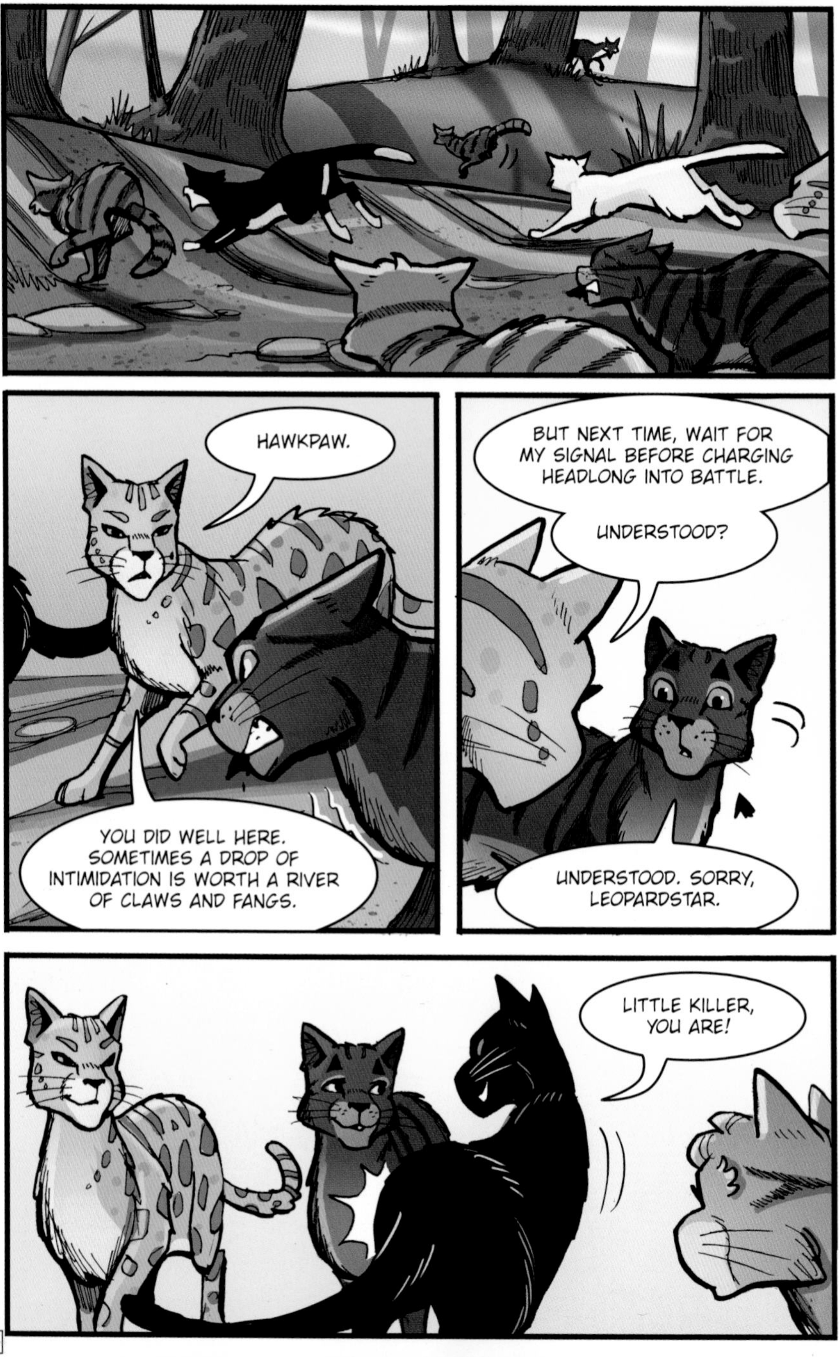
HAWKPAW.
YOU DID WELL HERE. SOMETIMES A DROP OF INTIMIDATION IS WORTH A RIVER OF CLAWS AND FANGS.
BUT NEXT TIME, WAIT FOR MY SIGNAL BEFORE CHARGING HEADLONG INTO BATTLE.
UNDERSTOOD?
UNDERSTOOD. SORRY, LEOPARDSTAR.
LITTLE KILLER, YOU ARE!

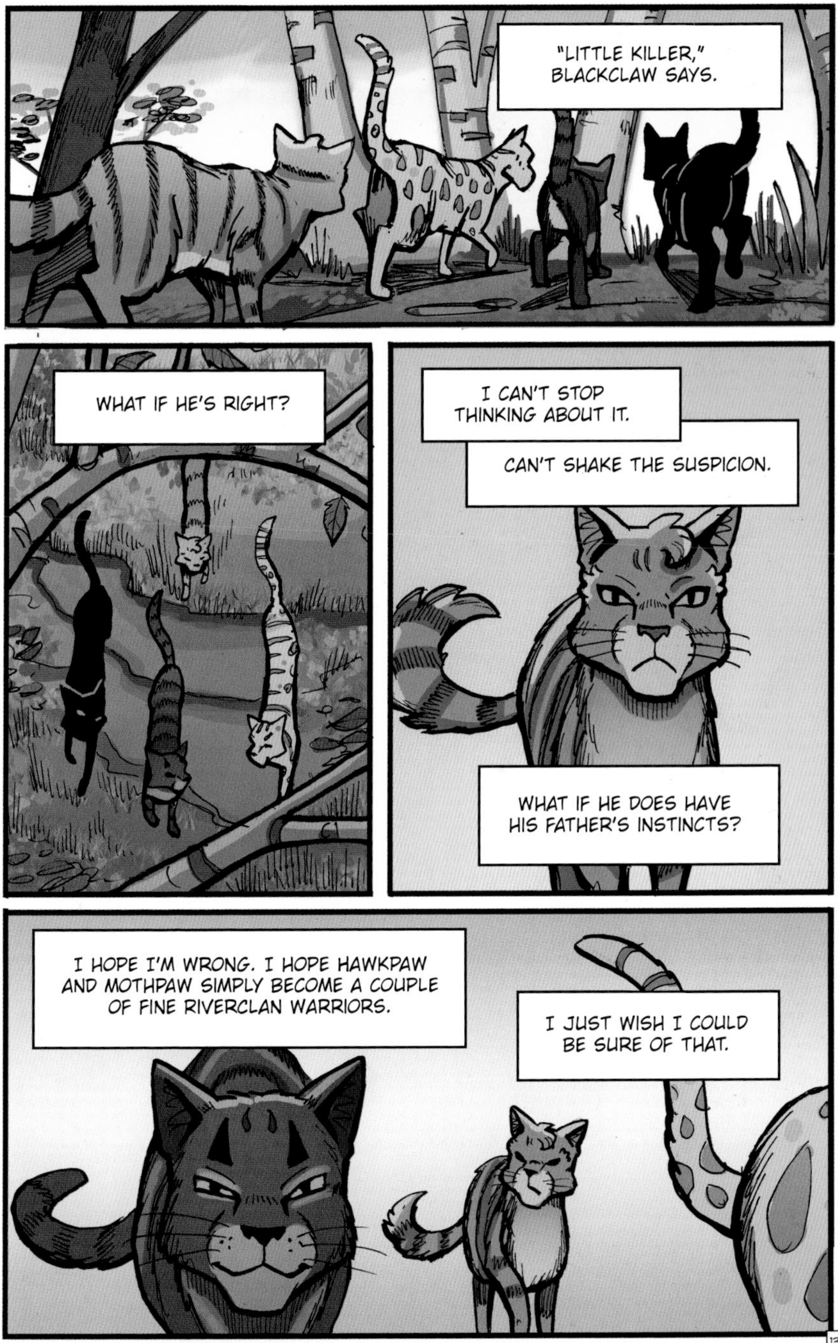
"LITTLE KILLER," BLACKCLAW SAYS.
WHAT IF HE'S RIGHT?
I CAN'T STOP THINKING ABOUT IT.
CAN'T SHAKE THE SUSPICION.
WHAT IF HE DOES HAVE HIS FATHER'S INSTINCTS?
I HOPE I'M WRONG. I HOPE HAWKPAW AND MOTHPAW SIMPLY BECOME A COUPLE OF FINE RIVERCLAN WARRIORS.
I JUST WISH I COULD BE SURE OF THAT.

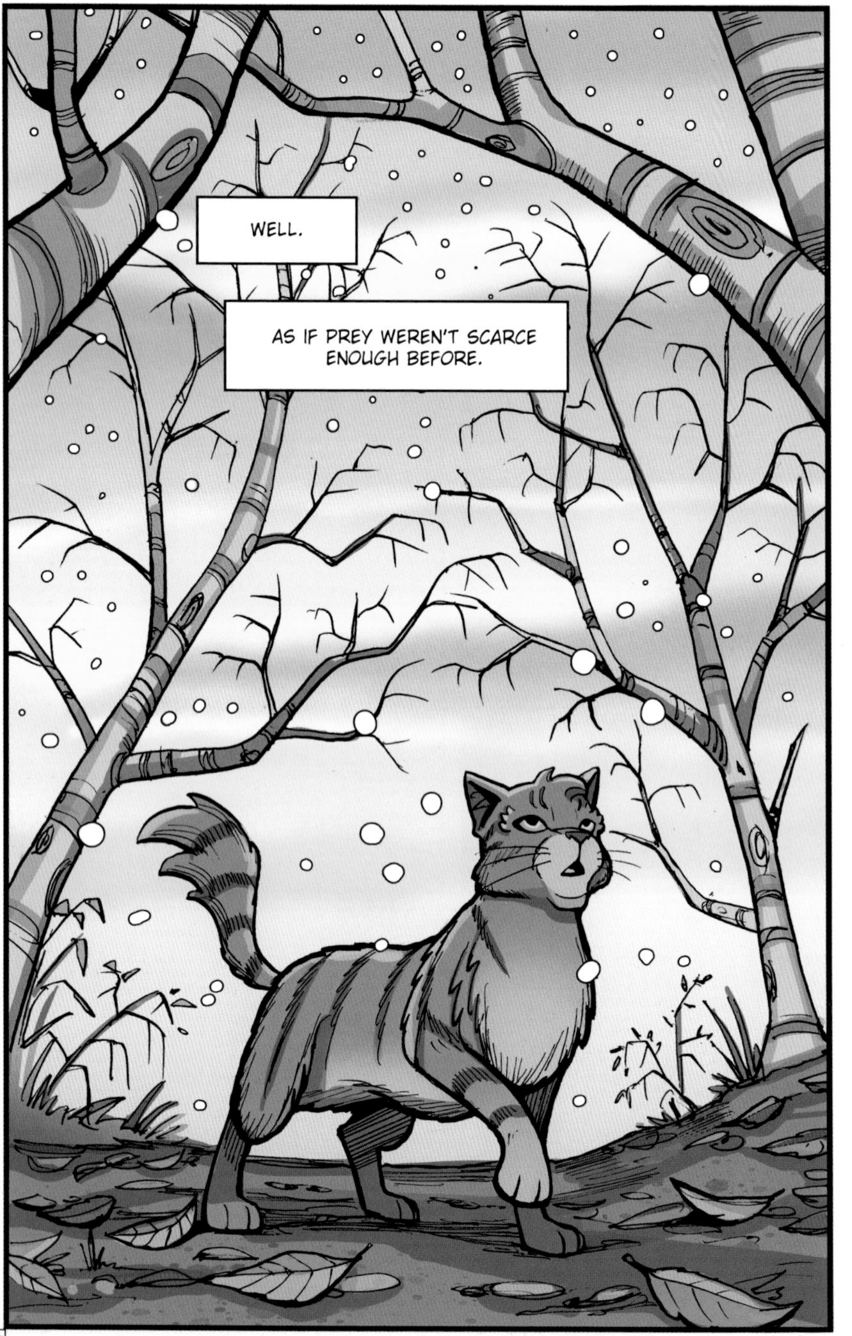
WELL.
AS IF PREY WEREN'T SCARCE ENOUGH BEFORE.

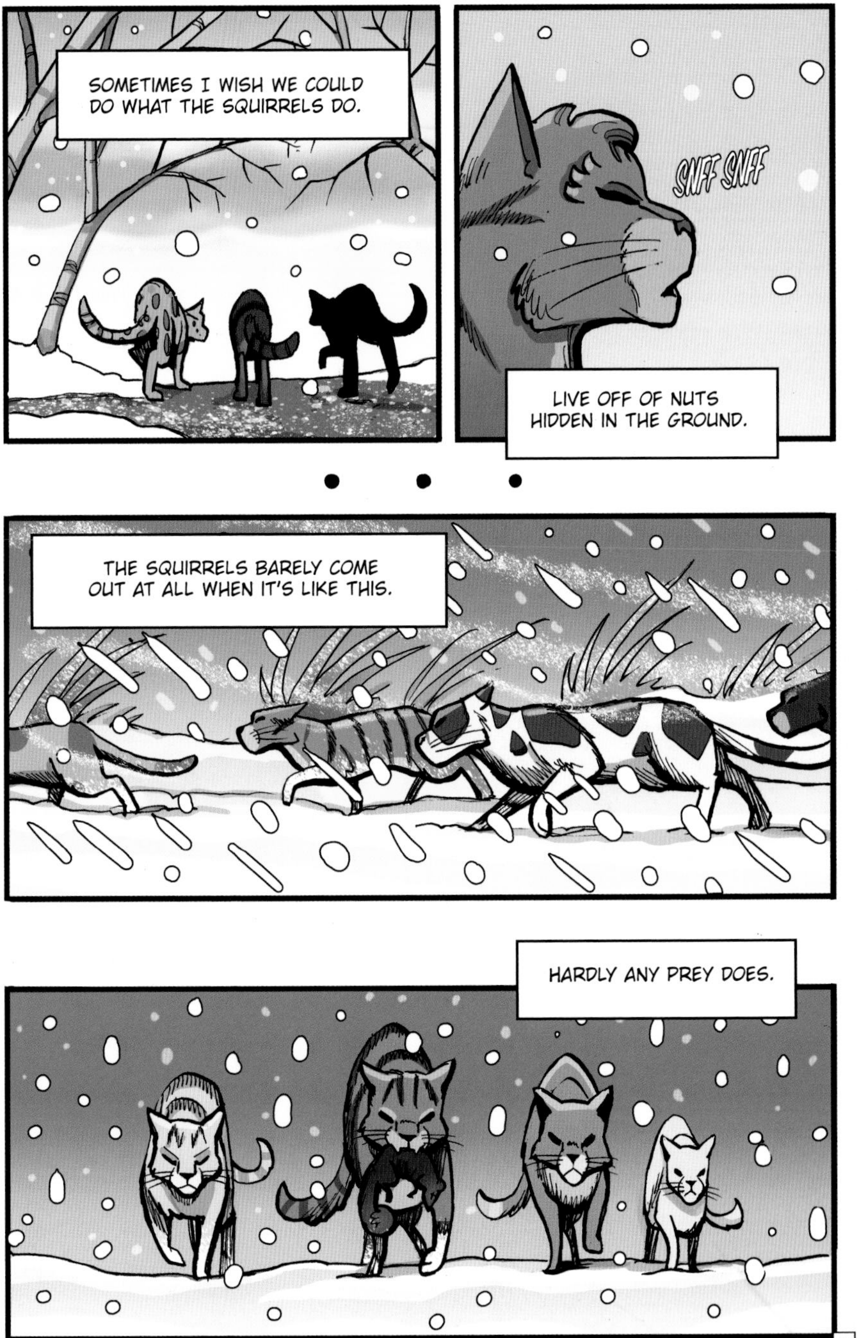
SOMETIMES I WISH WE COULD DO WHAT THE SQUIRRELS DO.
SNFF SNFF
LIVE OFF OF NUTS HIDDEN IN THE GROUND.
THE SQUIRRELS BARELY COME OUT AT ALL WHEN IT'S LIKE THIS.
HARDLY ANY PREY DOES.

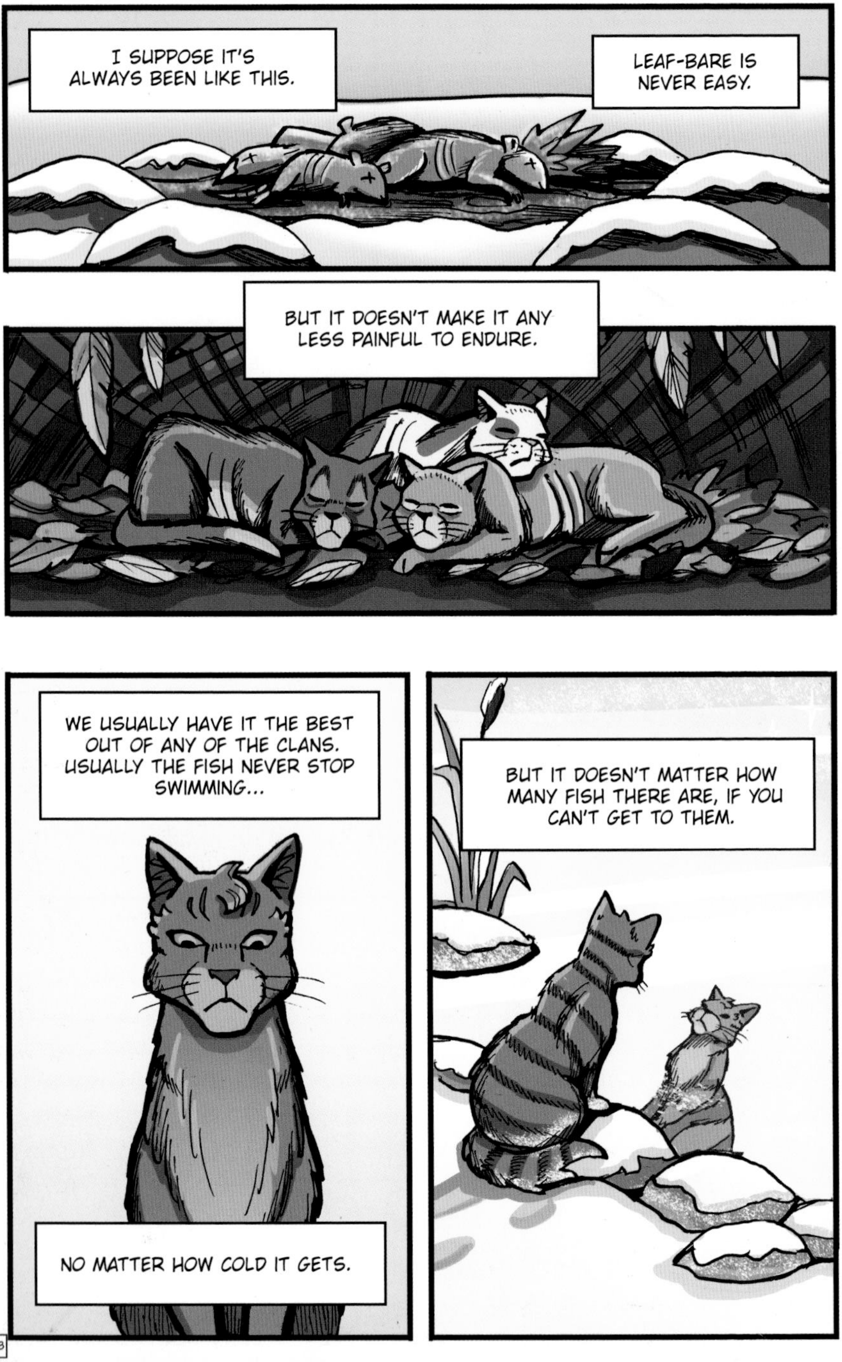

I SUPPOSE IT'S ALWAYS BEEN LIKE THIS.
LEAF-BARE IS NEVER EASY.
BUT IT DOESN'T MAKE IT ANY LESS PAINFUL TO ENDURE.
WE USUALLY HAVE IT THE BEST OUT OF ANY OF THE CLANS. USUALLY THE FISH NEVER STOP SWIMMING...
NO MATTER HOW COLD IT GETS.
BUT IT DOESN'T MATTER HOW MANY FISH THERE ARE, IF YOU CAN'T GET TO THEM.

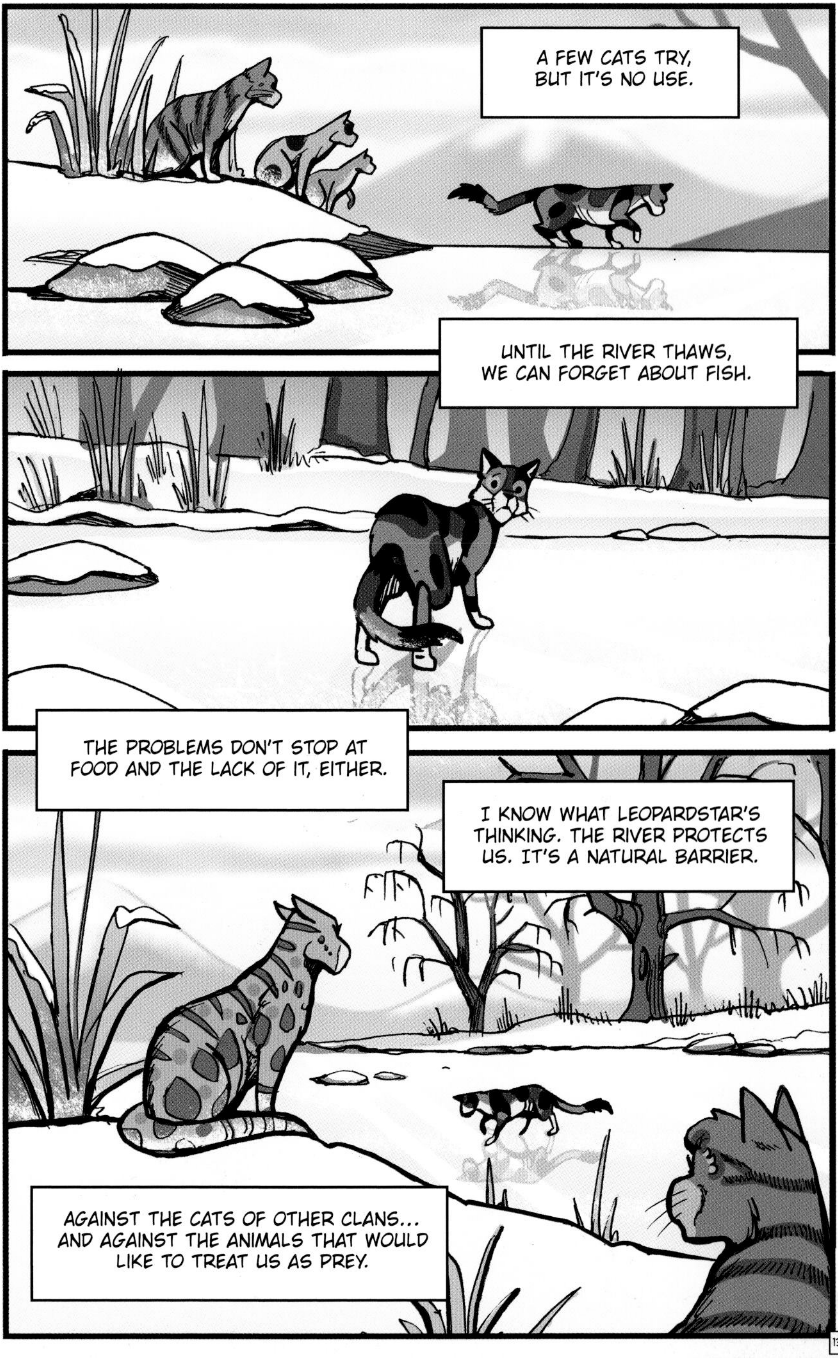
A FEW CATS TRY,
BUT IT'S NO USE.
UNTIL THE RIVER THAWS,
WE CAN FORGET ABOUT FISH.
THE PROBLEMS DON'T STOP AT
FOOD AND THE LACK OF IT, EITHER.
I KNOW WHAT LEOPARDSTAR'S
THINKING. THE RIVER PROTECTS
US. IT'S A NATURAL BARRIER.
AGAINST THE CATS OF OTHER CLANS...
AND AGAINST THE ANIMALS THAT WOULD
LIKE TO TREAT US AS PREY.

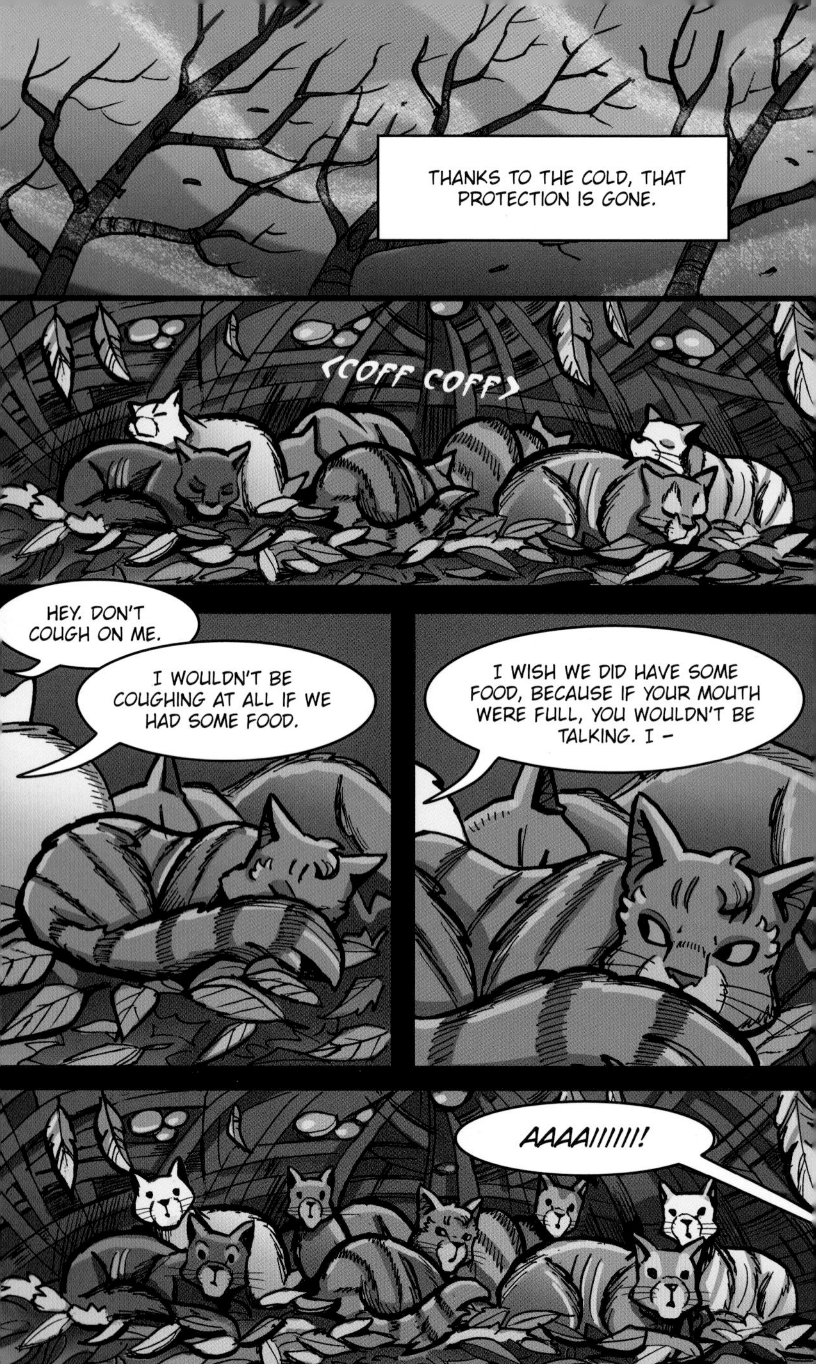
THANKS TO THE COLD, THAT PROTECTION IS GONE.
<COFF COFF>
HEY. DON'T COUGH ON ME.
I WOULDN'T BE COUGHING AT ALL IF WE HAD SOME FOOD.
I WISH WE DID HAVE SOME FOOD, BECAUSE IF YOUR MOUTH WERE FULL, YOU WOULDN'T BE TALKING. I –
AAAAIIIIIII!

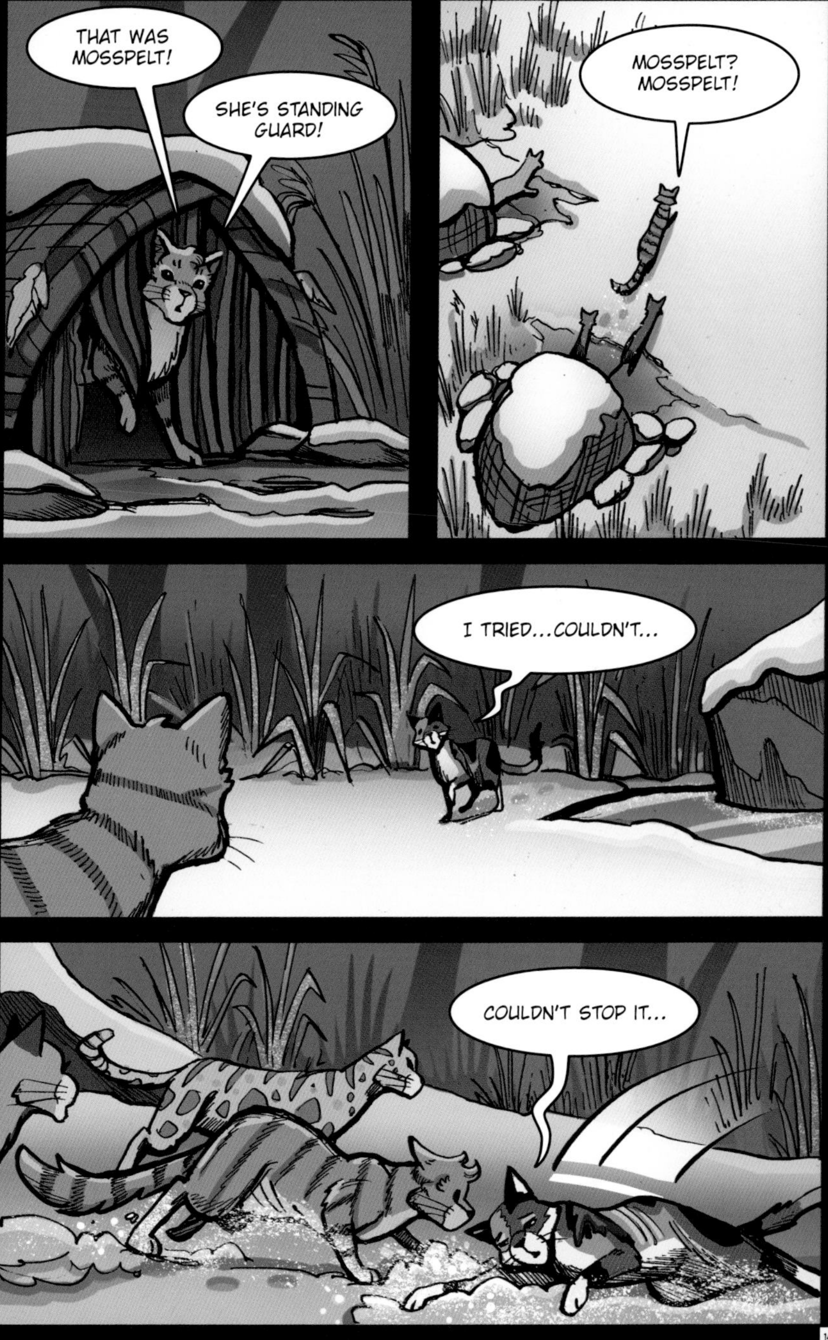
THAT WAS MOSSPELT!
SHE'S STANDING GUARD!
MOSSPELT? MOSSPELT!
I TRIED...COULDN'T...
COULDN'T STOP IT...

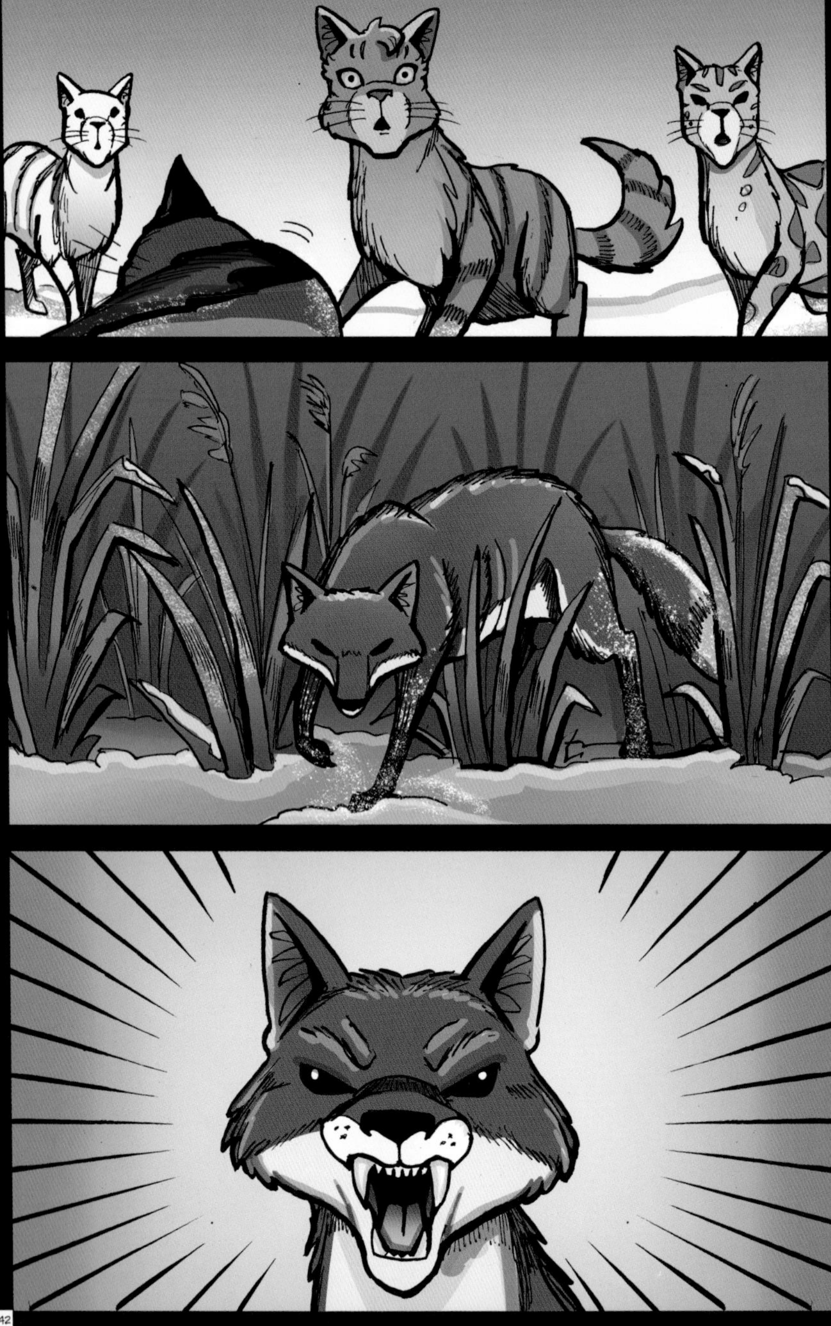

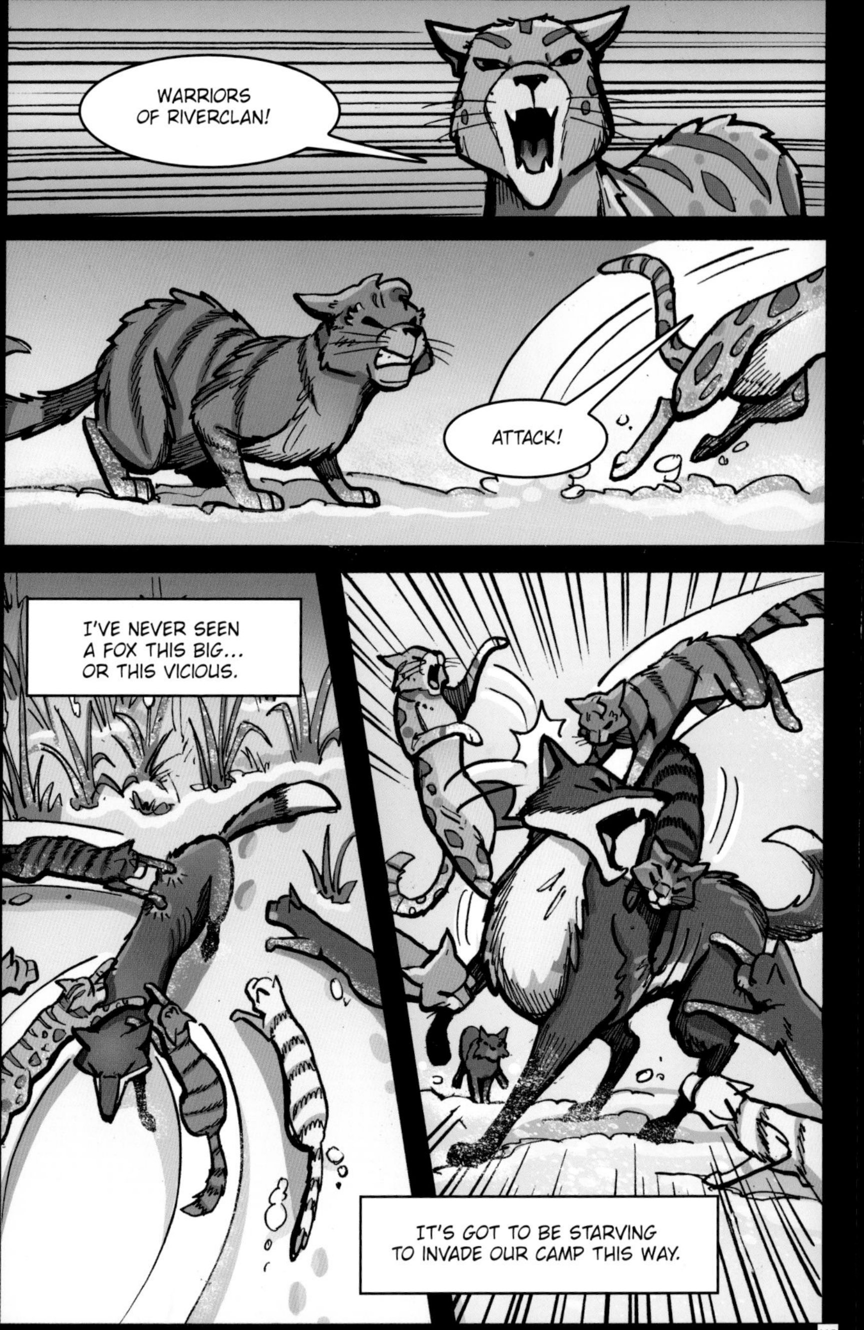
WARRIORS OF RIVERCLAN!
ATTACK!
I'VE NEVER SEEN A FOX THIS BIG... OR THIS VICIOUS.
IT'S GOT TO BE STARVING TO INVADE OUR CAMP THIS WAY.

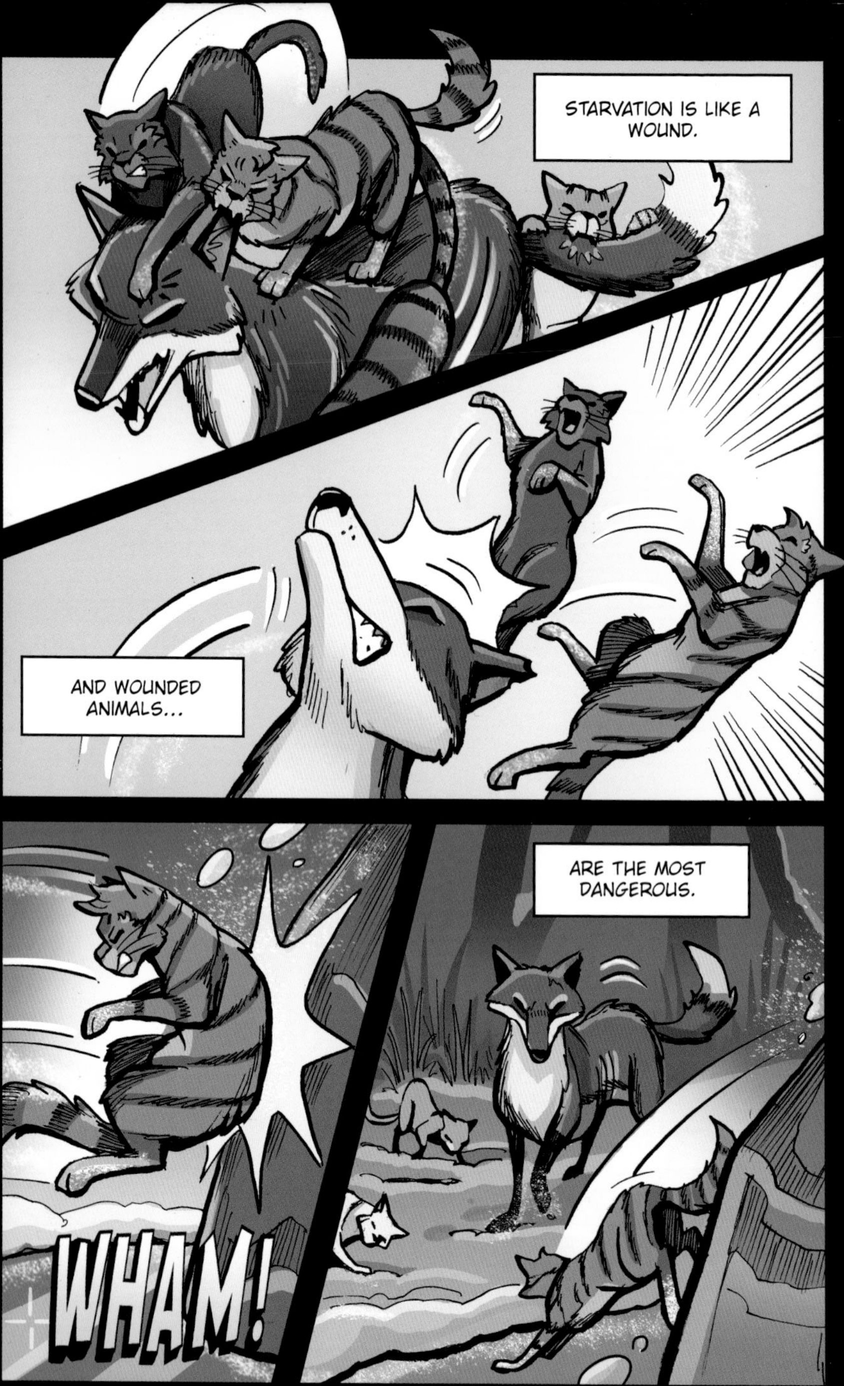
STARVATION IS LIKE A WOUND.
AND WOUNDED ANIMALS...
WHAM!
ARE THE MOST DANGEROUS.

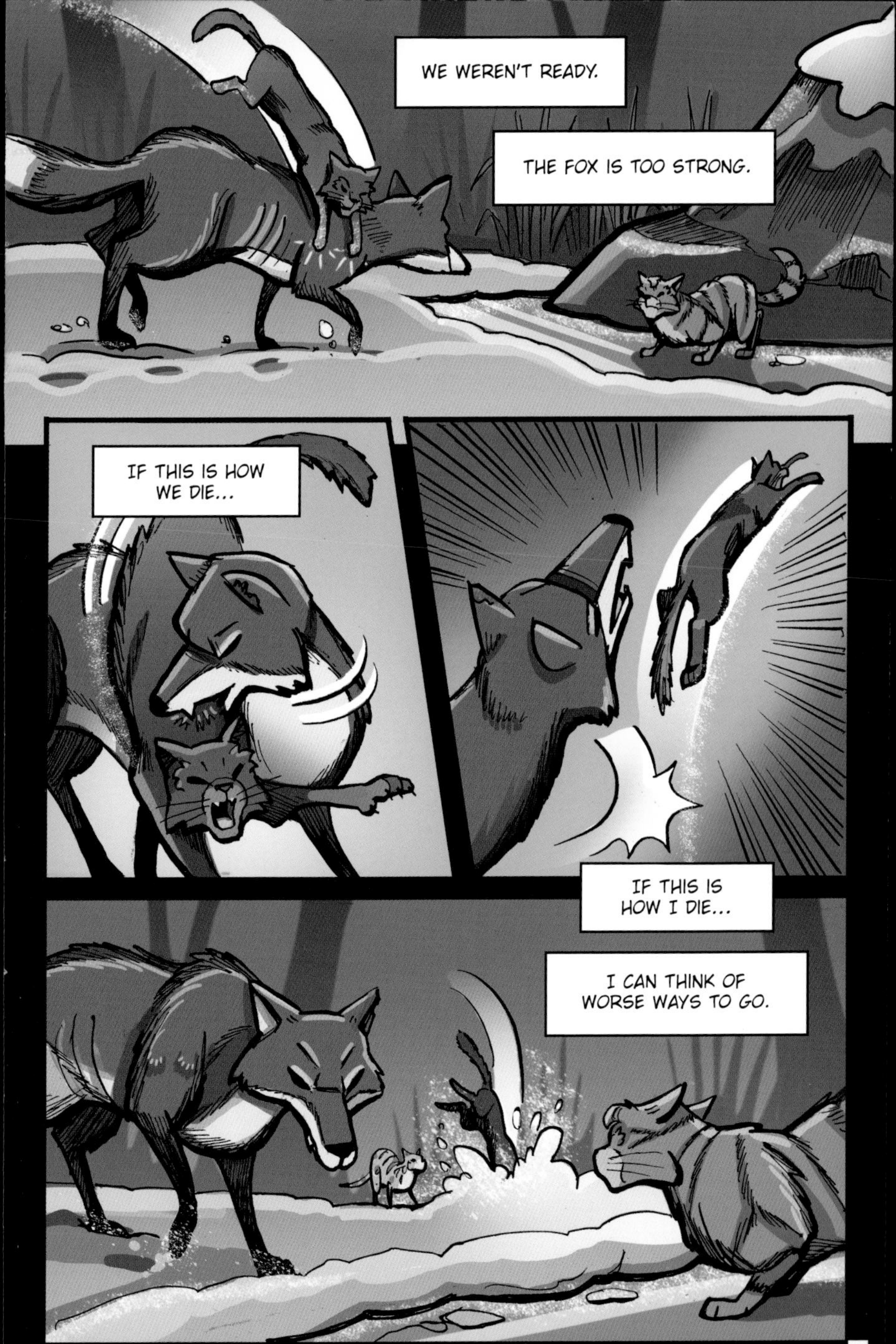
WE WEREN'T READY.
THE FOX IS TOO STRONG.
IF THIS IS HOW WE DIE...
IF THIS IS HOW I DIE...
I CAN THINK OF WORSE WAYS TO GO.

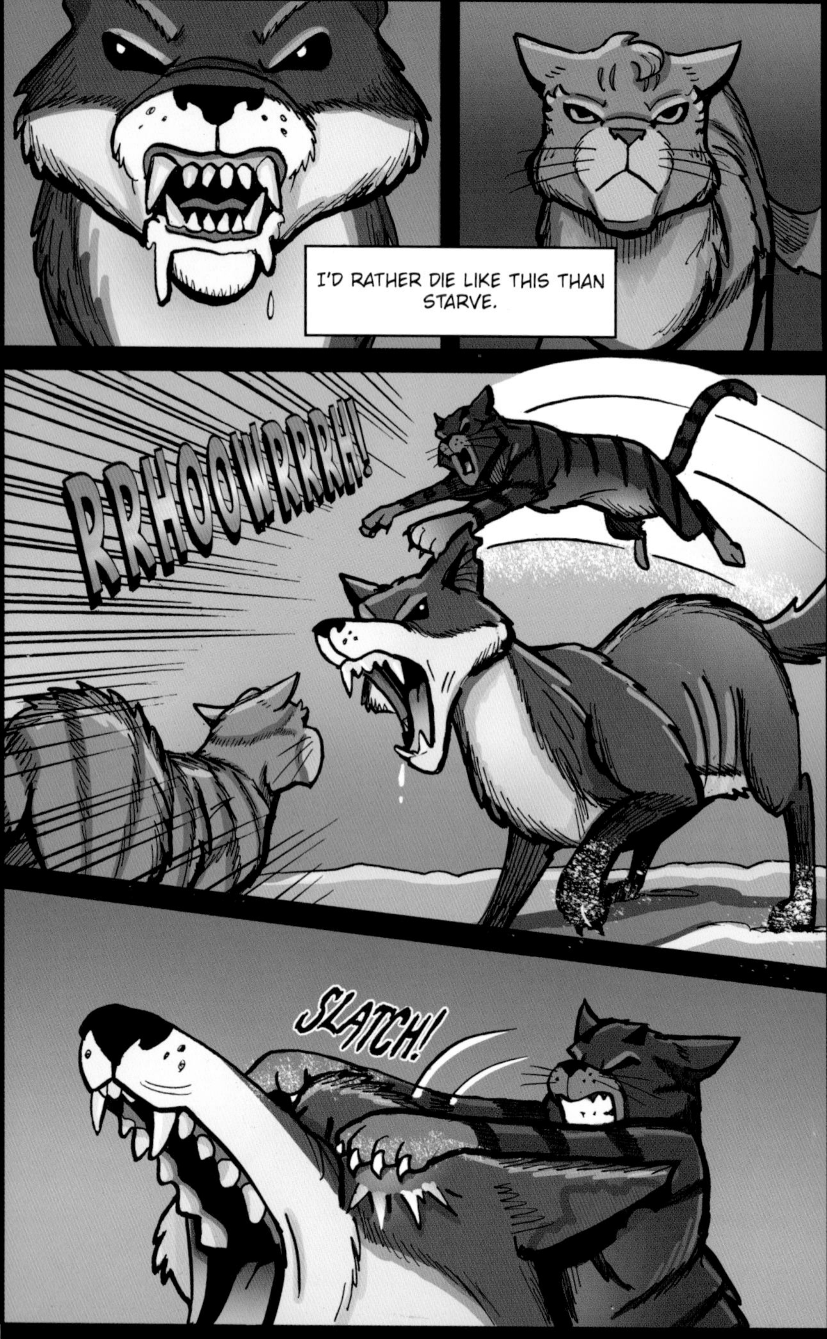
I'D RATHER DIE LIKE THIS THAN STARVE.
RRHOOWRRRH!
SLATCH!

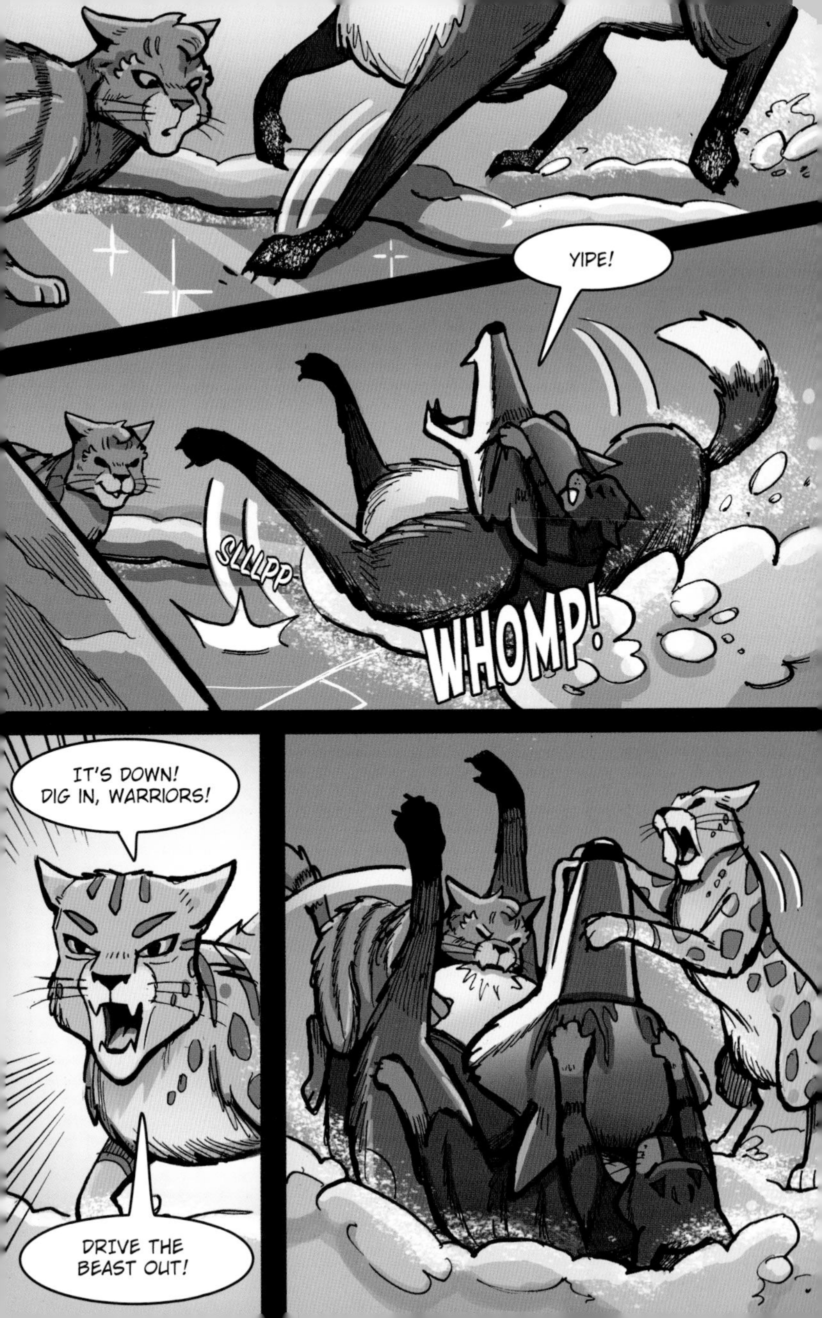
YIPE!
SLLLPP
WHOMP!
IT'S DOWN! DIG IN, WARRIORS!
DRIVE THE BEAST OUT!

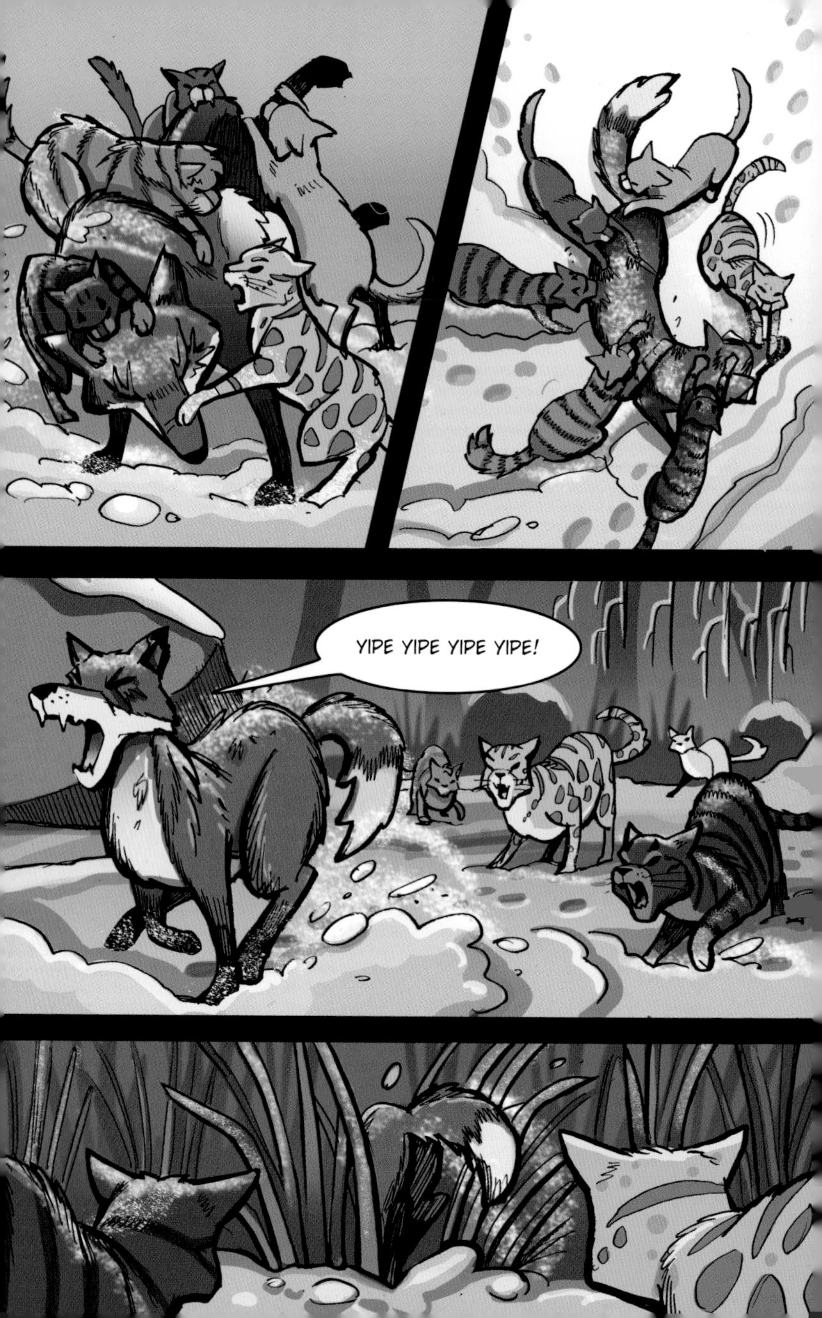
YIPE YIPE YIPE YIPE!

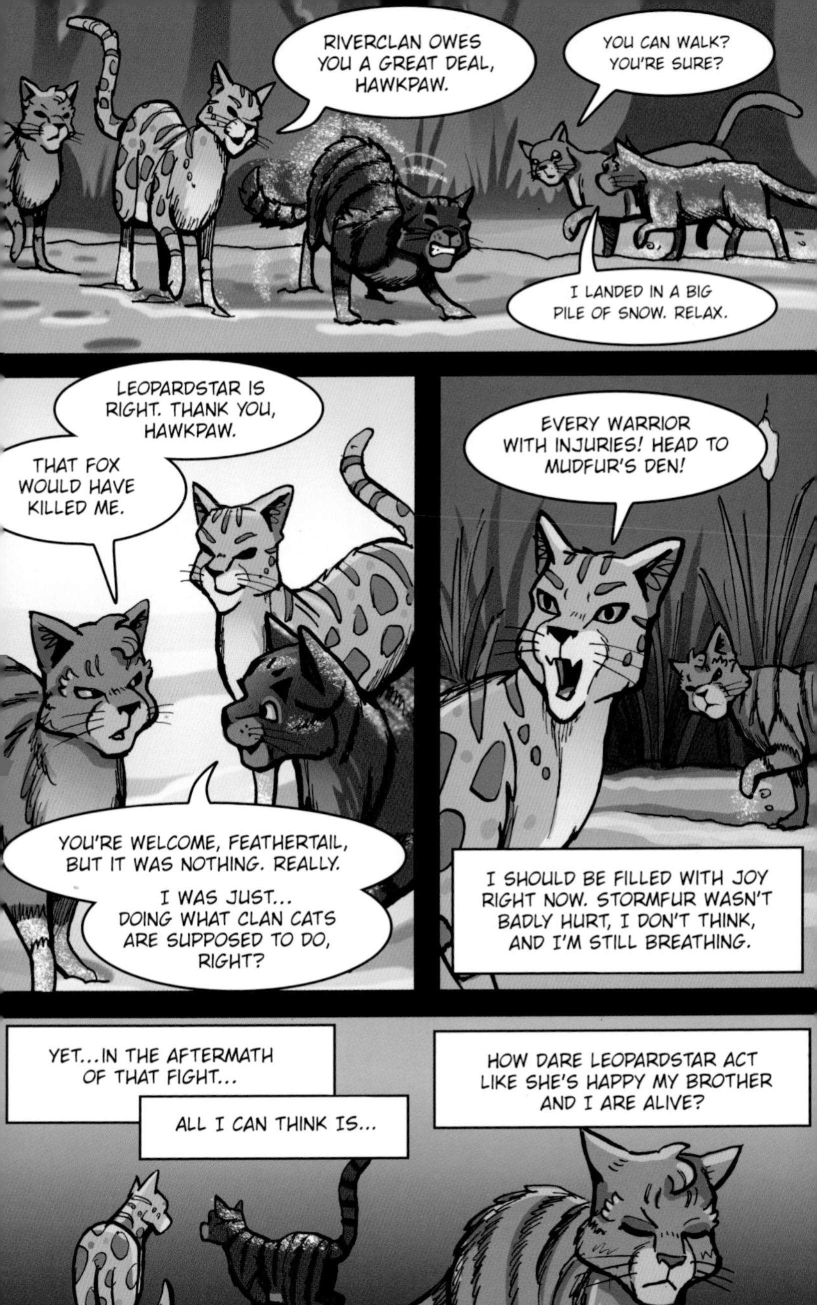
RIVERCLAN OWES YOU A GREAT DEAL, HAWKPAW.
YOU CAN WALK? YOU'RE SURE?
I LANDED IN A BIG PILE OF SNOW. RELAX.
LEOPARDSTAR IS RIGHT. THANK YOU, HAWKPAW.
THAT FOX WOULD HAVE KILLED ME.
YOU'RE WELCOME, FEATHERTAIL, BUT IT WAS NOTHING. REALLY.
I WAS JUST... DOING WHAT CLAN CATS ARE SUPPOSED TO DO, RIGHT?
EVERY WARRIOR WITH INJURIES! HEAD TO MUDFUR'S DEN!
I SHOULD BE FILLED WITH JOY RIGHT NOW. STORMFUR WASN'T BADLY HURT, I DON'T THINK, AND I'M STILL BREATHING.
YET...IN THE AFTERMATH OF THAT FIGHT...
ALL I CAN THINK IS...
HOW DARE LEOPARDSTAR ACT LIKE SHE'S HAPPY MY BROTHER AND I ARE ALIVE?

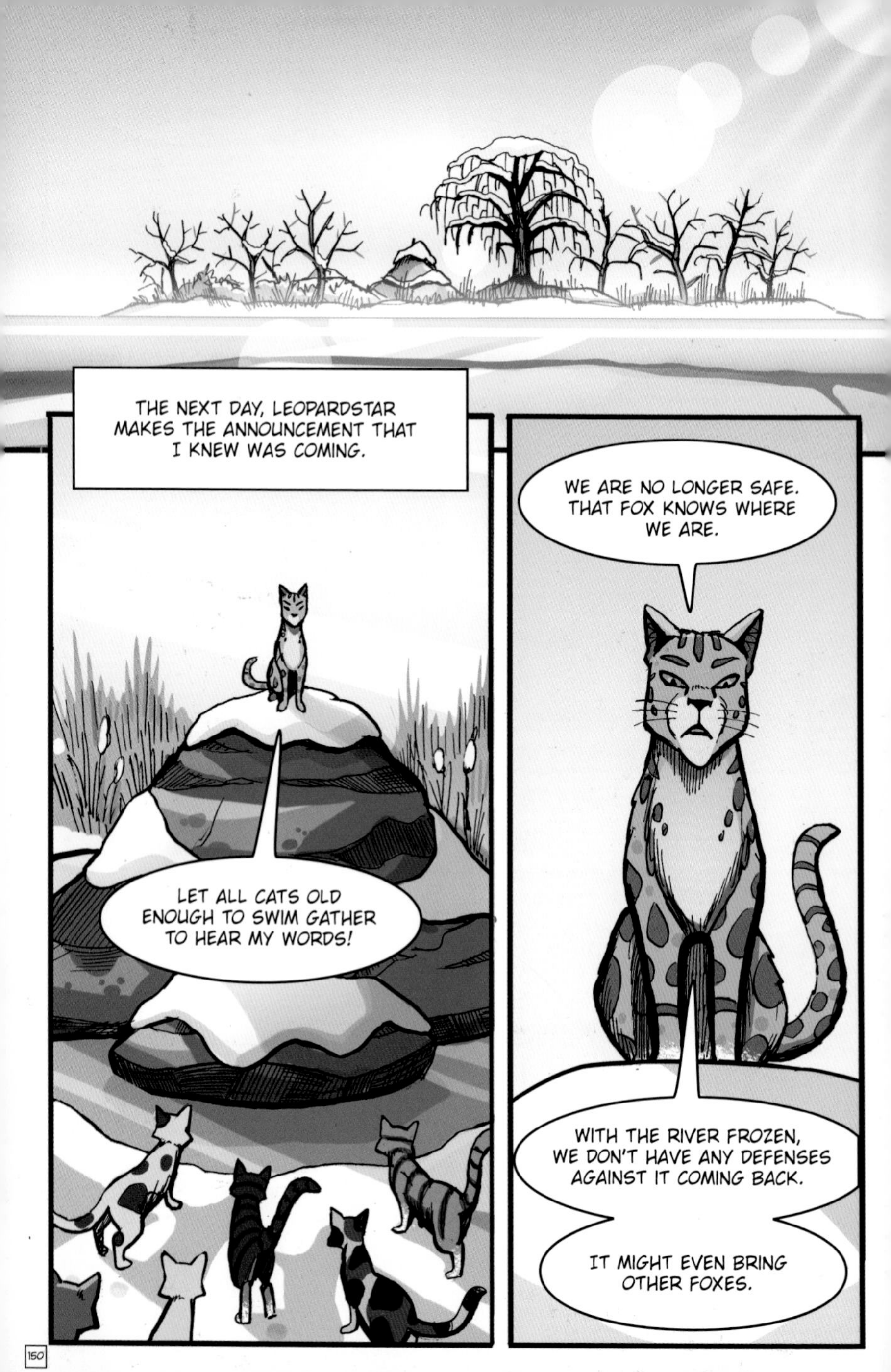
THE NEXT DAY, LEOPARDSTAR MAKES THE ANNOUNCEMENT THAT I KNEW WAS COMING.
LET ALL CATS OLD ENOUGH TO SWIM GATHER TO HEAR MY WORDS!
WE ARE NO LONGER SAFE. THAT FOX KNOWS WHERE WE ARE.
WITH THE RIVER FROZEN, WE DON'T HAVE ANY DEFENSES AGAINST IT COMING BACK.
IT MIGHT EVEN BRING OTHER FOXES.

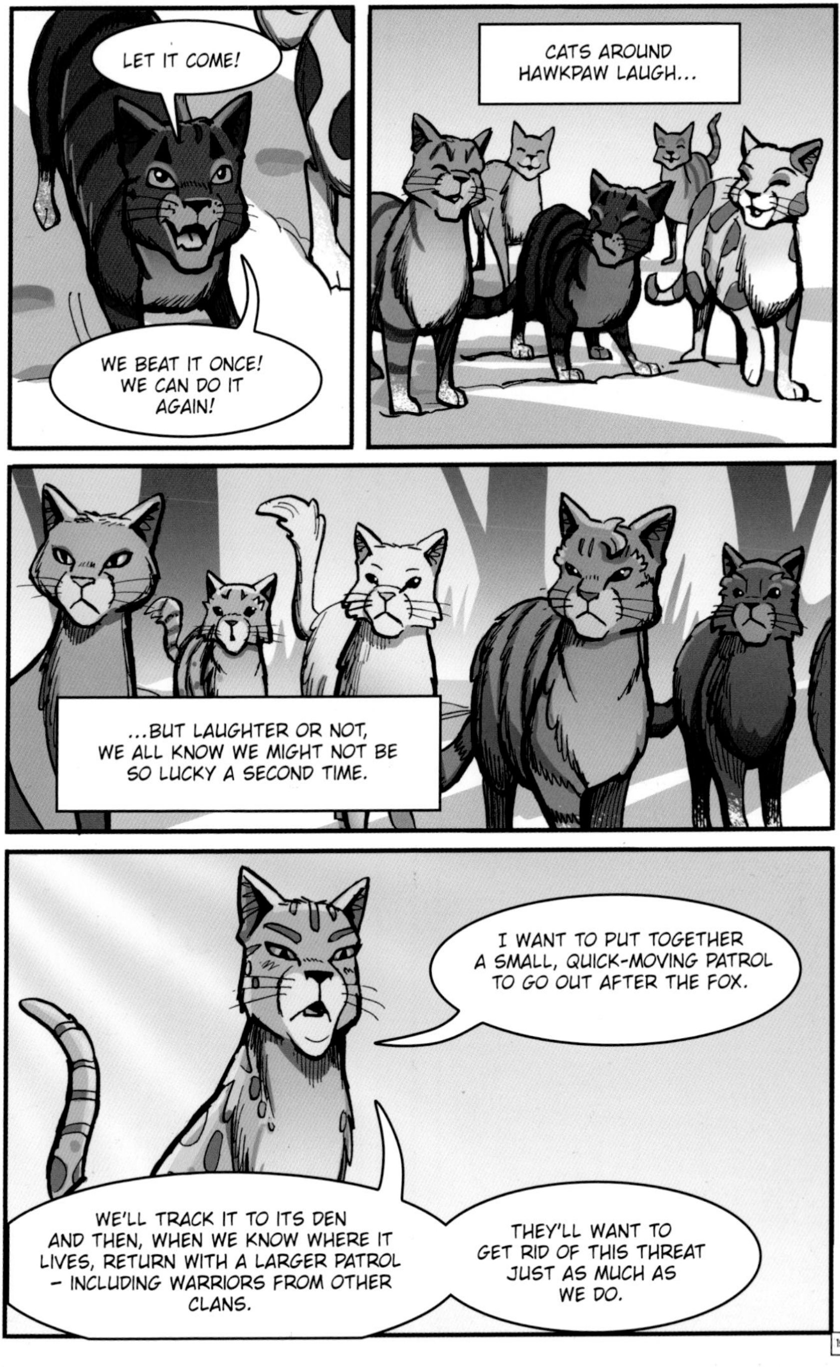
LET IT COME!
WE BEAT IT ONCE! WE CAN DO IT AGAIN!
CATS AROUND HAWKPAW LAUGH...
...BUT LAUGHTER OR NOT, WE ALL KNOW WE MIGHT NOT BE SO LUCKY A SECOND TIME.
I WANT TO PUT TOGETHER A SMALL, QUICK-MOVING PATROL TO GO OUT AFTER THE FOX.
WE'LL TRACK IT TO ITS DEN AND THEN, WHEN WE KNOW WHERE IT LIVES, RETURN WITH A LARGER PATROL – INCLUDING WARRIORS FROM OTHER CLANS.
THEY'LL WANT TO GET RID OF THIS THREAT JUST AS MUCH AS WE DO.

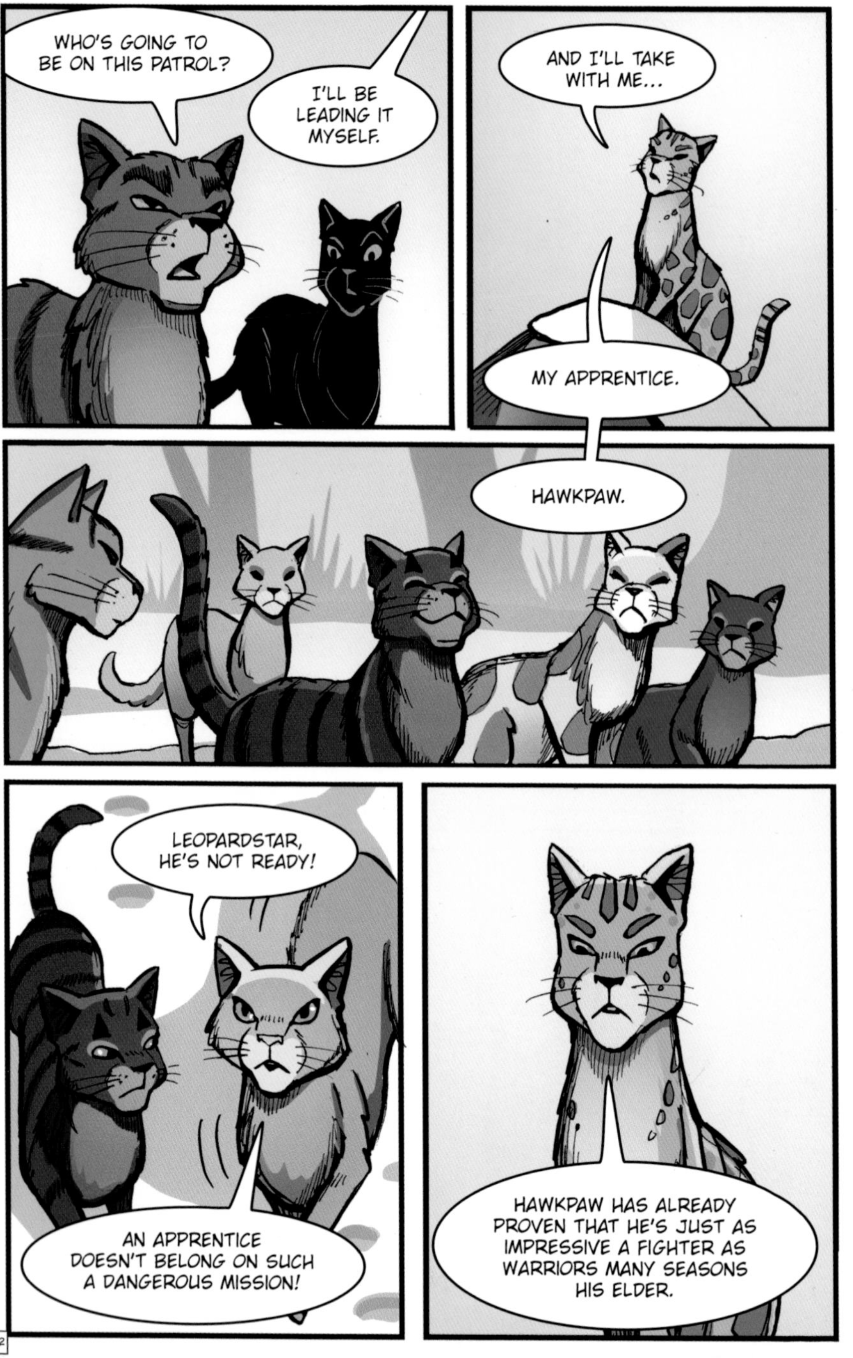
WHO'S GOING TO BE ON THIS PATROL?
I'LL BE LEADING IT MYSELF.
AND I'LL TAKE WITH ME...
MY APPRENTICE.
HAWKPAW.
LEOPARDSTAR, HE'S NOT READY!
AN APPRENTICE DOESN'T BELONG ON SUCH A DANGEROUS MISSION!
HAWKPAW HAS ALREADY PROVEN THAT HE'S JUST AS IMPRESSIVE A FIGHTER AS WARRIORS MANY SEASONS HIS ELDER.

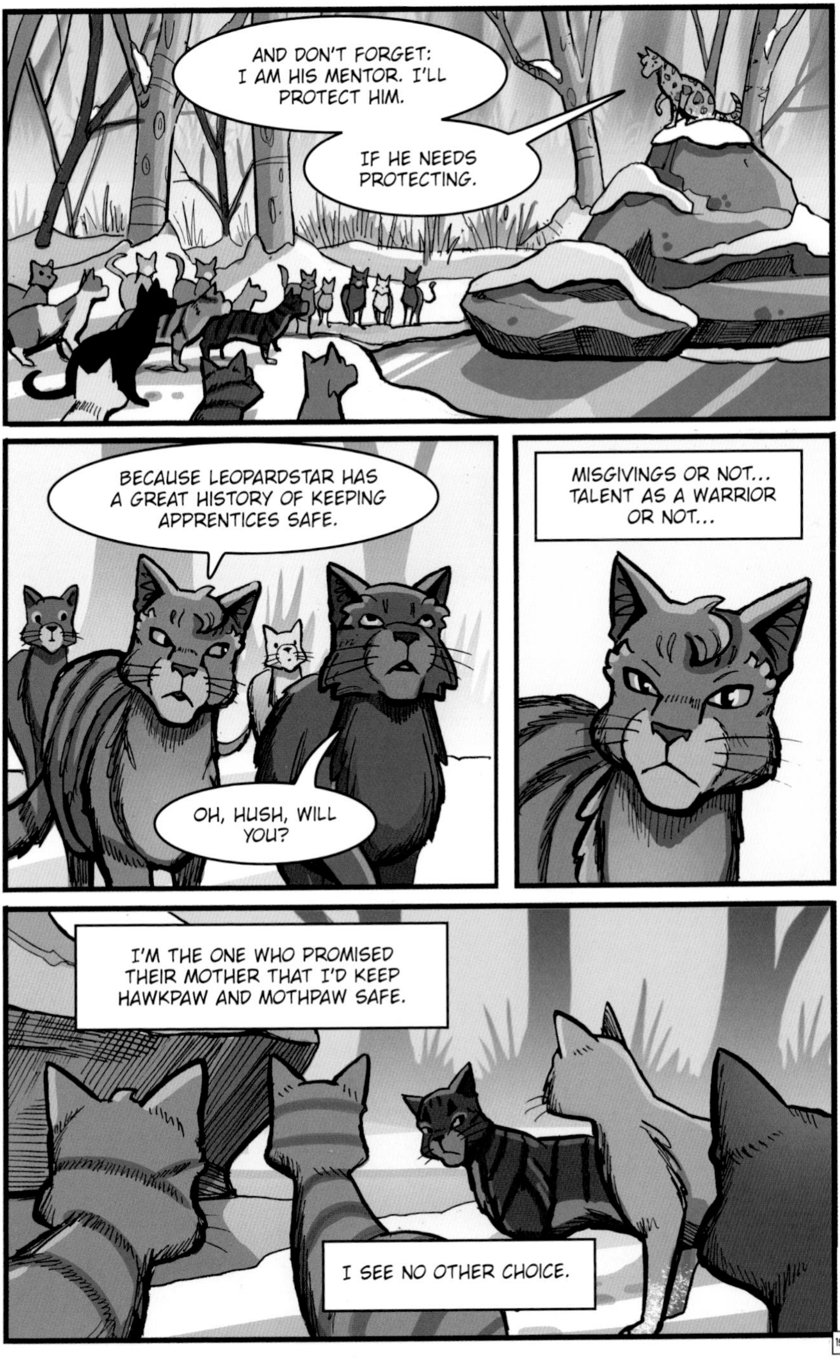
AND DON'T FORGET: I AM HIS MENTOR. I'LL PROTECT HIM.
IF HE NEEDS PROTECTING.
BECAUSE LEOPARDSTAR HAS A GREAT HISTORY OF KEEPING APPRENTICES SAFE.
OH, HUSH, WILL YOU?
MISGIVINGS OR NOT... TALENT AS A WARRIOR OR NOT...
I'M THE ONE WHO PROMISED THEIR MOTHER THAT I'D KEEP HAWKPAW AND MOTHPAW SAFE.
I SEE NO OTHER CHOICE.

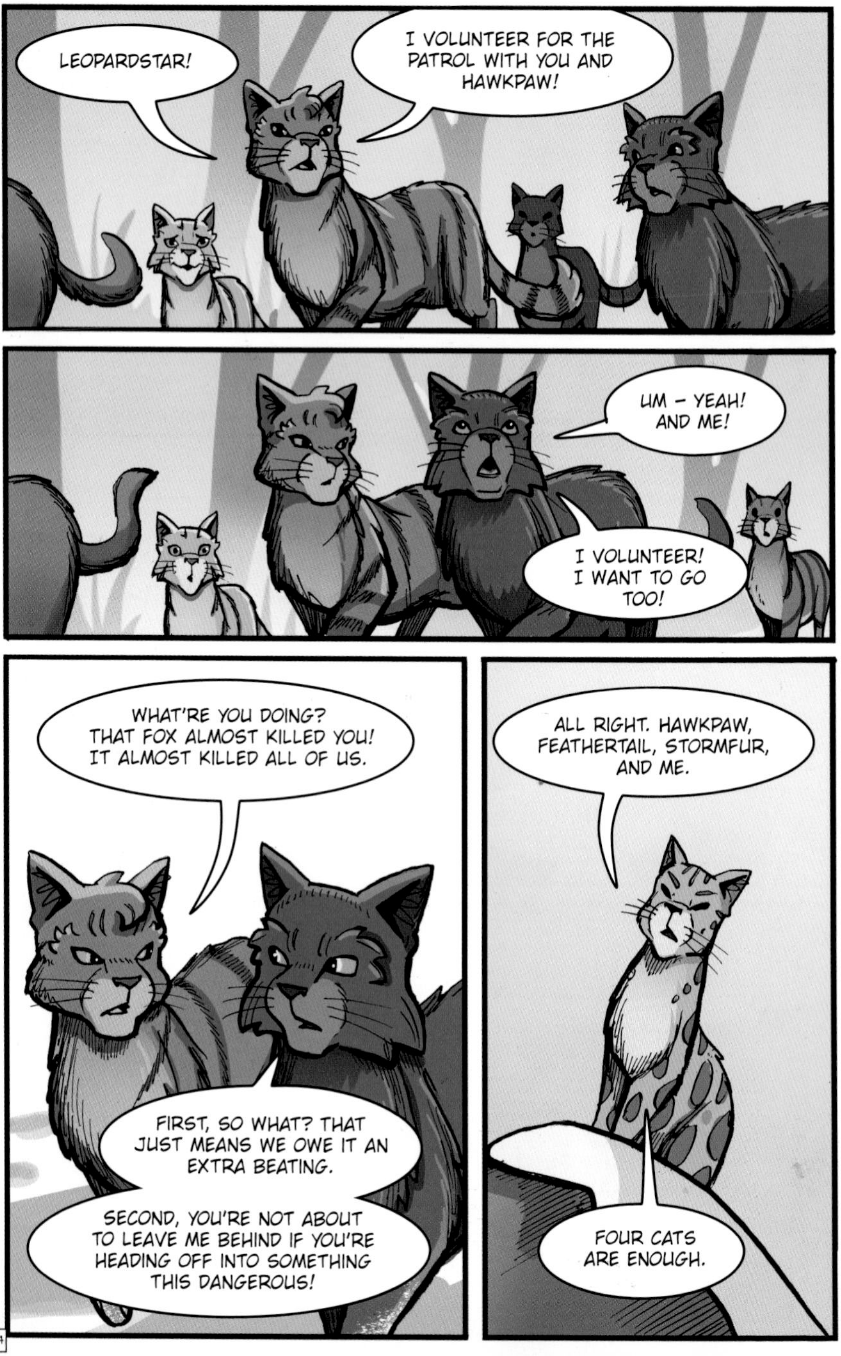
LEOPARDSTAR!
I VOLUNTEER FOR THE PATROL WITH YOU AND HAWKPAW!
UM - YEAH! AND ME!
I VOLUNTEER! I WANT TO GO TOO!
WHAT'RE YOU DOING? THAT FOX ALMOST KILLED YOU! IT ALMOST KILLED ALL OF US.
FIRST, SO WHAT? THAT JUST MEANS WE OWE IT AN EXTRA BEATING.
SECOND, YOU'RE NOT ABOUT TO LEAVE ME BEHIND IF YOU'RE HEADING OFF INTO SOMETHING THIS DANGEROUS!
ALL RIGHT. HAWKPAW, FEATHERTAIL, STORMFUR, AND ME.
FOUR CATS ARE ENOUGH.

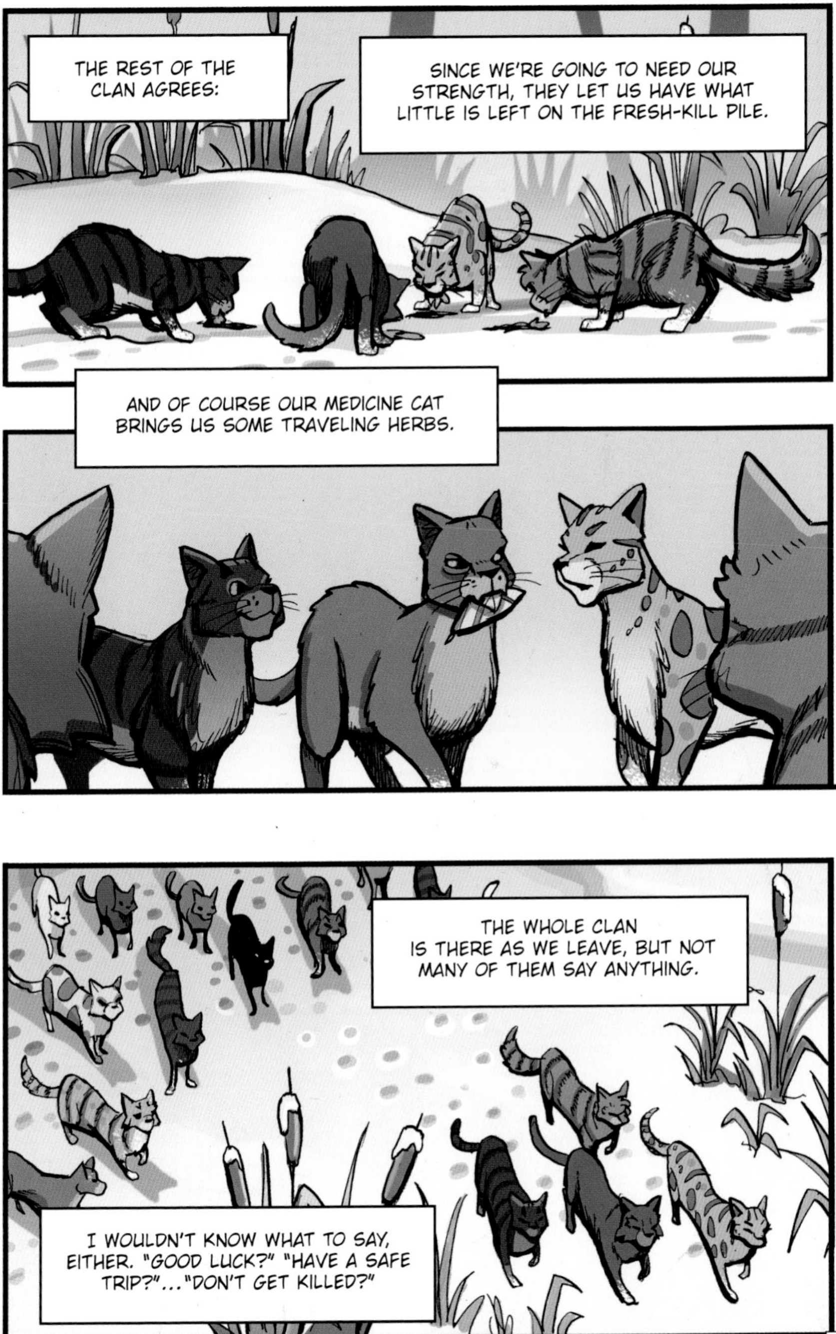
THE REST OF THE CLAN AGREES:
SINCE WE'RE GOING TO NEED OUR STRENGTH, THEY LET US HAVE WHAT LITTLE IS LEFT ON THE FRESH-KILL PILE.
AND OF COURSE OUR MEDICINE CAT BRINGS US SOME TRAVELING HERBS.
THE WHOLE CLAN IS THERE AS WE LEAVE, BUT NOT MANY OF THEM SAY ANYTHING.
I WOULDN'T KNOW WHAT TO SAY, EITHER. "GOOD LUCK?" "HAVE A SAFE TRIP?"..."DON'T GET KILLED?"

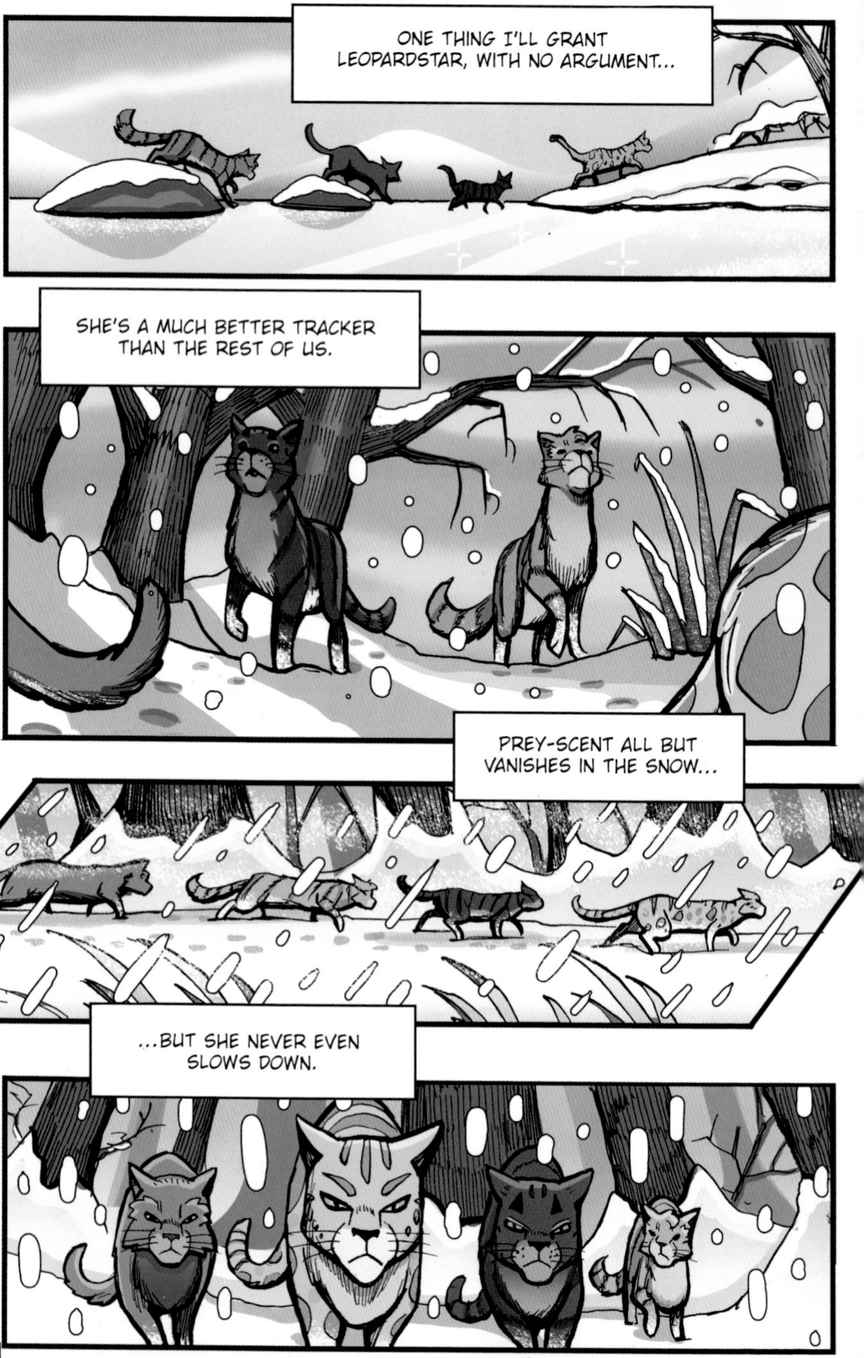
ONE THING I'LL GRANT LEOPARDSTAR, WITH NO ARGUMENT...
SHE'S A MUCH BETTER TRACKER THAN THE REST OF US.
PREY-SCENT ALL BUT VANISHES IN THE SNOW...
...BUT SHE NEVER EVEN SLOWS DOWN.

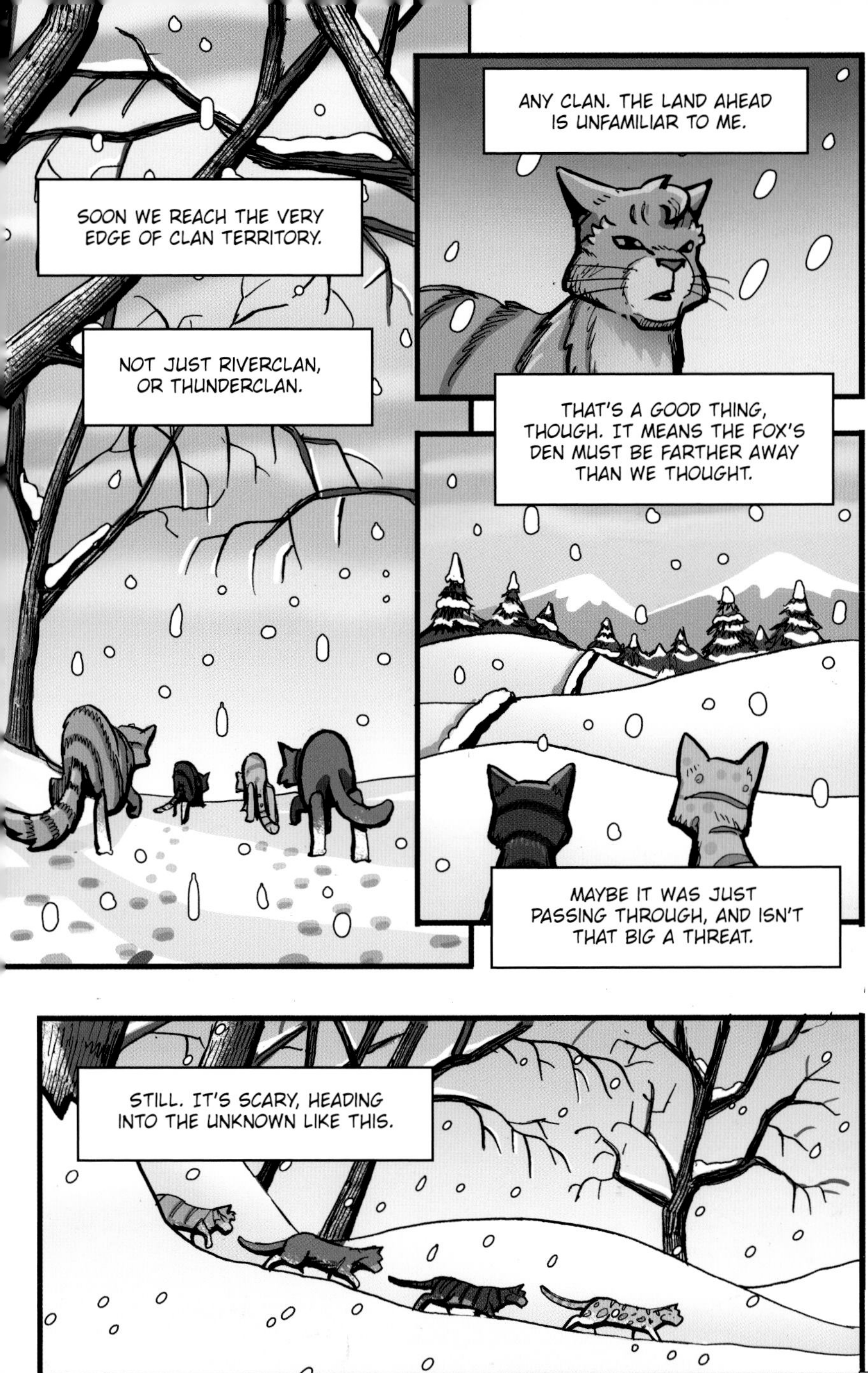
SOON WE REACH THE VERY EDGE OF CLAN TERRITORY.
NOT JUST RIVERCLAN, OR THUNDERCLAN.
ANY CLAN. THE LAND AHEAD IS UNFAMILIAR TO ME.
THAT'S A GOOD THING, THOUGH. IT MEANS THE FOX'S DEN MUST BE FARTHER AWAY THAN WE THOUGHT.
MAYBE IT WAS JUST PASSING THROUGH, AND ISN'T THAT BIG A THREAT.
STILL. IT'S SCARY, HEADING INTO THE UNKNOWN LIKE THIS.

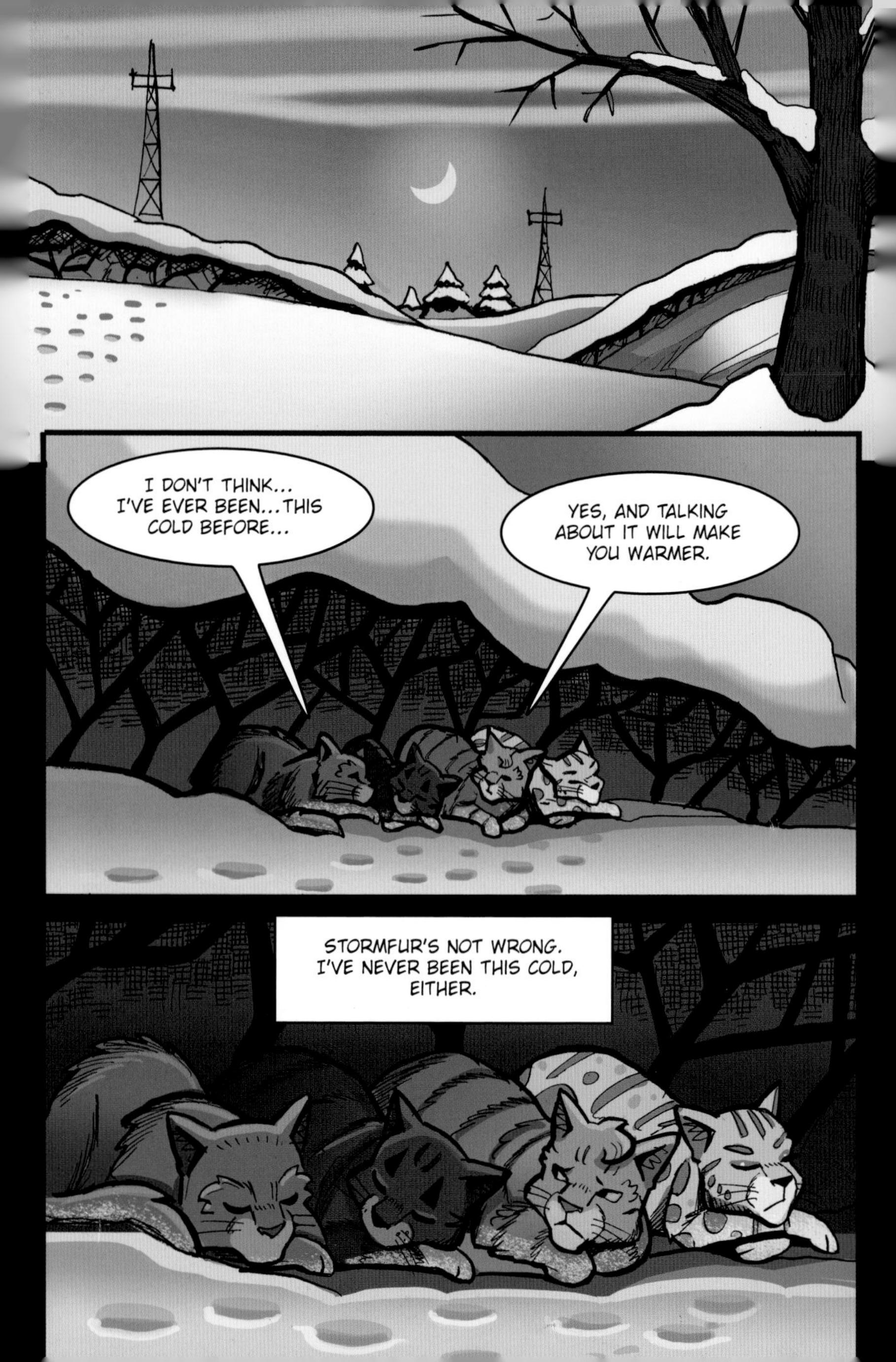

I DON'T THINK... I'VE EVER BEEN... THIS COLD BEFORE...
YES, AND TALKING ABOUT IT WILL MAKE YOU WARMER.
STORMFUR'S NOT WRONG. I'VE NEVER BEEN THIS COLD, EITHER.

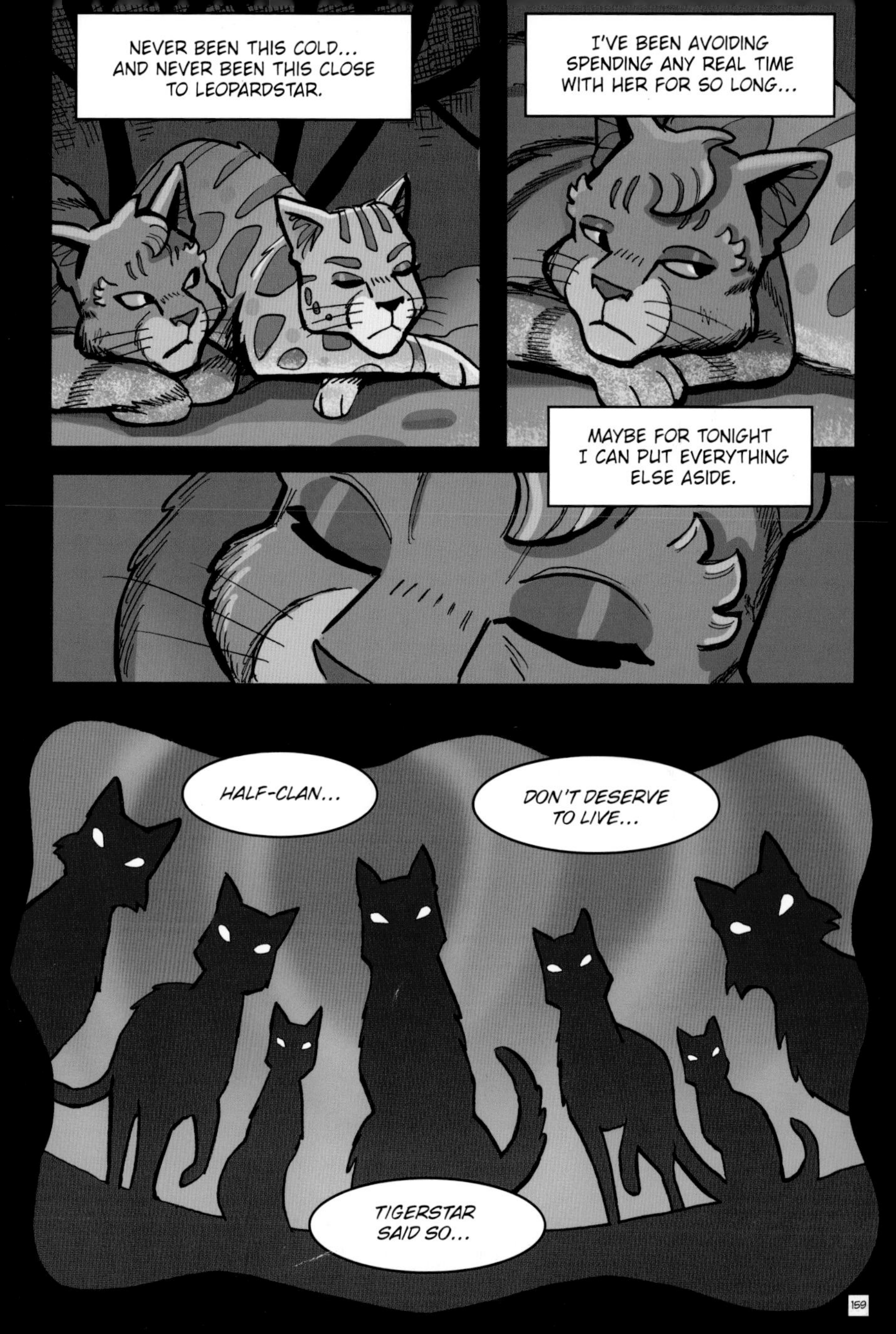
NEVER BEEN THIS COLD... AND NEVER BEEN THIS CLOSE TO LEOPARDSTAR.
I'VE BEEN AVOIDING SPENDING ANY REAL TIME WITH HER FOR SO LONG...
MAYBE FOR TONIGHT I CAN PUT EVERYTHING ELSE ASIDE.
HALF-CLAN...
DON'T DESERVE TO LIVE...
TIGERSTAR SAID SO...

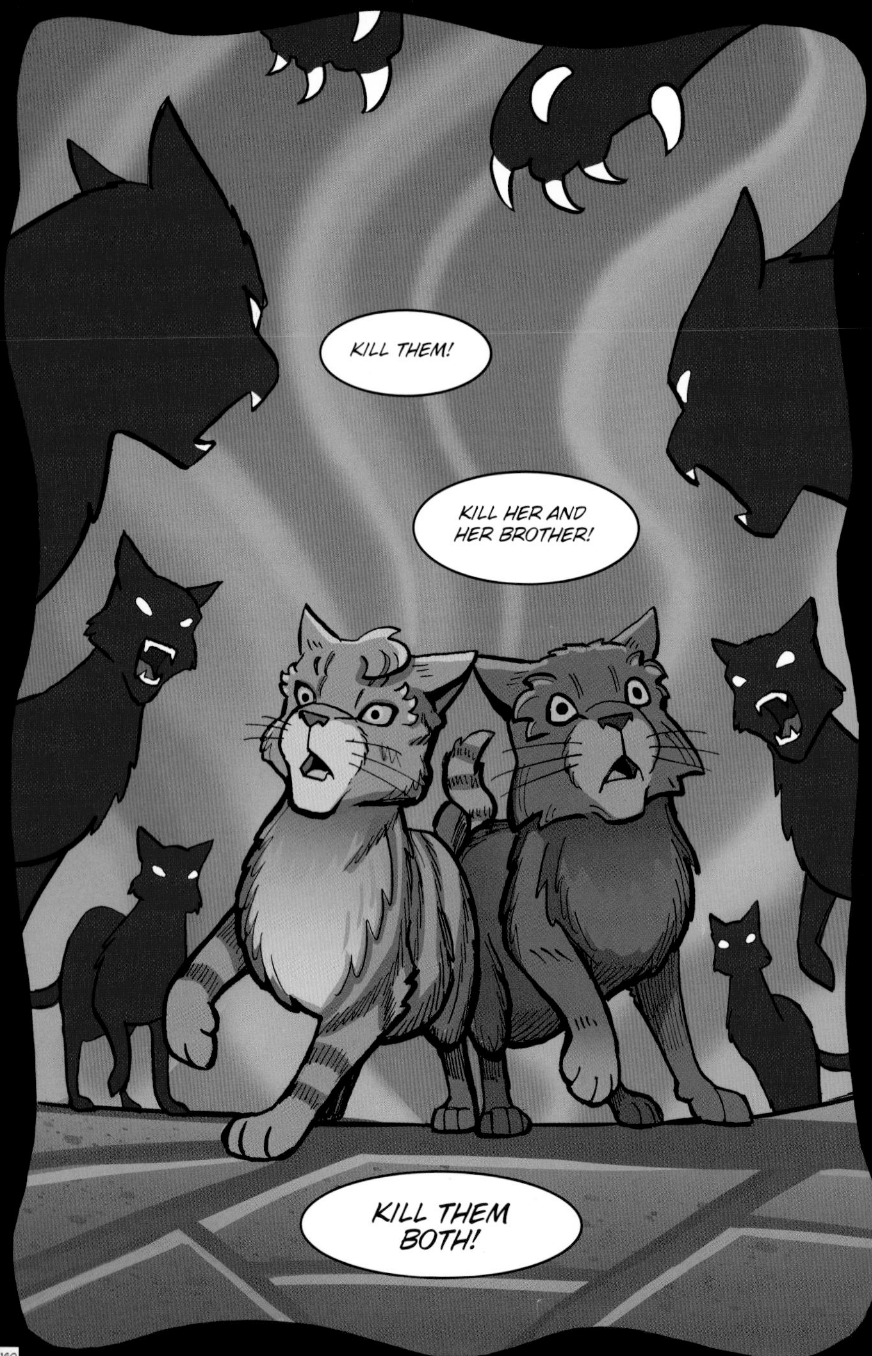
KILL THEM!
KILL HER AND HER BROTHER!
KILL THEM BOTH!

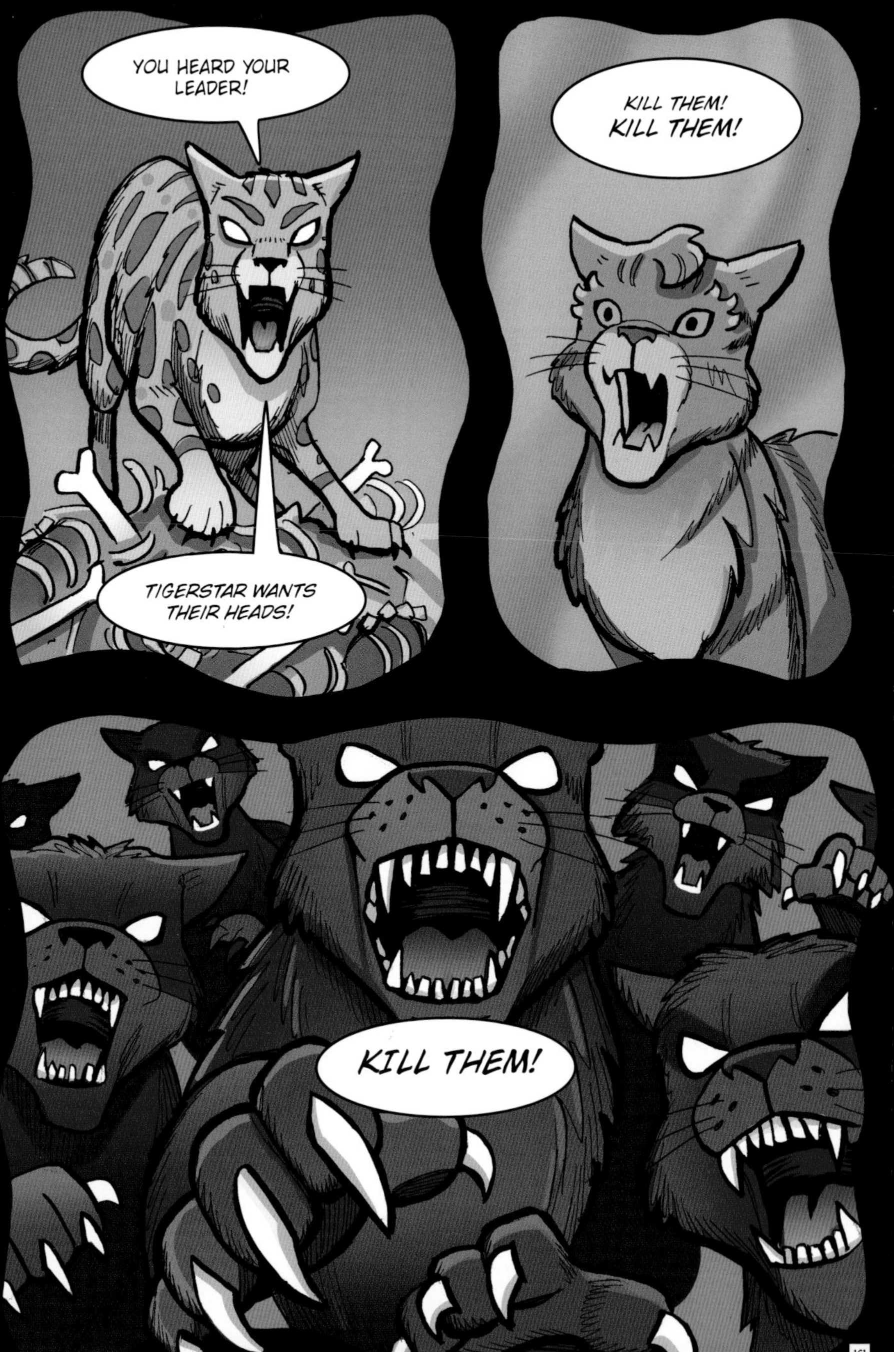
YOU HEARD YOUR LEADER!
TIGERSTAR WANTS THEIR HEADS!
KILL THEM! KILL THEM!
KILL THEM!

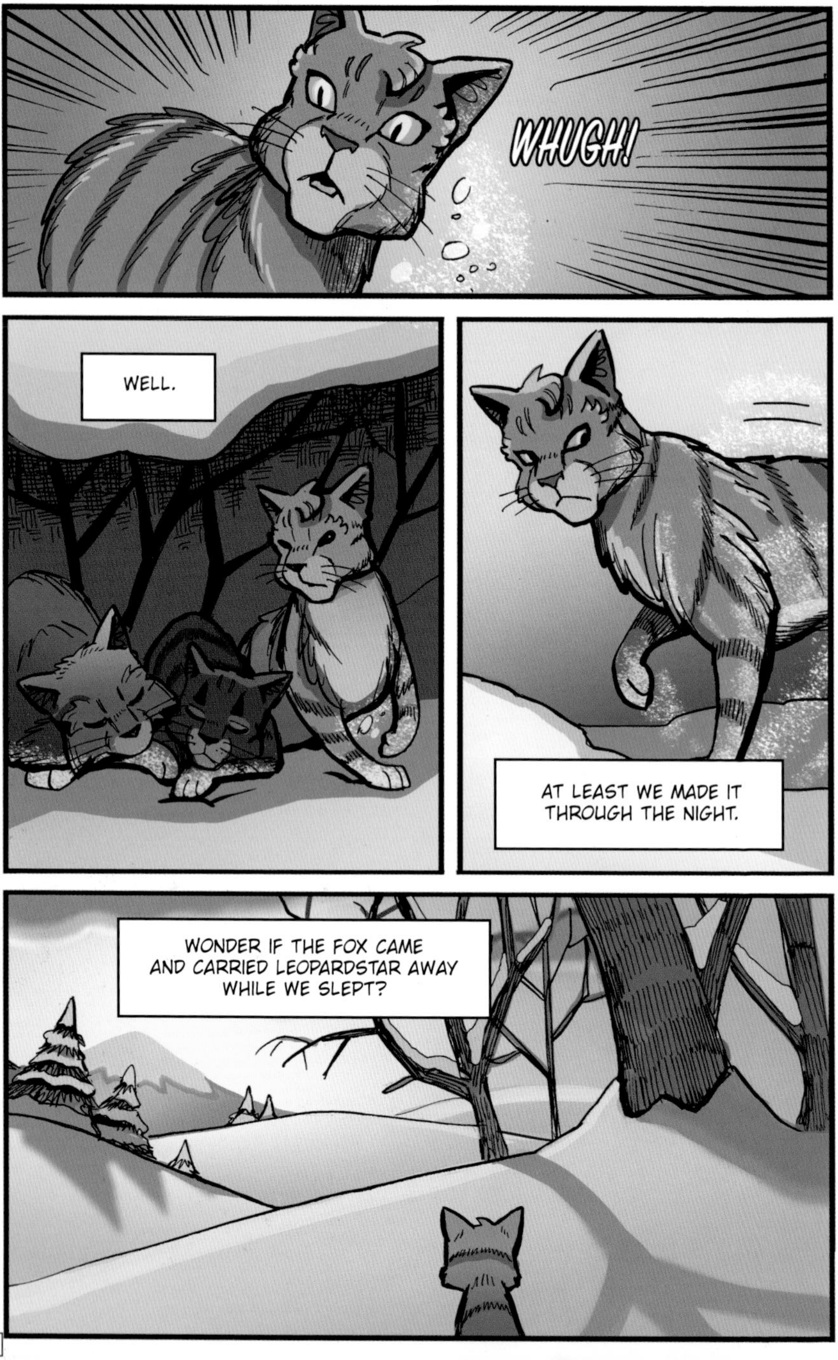
WHUGH!
WELL.
AT LEAST WE MADE IT THROUGH THE NIGHT.
WONDER IF THE FOX CAME AND CARRIED LEOPARDSTAR AWAY WHILE WE SLEPT?

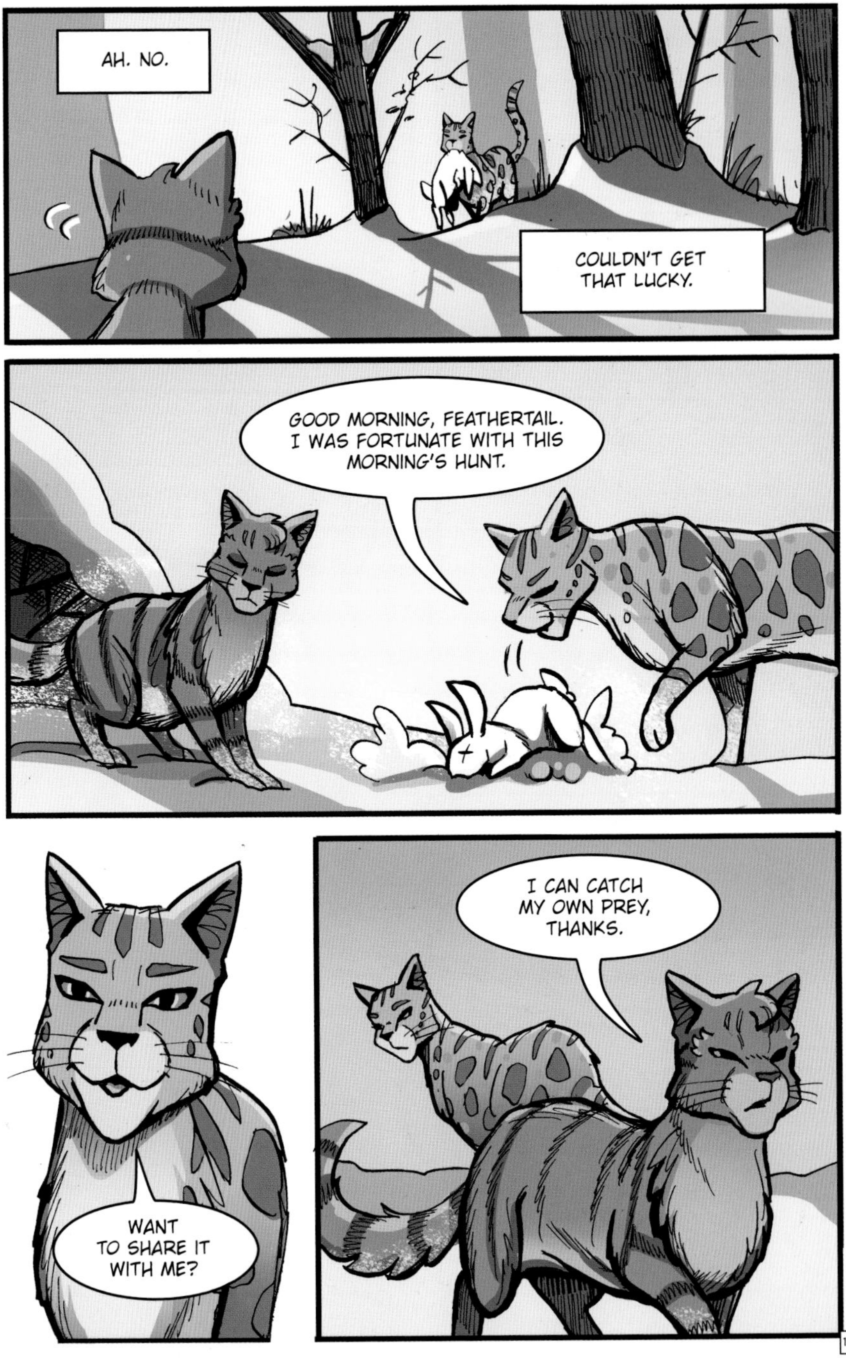
AH. NO.
COULDN'T GET THAT LUCKY.
GOOD MORNING, FEATHERTAIL. I WAS FORTUNATE WITH THIS MORNING'S HUNT.
WANT TO SHARE IT WITH ME?
I CAN CATCH MY OWN PREY, THANKS.

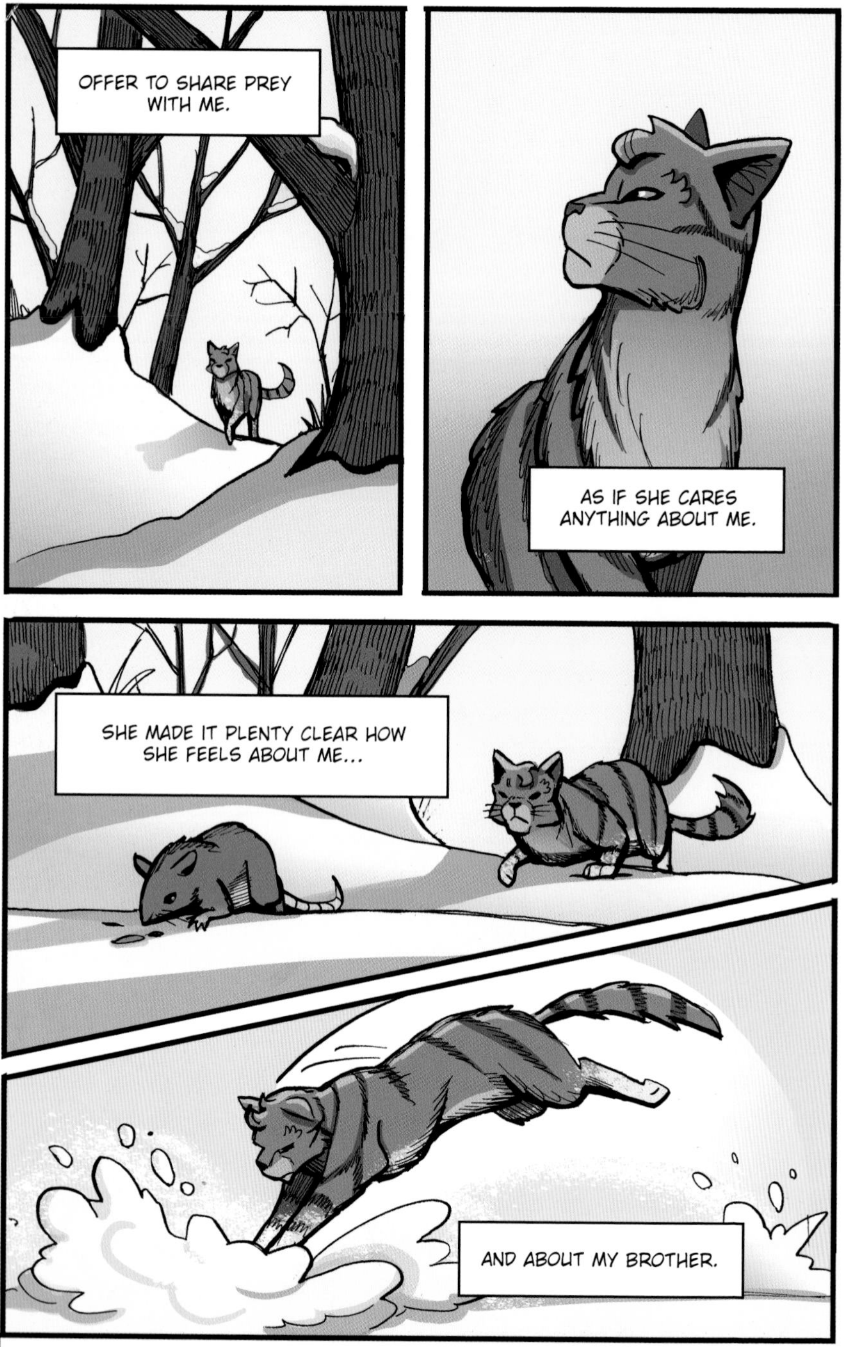
OFFER TO SHARE PREY WITH ME.
AS IF SHE CARES ANYTHING ABOUT ME.
SHE MADE IT PLENTY CLEAR HOW SHE FEELS ABOUT ME...
AND ABOUT MY BROTHER.

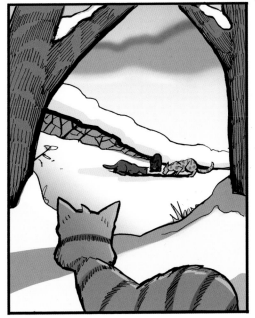

I WANT NOTHING FROM HER.

•  •  •

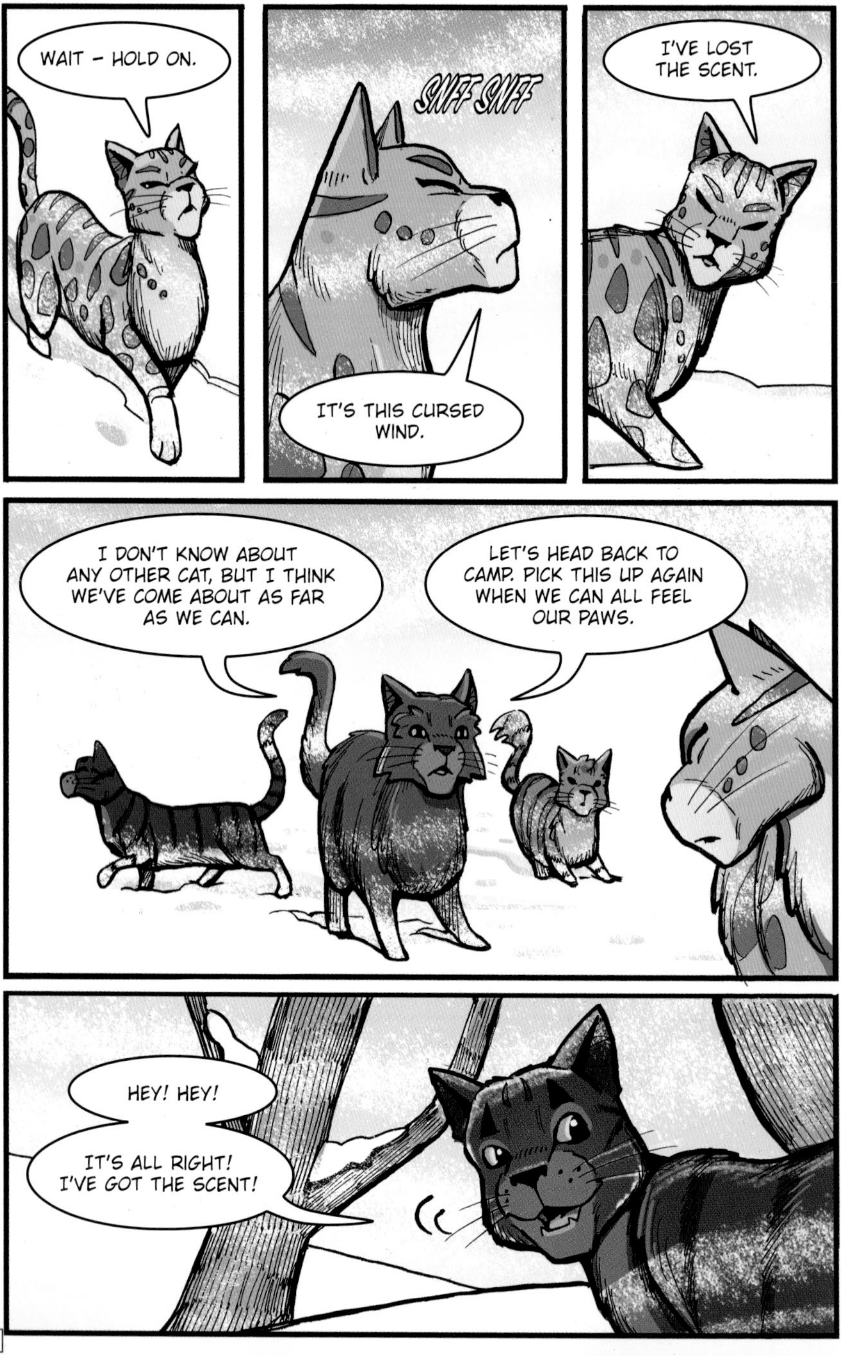
WAIT – HOLD ON.
SNIFF SNIFF
IT'S THIS CURSED WIND.
I'VE LOST THE SCENT.
I DON'T KNOW ABOUT ANY OTHER CAT, BUT I THINK WE'VE COME ABOUT AS FAR AS WE CAN.
LET'S HEAD BACK TO CAMP. PICK THIS UP AGAIN WHEN WE CAN ALL FEEL OUR PAWS.
HEY! HEY!
IT'S ALL RIGHT! I'VE GOT THE SCENT!

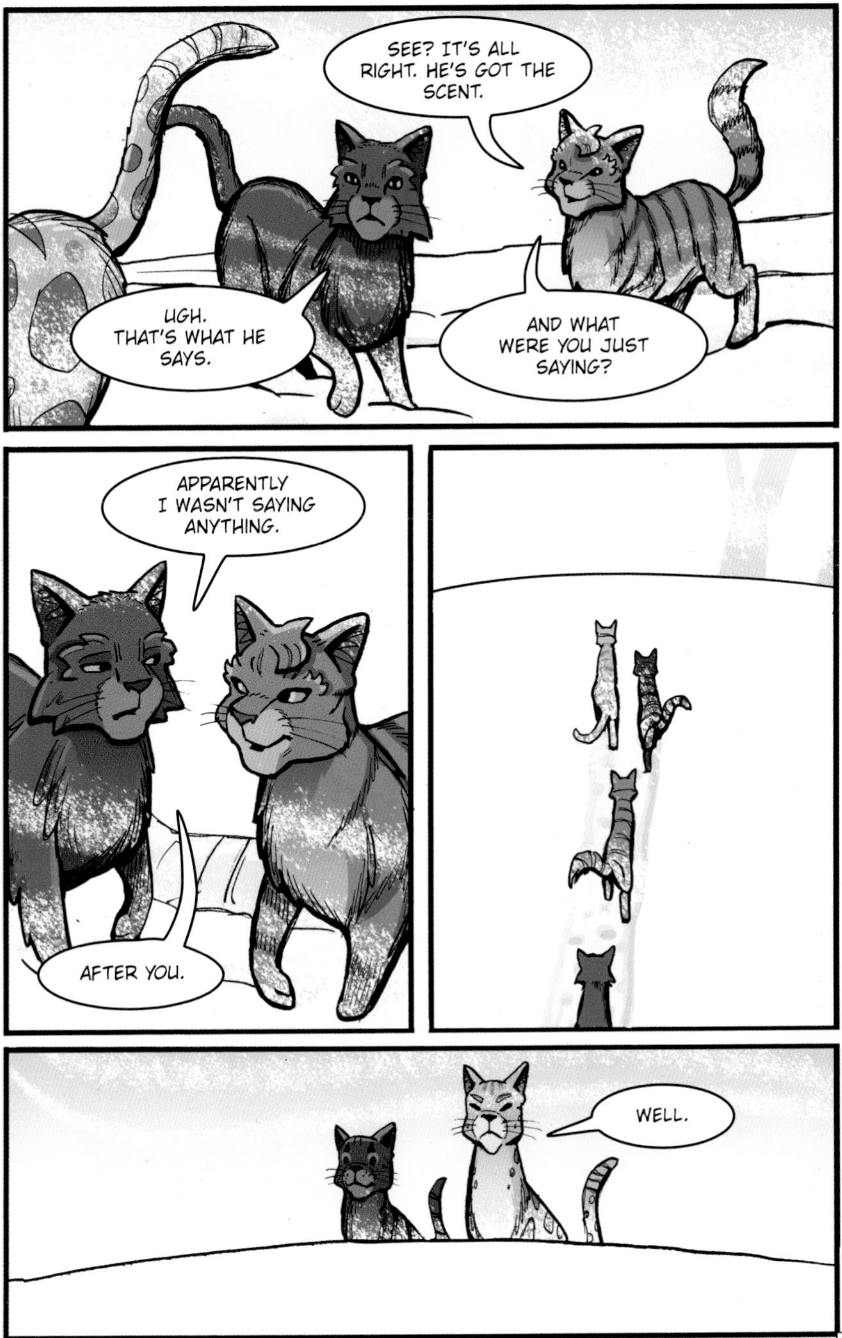
SEE? IT'S ALL RIGHT. HE'S GOT THE SCENT.
UGH. THAT'S WHAT HE SAYS.
AND WHAT WERE YOU JUST SAYING?
APPARENTLY I WASN'T SAYING ANYTHING.
AFTER YOU.
WELL.

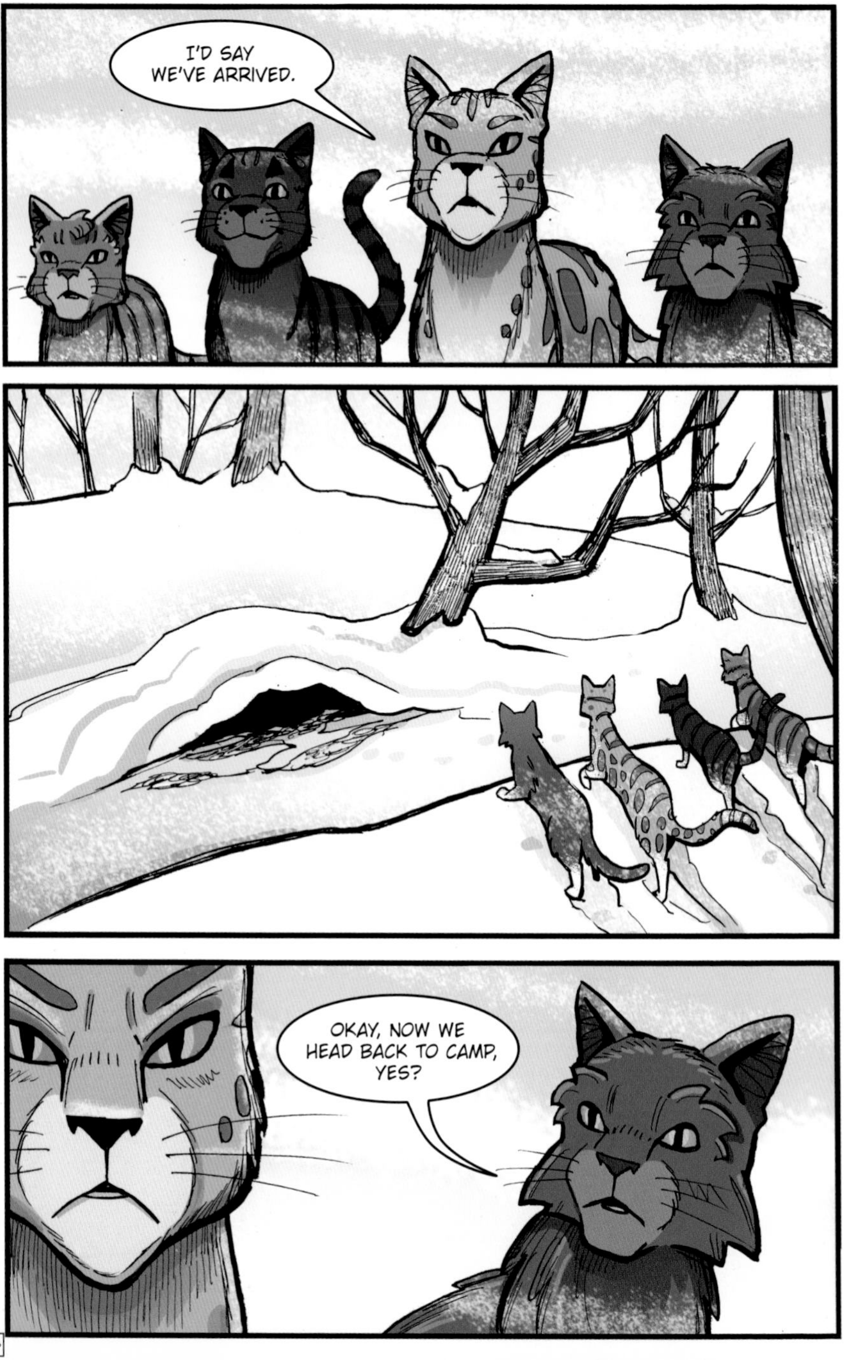
I'D SAY WE'VE ARRIVED.
OKAY, NOW WE HEAD BACK TO CAMP, YES?

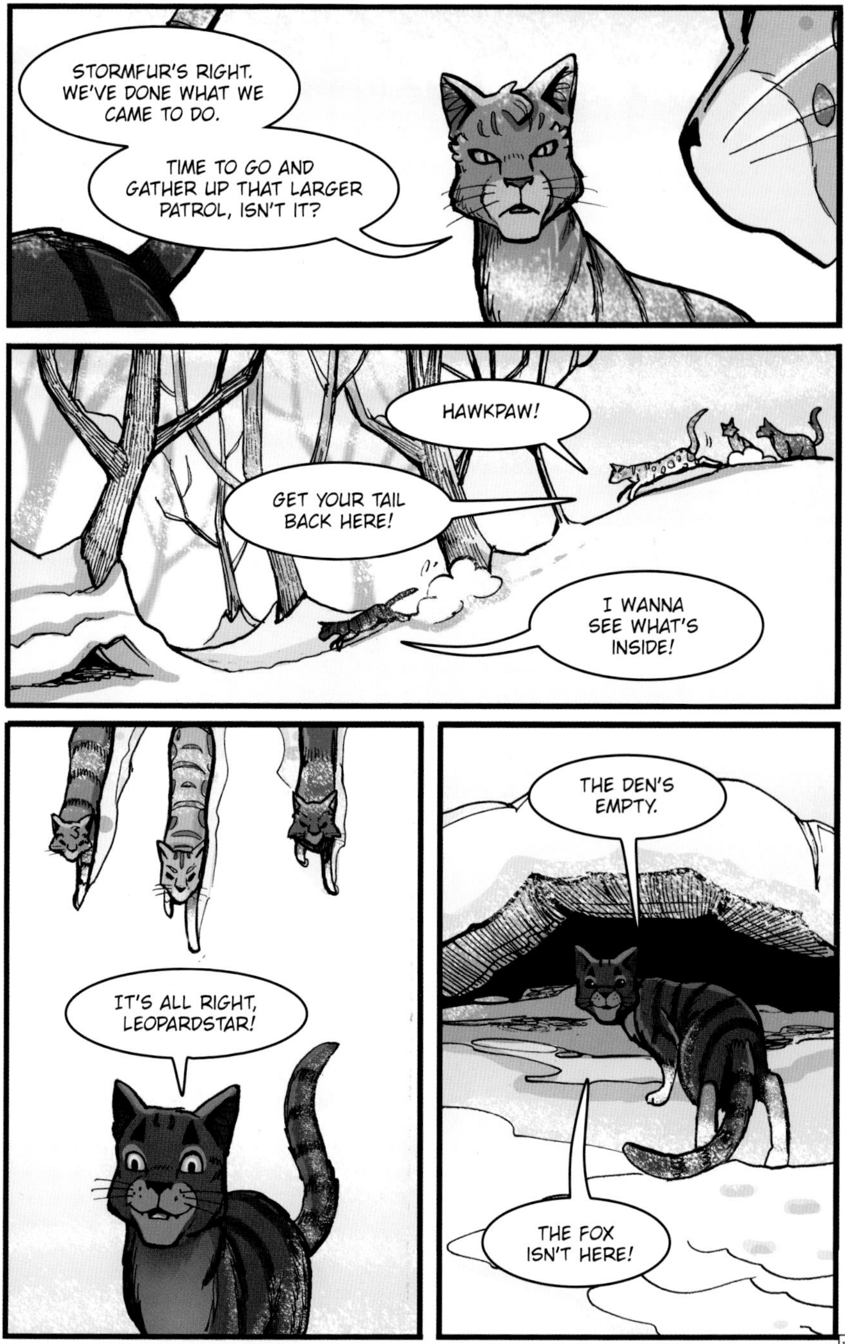
STORMFUR'S RIGHT. WE'VE DONE WHAT WE CAME TO DO.
TIME TO GO AND GATHER UP THAT LARGER PATROL, ISN'T IT?
HAWKPAW!
GET YOUR TAIL BACK HERE!
I WANNA SEE WHAT'S INSIDE!
IT'S ALL RIGHT, LEOPARDSTAR!
THE DEN'S EMPTY.
THE FOX ISN'T HERE!

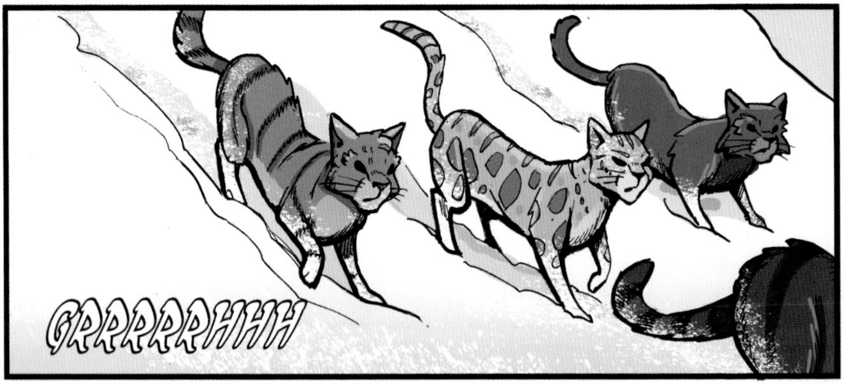
GRRRRRHHH

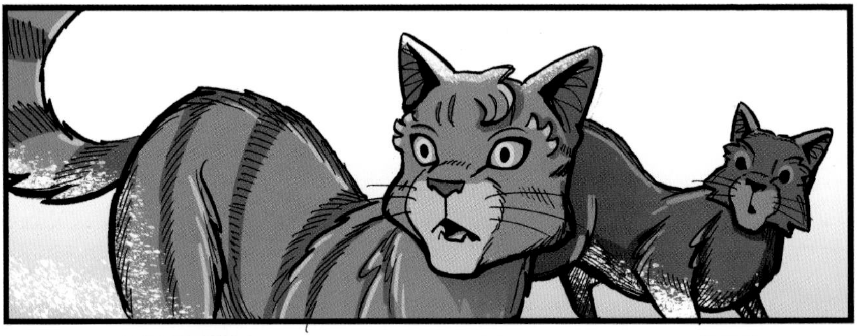

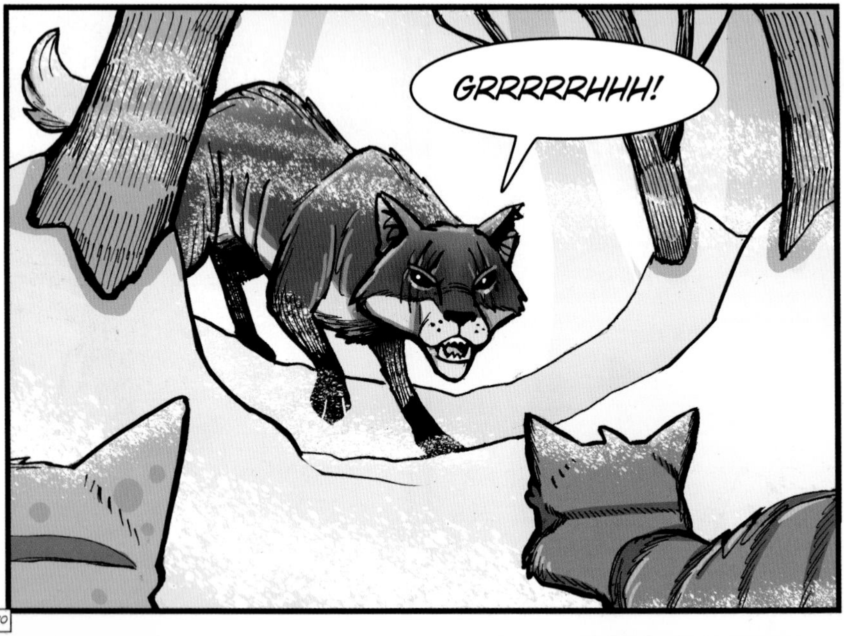
GRRRRRHHH!

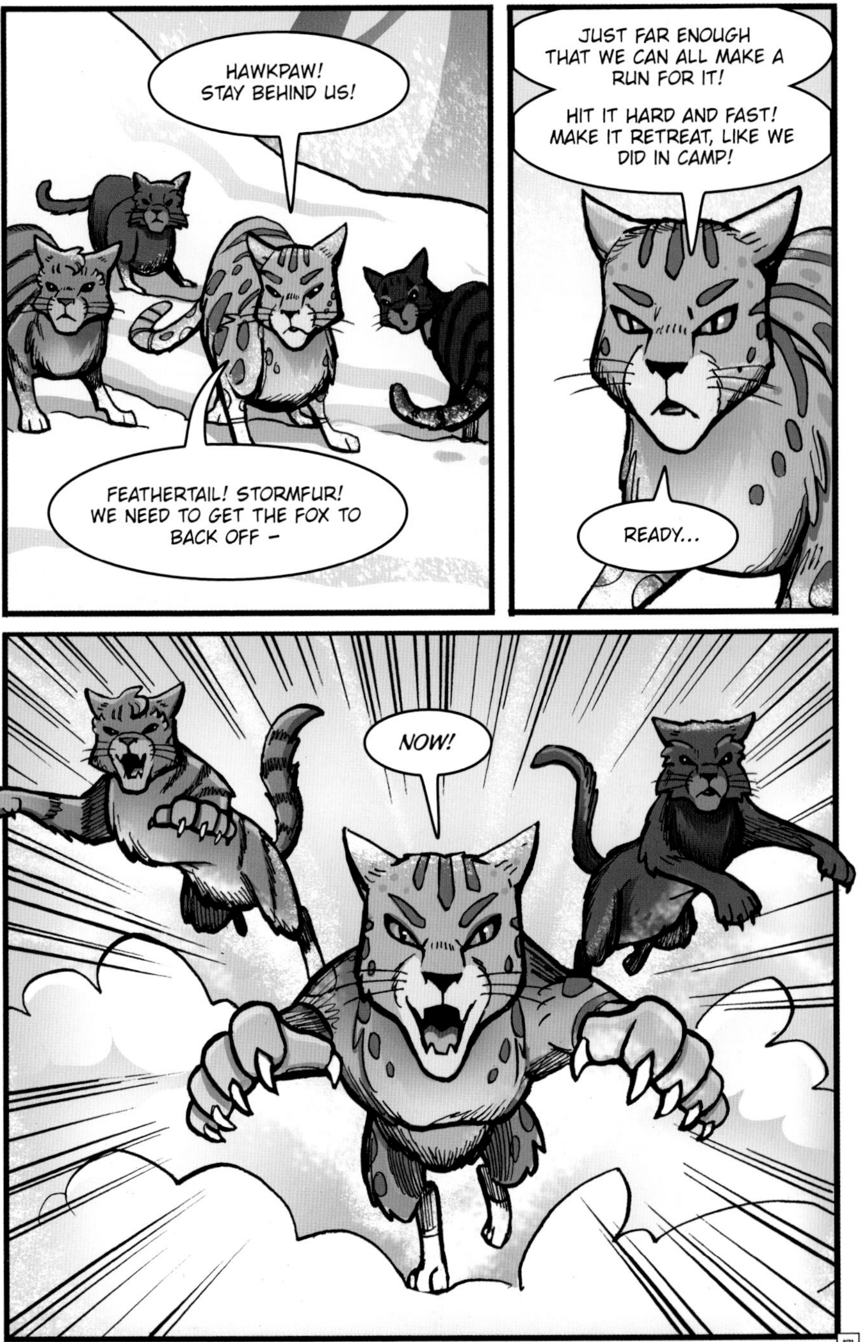
HAWKPAW! STAY BEHIND US!
FEATHERTAIL! STORMFUR! WE NEED TO GET THE FOX TO BACK OFF –
JUST FAR ENOUGH THAT WE CAN ALL MAKE A RUN FOR IT!
HIT IT HARD AND FAST! MAKE IT RETREAT, LIKE WE DID IN CAMP!
READY...
NOW!

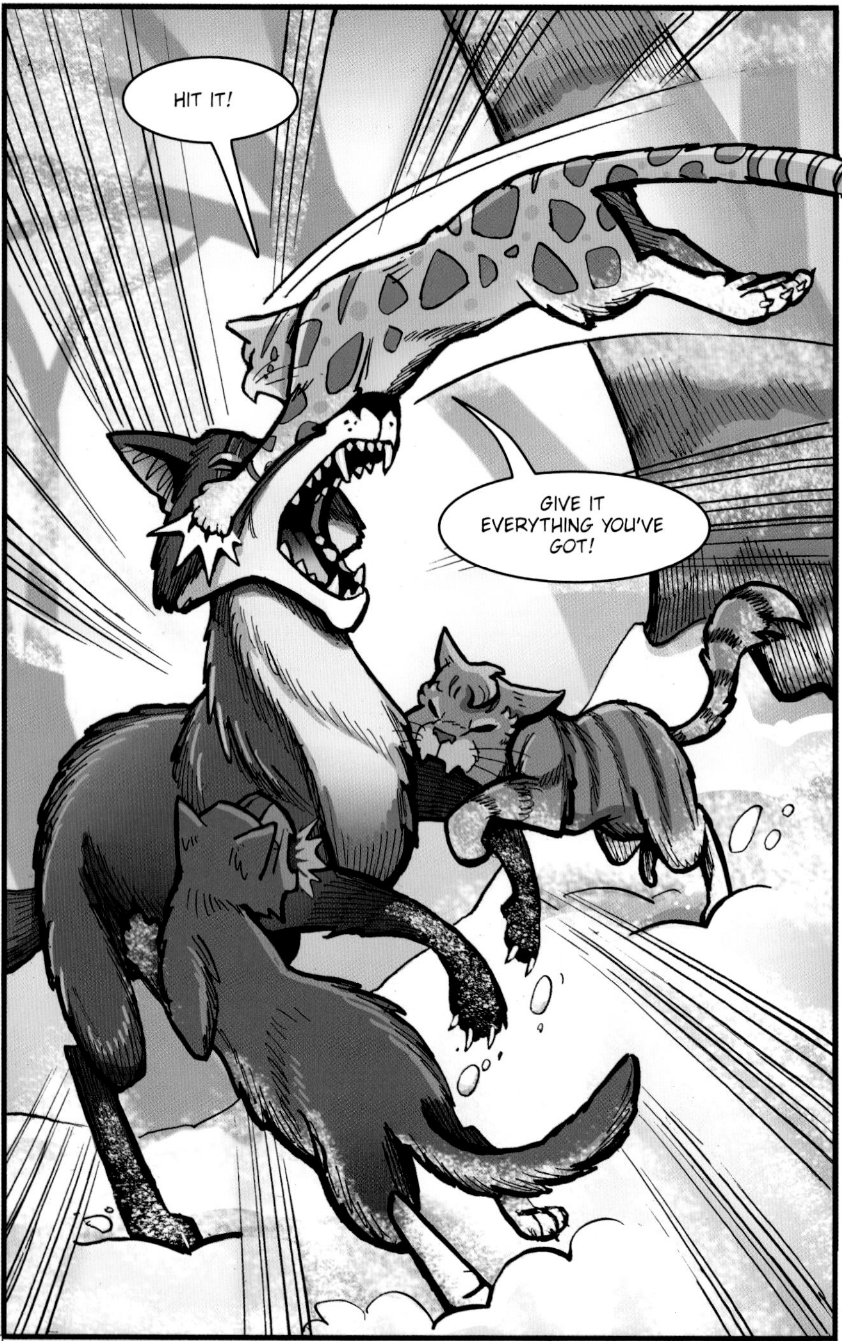
HIT IT!
GIVE IT EVERYTHING YOU'VE GOT!

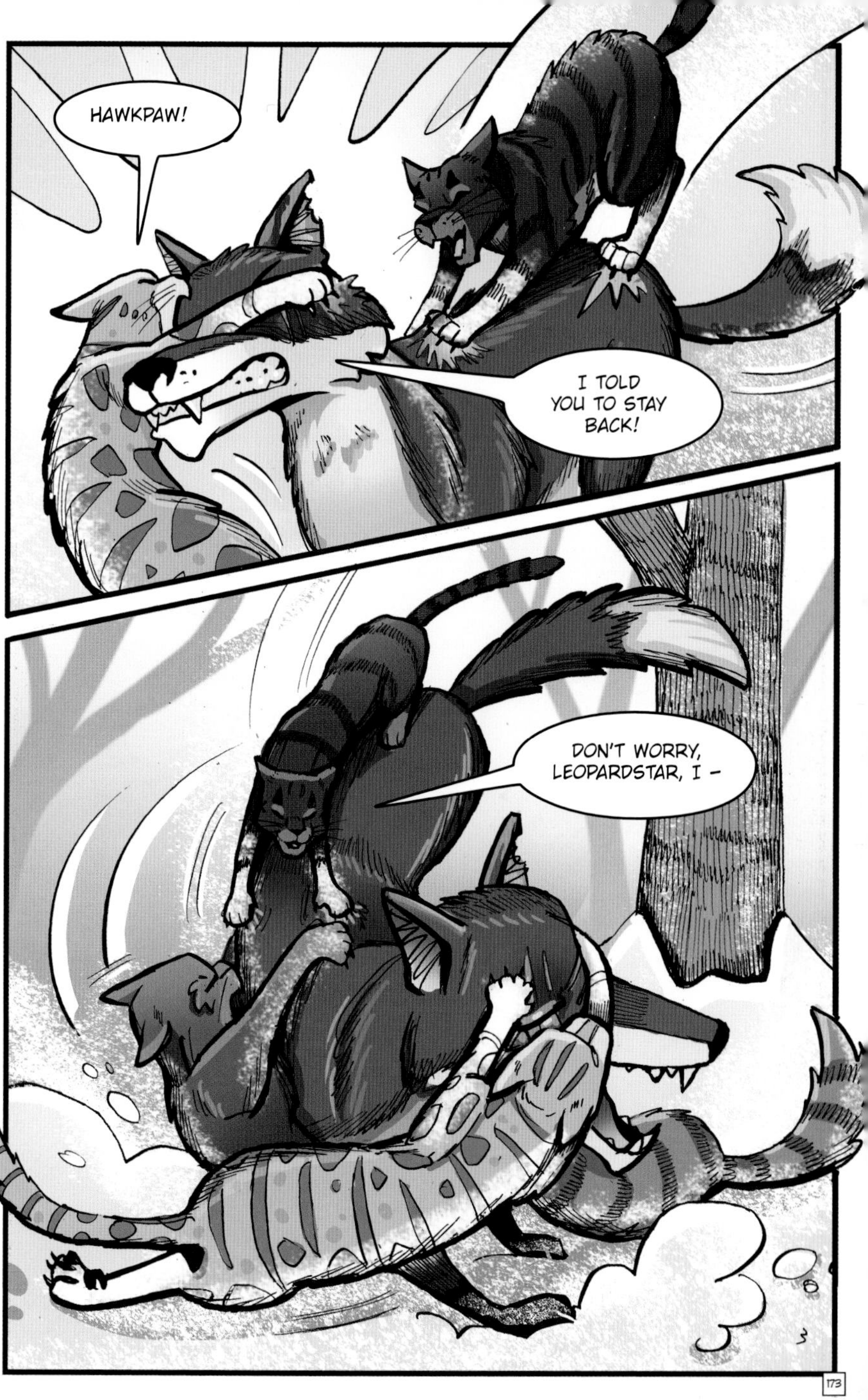
HAWKPAW!
I TOLD YOU TO STAY BACK!
DON'T WORRY, LEOPARDSTAR, I –

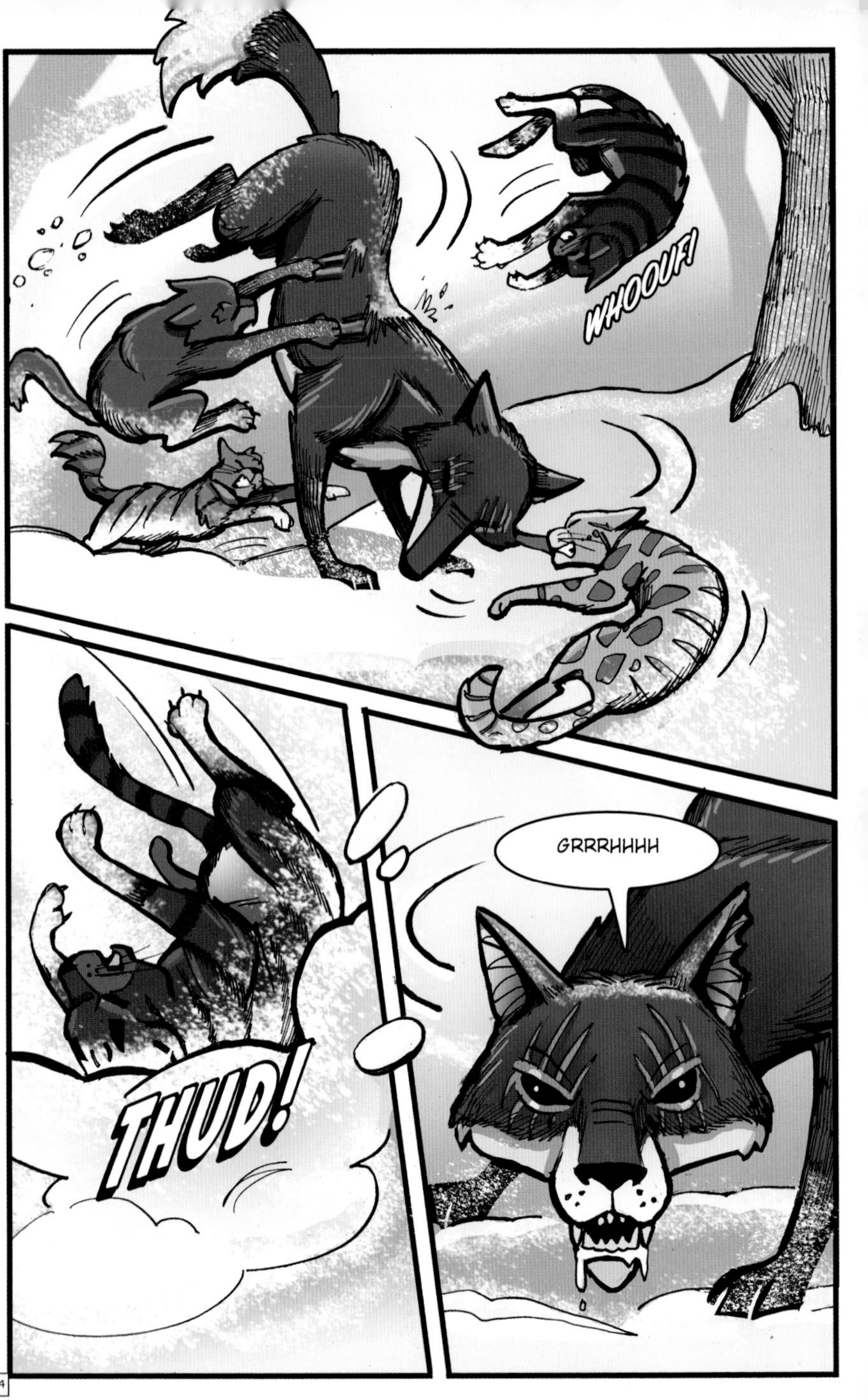
WHOOUF!
THUD!
GRRRHHHH

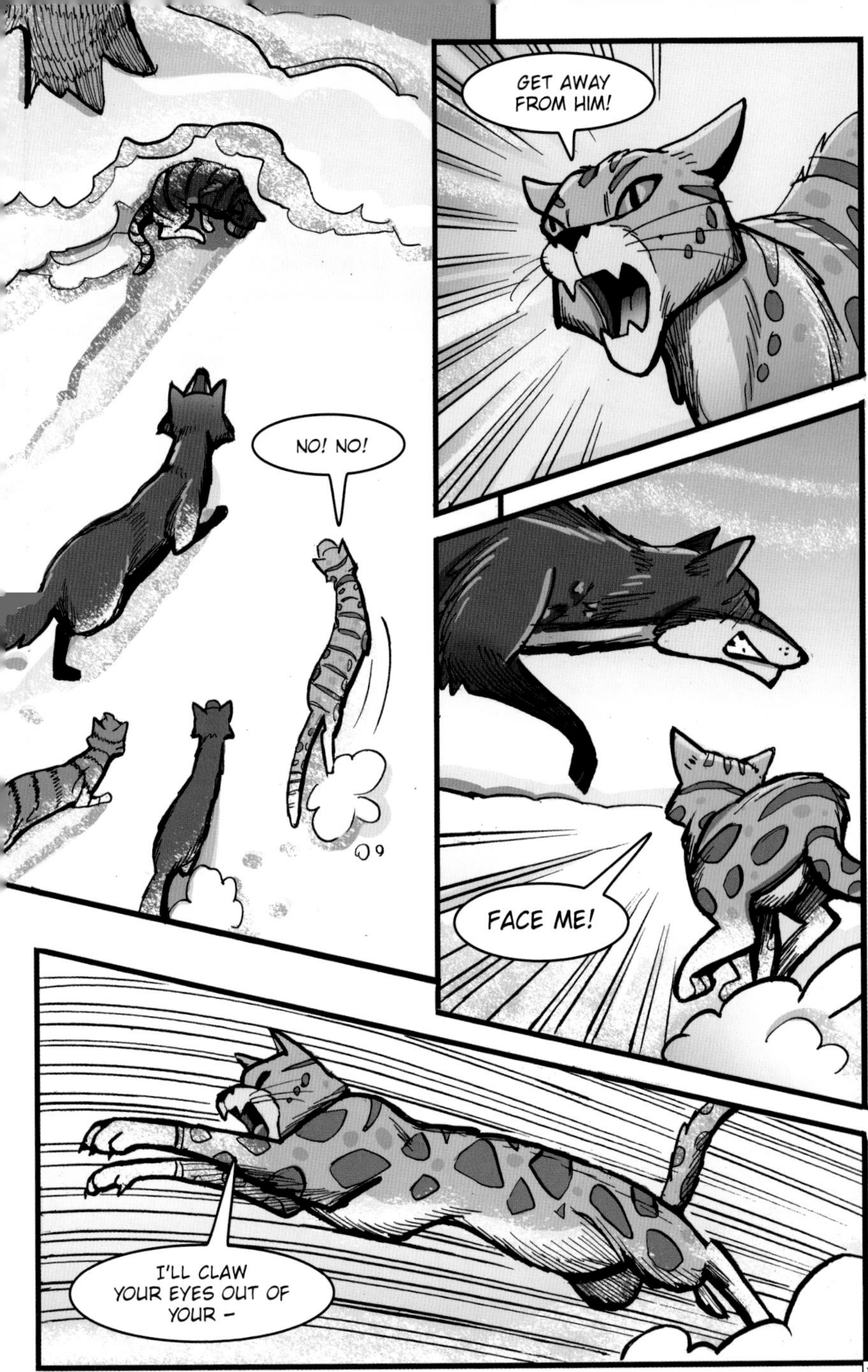
GET AWAY FROM HIM!
NO! NO!
FACE ME!
I'LL CLAW YOUR EYES OUT OF YOUR –

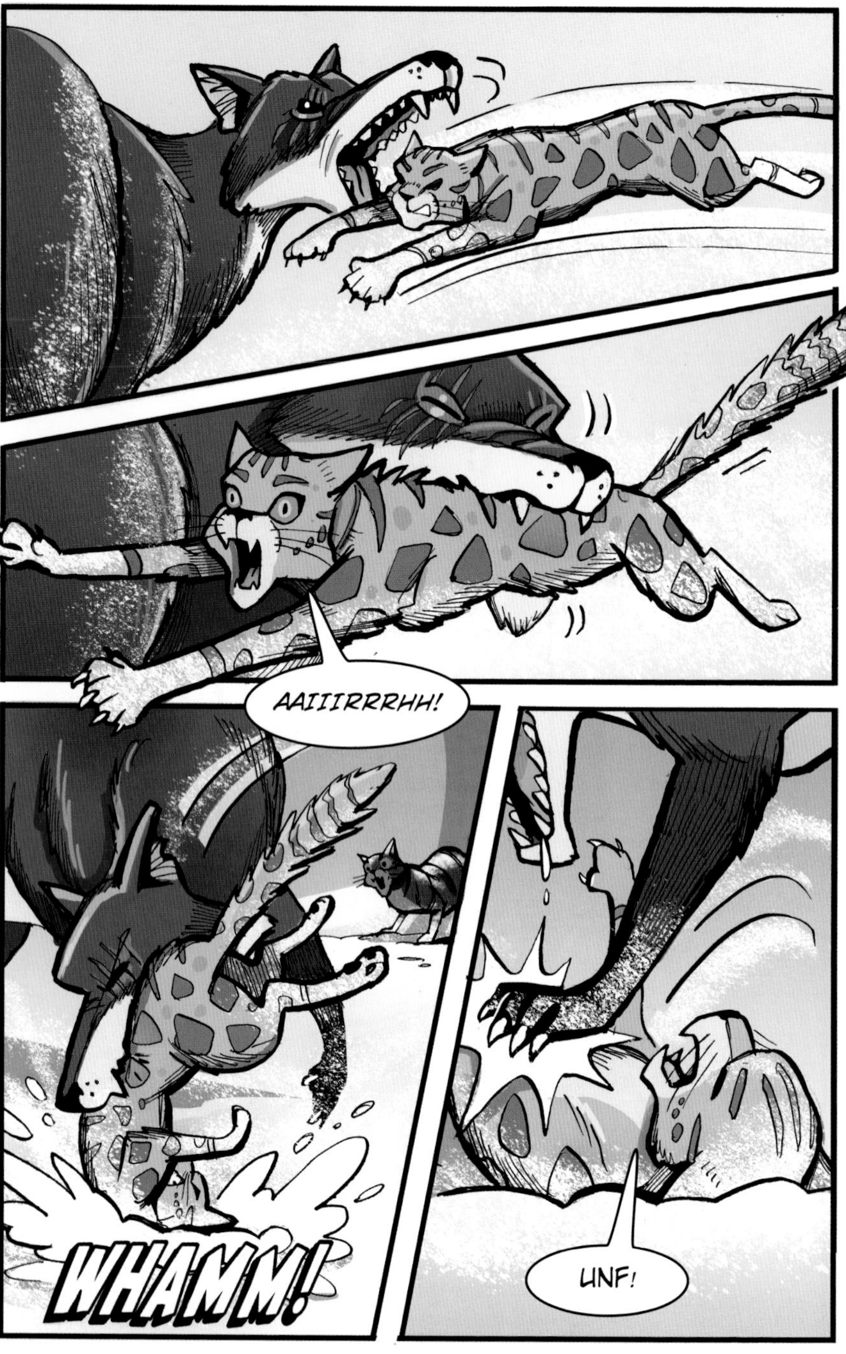
AAIIIRRRHH!
WHAMM!
UNF!

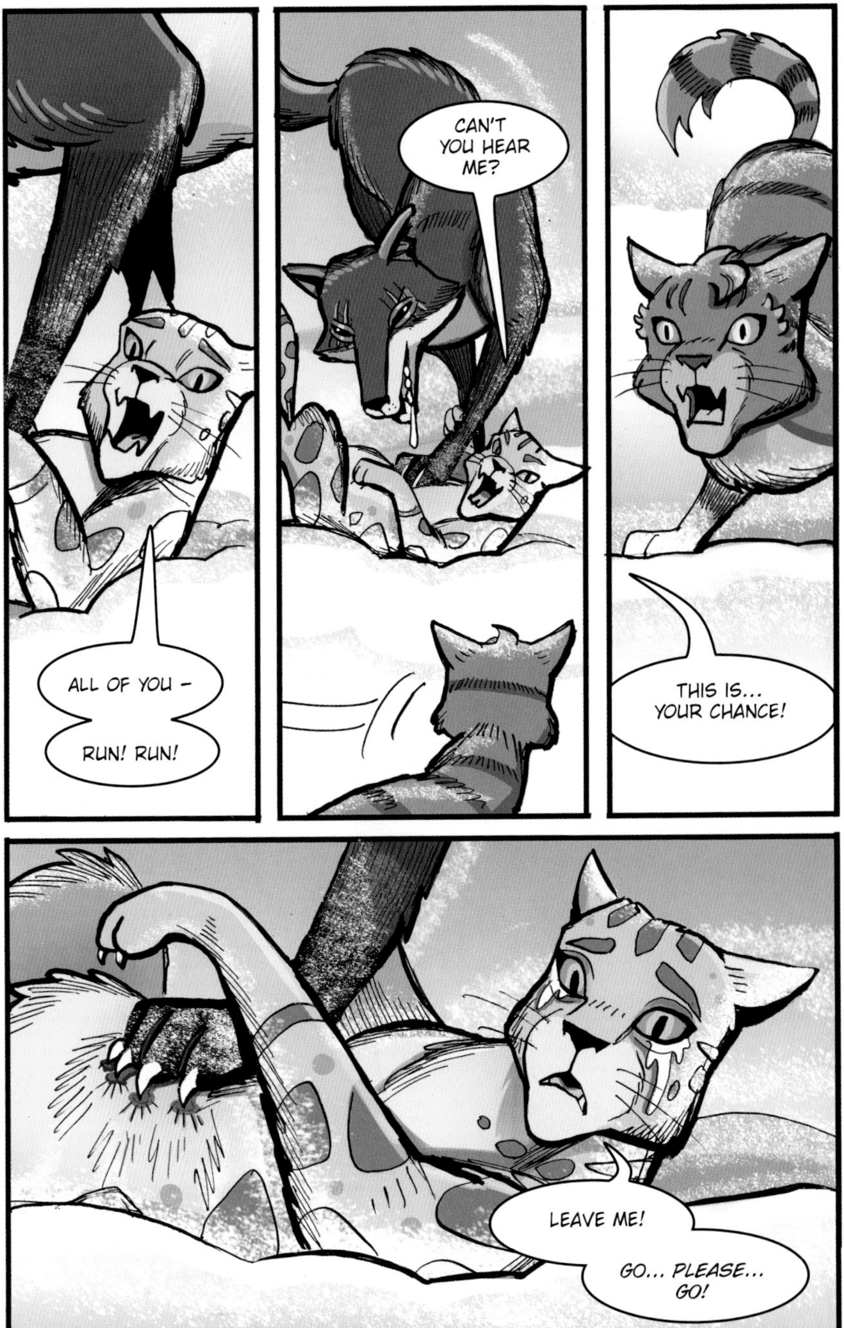
ALL OF YOU –
RUN! RUN!
CAN'T YOU HEAR ME?
THIS IS... YOUR CHANCE!
LEAVE ME!
GO... PLEASE... GO!

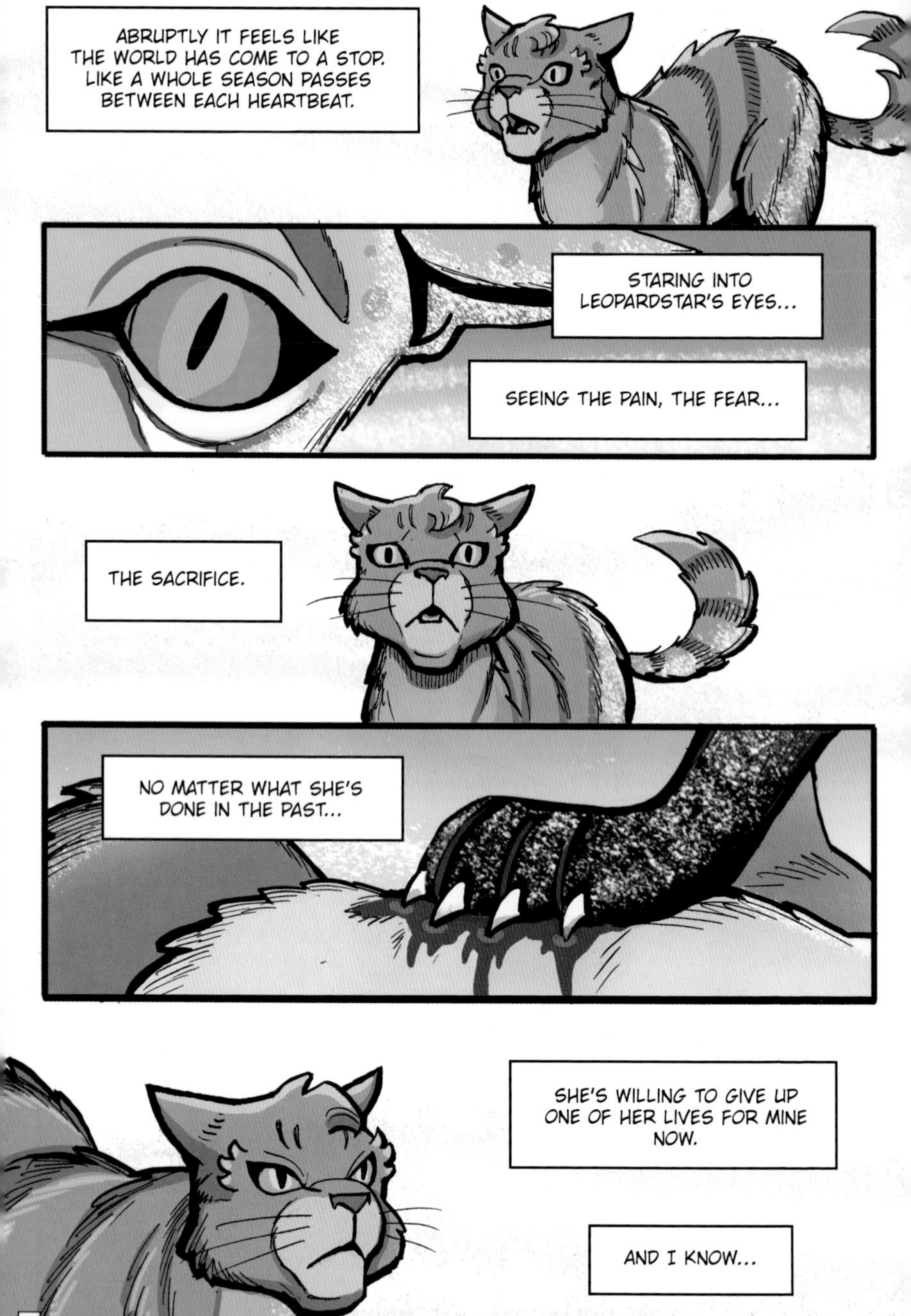
ABRUPTLY IT FEELS LIKE THE WORLD HAS COME TO A STOP. LIKE A WHOLE SEASON PASSES BETWEEN EACH HEARTBEAT.
STARING INTO LEOPARDSTAR'S EYES...
SEEING THE PAIN, THE FEAR...
THE SACRIFICE.
NO MATTER WHAT SHE'S DONE IN THE PAST...
SHE'S WILLING TO GIVE UP ONE OF HER LIVES FOR MINE NOW.
AND I KNOW...

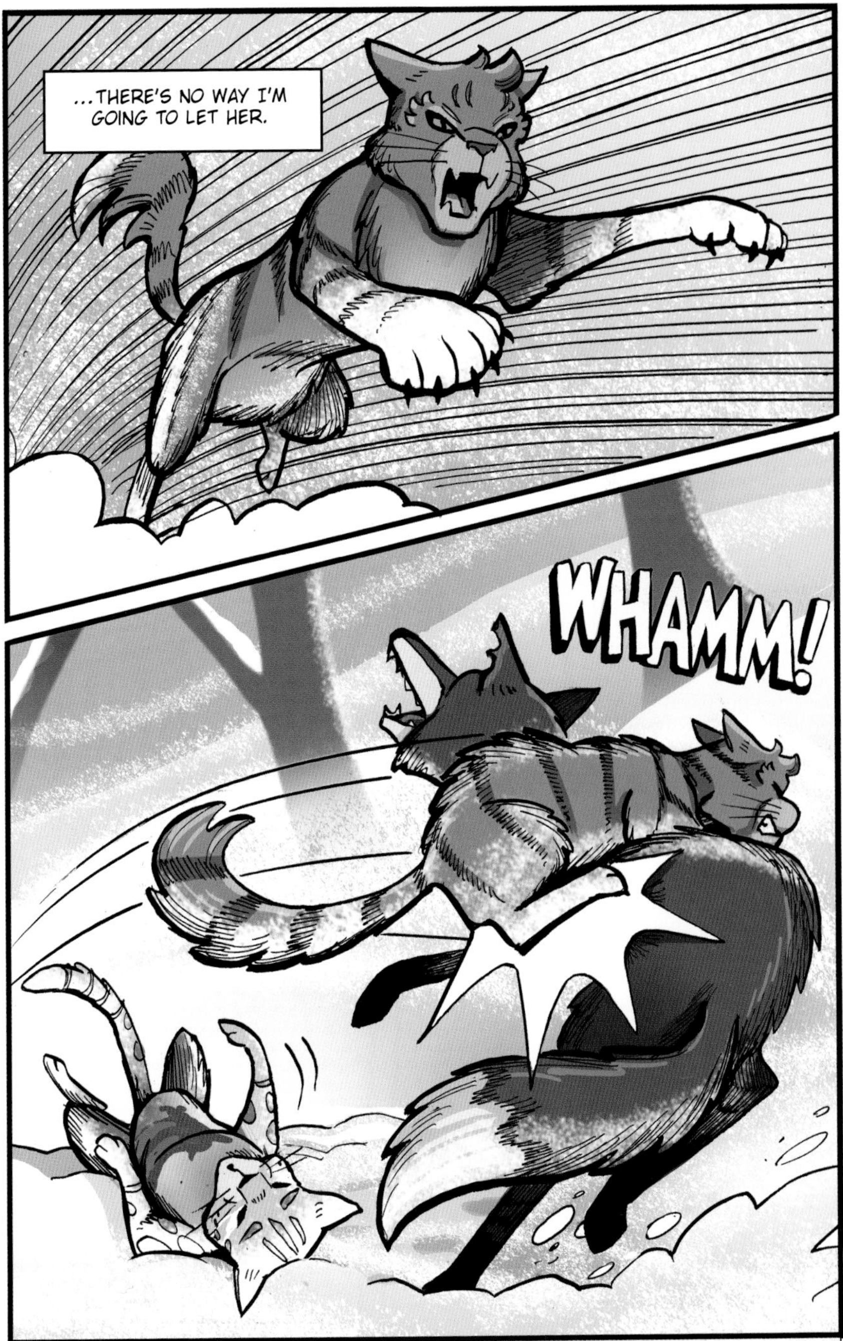
...THERE'S NO WAY I'M GOING TO LET HER.
WHAMM!

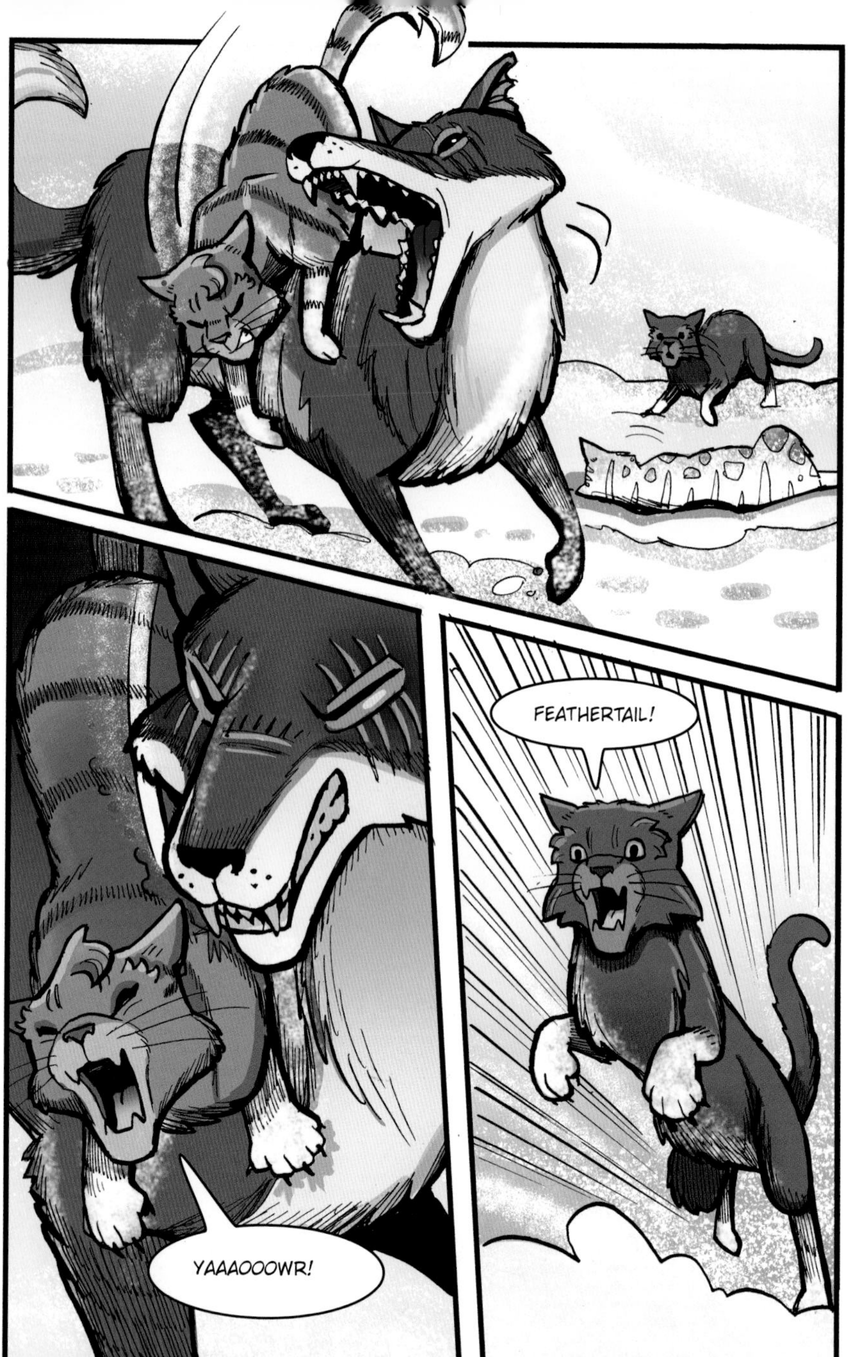
FEATHERTAIL!
YAAAOOOWR!

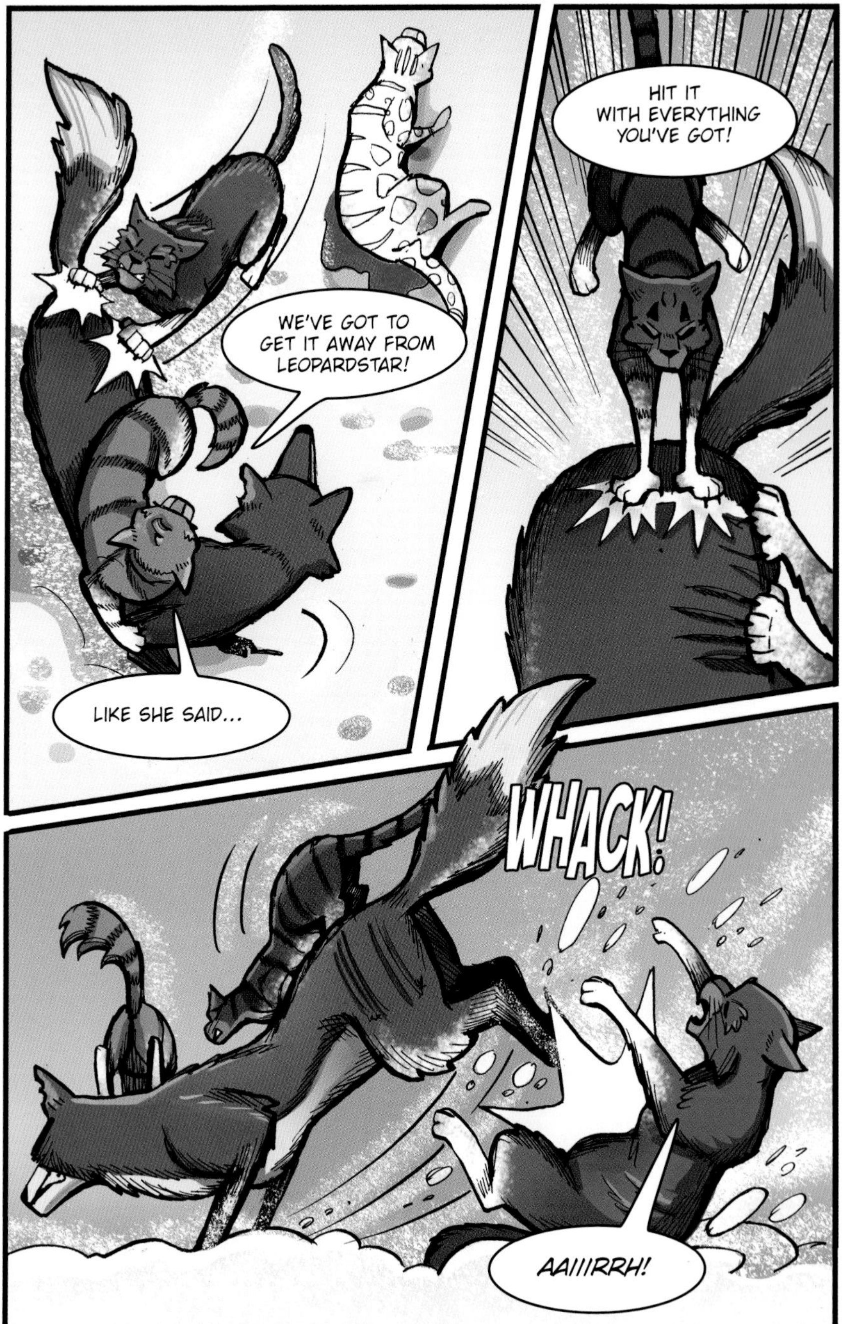
WE'VE GOT TO GET IT AWAY FROM LEOPARDSTAR!
LIKE SHE SAID...
HIT IT WITH EVERYTHING YOU'VE GOT!
WHACK!
AAIIIRRH!

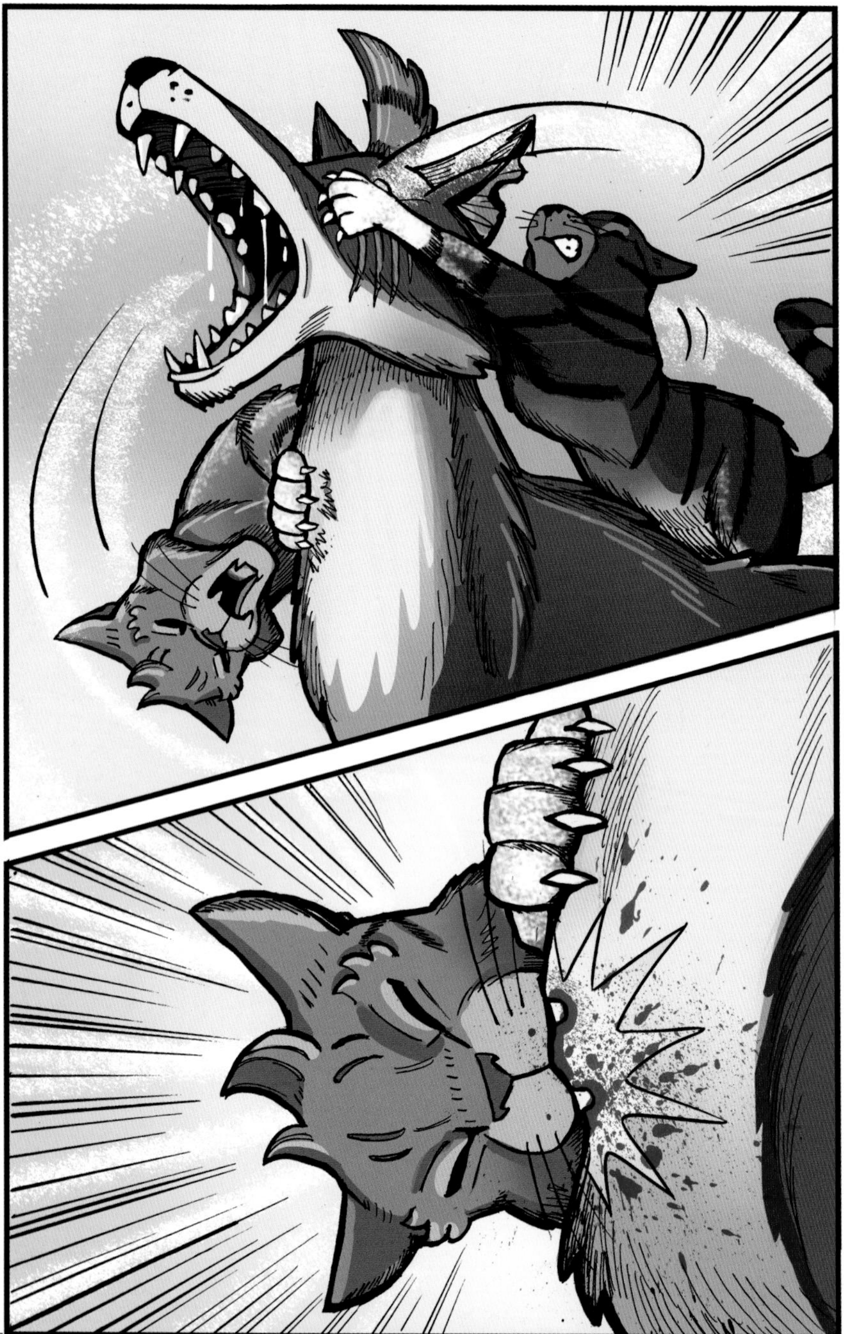

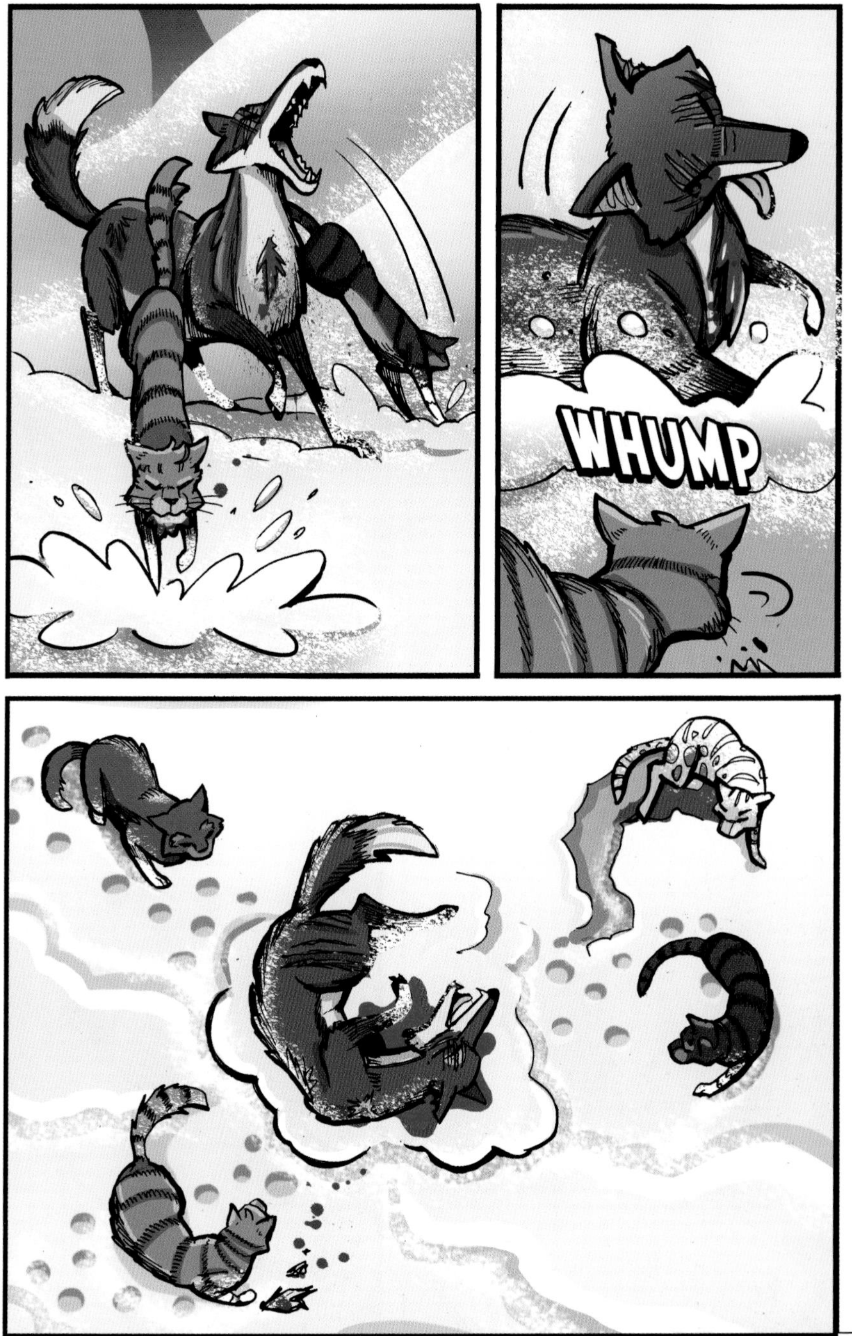
WHUMP

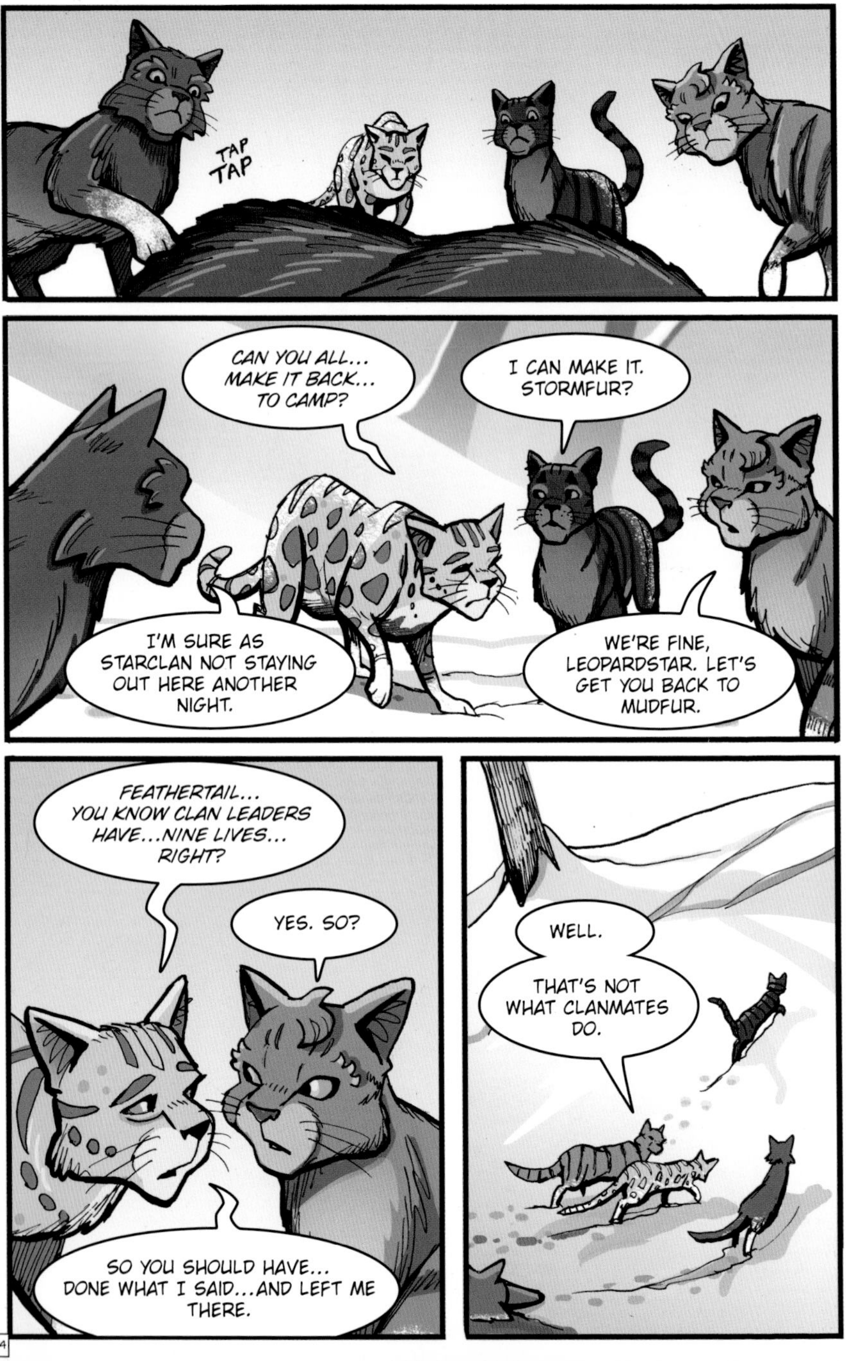
TAP TAP
CAN YOU ALL... MAKE IT BACK... TO CAMP?
I CAN MAKE IT. STORMFUR?
I'M SURE AS STARCLAN NOT STAYING OUT HERE ANOTHER NIGHT.
WE'RE FINE, LEOPARDSTAR. LET'S GET YOU BACK TO MUDFUR.
FEATHERTAIL... YOU KNOW CLAN LEADERS HAVE...NINE LIVES... RIGHT?
YES. SO?
SO YOU SHOULD HAVE... DONE WHAT I SAID...AND LEFT ME THERE.
WELL.
THAT'S NOT WHAT CLANMATES DO.

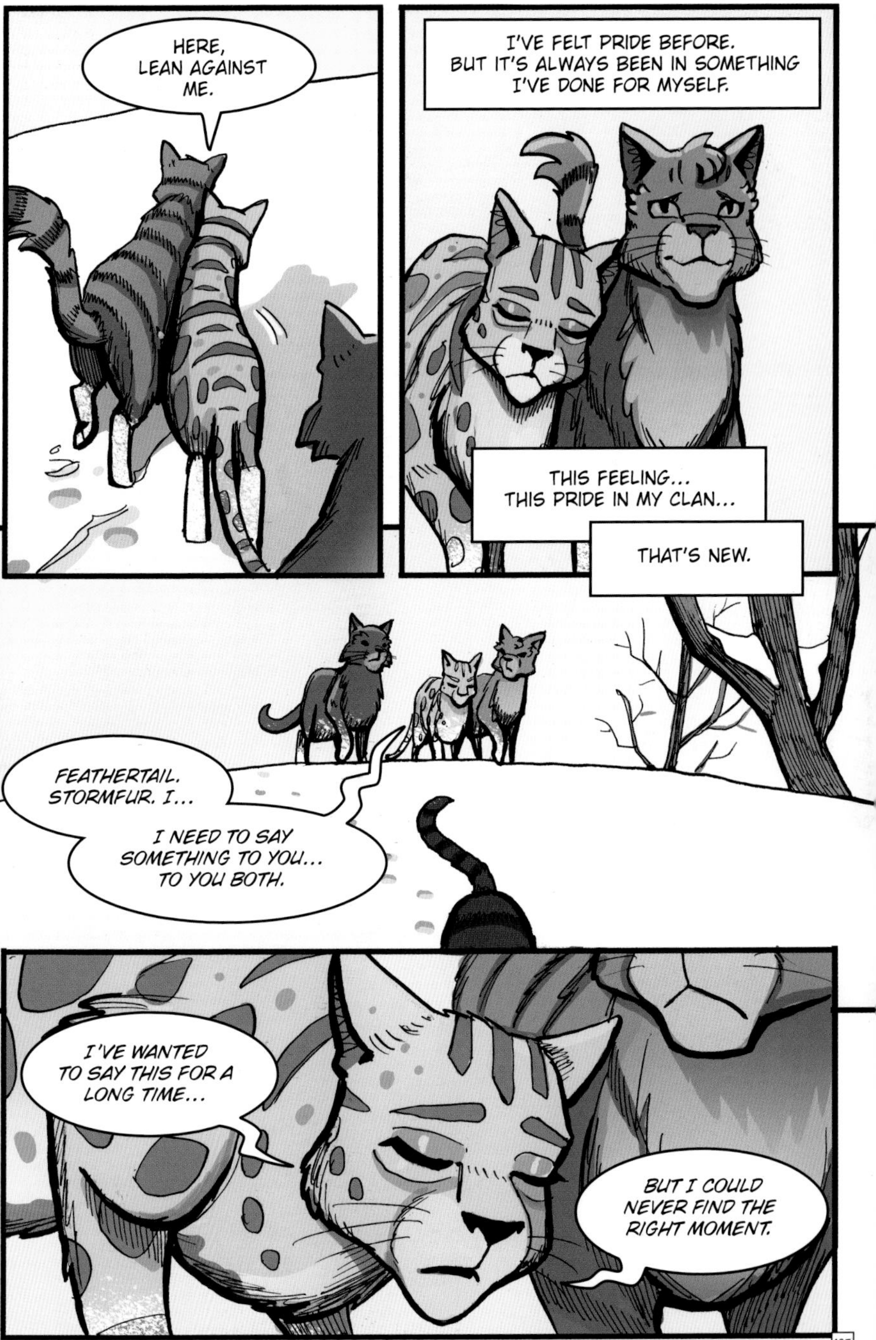
HERE, LEAN AGAINST ME.
I'VE FELT PRIDE BEFORE. BUT IT'S ALWAYS BEEN IN SOMETHING I'VE DONE FOR MYSELF.
THIS FEELING... THIS PRIDE IN MY CLAN...
THAT'S NEW.
FEATHERTAIL. STORMFUR. I...
I NEED TO SAY SOMETHING TO YOU... TO YOU BOTH.
I'VE WANTED TO SAY THIS FOR A LONG TIME...
BUT I COULD NEVER FIND THE RIGHT MOMENT.

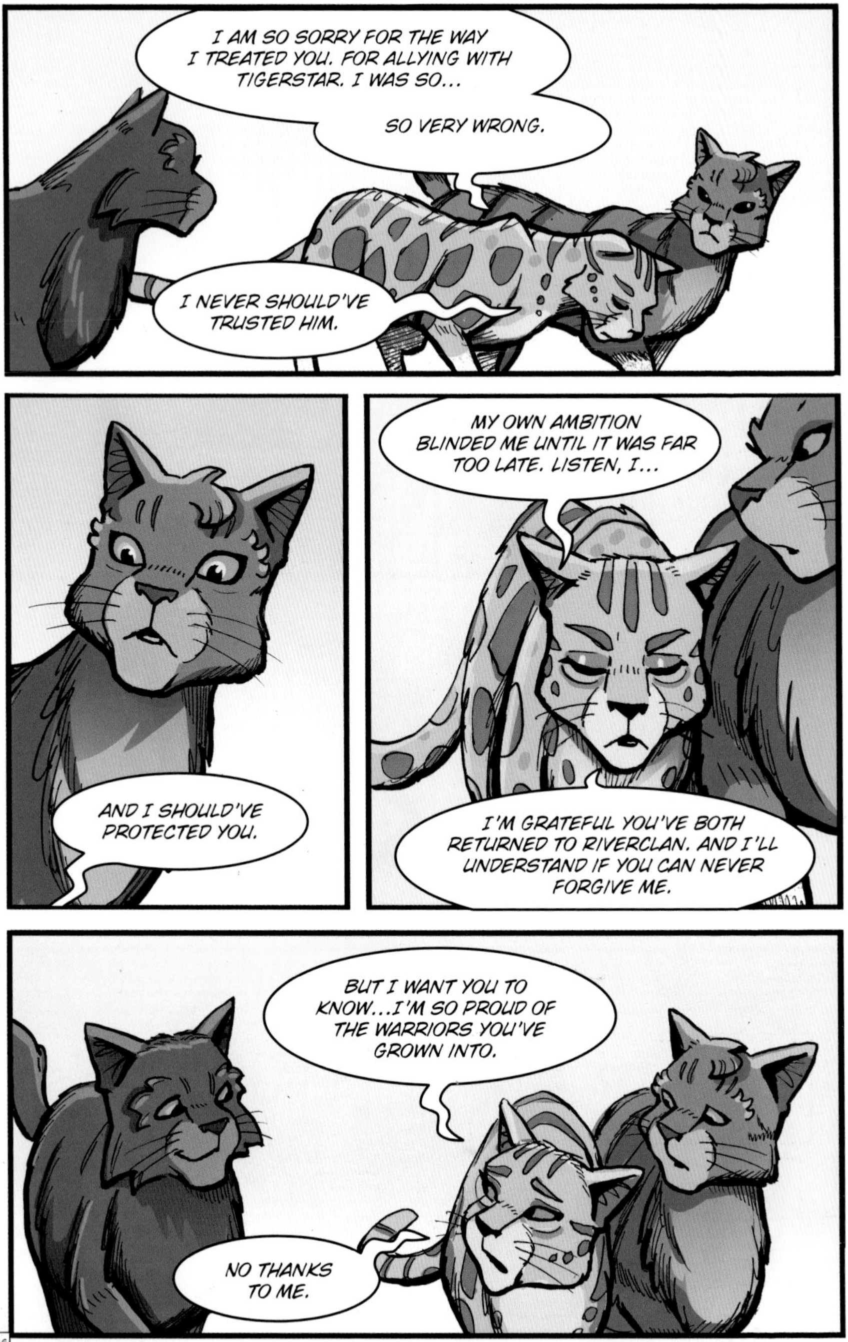
I AM SO SORRY FOR THE WAY I TREATED YOU. FOR ALLYING WITH TIGERSTAR. I WAS SO...
SO VERY WRONG.
I NEVER SHOULD'VE TRUSTED HIM.
AND I SHOULD'VE PROTECTED YOU.
MY OWN AMBITION BLINDED ME UNTIL IT WAS FAR TOO LATE. LISTEN, I...
I'M GRATEFUL YOU'VE BOTH RETURNED TO RIVERCLAN. AND I'LL UNDERSTAND IF YOU CAN NEVER FORGIVE ME.
BUT I WANT YOU TO KNOW...I'M SO PROUD OF THE WARRIORS YOU'VE GROWN INTO.
NO THANKS TO ME.

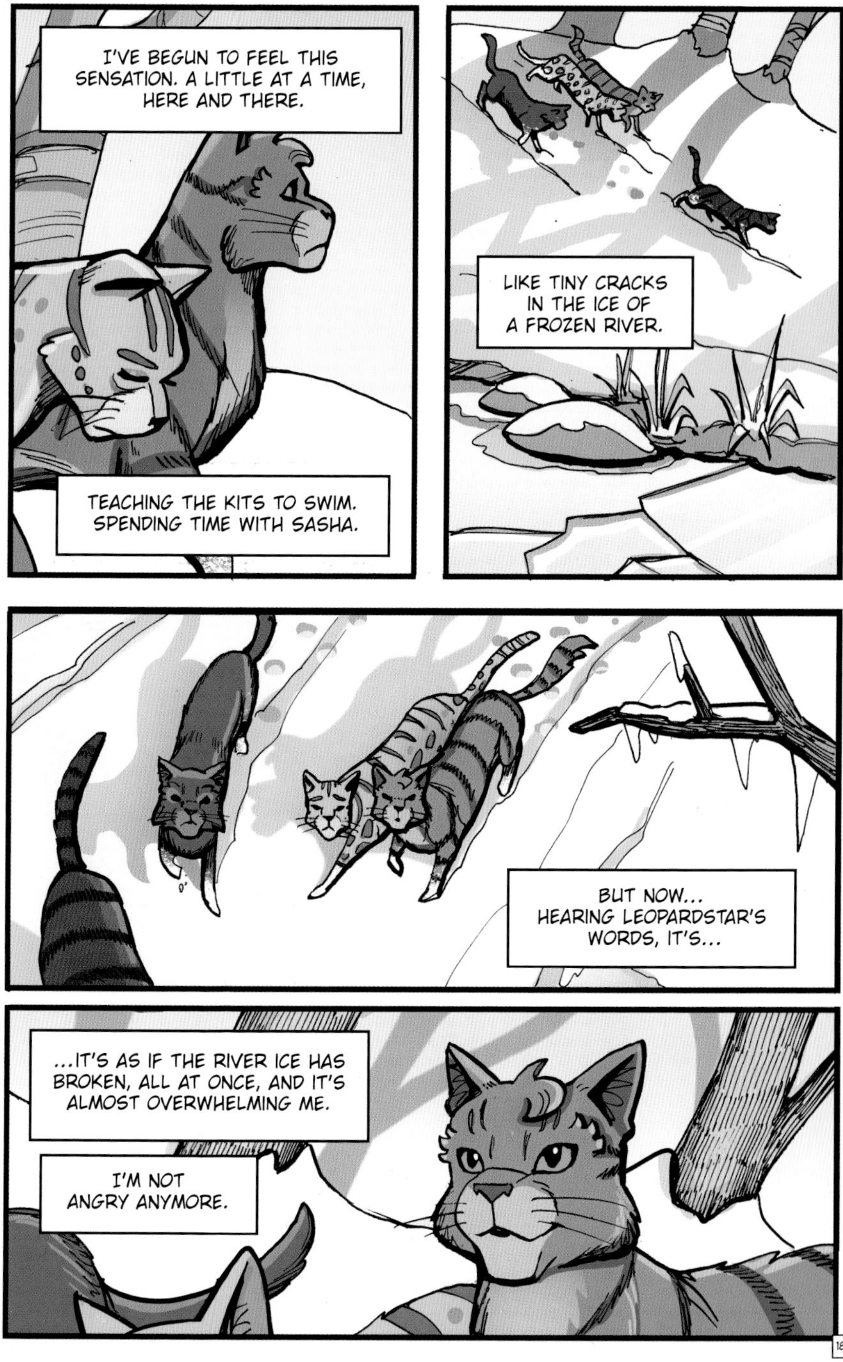
I'VE BEGUN TO FEEL THIS SENSATION. A LITTLE AT A TIME, HERE AND THERE.
TEACHING THE KITS TO SWIM. SPENDING TIME WITH SASHA.
LIKE TINY CRACKS IN THE ICE OF A FROZEN RIVER.
BUT NOW... HEARING LEOPARDSTAR'S WORDS, IT'S...
...IT'S AS IF THE RIVER ICE HAS BROKEN, ALL AT ONCE, AND IT'S ALMOST OVERWHELMING ME.
I'M NOT ANGRY ANYMORE.

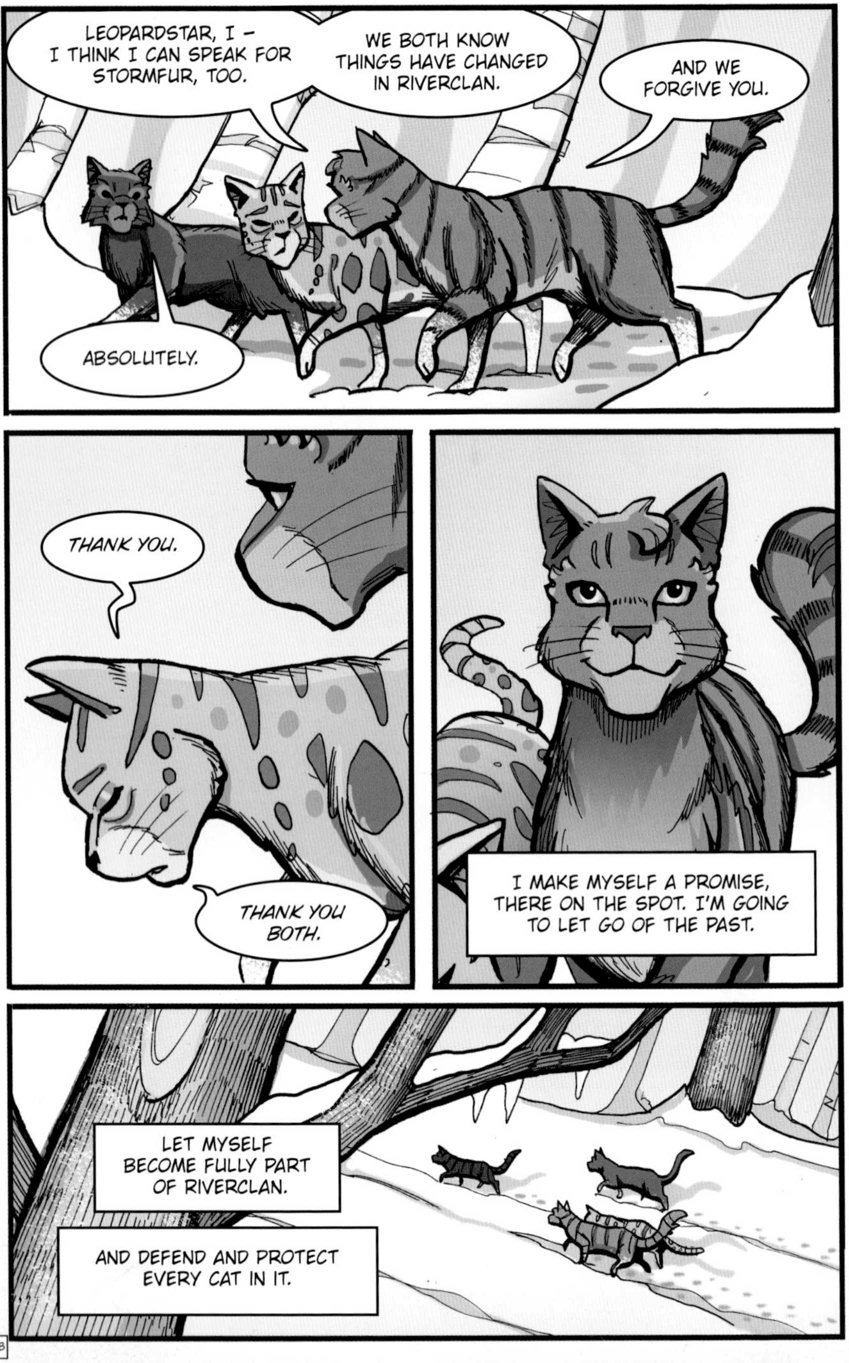
LEOPARDSTAR, I – I THINK I CAN SPEAK FOR STORMFUR, TOO.
WE BOTH KNOW THINGS HAVE CHANGED IN RIVERCLAN.
AND WE FORGIVE YOU.
ABSOLUTELY.
THANK YOU.
THANK YOU BOTH.
I MAKE MYSELF A PROMISE, THERE ON THE SPOT. I'M GOING TO LET GO OF THE PAST.
LET MYSELF BECOME FULLY PART OF RIVERCLAN.
AND DEFEND AND PROTECT EVERY CAT IN IT.

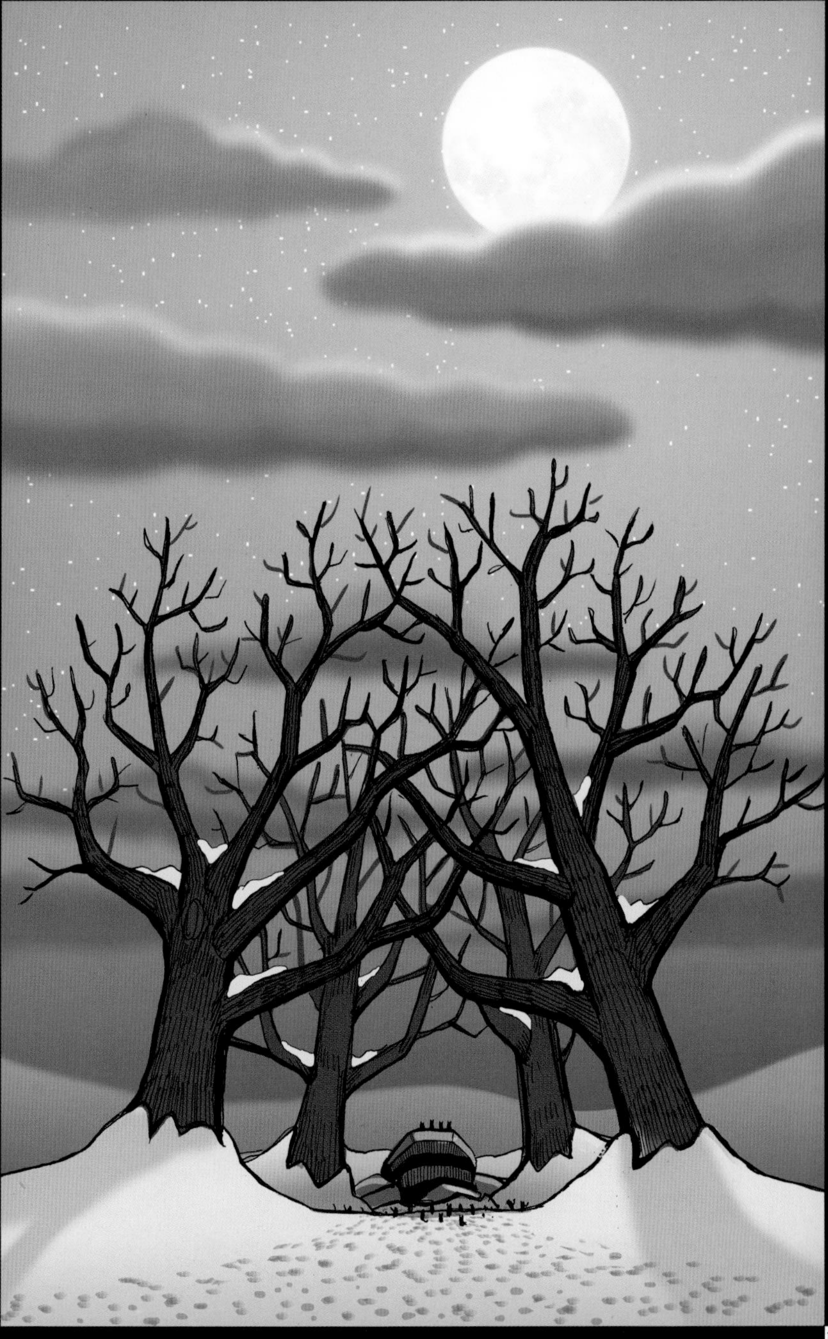

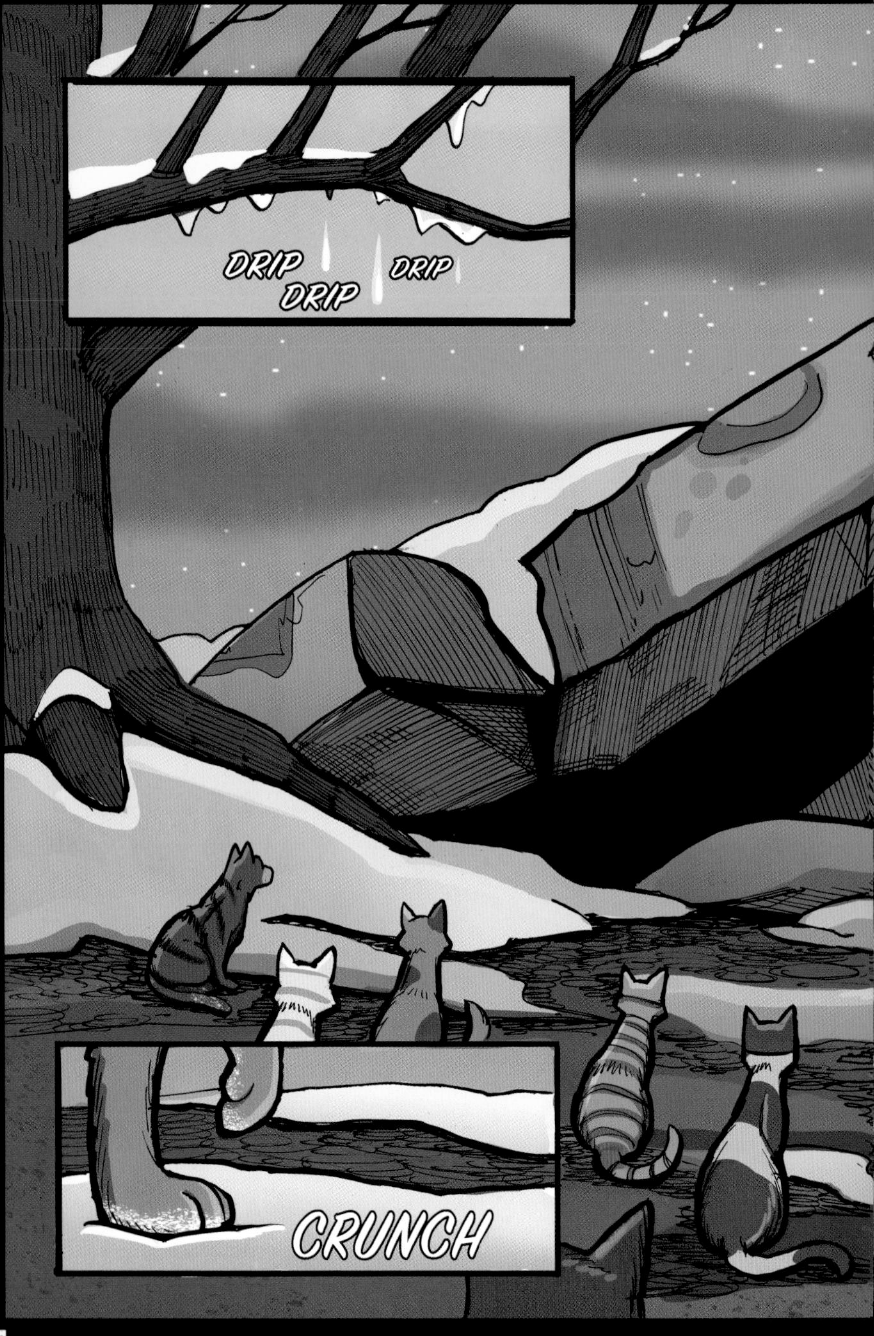
DRIP
DRIP
DRIP
CRUNCH

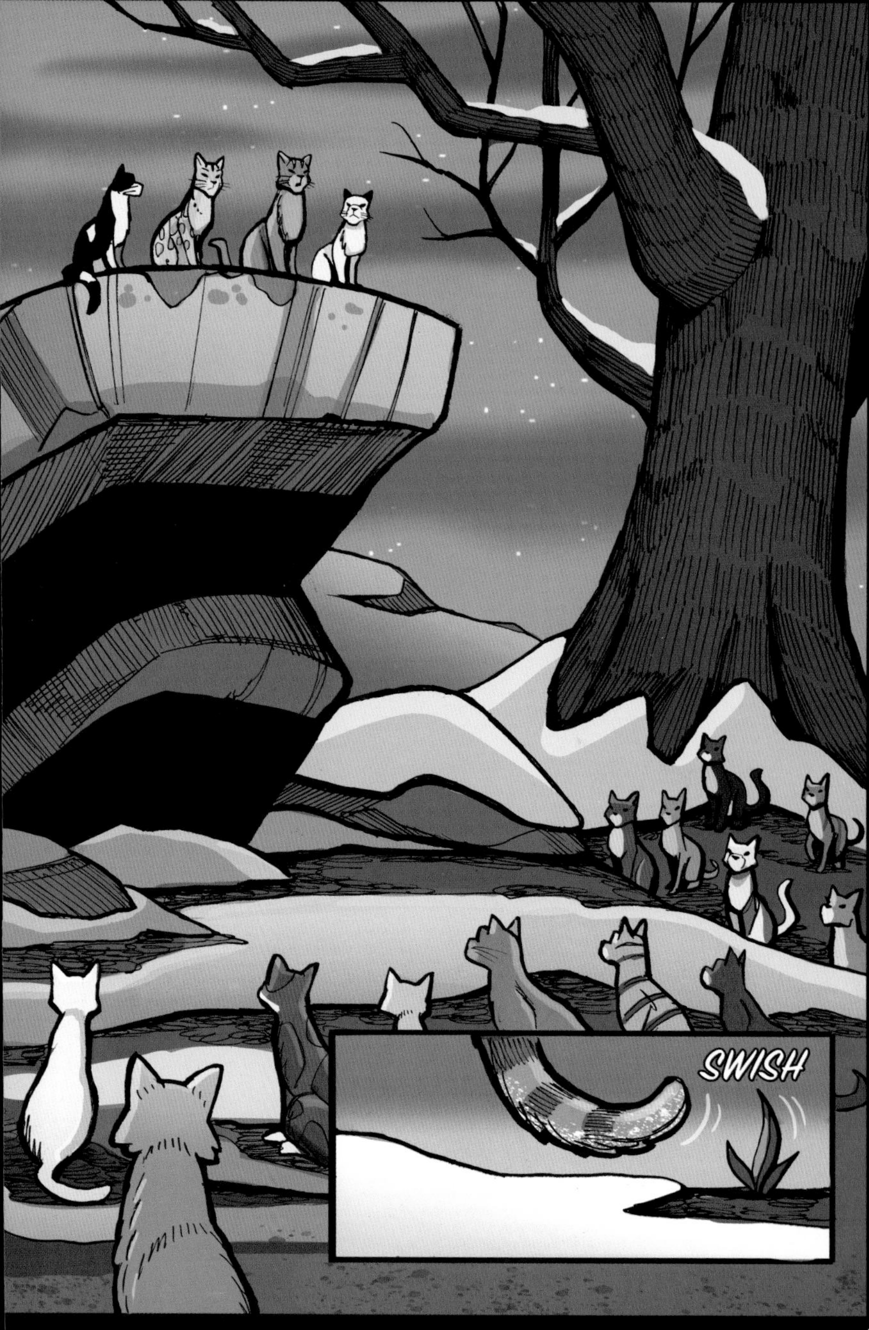
SWISH

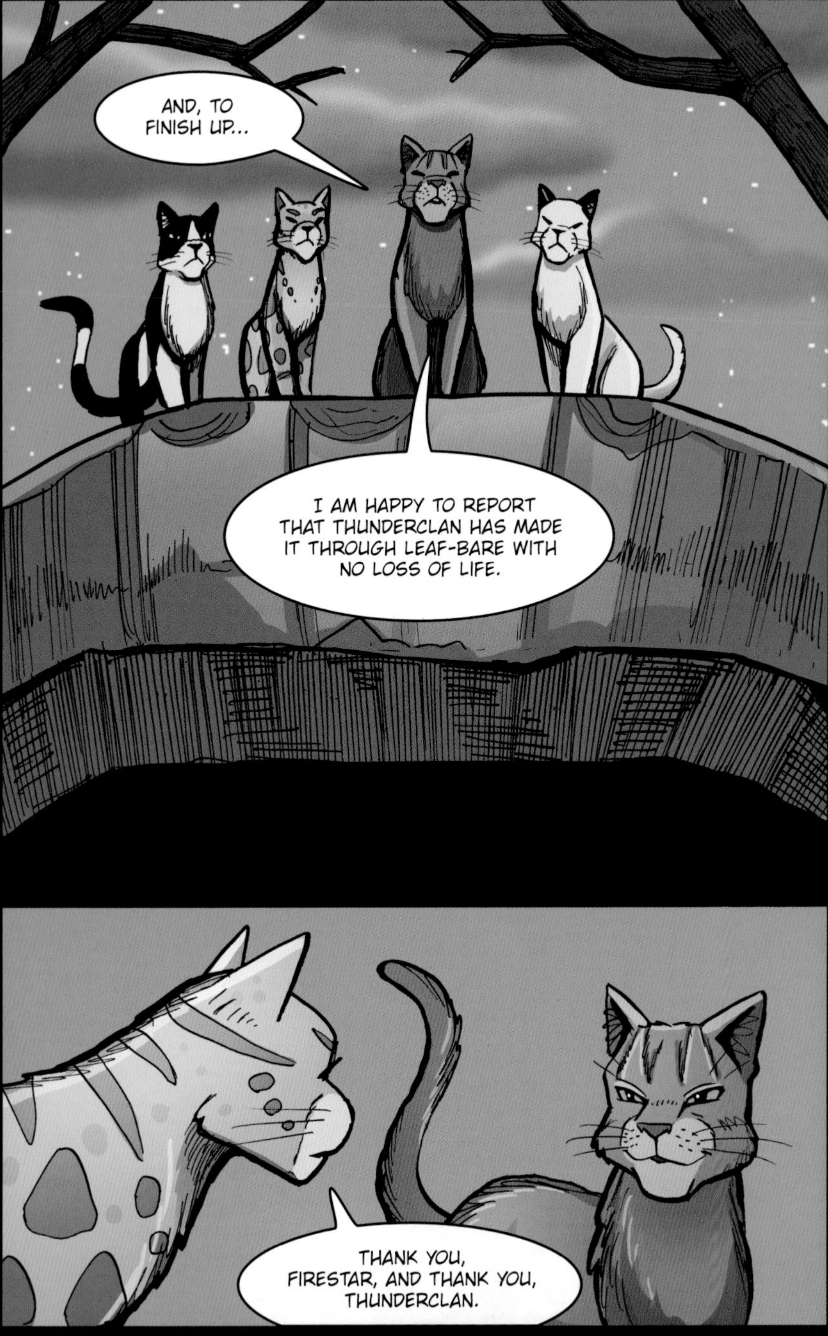
AND, TO FINISH UP...
I AM HAPPY TO REPORT THAT THUNDERCLAN HAS MADE IT THROUGH LEAF-BARE WITH NO LOSS OF LIFE.
THANK YOU, FIRESTAR, AND THANK YOU, THUNDERCLAN.

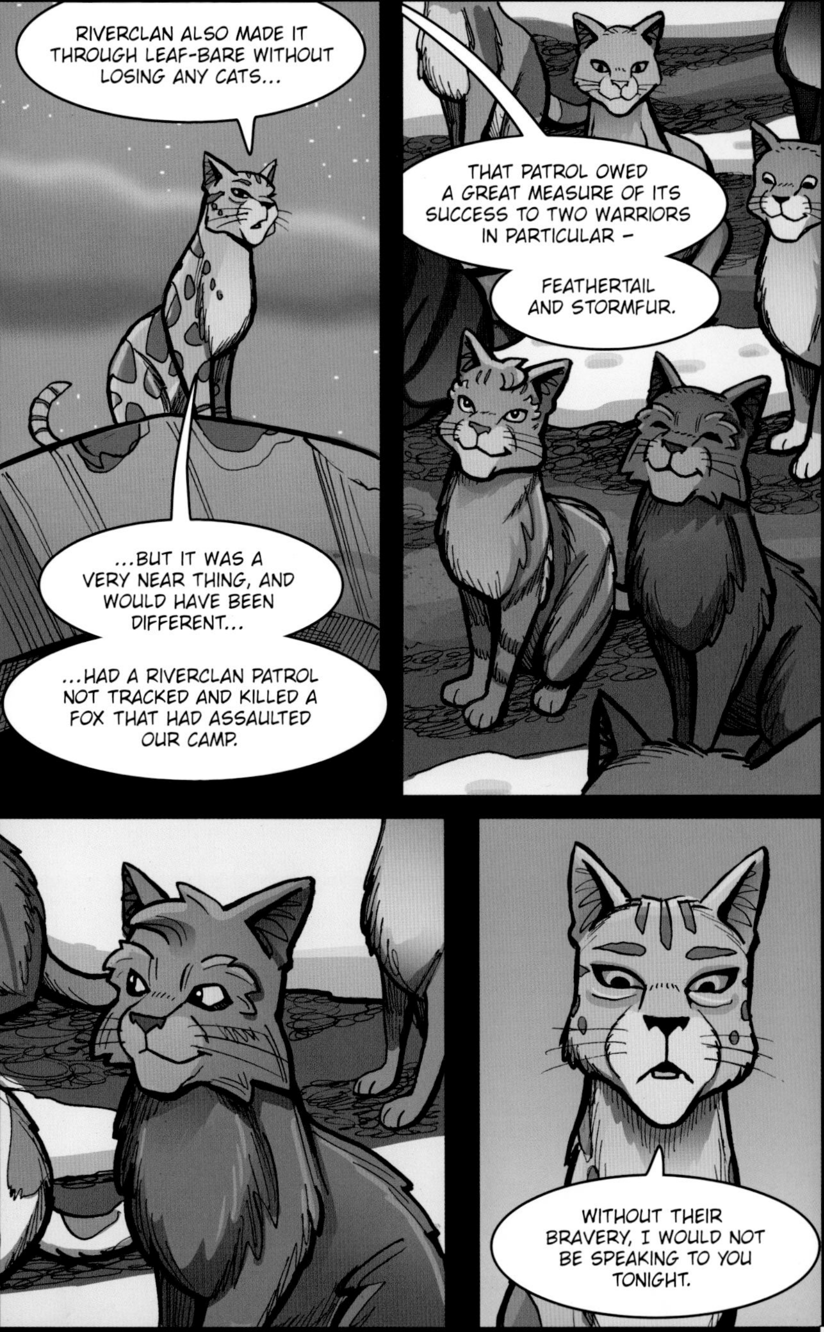
RIVERCLAN ALSO MADE IT THROUGH LEAF-BARE WITHOUT LOSING ANY CATS...
...BUT IT WAS A VERY NEAR THING, AND WOULD HAVE BEEN DIFFERENT...
...HAD A RIVERCLAN PATROL NOT TRACKED AND KILLED A FOX THAT HAD ASSAULTED OUR CAMP.
THAT PATROL OWED A GREAT MEASURE OF ITS SUCCESS TO TWO WARRIORS IN PARTICULAR -
FEATHERTAIL AND STORMFUR.
WITHOUT THEIR BRAVERY, I WOULD NOT BE SPEAKING TO YOU TONIGHT.

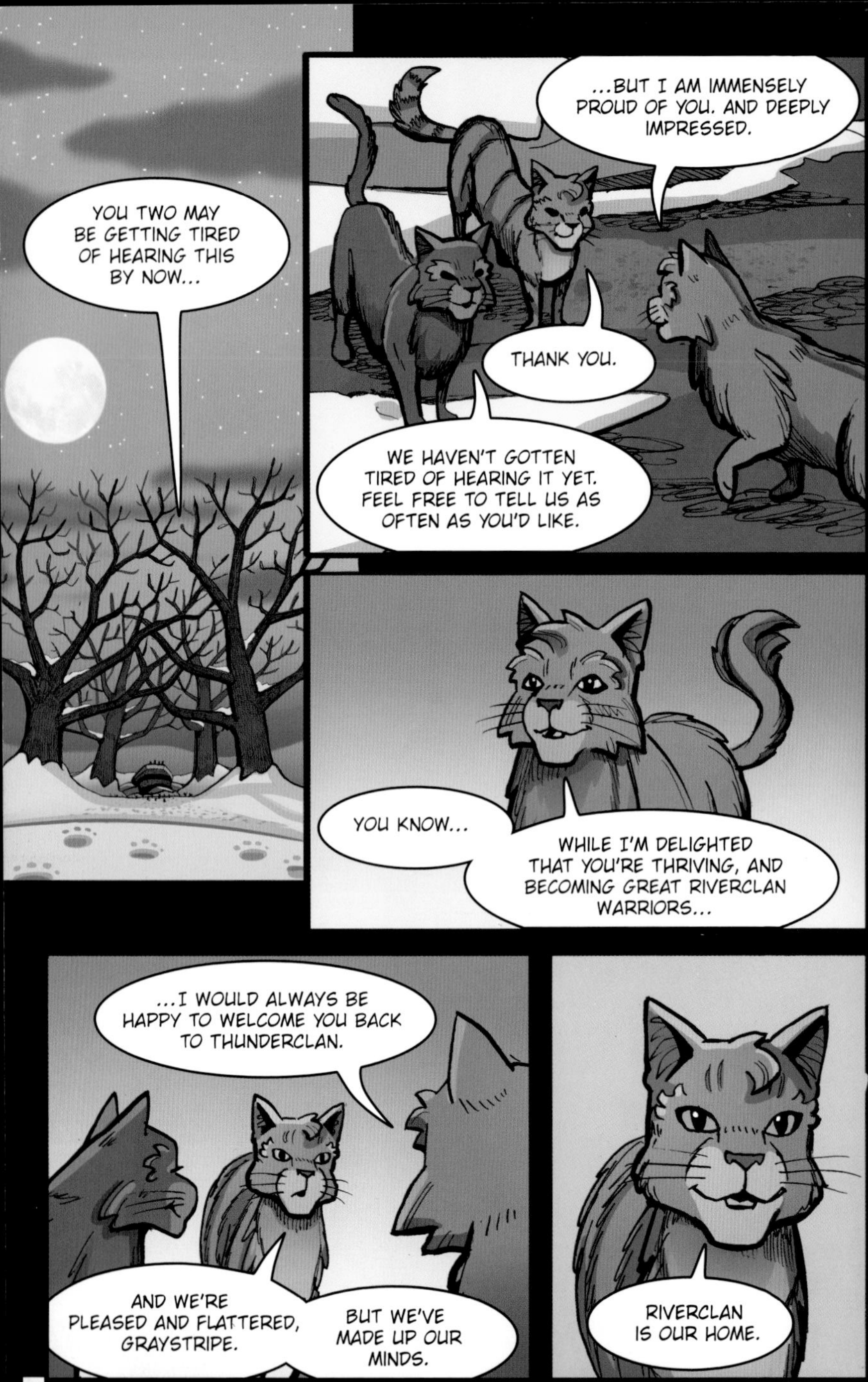
YOU TWO MAY BE GETTING TIRED OF HEARING THIS BY NOW...
...BUT I AM IMMENSELY PROUD OF YOU. AND DEEPLY IMPRESSED.
THANK YOU.
WE HAVEN'T GOTTEN TIRED OF HEARING IT YET. FEEL FREE TO TELL US AS OFTEN AS YOU'D LIKE.
YOU KNOW...
WHILE I'M DELIGHTED THAT YOU'RE THRIVING, AND BECOMING GREAT RIVERCLAN WARRIORS...
...I WOULD ALWAYS BE HAPPY TO WELCOME YOU BACK TO THUNDERCLAN.
AND WE'RE PLEASED AND FLATTERED, GRAYSTRIPE.
BUT WE'VE MADE UP OUR MINDS.
RIVERCLAN IS OUR HOME.

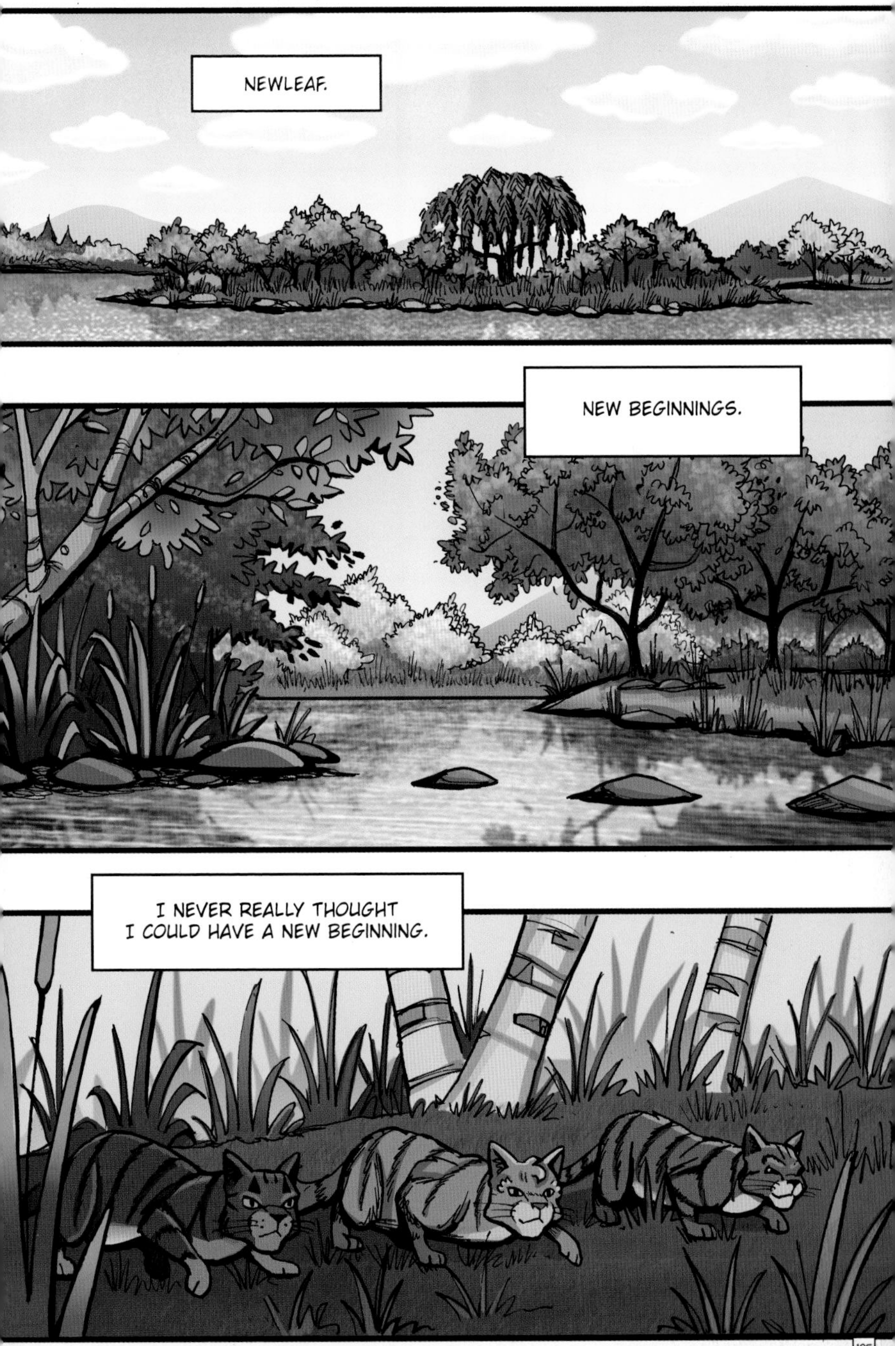
NEWLEAF.
NEW BEGINNINGS.
I NEVER REALLY THOUGHT I COULD HAVE A NEW BEGINNING.

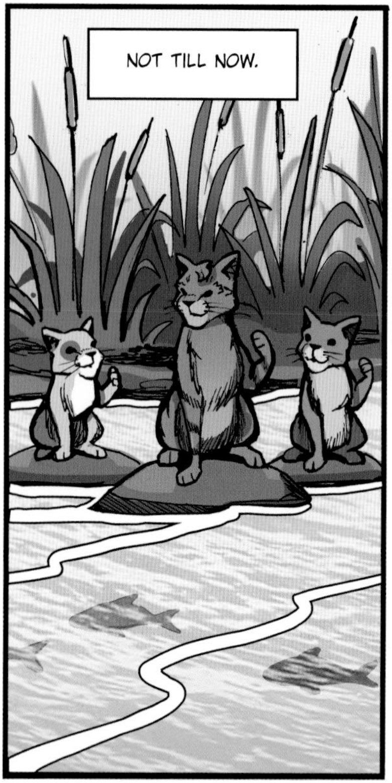
NOT TILL NOW.

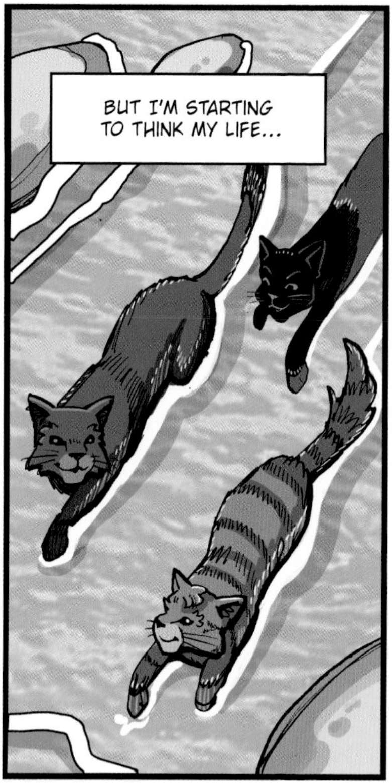
BUT I'M STARTING TO THINK MY LIFE...

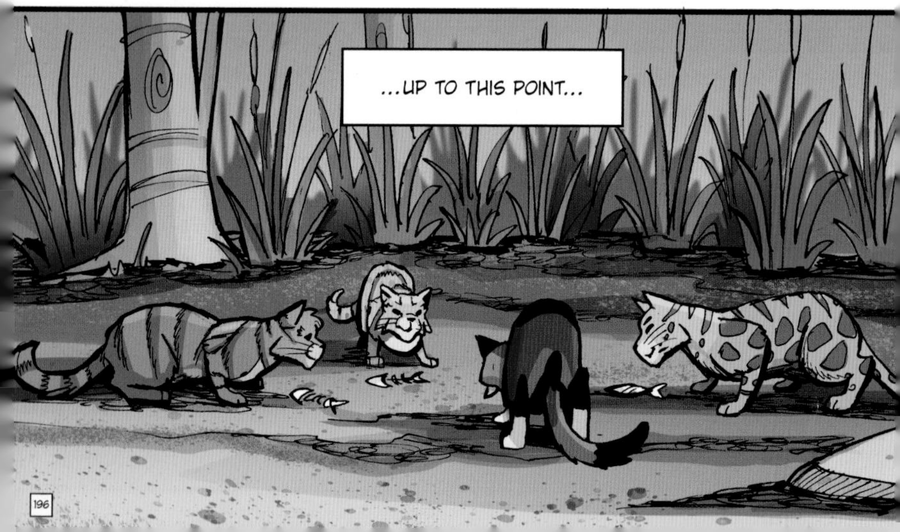
...UP TO THIS POINT...

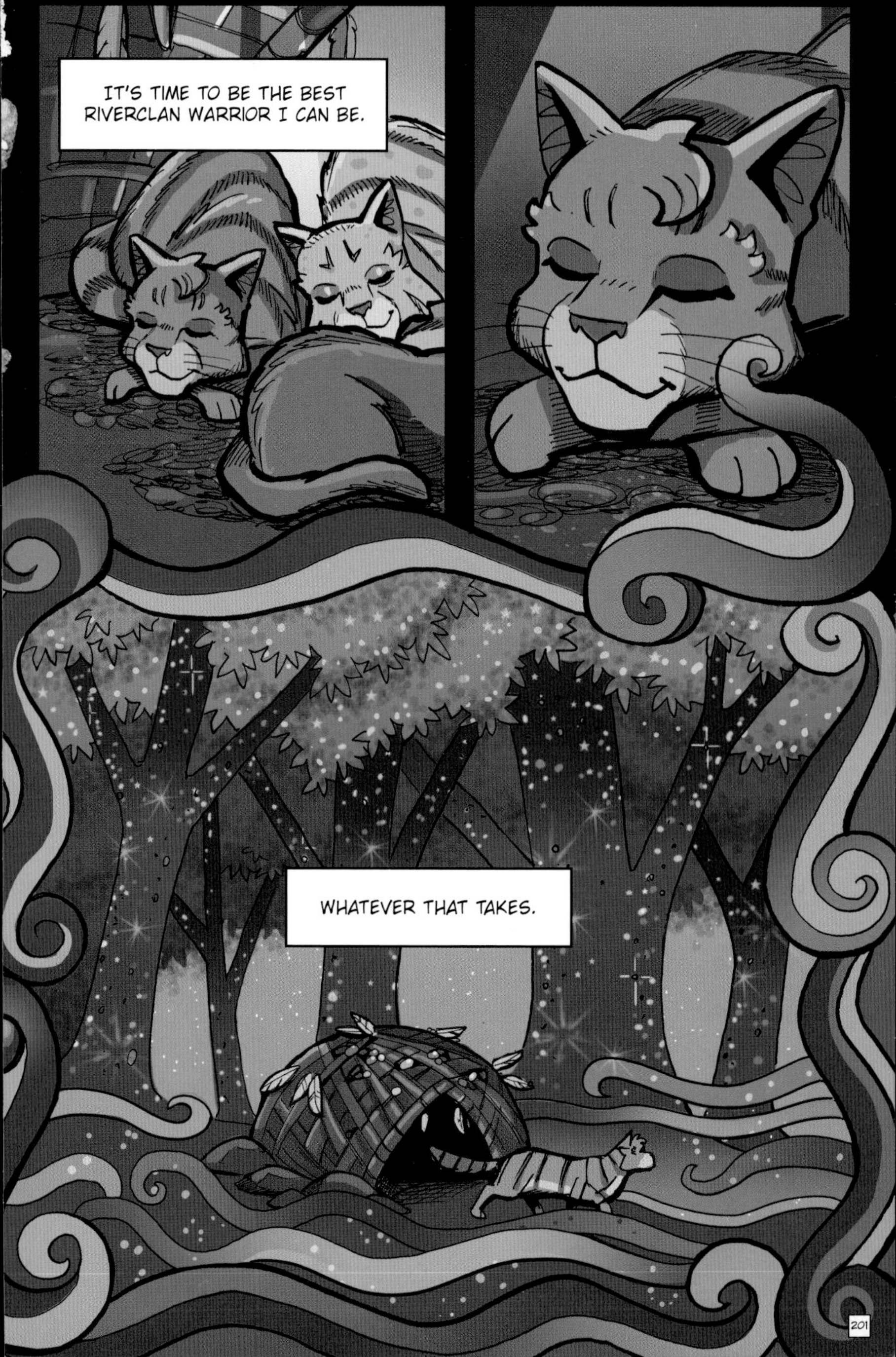
IT'S TIME TO BE THE BEST RIVERCLAN WARRIOR I CAN BE.
WHATEVER THAT TAKES.

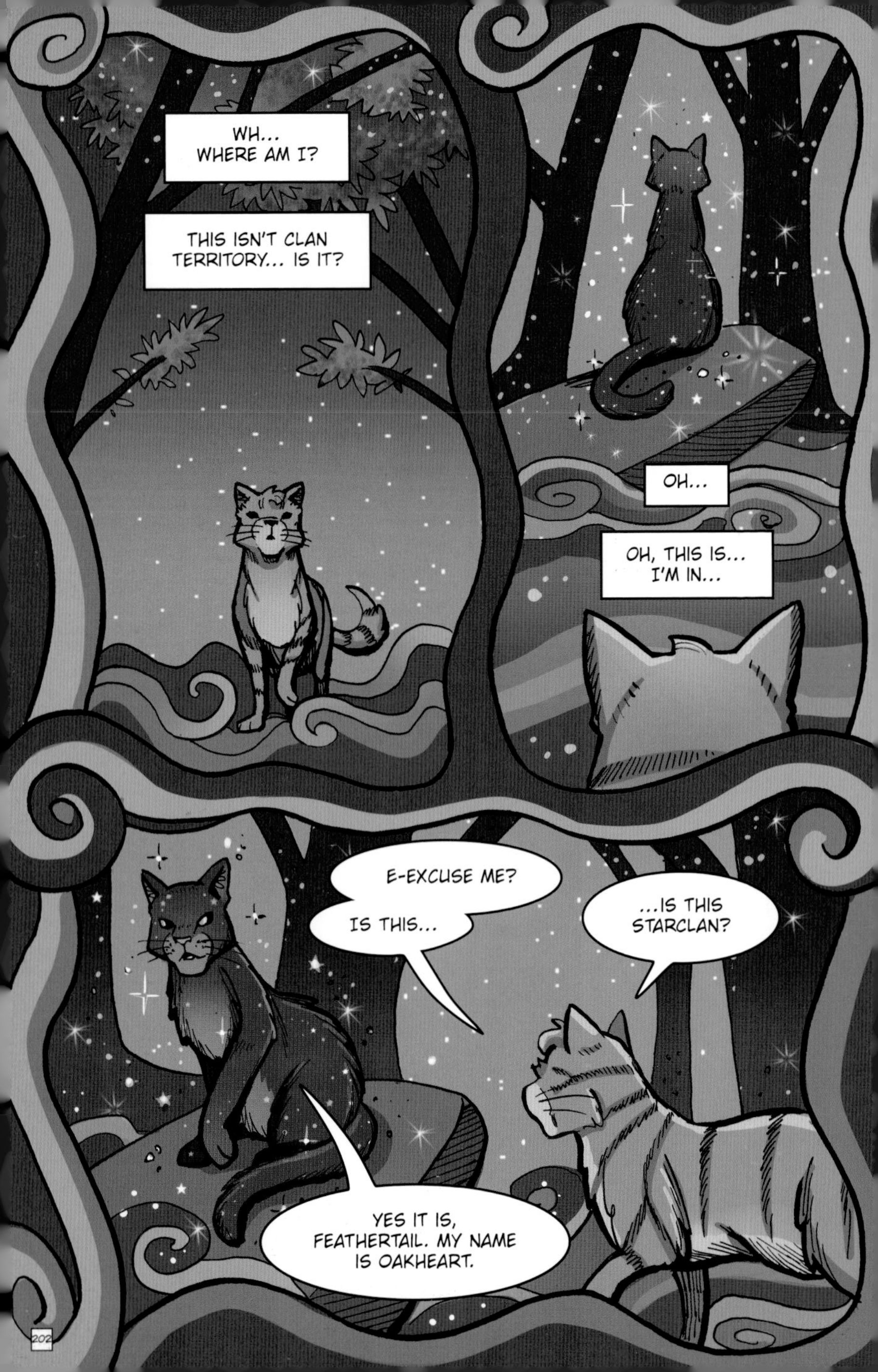
WH...
WHERE AM I?
THIS ISN'T CLAN TERRITORY... IS IT?
OH...
OH, THIS IS... I'M IN...
E-EXCUSE ME?
IS THIS...
...IS THIS STARCLAN?
YES IT IS, FEATHERTAIL. MY NAME IS OAKHEART.

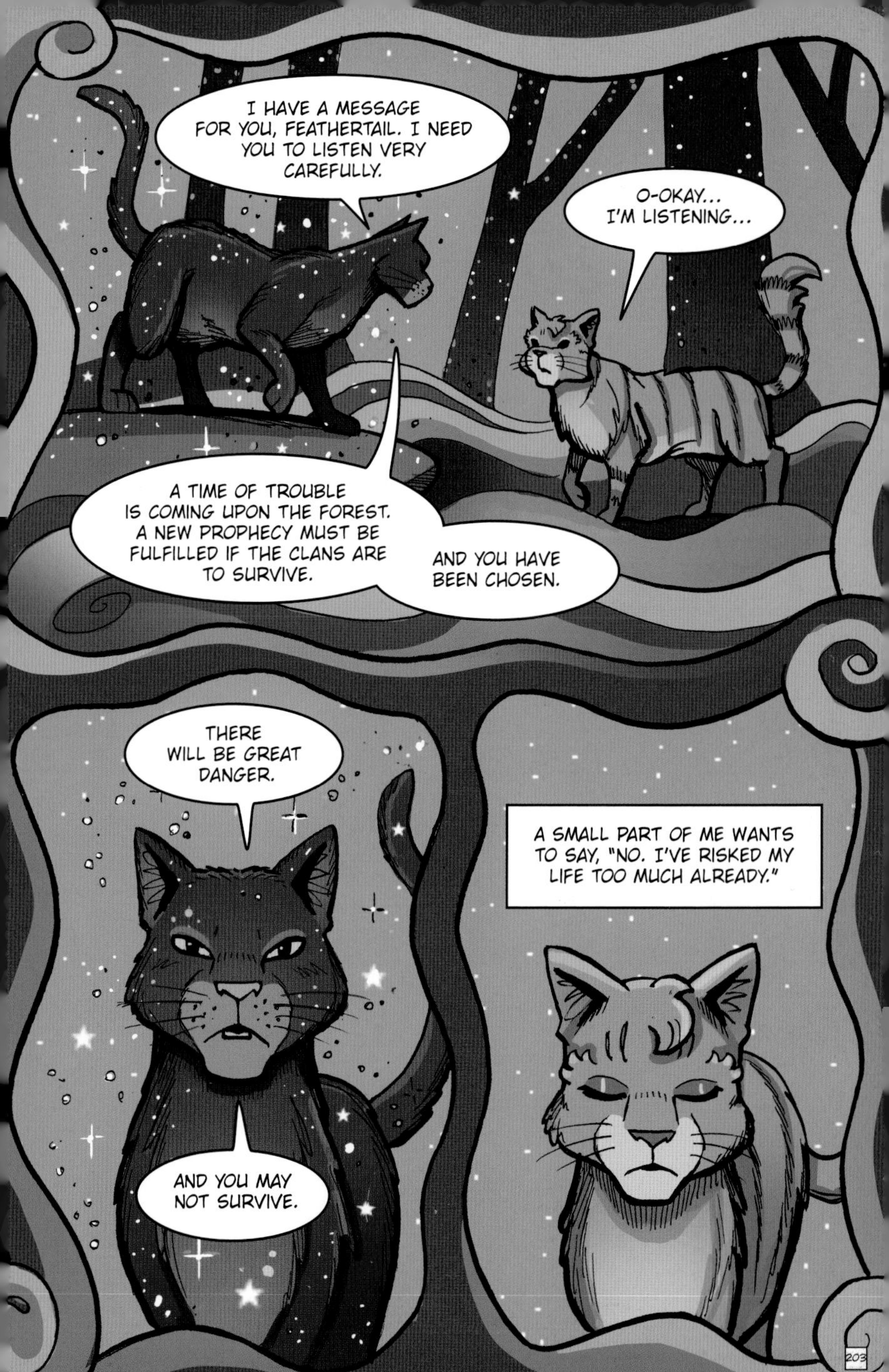

I HAVE A MESSAGE FOR YOU, FEATHERTAIL. I NEED YOU TO LISTEN VERY CAREFULLY.
O-OKAY... I'M LISTENING...
A TIME OF TROUBLE IS COMING UPON THE FOREST. A NEW PROPHECY MUST BE FULFILLED IF THE CLANS ARE TO SURVIVE.
AND YOU HAVE BEEN CHOSEN.
THERE WILL BE GREAT DANGER.
AND YOU MAY NOT SURVIVE.
A SMALL PART OF ME WANTS TO SAY, "NO. I'VE RISKED MY LIFE TOO MUCH ALREADY."

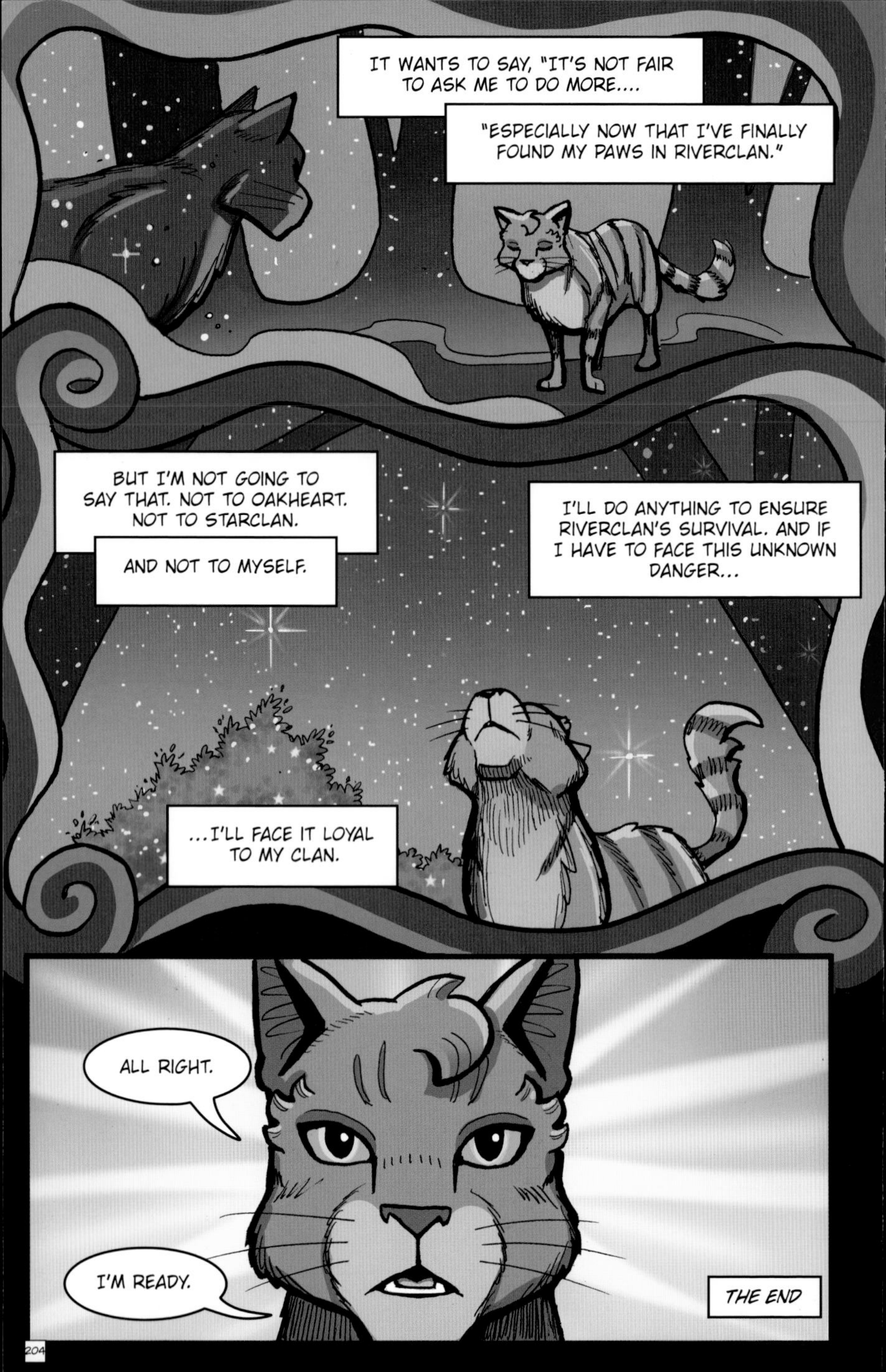
IT WANTS TO SAY, "IT'S NOT FAIR TO ASK ME TO DO MORE....
"ESPECIALLY NOW THAT I'VE FINALLY FOUND MY PAWS IN RIVERCLAN."
BUT I'M NOT GOING TO SAY THAT. NOT TO OAKHEART. NOT TO STARCLAN.
AND NOT TO MYSELF.
I'LL DO ANYTHING TO ENSURE RIVERCLAN'S SURVIVAL. AND IF I HAVE TO FACE THIS UNKNOWN DANGER...
...I'LL FACE IT LOYAL TO MY CLAN.
ALL RIGHT.
I'M READY.
THE END

DON'T MISS THIS WARRIORS GRAPHIC NOVEL ADVENTURE

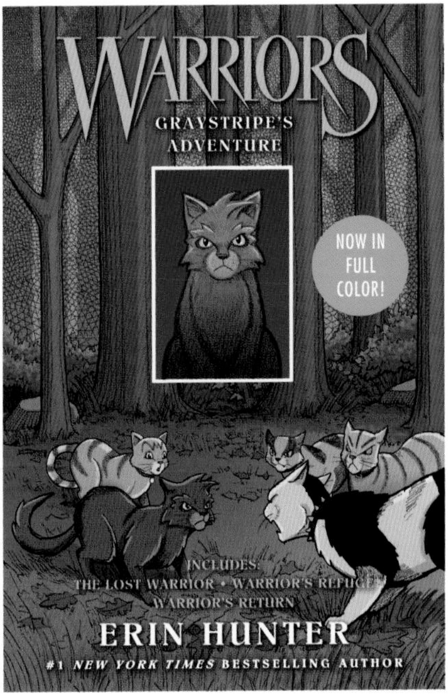
WARRIORS
GRAYSTRIPE'S ADVENTURE
NOW IN FULL COLOR!
INCLUDES:
THE LOST WARRIOR • WARRIOR'S REFUGE
WARRIOR'S RETURN
ERIN HUNTER
#1 NEW YORK TIMES BESTSELLING AUTHOR

**Keep reading for a sneak peek!**

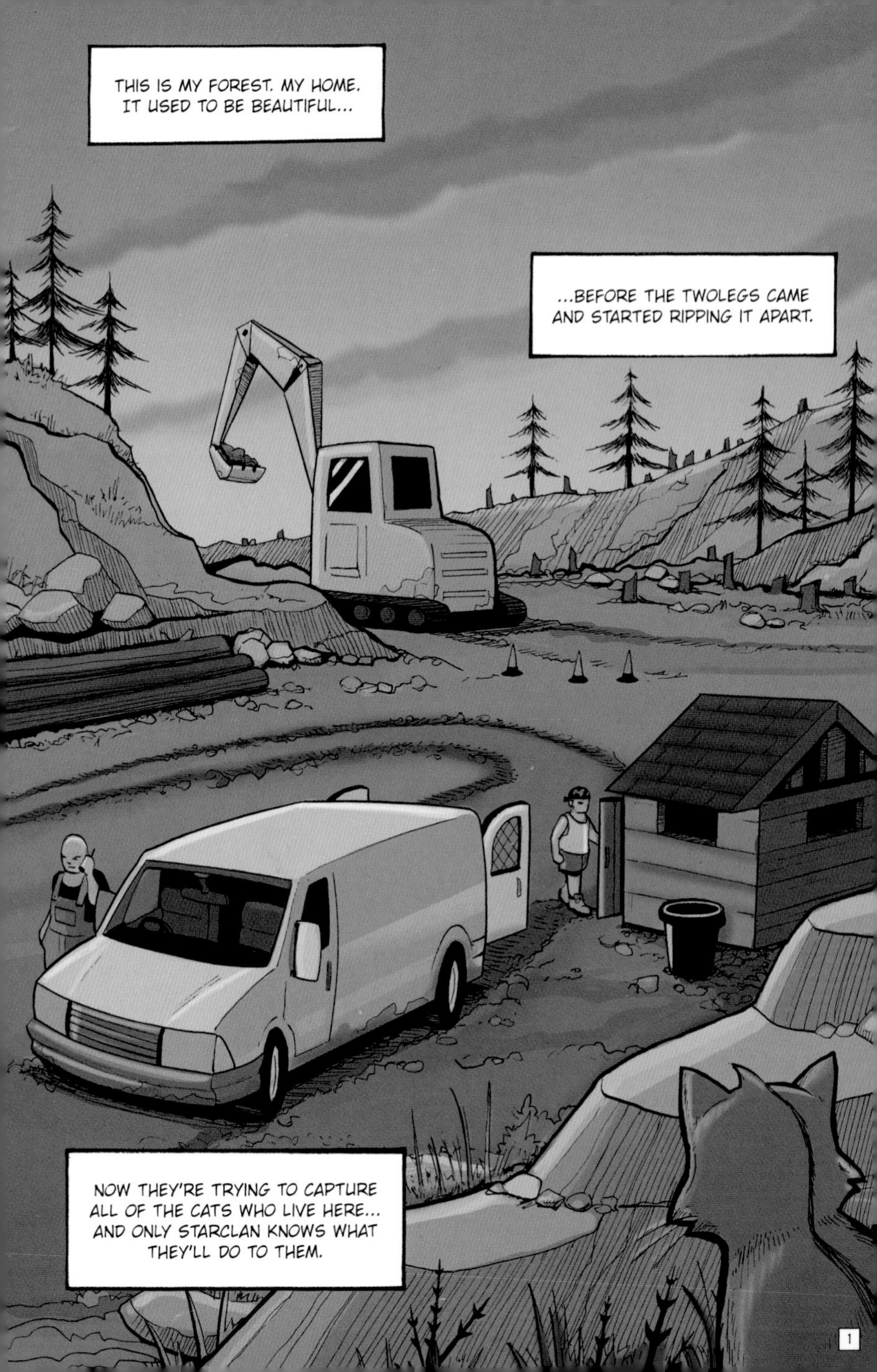
THIS IS MY FOREST. MY HOME. IT USED TO BE BEAUTIFUL...
...BEFORE THE TWOLEGS CAME AND STARTED RIPPING IT APART.
NOW THEY'RE TRYING TO CAPTURE ALL OF THE CATS WHO LIVE HERE... AND ONLY STARCLAN KNOWS WHAT THEY'LL DO TO THEM.

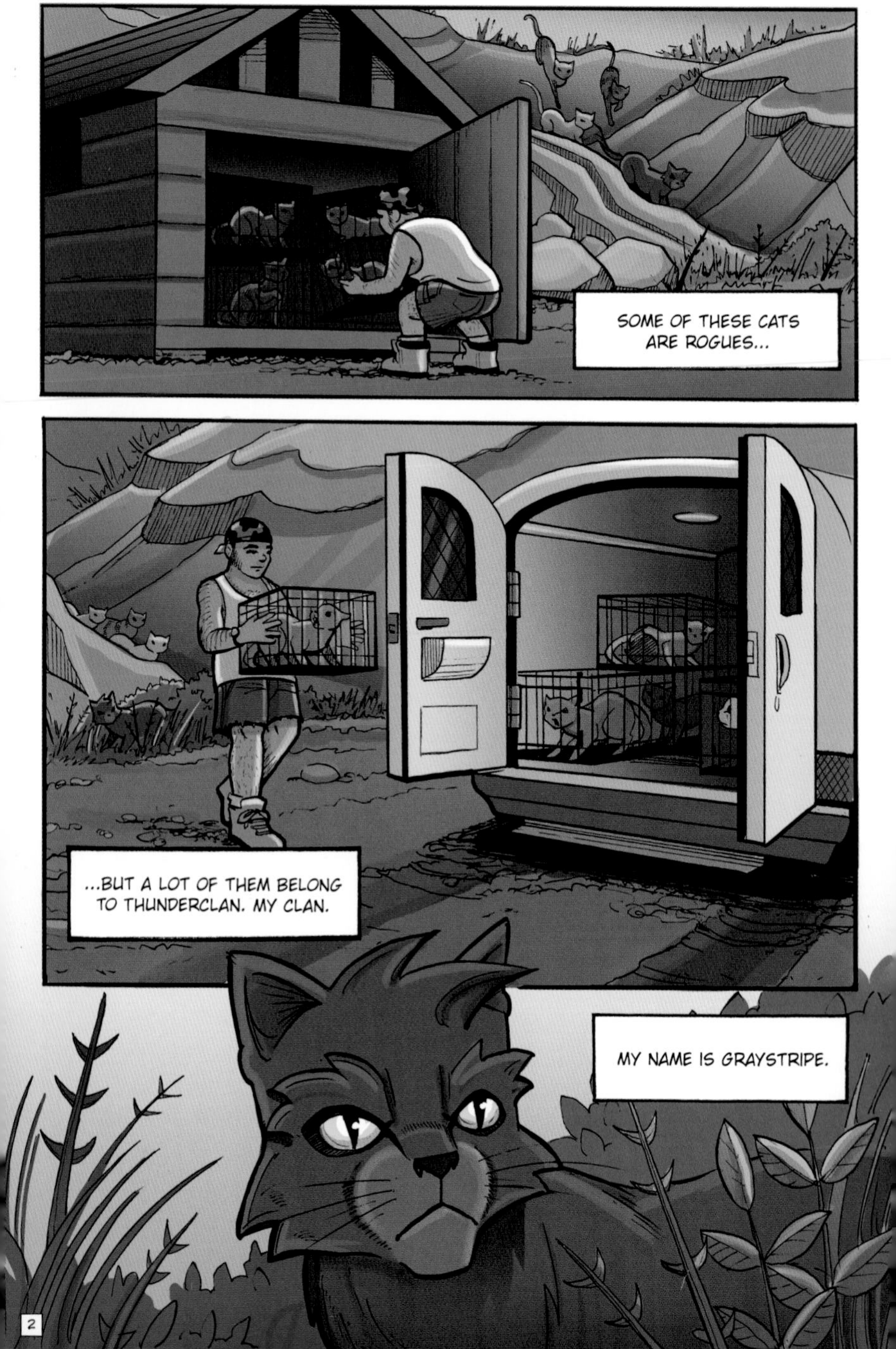
SOME OF THESE CATS ARE ROGUES...
...BUT A LOT OF THEM BELONG TO THUNDERCLAN. MY CLAN.
MY NAME IS GRAYSTRIPE.

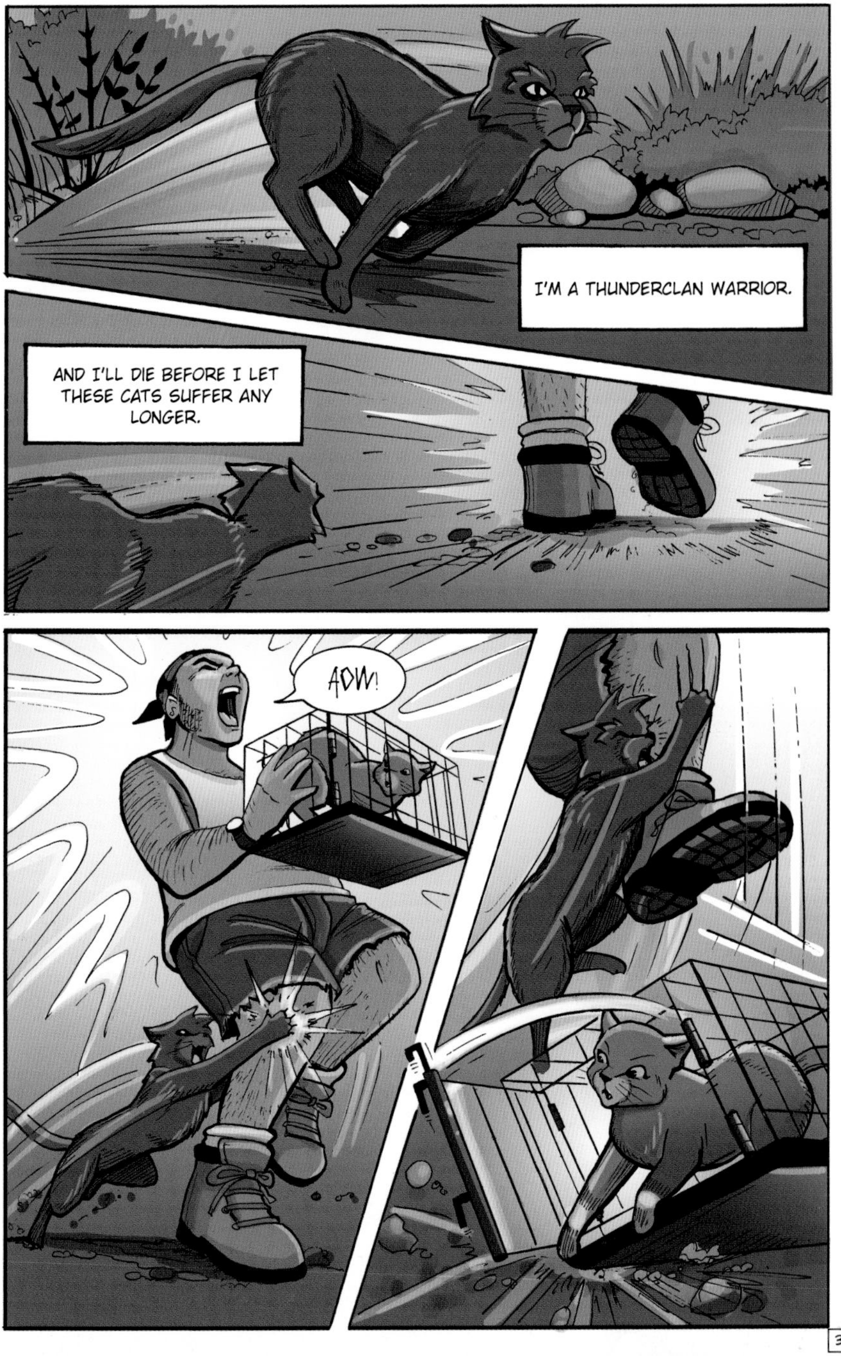
I'M A THUNDERCLAN WARRIOR.
AND I'LL DIE BEFORE I LET THESE CATS SUFFER ANY LONGER.
ADW!

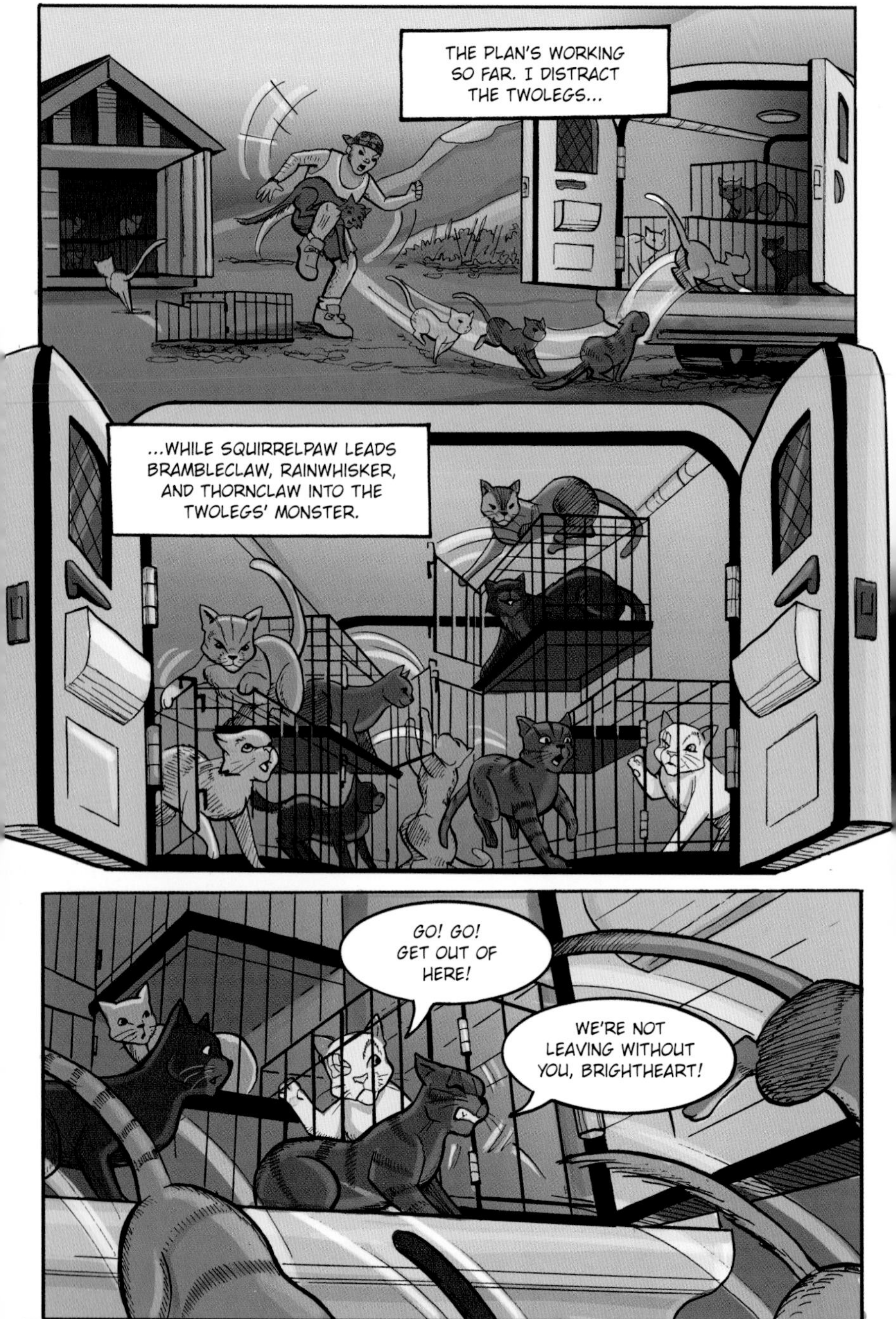

THE PLAN'S WORKING SO FAR. I DISTRACT THE TWOLEGS...
...WHILE SQUIRRELPAW LEADS BRAMBLECLAW, RAINWHISKER, AND THORNCLAW INTO THE TWOLEGS' MONSTER.
GO! GO! GET OUT OF HERE!
WE'RE NOT LEAVING WITHOUT YOU, BRIGHTHEART!

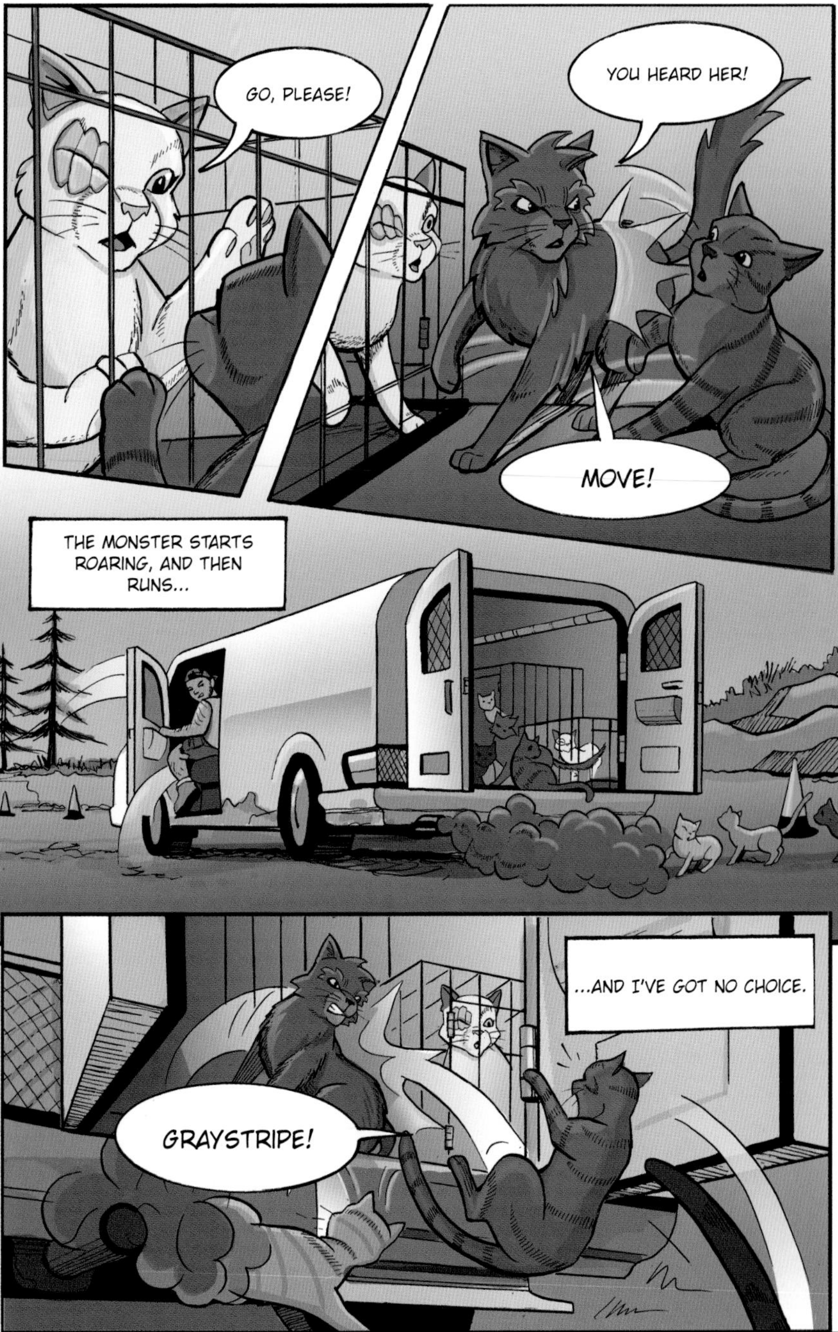
GO, PLEASE!
YOU HEARD HER!
MOVE!
THE MONSTER STARTS ROARING, AND THEN RUNS...
...AND I'VE GOT NO CHOICE.
GRAYSTRIPE!

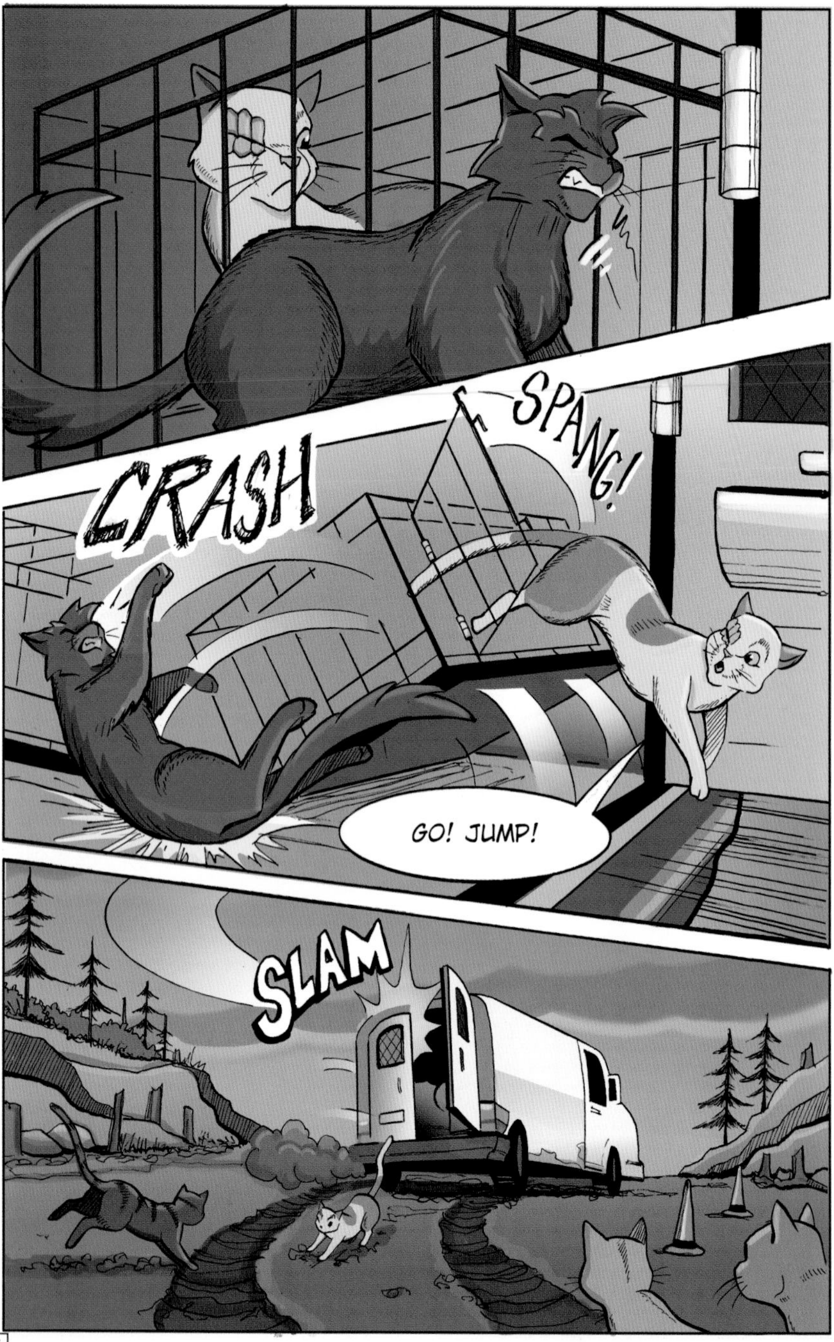

SPANG!
CRASH
GO! JUMP!
SLAM

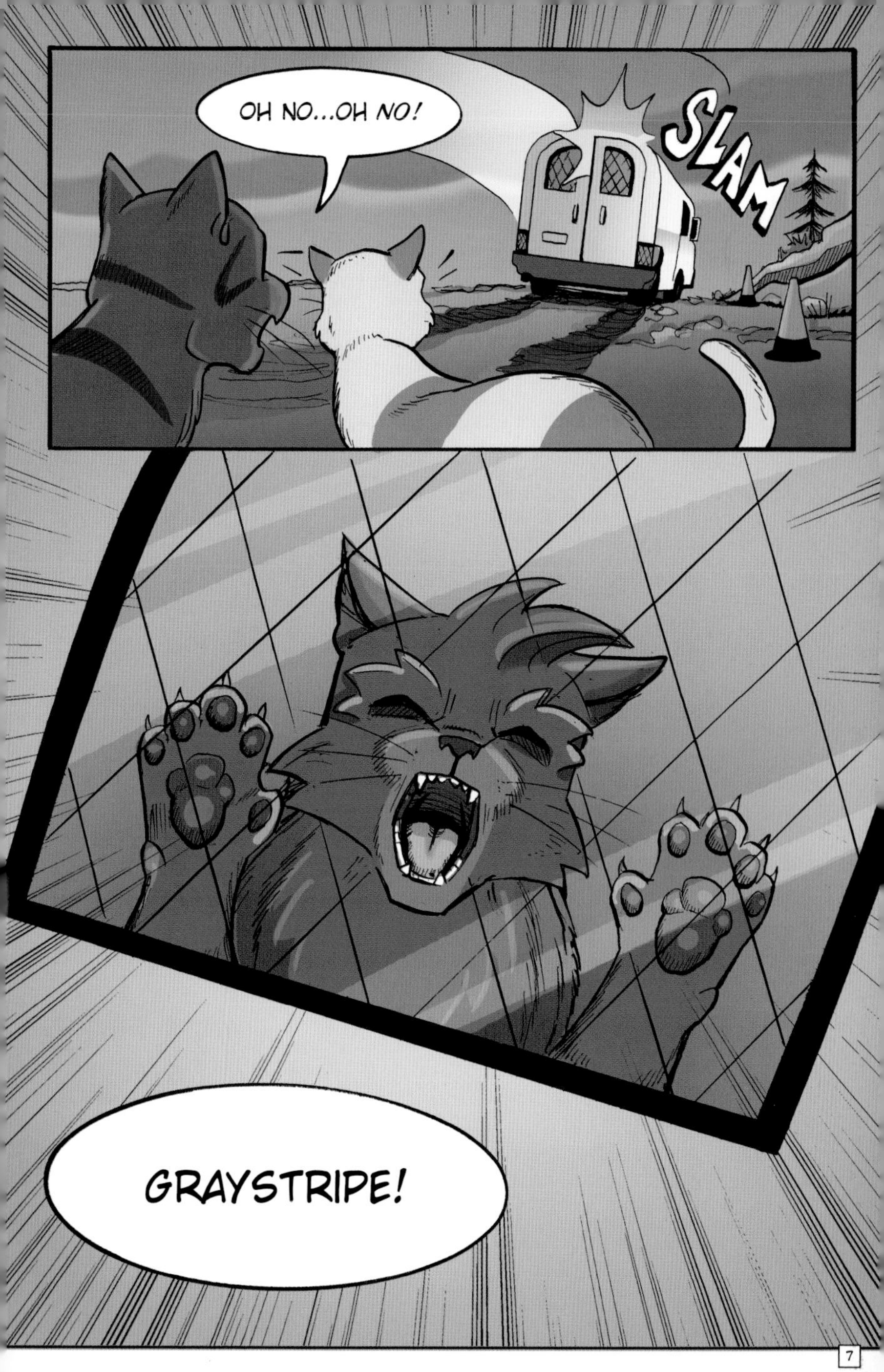
OH NO...OH NO!
SLAM
GRAYSTRIPE!

# CHAPTER 1

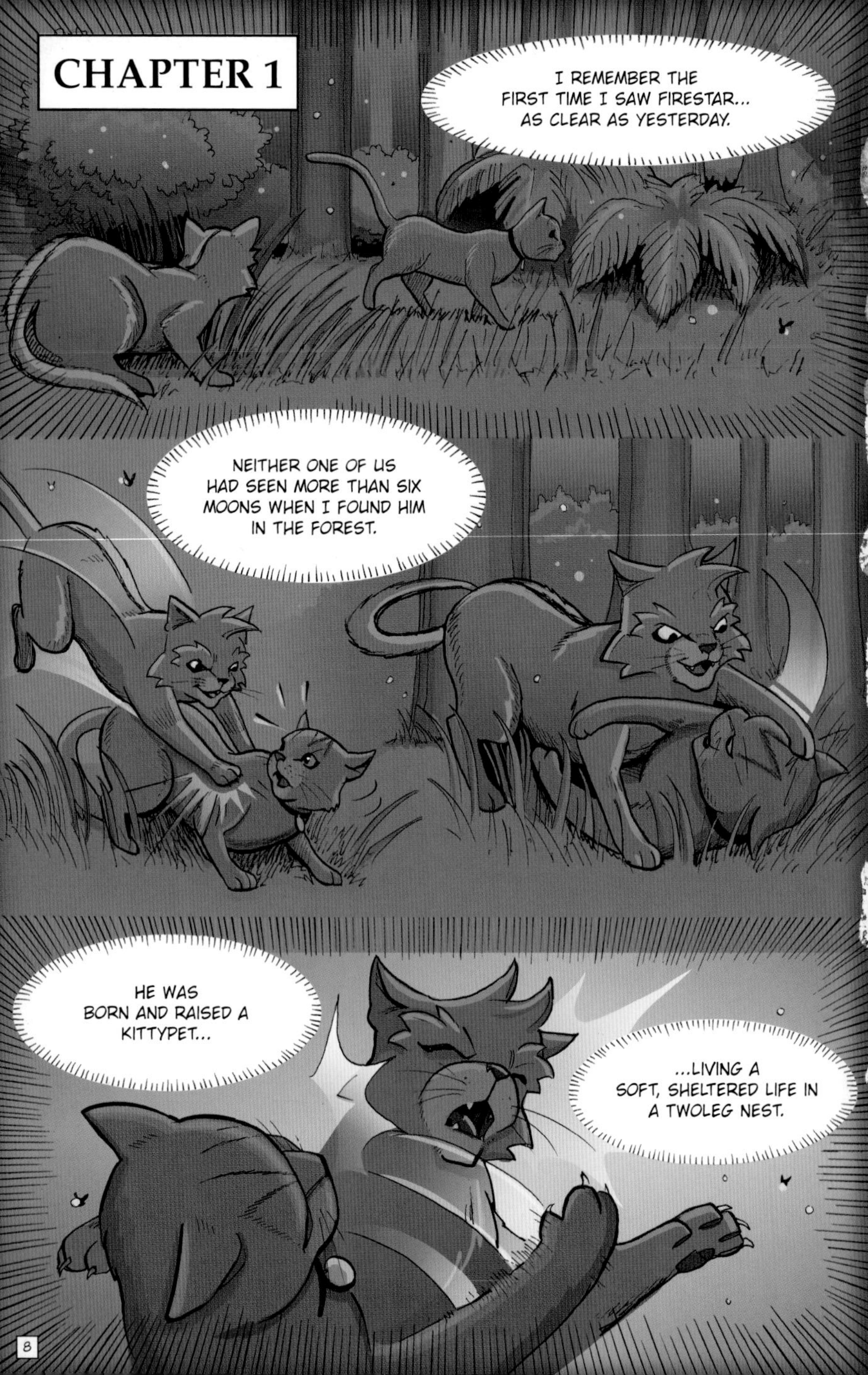
I REMEMBER THE FIRST TIME I SAW FIRESTAR... AS CLEAR AS YESTERDAY.
NEITHER ONE OF US HAD SEEN MORE THAN SIX MOONS WHEN I FOUND HIM IN THE FOREST.
HE WAS BORN AND RAISED A KITTYPET...
...LIVING A SOFT, SHELTERED LIFE IN A TWOLEG NEST.

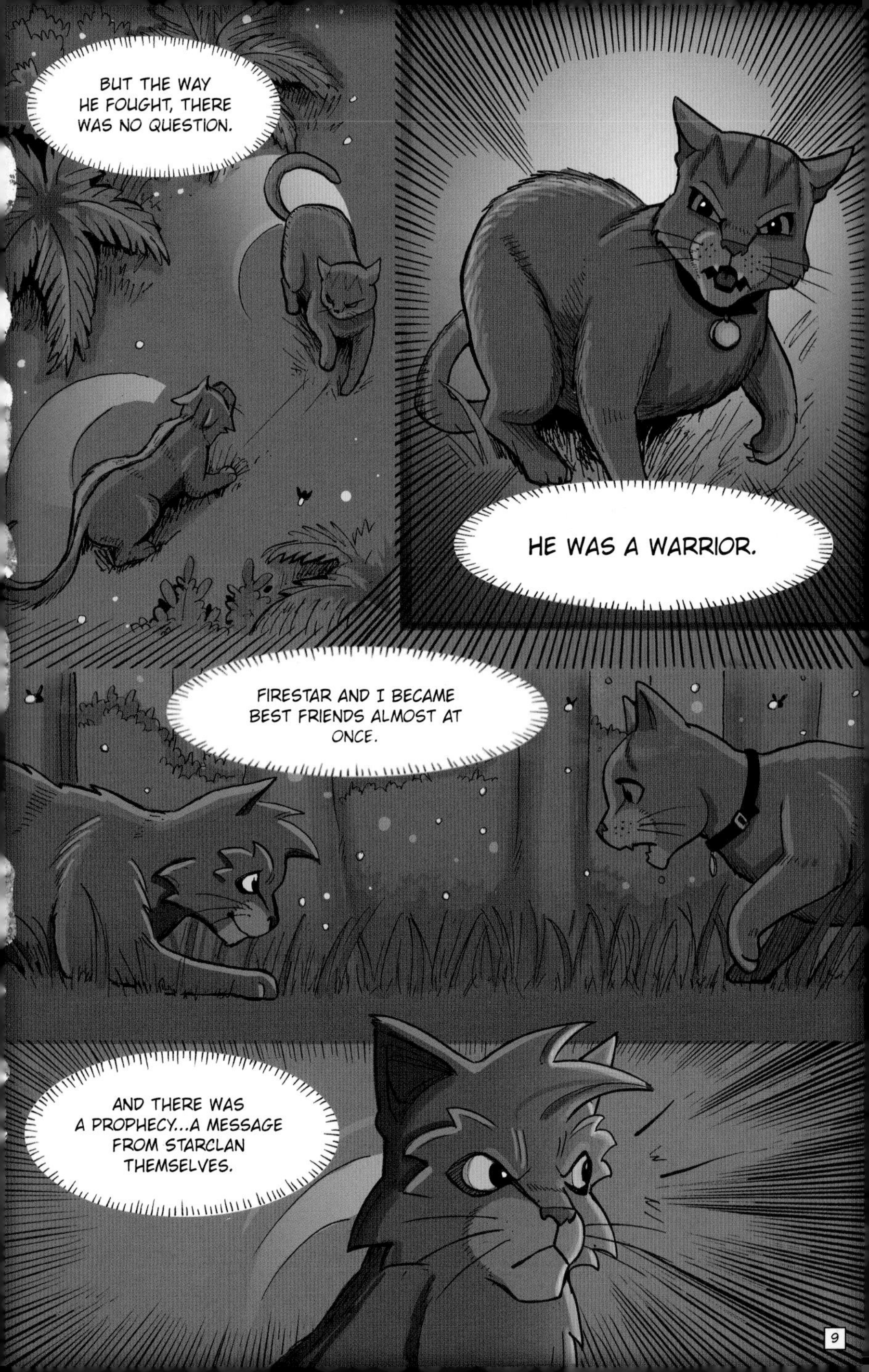
BUT THE WAY HE FOUGHT, THERE WAS NO QUESTION.
HE WAS A WARRIOR.
FIRESTAR AND I BECAME BEST FRIENDS ALMOST AT ONCE.
AND THERE WAS A PROPHECY...A MESSAGE FROM STARCLAN THEMSELVES.

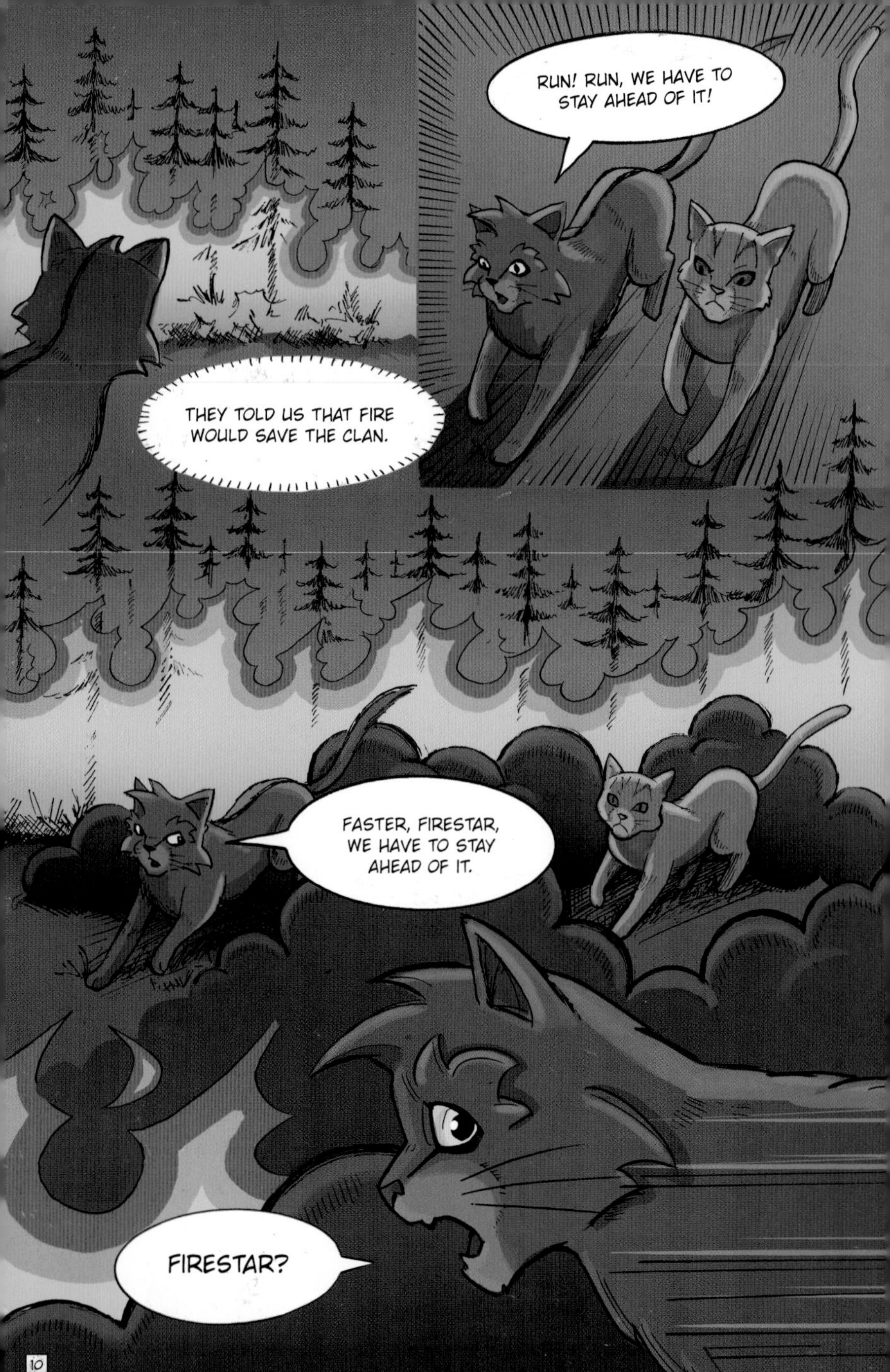
THEY TOLD US THAT FIRE WOULD SAVE THE CLAN.
RUN! RUN, WE HAVE TO STAY AHEAD OF IT!
FASTER, FIRESTAR, WE HAVE TO STAY AHEAD OF IT.
FIRESTAR?

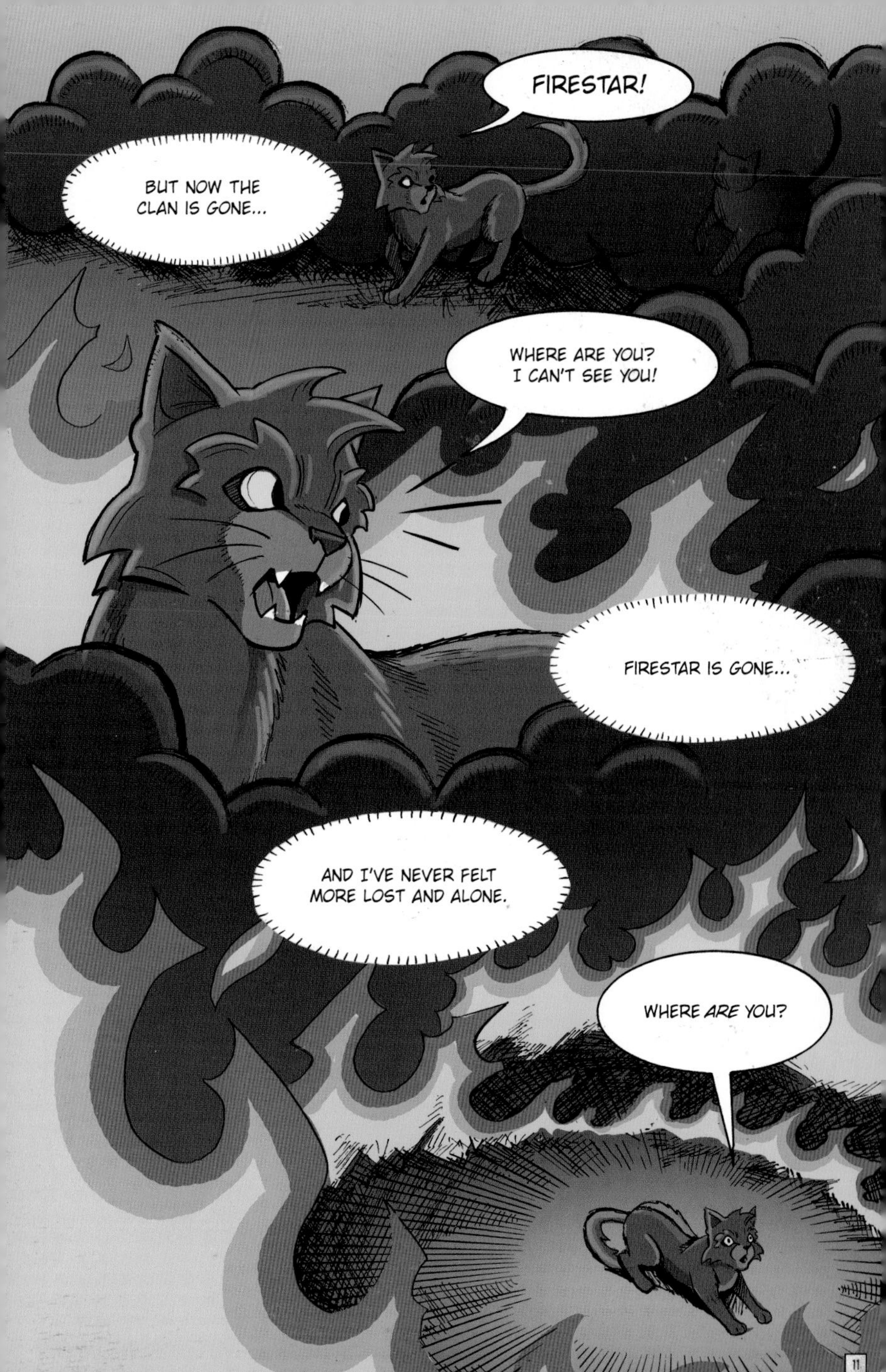
FIRESTAR!
BUT NOW THE CLAN IS GONE...
WHERE ARE YOU? I CAN'T SEE YOU!
FIRESTAR IS GONE...
AND I'VE NEVER FELT MORE LOST AND ALONE.
WHERE *ARE* YOU?

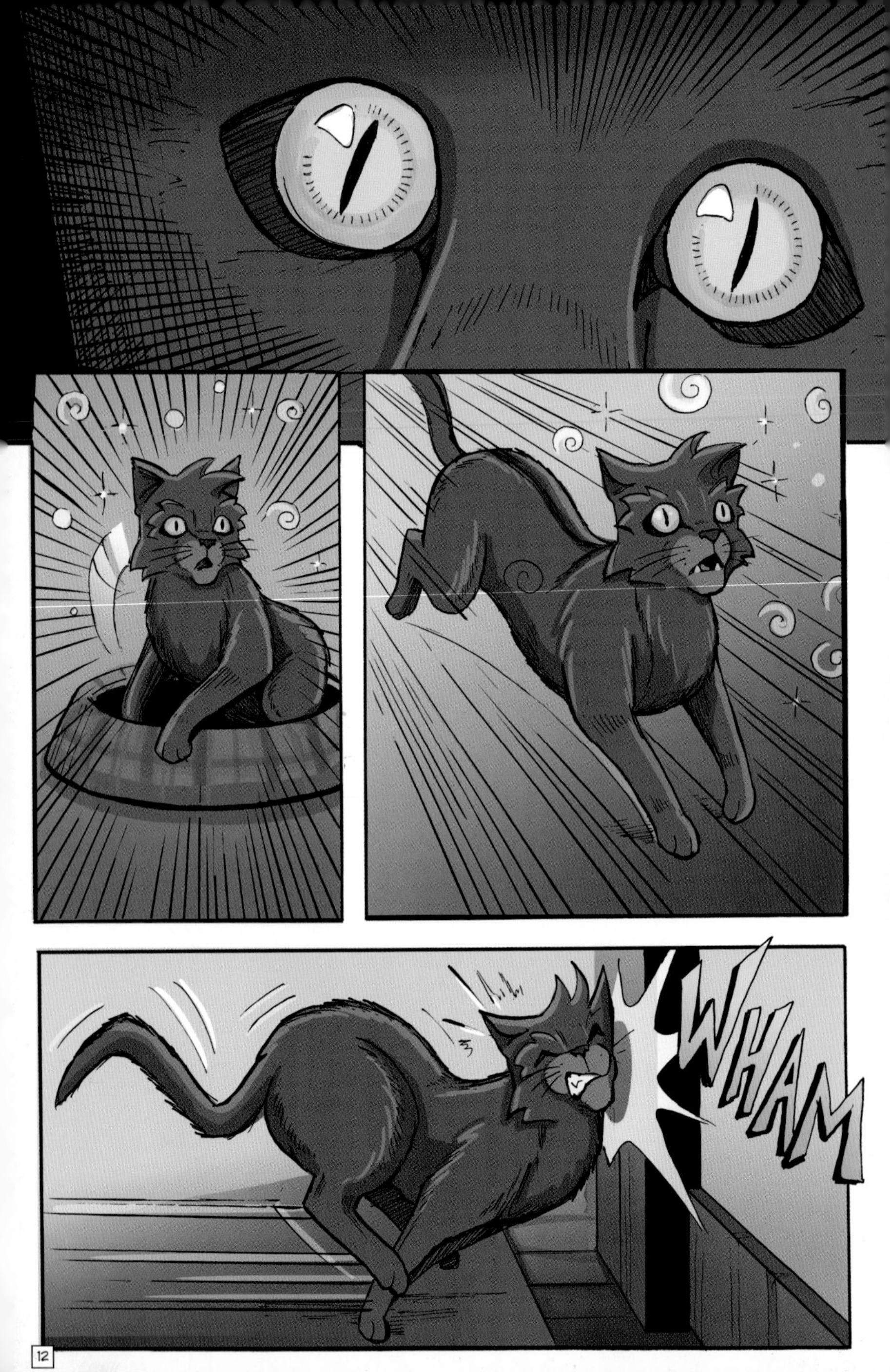
WHAM

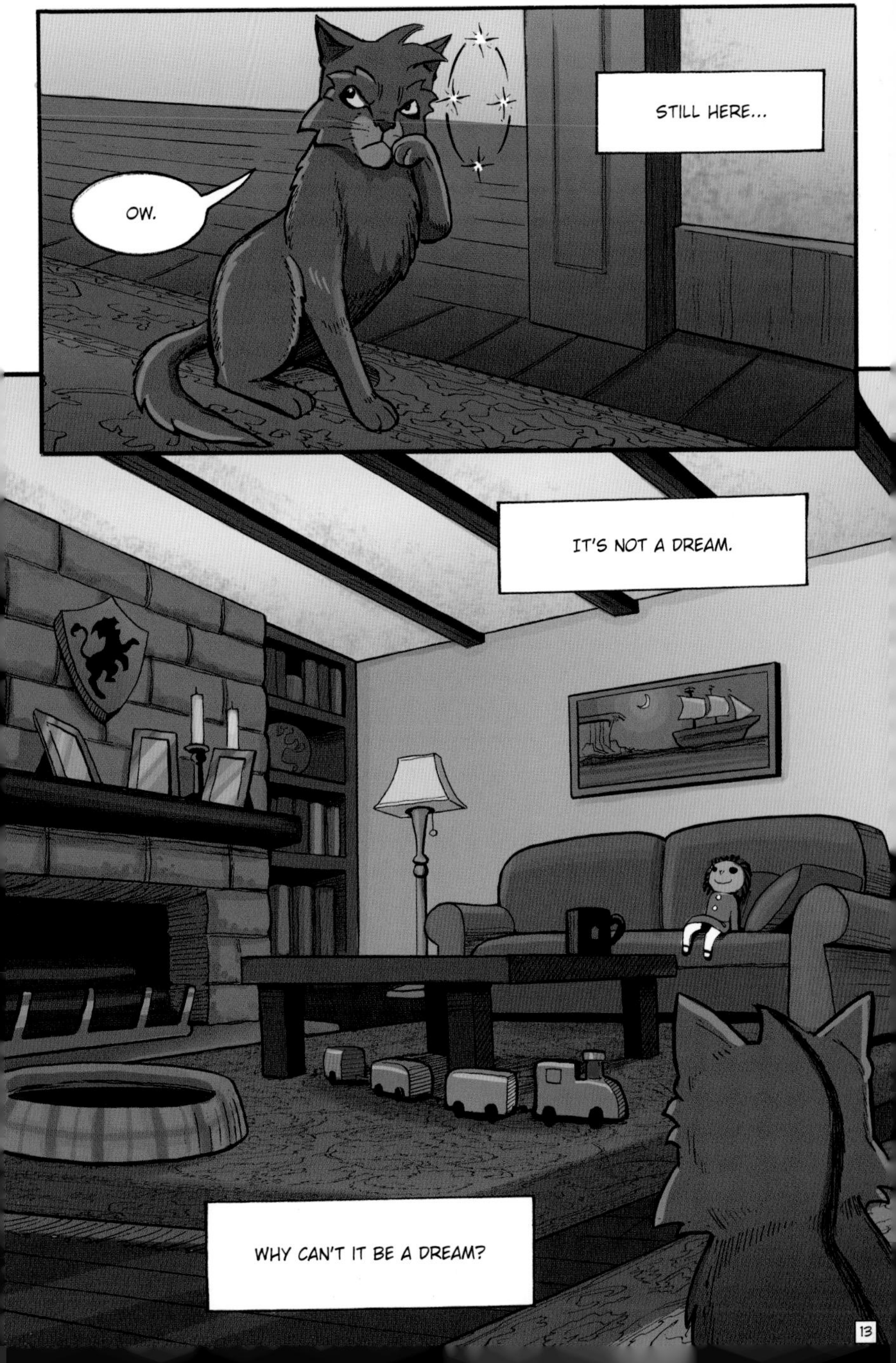
STILL HERE...
OW.
IT'S NOT A DREAM.
WHY CAN'T IT BE A DREAM?

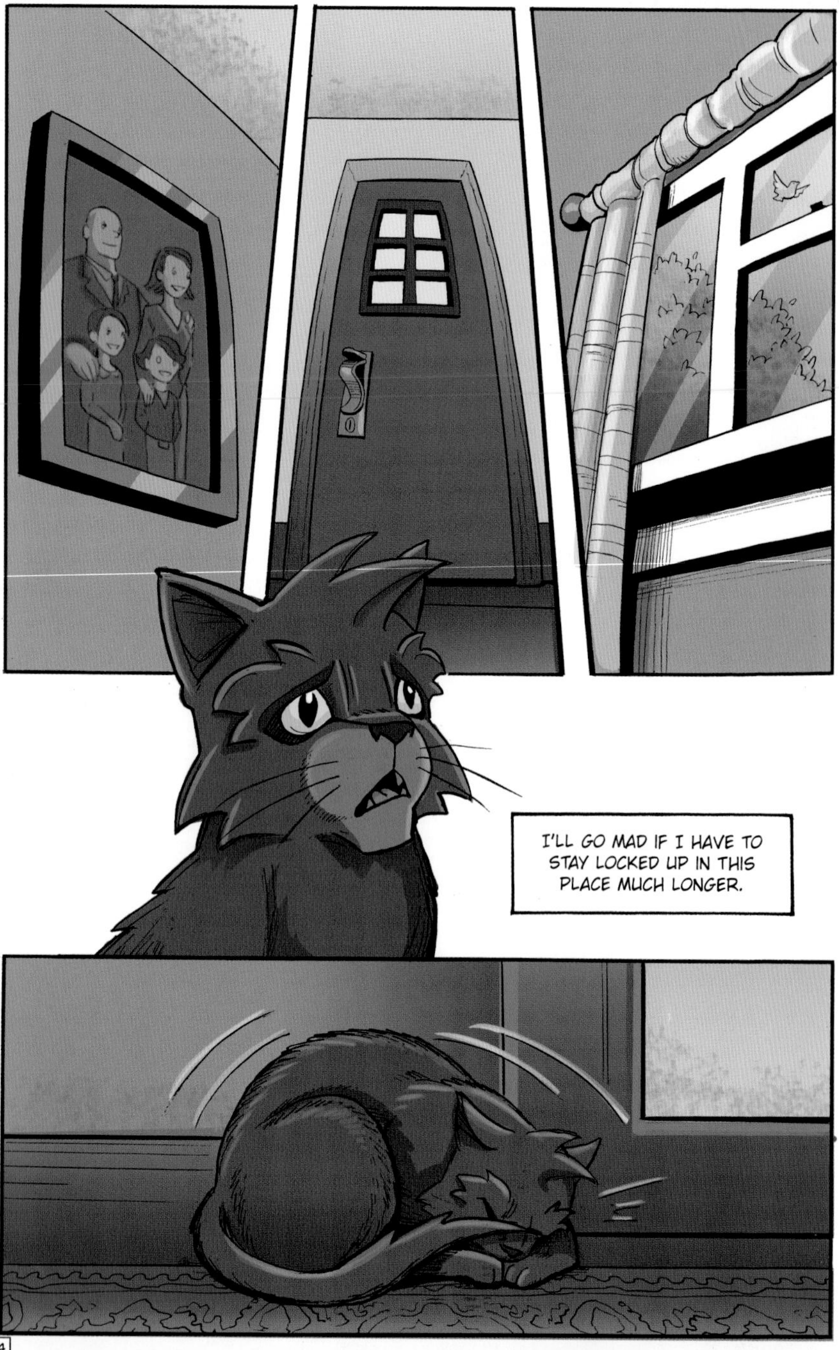
I'LL GO MAD IF I HAVE TO STAY LOCKED UP IN THIS PLACE MUCH LONGER.

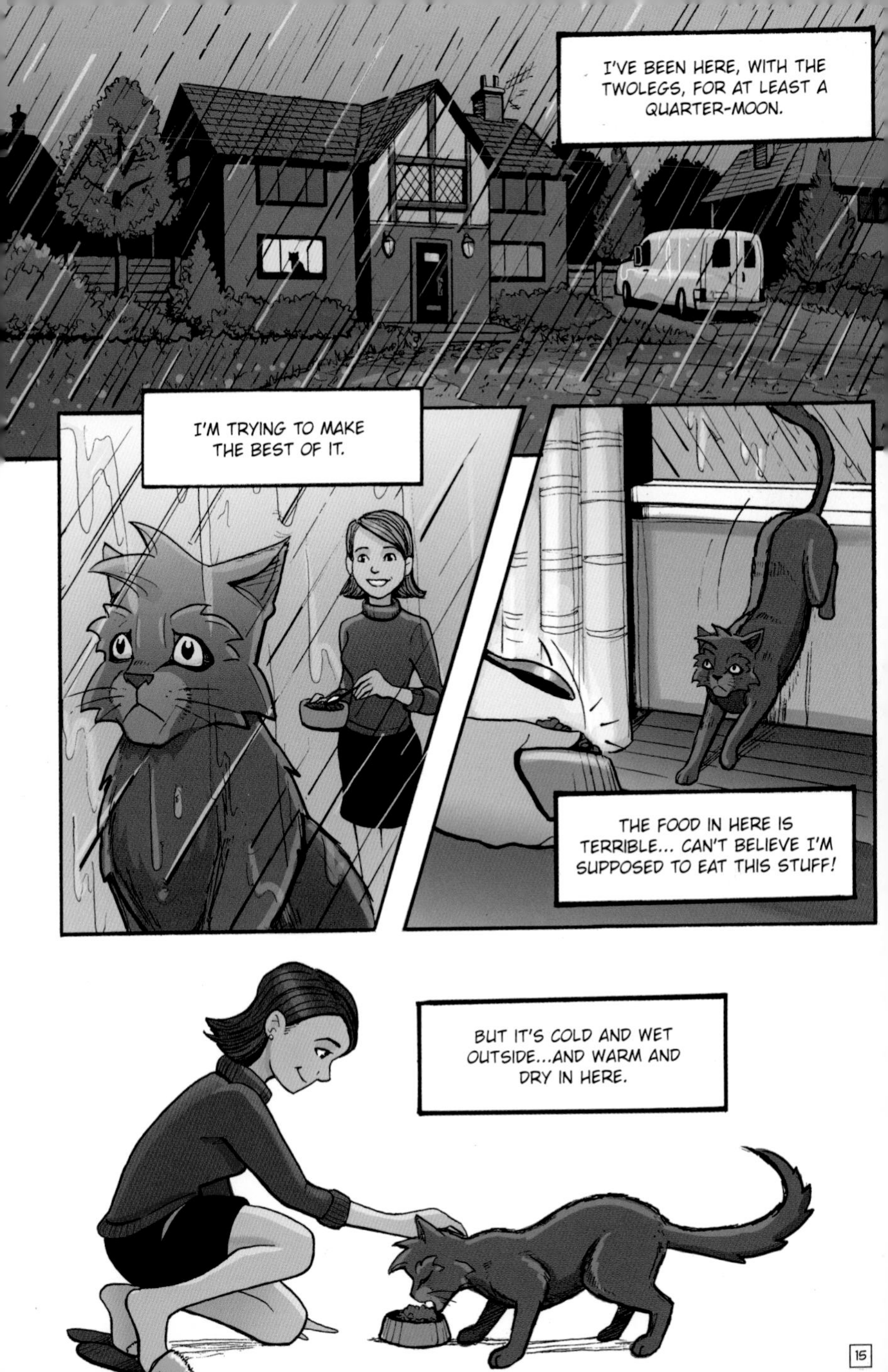
I'VE BEEN HERE, WITH THE TWOLEGS, FOR AT LEAST A QUARTER-MOON.
I'M TRYING TO MAKE THE BEST OF IT.
THE FOOD IN HERE IS TERRIBLE... CAN'T BELIEVE I'M SUPPOSED TO EAT THIS STUFF!
BUT IT'S COLD AND WET OUTSIDE...AND WARM AND DRY IN HERE.

# ERIN HUNTER

is inspired by a fascination with
the ferocity of the natural world.
As well as having great respect for
nature in all its forms, Erin enjoys
creating rich, mythical explanations
for animal behavior. She is also the
author of the Survivors, Seekers, and
Bravelands series.

Find out more online at
www.warriorcats.com.

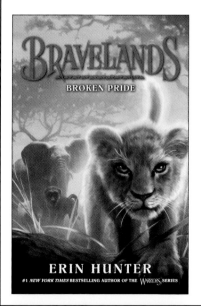

# A new WARRIORS arc!

# WARRIORS:
## THE BROKEN CODE

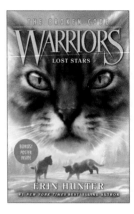

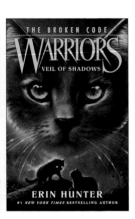

## Have you read them all?

○ #1: Lost Stars

○ #2: The Silent Thaw

○ #3: Veil of Shadows

# WARRIORS

# How many have you read?

**Dawn of the Clans** 
- ◯ #1: The Sun Trail
- ◯ #2: Thunder Rising
- ◯ #3: The First Battle
- ◯ #4: The Blazing Star
- ◯ #5: A Forest Divided
- ◯ #6: Path of Stars

**Power of Three** 
- ◯ #1: The Sight
- ◯ #2: Dark River
- ◯ #3: Outcast
- ◯ #4: Eclipse
- ◯ #5: Long Shadows
- ◯ #6: Sunrise

**The Prophecies Begin** 
- ◯ #1: Into the Wild
- ◯ #2: Fire and Ice
- ◯ #3: Forest of Secrets
- ◯ #4: Rising Storm
- ◯ #5: A Dangerous Path
- ◯ #6: The Darkest Hour

**Omen of the Stars**
- ◯ #1: The Fourth Apprentice
- ◯ #2: Fading Echoes
- ◯ #3: Night Whispers
- ◯ #4: Sign of the Moon
- ◯ #5: The Forgotten Warrior
- ◯ #6: The Last Hope

**The New Prophecy**
- ◯ #1: Midnight
- ◯ #2: Moonrise
- ◯ #3: Dawn
- ◯ #4: Starlight
- ◯ #5: Twilight
- ◯ #6: Sunset

**A Vision of Shadows** 
- ◯ #1: The Apprentice's Quest
- ◯ #2: Thunder and Shadow
- ◯ #3: Shattered Sky
- ◯ #4: Darkest Night
- ◯ #5: River of Fire
- ◯ #6: The Raging Storm

## Select titles also available as audiobooks!

**HARPER**
*An Imprint of HarperCollinsPublishers*

www.warriorcats.com • www.shelfstuff.com

## SUPER EDITIONS

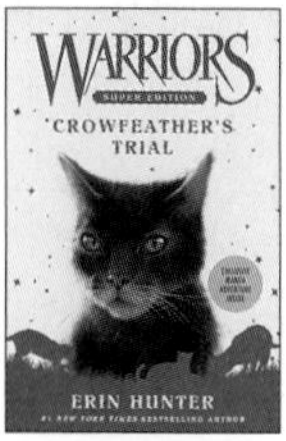
WARRIORS
SUPER EDITION
CROWFEATHER'S TRIAL
ERIN HUNTER

- ❍ Firestar's Quest
- ❍ Bluestar's Prophecy
- ❍ SkyClan's Destiny
- ❍ Crookedstar's Promise
- ❍ Yellowfang's Secret
- ❍ Tallstar's Revenge
- ❍ Bramblestar's Storm
- ❍ Moth Flight's Vision
- ❍ Hawkwing's Journey
- ❍ Tigerheart's Shadow
- ❍ Crowfeather's Trial
- ❍ Squirrelflight's Hope

## GUIDES

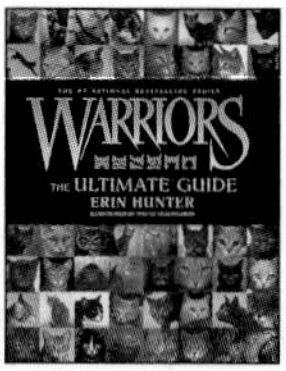
WARRIORS
THE ULTIMATE GUIDE
ERIN HUNTER

- ❍ Secrets of the Clans
- ❍ Cats of the Clans
- ❍ Code of the Clans
- ❍ Battles of the Clans
- ❍ Enter the Clans
- ❍ The Ultimate Guide

## FULL-COLOR GRAPHIC NOVELS

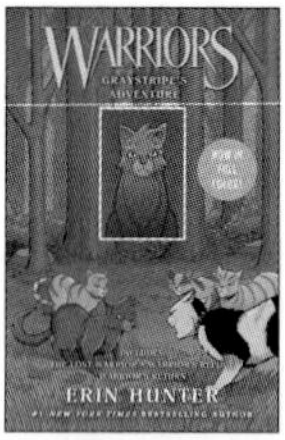
WARRIORS
GRAYSTRIPE'S ADVENTURE
ERIN HUNTER

- ❍ Graystripe's Adventure
- ❍ Ravenpaw's Path
- ❍ SkyClan and the Stranger
- ❍ A Shadow in RiverClan

## EBOOKS AND NOVELLAS

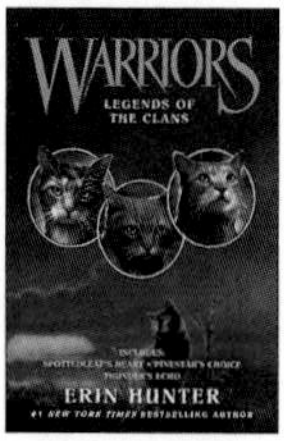
WARRIORS
LEGENDS OF THE CLANS
ERIN HUNTER

**The Untold Stories**
- ❍ Hollyleaf's Story
- ❍ Mistystar's Omen
- ❍ Cloudstar's Journey

**Shadows of the Clans**
- ❍ Mapleshade's Vengeance
- ❍ Goosefeather's Curse
- ❍ Ravenpaw's Farewell

**Path of a Warrior**
- ❍ Redtail's Debt
- ❍ Tawnypelt's Clan
- ❍ Shadowstar's Life

**Tales from the Clans**
- ❍ Tigerclaw's Fury
- ❍ Leafpool's Wish
- ❍ Dovewing's Silence

**Legends of the Clans**
- ❍ Spottedleaf's Heart
- ❍ Pinestar's Choice
- ❍ Thunderstar's Echo

**A Warrior's Spirit**
- ❍ Pebbleshine's Kits
- ❍ Tree's Roots
- ❍ Mothwing's Secret

HARPER
*An Imprint of* HarperCollins*Publishers*

www.warriorcats.com • www.shelfstuff.com